BOOK THREE IN THE MILKY WAY REPO SERIES

THE UNWORTHY

MICHAEL PRELEE

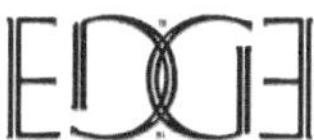

EDGE SCIENCE FICTION AND FANTASY PUBLISHING
An Imprint of HADES PUBLICATIONS, INC.
CALGARY

The Unworthy
Book Three in The Milky Way Repo Series

Copyright © 2023 by Michael Prelee

EDGE SCIENCE FICTION AND FANTASY PUBLISHING
An Imprint of HADES PUBLICATIONS, INC.
P.O. Box 1414, Calgary, Alberta, T2P 2L6, Canada

The EDGE Team:
Producer: Brian Hades
Edited by: Kathryn Shalley
Cover Design: Brian Hades
Cover Art: David Wilicome
Book Design: Mark Steele

ISBN: 978-1-77053-229-8

EDGE Science Fiction and Fantasy Publishing and Hades Publications, Inc. acknowledges the ongoing support of the Alberta Foundation for the Arts and the Canada Council for the Arts for our publishing programme.

Library and Archives Canada Cataloguing in Publication

Title: The unworthy / Michael Prelee.
Names: Prelee, Michael, author.
Description: Series statement: The Milky Way repo series ; book three
Identifiers: Canadiana (print) 20230492835 | Canadiana (ebook) 2023049286X | ISBN 9781770532328 (hardcover) | ISBN 9781770532298 (softcover) | ISBN 9781770532281 (EPUB)
Classification: LCC PS3616.R44 U59 2023 | DDC 813/.6—dc23

FIRST EDITION
(20230726)
Printed in USA
www.edgewebsite.com

Publisher's Note:

Thank you for purchasing this book. It began as an idea, was shaped by the creativity of its talented author, and was subsequently molded into the book you have before you by a team of editors and designers.

Like all EDGE books, this book is the result of the creative talents of a dedicated team of individuals who all believe that books (whether in print or pixels) have the magical ability to take you on an adventure to new and wondrous places powered by the author's imagination.

As EDGE's publisher, I hope that you enjoy this book. It is a part of our ongoing quest to discover talented authors and to make their creative writing available to you.

We also hope that you will share your discovery and enjoyment of this novel on social media through Facebook, Twitter, Goodreads, Pinterest, etc., and by posting your opinions and/or reviews on Amazon and other review sites and blogs. By doing so, others will be able to share your discovery and passion for this book.

Brian Hades, publisher

Dedication

For Tina and the boys

Acknowledgement

Writing a book is not a bootstrap project. It takes plenty of help and assistance to get it just right. I'd like to thank my wife Tina for doing everything I couldn't while I was hunched over the keyboard gnashing my teeth and grinding out the words. Without her this book and its two predecessors wouldn't exist.

I would also like to thank Kathryn Shalley for editing this book. Her insight and suggestions were instrumental in shaping it into a much better story than the one we started with.

Thanks too for the amazing cover art by David Willicome.

Finally, I would like to thank Brian Hades for taking another chance on myself, Nathan, and the crew. I enjoyed writing this story, so it's gratifying that someone else has faith in it becoming a success.

1.

Nathan Teller, owner of Milky Way Repossessions — a company that tracked down and repossessed starships — lay on the large sectional couch in his employee, Cole's, living room, listening to Cole thump around the kitchen. At a pause in the clatter, Nathan rolled his head to look towards the kitchen and saw Cole glowering at him.

He caught the smell of freshly brewed coffee and noticed the machine on the counter slowly filling the pot. Cole laid out mugs but his eyes zeroed in on Nathan as he went about the task. Knowing his friend well enough to realize trouble was on the horizon, he broke the ice.

"Coffee smells great," he said.

"I need you, Kimiyo and I need you, to get the hell out of our house," Cole said from behind the counter. He used the voice Nathan had heard many times. It was his, "I'm asking as nicely as possible for you to do something you don't want to do," voice. Cole's job at Milk Way Repo was to track down people who didn't want to be found and Nathan usually heard that voice directed at starship owners who entertained the thought of using force to keep their repossessed ships. Commands given in this voice with the accompanying look Nathan was getting right now were usually enough to convince them to follow directions.

Cole and Kimiyo owned a two-hundred-acre ranch about ten kilometers outside Go City, New Mexico. It wasn't a working ranch, but Nathan thought Cole liked the feeling he got when he told people he owned a ranch. Go City was the premier location for starship manufacturing in North America.

Their house sat in the middle of the property at the end of a long access road. A single-story affair, the home had four bedrooms and two bathrooms. Cole and Kimiyo shared one bedroom and Nathan and his girlfriend, Tricia, were staying in another.

The house was decorated in a mid-nineteenth century western theme. Exposed, rough-hewn cedar beams ran the length of the ceiling and the furniture had a faux-distressed look. The heavy wood frames for the chairs and couches were cut rough and the cushions were bright reds, yellows, and greens. Nathan was almost positive the furniture wasn't five-hundred years old, but it was authentic wood. The living room was sunken two steps which gave Cole a height advantage in their conversation. Rolling off the sectional and dodging a coffee table, Nathan stepped up into the kitchen and took a seat at one of the tall, counter stools.

"You know I want out of your guest room, right?"

"I know you're still in it," Cole said.

Nathan crossed his arms on the counter and dropped his head. "Come on, man, there's a mob enforcer chasing me who can quite literally light himself on fire. These are not normal circumstances. I'm working on resolving the situation."

"You've been on the run for six months. That's not a plan. Getting your ship back so we can go to work is a plan." He poured a cup of coffee and set it down in front of his boss.

Nathan lifted his head and spied the mug. "Thank you." He took a sip and started to feel like a real human being again. "Look, I don't want to be here either, but being chased by Atomic Jack has definitely screwed up my life."

"We should just kill him," Cole said. Nathan eyed him and couldn't tell whether he was serious or not.

"If we killed him the Syndicate would just send someone else."

"Then we'd kill them, too. Eventually, they'd get the idea that screwing with us is a bad idea."

"No, eventually we'd be dead. The Syndicate has more guys with guns than they know what to do with. This isn't a problem we can solve with bullets."

"Why not? It's how we got into it."

Nathan had to concede that Cole was right. "Hey, they started it. They almost killed Marla, Richie, and Tricia and they crashed my ship. That couldn't go unanswered."

"I know, and I know local law enforcement wasn't up to the task of arresting them, but you're running out of places to hole up."

"I know."

"And I need some money. I'm getting by on security side jobs but none of them pay as well as repossessing starships. The mortgage on this place is very real so we need to get back in the game."

"I know," Nathan said again.

"So, what's the plan?"

Nathan smiled. "I don't know."

Cole gestured toward him with his mug. "Look, you're the guy who plans shit out. That's what you're good at. You see a problem and you solve a problem, but lately, it hasn't been that way. It's like you can't see the angles anymore. When we first met, I was impressed at how easily all that kind of stuff came to you. Every time we ran into a brick wall, you found a way over it or under it. But these last few years it's like you started digging a hole and you just won't stop shoveling."

Nathan conceded Cole's point to himself. When he'd put his crew together, all of them were dealing with problems, but all he saw were diamonds in the rough. One-by-one he'd found them and gave them a second chance to succeed, and in every case, he'd been right. They'd all excelled.

Cole and Kimiyo were building a life in this very house after meeting on a job he'd accepted from a billionaire named Saji Vy. His engineer Duncan Jax and co-pilot Marla were getting ready to celebrate their seventh wedding anniversary this summer. Even his machinist mate, Richie Pearson, was doing well after beating a gambling addiction.

For as much personal growth as his crew showed, Nathan's life had gone the other way. He was divorced, broke, his business was on the verge of failing, and now he was on the run from the Syndicate. He wasn't sure why Tricia was still with him, any hospital would have taken on an experienced ER nurse like herself. Cole was right, something had to change. It was ridiculous to live this way. The only place to go from here was living on the street.

The thing that bothered him most was that as bad as things were, he was so very close to getting them right again. His crew were biding their time with temporary jobs until he got his act together. He didn't want to tell Cole and Kimiyo just yet, in case things went wrong, but today was different, today his ship was fully repaired and all he had to do to get it back was pay off the shipyard. He just needed one break to get things rolling his way.

"I want you to know that I'm trying to get things working," Nathan said. "I've put some feelers out with banks and lenders, letting them know we're available for work."

Cole took a sip of coffee. "How are we going to work without a ship?"

"I can go to the shipyard today," he said. "I'll pay off the repairs on the *Blue Moon Bandit* and get things in gear."

Cole's eyes narrowed. "Where did you get the credits for that?"

"The repairs have been done for a while and when I got the call that it was done, I realized that I was using the excuse of not having a ship as a reason to keep hiding out. I don't have to worry about Syndicate hitmen if they can't find me.

"A few days ago, though, Tricia and I were talking. She's had enough and needs things to change." He exhaled heavily.

"Is she leaving you?" Cole asked.

"She didn't say that explicitly, but only because she's giving me one more chance to get my act together. I don't blame her. This is no way to live. So, I bit the bullet and went to Lucy Bega at Amalgamated Logistics for the money."

"I thought you hated using factoring companies."

Nathan did. Factoring companies gave haulers credits up front in exchange for getting it back, plus a fee, once the work was complete. The problem was that their bite was so big that ship owners ended up using them over and over in cycles. That could lead to ship owners working their asses off and still going out of business.

"What else could I do?" Nathan said. "I don't want to lose her, I don't want to lose the crew, and I want my ship back."

Nathan heard steps clicking on the floor behind him and turned to see Kimiyo Himura moving gracefully across the living room. Kimiyo's dark blue hair caught the morning light with an iridescent flash as she crossed in front of the living room windows. She was dressed in her work clothing: a black pantsuit and low, stylish heels. Nathan could tell the outfit was designer from the quality of the material and the way it was tailored, but he had no idea who made it. All he knew about fashion was that he was legally required to keep his ass covered in public. For him, flight suits and jeans usually did the trick.

"Good morning, boys," she said.

Cole leaned across the counter and gave her a kiss on the cheek as he slipped her a travel mug full of coffee. "Morning, honey."

"What's the plan for today?" she asked.

Kimiyo was an assistant to Saji Vy, the same billionaire industrialist whom the crew had been working for when she and Cole had first met. Saji Vy had earned billions of credits manufacturing starship parts and now there wasn't a ship flying that wasn't fitted with SajiCo reactors, filters, seals, or one of another thousand parts.

"Good news, Kimiyo," Cole said. "Nathan thinks he can get us some repo jobs."

She looked at Nathan and he could see the skepticism in her eyes. "You're really looking for a repo job?"

"Sure am," he said. "You know of any?"

"I can ask around. Saji may have something."

"That would be great."

She smiled sweetly. "Well, whatever gets you out of our guest room, right?"

He tried returning her smile but was pretty sure he just grimaced. "Right."

She walked around the counter and kissed Cole again. "See you tonight." Then she walked out the side door to leave for work.

Cole turned back to Nathan. "Find something today."

2.

A couple hours later, dust from the desert hardpan collected around Nathan's boots in a thin cloud as he and Duncan walked through the gates of the shipyard where his ship was being repaired. The sign over the gate announced they were entering the Western Dune Shipyards, which looked like it had been repairing starships as long as people had been launching them from this part of New Mexico. The facility was measured in square kilometers, and space vehicles in various states of repair sat on concrete pads for as far as Nathan could see.

Blue Moon Bandit had started life as a hazardous waste hauler, built strongly enough to contain its cargo in case of a mishap. After crashing at the Bad Rock settlement, the *Blue Moon Bandit* had been ferried home and then shuttled down to this place, outside Go City. As always, the *Bandit* reminded Nathan of a predator, with its aft section sitting higher than the bow, as if it were preparing to pounce on some unwary prey.

They walked around the ship, admiring the repair work that had been completed. The cockpit retained the wide canopy that he loved but the polycarbonate-acrylic cover was all new because the previous one had been cracked when a madman slammed a drone into the portside engine cowling. That too was new, as was the engine behind it.

They came to the rear of the ship and saw the hull had been repaired where a heavy-duty rescue bot had shredded it. Nathan thumbed the ramp control and it lowered between the ship's two engines. Brand new lights came on, as if Nathan was being invited inside.

They mounted the ramp and he remembered that the last time he'd seen the ship, this whole section was missing. It had been torn apart during the rescue after the crash. He ran a hand over the ramp struts and climbed up into the ship.

The first thing that struck him was how clean it was. It wasn't that he kept a dirty ship, it was just that so much of it was new.

The deck plating wasn't scuffed from decades of having cargo containers dragged across it and the bulkheads weren't covered with dings from having all manner of equipment banged into them. They were like blank pages, waiting for new stories to be written.

Nathan turned to Duncan. "What do you think?"

The engineer was staring at the new work. Nathan knew Duncan's eyes were modified to give him a greater range of vision, allowing him to see in low light and detect ambient forms of radiation. He wasn't just looking at the patches, he was examining them on a microscopic level that let him see cracks or holes in the welds. After a moment he nodded at Nathan. "I like what I see. They did a good job."

"Well, what did you expect?" a voice boomed from outside. Nathan turned to see the owner of the shipyard, Bruce Corbin, approaching up the loading ramp. He was a large man, two meters tall and almost half as wide. His dark blue coveralls were stretched out around a sizeable belly and he carried a plastic bottle. "We don't do bad work around here."

Nathan greeted him at the top of the ramp. "She looks good so far, Bruce."

"It was a job and a half, let me tell you," he said. "There were more than a few times when I thought about calling you to tell you she was a lost cause. The damage done by the initial collision destroyed the engine on that side, which was bad enough, but slamming her onto concrete during the crash landing really hurt her. If it wasn't for the structure already being reinforced, she would have been totaled out."

Duncan gave him a side eyed look. "Marla didn't have much choice, under the circumstances."

Bruce wiped sweat from his glistening bald head with a blue bandana. "I'm not casting any aspersions on your wife. I'm just telling you what we were dealing with. We did a lot of frame straightening and replaced a lot of metal that was too twisted or cracked to keep." He slapped a bulkhead. "She's straight now, though. Give her a good look and you'll see." He spit tobacco juice into his bottle.

"I'll tell you what," Nathan said. "Why don't we let Duncan give her the once over while you and I go talk business in your office? I assume it's air conditioned."

"Sounds good to me."

Bruce's office was a cargo container sitting on some short concrete pylons. A metal desk cluttered with tablets, starship parts, and tools sat at one end. Bruce dropped into a large chair behind it and pointed at a smaller one in front for Nathan.

"I appreciate the work your team was able to do," Nathan said. "The *Bandit* looks great."

"She'll fly," Bruce said, and picked up a tablet. After tapping a few times, he threw up a hologram over the desk. "This is everything we did to her. I'll skip the piddly little bits and get to the important stuff."

"All right." Nathan started to get a bad feeling. The *Bandit* had been torn up good when he dropped it off.

"You paid for the good insurance so you get full replacement on everything. That means factory original parts rather than rebuilt crap out of a salvage yard."

"Good."

"You got yourself a replacement engine for the one that was destroyed, the undercarriage was straightened and strengthened, the missing rear structure was replaced, and the plasma thruster distribution network was repaired. We also got you a new canopy made of ballistics resistant composite and completely inspected your fusion reactors, flight control systems and repaired any hull defects we found."

"Sounds like a lot of work."

"Like I said, we almost scrapped it, but the work came in right under the line so your insurance company said to keep it flying."

"What about the goose?" Nathan said. "It's going to make my job hard if I can't make light speed jumps." The goose was the component that made faster-than-light jumps possible.

"You got a new one. I would have liked to have the old one to rebuild but we couldn't find it."

"Lost in the crash, I expect," Nathan said. In reality, he and his crew had used it to destroy a building housing a drug lab at the Bad Rock settlement. That goose was probably still under a few hundred tons of block and steel. "So, what do I owe you?"

Bruce tapped his tablet and an invoice appeared. "The insurance has already paid up. Your share, including deductible and storage fees comes to fifty-five thousand credits."

Nathan almost fell off his chair. "Wait, what? My share was supposed to be forty thousand."

"It is," Bruce said, "for the repairs. You owe fifteen thousand in storage fees."

"That can't be right."

"It's right. The work was completed three months ago. Storage fees are five thousand a month. Five thousand times three months is fifteen thousand."

Nathan sank down in his chair. He'd left the *Bandit* here while he hid to keep it safe from Atomic Jack and his Syndicate goons. He hadn't counted on the storage fees being so high. He had enough credits to cover his deductible, but not the storage fees.

"I'm going to be honest with you, I can pay fifty thousand and that's all. Will that do it?"

Bruce shook his head. "I can't give you a discount like that. I left you messages and you never responded."

"I know, but I had some stuff going on. Believe me, I wanted to get it when the repairs were completed."

"Your problems with Atomic Jack and the Syndicate aren't my problems," Bruce said. "You have a price on your head. If that means you leave your ship here, I get paid for holding on to it."

Nathan rubbed his forehead and calmly counted to ten so he didn't lose his cool. This wasn't how he wanted his new start to begin. Any endeavor worth pursuing was going to have obstacles to overcome. He smiled. "Bruce, I get what you're saying. Is there anything we can do? Some agreement we could come to?"

"Like what?"

"My crew and I are ready to start working as soon as we get the ship back. I can give you fifty now and the remaining five over the course of a couple jobs. It'll be a couple months at the most. What do you think?"

Bruce leaned forward. "I think you can have your ship back when you pay the bill in full. That's the way this works."

"Come on, Bruce."

Bruce stood up behind the desk. "You come on, Nathan. I can't run my business on promises. You come up with the credits, you get your ship."

Nathan stood up. "I'm good for it. With everything you've made off this deal so far you can spot me five grand."

Bruce laughed. "I don't know you beyond this job, so I don't know what you're good for. I'm already doing you a solid by not cashing in the reward the Syndicate is offering on your head. Hell, I didn't even tell them your ship was here. You're lucky there aren't a dozen guys staking the place out waiting for you to show up. I get the credits, you get the ship."

Nathan wanted to take his ship and leave, tell Bruce to eat his fees, but that would mean compounding his problems instead of solving them. Earning five thousand credits couldn't be that difficult. One job at most.

"Fine, I'll get it."

"Do it quick," Bruce said. "The repair agreement says that after four months I can auction off the ship to recoup my costs."

Nathan pointed at him. "Don't do anything stupid. I'll get the credits."

Bruce shrugged. "I get paid either way."

Without another word, Nathan turned and left the office, storming back to the pad where the *Blue Moon Bandit* sat. Duncan stood at the bottom of the ramp.

"Are we good?" he asked. "The ship checks out. We could fly her out of here right now."

Nathan threw a look over his shoulder toward the office. Bruce stood there by the door, smoking a cigarette. "Not quite. Let's go meet up with everyone and I'll explain."

<h1 style="text-align:center">3.</h1>

At that moment, the mob enforcer known as Atomic Jack sat on a table in a very special exam room inside Our Lady of Mercy hospital. The hospital was located downtown in Go City, in a section of the city populated by clinics and doctor's offices. This particular examination room was on the ninth floor of the twelve-story hospital and had several unique properties. In this case, the room's atmosphere could be controlled, which was vitally important to the patient.

Atomic Jack wasn't his real name, of course. That was Jack Murphy, but no one called him that, unless he was within these healing walls. Anyone used to seeing Jack would be shocked at his current appearance. He was thinner than people thought, weighing in at a wiry eighty kilograms. His affliction normally confined him to a bulky pressure suit, which gave him a more robust and fearsome presence. Now he sat on an exam table, unencumbered by anything except a thin cotton johnnie that was pulled down to his waist. He wanted to feel as free as possible.

The normal concentration of oxygen in the atmosphere, about 18%, combined with the unusual radiation settled deep in his bones, resulted in his body's tissue combusting. The pressure suit he normally wore maintained the atmospheric concentration of oxygen at a level that prevented ignition. Sitting in a room like this was the only way he could be free of it.

He looked down at his mottled skin and touched it gingerly. A faint orange glow radiated through his skin, but it was dimmer in places where thick callouses had formed from rubbing against the interior of the suit. His joints, especially his elbows and knees, ached from years of confinement. It was his hands, though, that caused him the most grief.

He examined them under the harsh white lights of the exam room. The skin on his fingers and palms was thicker than it used to be, due to the number of times the skin there had been regrown. Monstrous hands like these would never have been able to do the fine work he had performed in his youth. Before the accident Jack's hands had been thin, his fingers so nimble he had no problem working on fusion reactors. Now, his affliction drove him to other, less legal pursuits.

As an enforcer for the Syndicate, having the ability to light oneself on fire was useful. Very few people failed to pay up when Atomic Jack made the scene. Those that thought they were tough enough to resist, cowered once he took off a glove and held their face in his flaming hand. He'd seen the fear of burning alive in the faces of a hundred men and women who'd thought they were brave, who'd thought they could tell the vaunted enforcer to fuck off and not pay the debts they owed. In the end, with a flaming hand squeezing their jaw, they always understood; you owe, you pay.

Now, though, something was wrong. He didn't know what, but he could feel it. In addition to maintaining the atmosphere he needed, the suit had tissue regeneration capabilities. If he took damage from exposure to a regular atmosphere, the suit helped him heal, re-growing skin and muscle lost to combustion. He looked at his hands again and saw patchy areas of regenerated skin that more closely resembled the rippled tissue of an alligator.

The airlock door to the room hissed open and Doctor Charbonneau entered. The oncologist, considered one of the best in the world, wore a neatly trimmed pencil-thin mustache with a pointy goatee under a respirator that let him function in the low oxygen atmosphere of the examination room. This man had done more to keep Jack Murphy alive than anyone else, but right now, Jack didn't like the look in his doctor's eyes.

Doctor Charbonneau approached and attached a small, silver metallic disc to Jack's bare right shoulder. The diagnostic reader activated upon contact and Jack's vital signs displayed on a wall to his left. Without saying anything, the doctor studied them and seemed to find them acceptable.

"Mr. Murphy, I have your test results," the small doctor said in English that carried a heavy Nigerian-French accent. "I'm afraid the news is not as good as we hoped."

Jack swallowed. Usually, he was the one giving people bad news. His eyes narrowed and zeroed in on the doctor. "What is it?"

Doctor Charbonneau licked his lips as a prelude to answering, an irritating habit that bothered Jack, but one that he'd never brought up. When there were only a few specialists in the solar system who could keep you alive, you learned to overlook the little things. "The news is not good and I dislike having to deliver it."

Jack nodded. There was little he could say. "How bad?"

Doctor Charbonneau licked his lips again, then said, "Your suit's regenerative capabilities deal with any … accidental exposure you may have to a regular atmosphere by re-growing your tissue. In addition, the suit has been slowing the expansion of cancerous tumors while promoting the growth of healthy cells."

Jack's head nodded up and down like a kid's toy, agreeing with everything the doctor said and knowing that somewhere there was going to be a "but" that delivered a hammer blow of bad news. "Right, I get it. The suit has been keeping me alive. I never take it off, doc, unless I'm in here with you."

The doctor gripped the tablet he carried with both hands, the tips of his fingers were tight and lightened against its edge with stress. "Your cancer has accelerated. It's reached stage four, and you know, we both know, there is no stage five."

Jack looked at the floor and he heard the sound of his vital signs on the wall display tick up as his heart raced and his breath quickened. He reached up and peeled the monitoring device from his shoulder and the display ceased. "What does that mean?"

Charbonneau took a step back and his eyes slid toward the door before looking back to Jack. "The cancer caused by your accident has never gone away, it has never even gone into remission. Between the oncology drugs and the regenerative properties of the suit, we have managed an uneasy stalemate with the disease. We have now reached a point where our efforts are no longer sufficient to stave off the aggressive nature of your cancer."

Jack looked down at his scarred hands again. "So, it's spreading again?"

Doctor Charbonneau nodded. "We successfully contained it there for more than a decade. I know this is devastating news to hear, but you must realize that you've had more time than anyone ever thought you'd have."

Time was the one thing Jack knew he didn't have. As far as he was concerned, the accident and the intervening decade had flown by in the blink of an eye. It was as if everything had taken no more than a couple weeks, not years. "Where has it spread to?"

Doctor Charbonneau took a deep breath from the regulator and the glass of his mask fogged slightly around the nose piece when he exhaled. "It's in every internal organ. Frankly, I'm amazed you came in complaining of simply not feeling well. You must be having trouble breathing, seeing and even thinking." He stopped speaking for a moment, letting the news sink in.

Jack looked up and caught his reflection in the mirror over the sink behind the doctor. His cheeks were flushed and glowed orange against the brilliant white of the sterile examination room. His poker face was just one more thing the accident had taken away from him. It was hard to control your emotions when your face glowed like a lantern. "So, what do I do now? What are my options?"

"Medically, we've reached a point where we are out of options, so I recommend hospice care. We can make you comfortable in a facility like this."

He didn't understand what Doctor Charbonneau was saying. There was always one more rabbit to pull out of the hat. One more treatment, one more course of harsher medication.

"I don't accept that."

"Mon ami, there is nothing more I can do for you. What we have accomplished so far is nothing short of miraculous. Please, let us make you comfortable in your remaining time."

Mon ami? Jack thought and studied the doctor. Jack knew that he had been nothing more than a treasure trove of interesting data to the doctor, that the man was waiting for the conclusion of his life so he could write journal articles. That had been the deal; no publishing until after he'd died. Jack didn't want the pity that came with notoriety.

Doctor Charbonneau dodged Jack's eye contact and fidgeted with his tablet. Jack's second career, as an enforcer for the Syndicate, had taught him to read people. He knew when people were lying about not being able to pay their debts, about where they had been when he was trying to find them, and about any other thing he wanted to know. People lied all the time and right now he could sense deception coming off the doctor in waves. The man was no friend, and he certainly wasn't telling Jack everything.

"Doc, don't lie to me."

Doctor Charbonneau looked at the floor. "I know this can be difficult news to hear, but you must understand, the treatments work, and then eventually the cancer finds its way around them. Believe me, I wish it wasn't so. I wish I had another option, for all my patients' sakes."

Jack saw the doctor's attention blink away for just a moment like something was on the tip of his tongue. Charbonneau was clearly holding something back. Jack slid off the table and the johnnie slipped to the floor. He stood there, his gaunt frame covered by nothing but his sagging boxer shorts. Anyone else might have looked pathetic, but with skin glowing a sallow orange and bones visible just under his skin, Atomic Jack looked like the most dangerous man alive.

A quick look at the door told him no one was outside. No nurses coming to check on the doc, and no orderlies standing by in case things went wrong. It was just the two of them, alone. He reached out and caught the doctor by the throat with one hand and tore the breathing mask away with the other.

As Charbonneau looked at him with wide, shocked eyes, Jack tightened his grip on the doc's throat for the briefest of seconds and then dropped him back to the floor.

"There's something you want to tell me, Doctor Charbonneau. I suggest you do it or I'm going to watch you pass out from lack of oxygen and then I'm going to watch you die. After that, I'm going to leave the hospital while your body lays on the floor waiting for someone to find it. Do you understand me?"

Gasping, the doctor nodded. Jack thought it must be strange for him, to be able to take full, deep breaths but still feel the effects of oxygen deprivation. It was going to get worse if he didn't get the answer he wanted.

Charbonneau reached for the mask in Jack's hand but he pulled it back. "You gonna tell me what I want to know?"

The doctor nodded his assent violently and lurched again for the mask. Jack held it farther away to reinforce his point, then handed it to the man. The doctor strapped it on and breathed deeply, sucking in air to getting himself under control.

"It's a rumor," Charbonneau said. "I don't have firsthand experience with it."

"Something you heard from someone?"

"That's right, it was about a year ago. It was another doctor, one with wealthy clients. A group staffed by people working on cutting edge treatments, things that are much further ahead of the work being done on Earth."

"Something that could help me?" Jack said. He didn't like how needy he sounded.

Charbonneau shrugged. "I don't know for sure. Your condition is so unique, but maybe. What was described to me seemed fantastic."

"Where is this place?"

"Off planet," Charbonneau said. "I just know it's out in the far reaches, where no one ever goes. A ship. That's all she knew."

Jack glanced up at the ceiling, thinking about it for a moment. "Whatever this group is working on, it's not legal, is it? That's why they're hiding out there."

Charbonneau swallowed hard. "That was the impression I got. Their methods, the way they are conducting the experiments, it didn't sound ethical."

"I need the location."

"I don't know it," Charbonneau said, and Jack grabbed his throat again. "I'm sorry, she didn't know herself."

Jack pulled him to a small rolling stool and pushed him down on it. He thought for a moment and then turned to the doctor. "How did this other doctor find out? If they need to stay hidden, how did she know?"

"They needed samples from her lab."

"What kind of samples?"

"She's a zoologist. They needed exotic cell samples. I don't know why."

Jack leaned back against the exam table and considered what Charbonneau was telling him. If this other doctor was sending things to this group, there had to be transportation involved, and probably not the kind legitimate folks use.

"I need information about your friend."

Charbonneau recoiled in horror. "Can't we leave her out of this?"

Jack shook his head and retrieved his mobi from his pressure suit. He held it out to the doctor. "Get on with it."

"Don't harm her," he said as he entered her contact information with shaking fingers. "You owe me that much."

Jack took the mobi from him. "I'll leave that up to you. Don't contact her, don't warn her, and she'll be fine. If she runs before I get there and I have to hunt her down or I find her surrounded by Protective Services, things will get ugly." He moved closer and drew a finger down the doctor's face. "You understand me?"

Charbonneau shrank away on the stool, sweat dripped from beneath his slick goatee, but he nodded.

"Good."

4.

Kimiyo Himura approached Saji Vy's office. The obelisk-like tower dominated downtown Go City; made from volcanic glass, it rose, twisting around four times from the ground floor to the uppermost level. The crystalline structure of the building drank in sunlight to power itself. Saji's public profile narrated a wonderous story of someone who had emigrated from Mumbai with parents who owned a small business that refurbished starship components for resale. From that humble beginning their only son, Saji, built SajiCo, one of the largest corporations on Earth. Kimiyo was a personal assistant, in charge of special projects.

The company was publicly traded, but Saji Vy was the only CEO it had ever known. Over the decades there had been several takeover attempts but Kimiyo knew Saji had fended off each in turn. Sometimes using acceptable business strategies, and other times using whatever means he viewed as necessary.

Kimiyo had been with SajiCo for about six years. In her first assignment, she'd overseen the payment of ransom to retrieve one of Saji's starship crews being held hostage. That's where she'd met Cole Seger and the two of them had been together ever since.

Once inside and up to the staggering top floor, Kimiyo rounded the corner in the executive suites and stepped into a small anteroom outside of Saji's office, in which there were two administrative assistants. Kimiyo nodded to the assistants and proceeded to enter Saji's immaculate office.

Black and white industrial prints hung on the walls sparingly, displaying images of SajiCo starship components. The images were shot close up to avoid showing the entirety of the piece and instead create an abstract view of the company's inventory. Wherever one looked in this office they were reminded of what Saji built.

Past the central conference table — large enough to comfortably accommodate twenty — Saji had set up his personal workspace by the floor-to-ceiling window with his desk and a more intimate set of chairs for visitors.

No personal mementos decorated the heavy, square desk; no holos of children because he didn't have any, and no images of a wife because he was currently divorced. In Kimiyo's opinion, the desk sat there looking like it had just come out of its shipping box. The two chairs facing the desk were a low backed design upholstered in deep gray fabric with pencil-thin legs set at forty-five-degree angles from the center of the chair. Kimiyo had seen larger framed visitors to the office sit down gingerly in the chairs as if they expected the wiry legs to collapse at any moment.

When Kimiyo entered, Saji's own highbacked chair faced the window and subsequent bird's eye view of Go City. She approached the desk and stood quietly. Saji was pleasant enough for a boss, but he had the annoying habit of tripping on his own power. He could be petty in that way, enjoying these little moments where he could make subordinates wait at his leisure. Finally, after a long moment, the chair swiveled and revealed the man himself.

Saji was small, standing just a few centimeters taller than her. He had dark skin and wrinkles gathered all around his eyes and mouth. This wizened visage gave him an air of superiority and betrayed just how many decades he'd walked the Earth. Kimiyo knew he was approaching his eighty-third birthday, a remarkable achievement of medicine and expensive life lengthening treatments. Of course, for a man sitting on a throne atop a tower in the middle of a city dedicated to visiting other planets and far-flung stars, expenses were hardly worth considering. He wore a lightweight charcoal grey suit in the current cut as if he aspired to camouflage with the décor of the office.

A small smile crossed his thin lips. "So good to see you, Kimiyo. Please, take a seat."

She sat and held up a small tablet. "I have the itinerary for your conference prepared for review, sir."

He took the offered device and scrolled through it. After a moment he handed it back. "This all looks fine. Thank you for all your hard work, Kimiyo," he said. "I know coordinating this conference with so many different companies was extraordinarily difficult for you."

She rose and nodded. "No problem at all, sir." In fact, the conference for manufacturers of starship components would be a global meeting that had taken months to put together.

Instead of turning to leave, though, she remained standing in front of the desk. "If you don't mind, there is one more thing I'd like to discuss."

"Yes?"

"You remember Nathan Teller, don't you?"

Saji sat back in his chair. "I do. He retrieved the *Charon* for us a few years ago from that cult that hijacked it."

"That's right, sir. Well, my partner is, or rather was, a member of his crew—"

"Mr. Seger, correct?"

Kimiyo paused before answering. She was relatively sure she had never discussed her personal life with him. "Yes, sir. Well, Nathan has had a bit of bad luck recently and I told him I'd see if there were any opportunities available with the company."

Saji raised his eyebrows as if he were surprised by the request. "Well, that is certainly unexpected. Captain Teller seemed more resourceful in our previous meetings."

"I suppose everyone falls on hard times, sir," Kimiyo said. That was as far as she was willing to go in describing Nathan's current state of affairs.

Saji crossed one thin leg over the other and folded his hands in his lap. His brow gathered in deep concentration and he looked past Kimiyo. She stood still, waiting for him to speak. Just as the silence grew uncomfortable, he cleared his throat.

"It's funny you should bring this up right now," he said. "There is a special project that has recently become rather more pressing. Do you think Captain Teller would be available immediately?"

"I believe so."

"Good," he said as he typed on a mobi he produced from a jacket pocket. "I'm sending you the details. Tell Captain Teller I'll need a quote and the time frame is short. I'll need it completed prior to my departure for the conference."

"Thank you, sir. I'll contact him immediately."

"Of course, and thank you for bringing this to my attention," he said. "If this works out it will make me very happy."

5.

Atomic Jack and his driver were on the edge of Go City; he sat in the passenger's side of a float car outside the lab complex where Doctor Susan Park worked as the sun dipped low on the western horizon. It had taken Jack a week to learn everything he needed to know about the good doctor.

The lab complex was made up of five squat buildings; the tallest of which was four stories, all in the usual adobe-esque, synthetic material builders used to blend in with the aesthetics of the environment.

What drew his eye was the berm of soil and indigenous plants that surrounded the complex. To a casual passerby, it would look like expensive landscaping meant to dress up the place. What it really did was form a wall with only two gaps. The first faced the highway and had a sliding gate with a small guardhouse. The other gap was in the rear for deliveries. It was wider to allow truck access, but equally well guarded.

"I don't like it," Jack said after sitting quietly for a few minutes. "We could get in there, but it looks crowded. I don't need a bunch of people poking their heads in while the doctor and I are talking."

The driver nodded. He was a slight man named Jojo, and he came from downtown. Jack's regular two-man crew had been busted six months ago in a deal involving Nathan Teller. One of his guys was dead and the other was in a prison hospital ward re-growing his groin. Jack preferred not to work alone, so he'd been working with the new guy ever since. As far as Jojo knew, Doctor Park was just another deadbeat to be leaned on. He did what Jack asked and didn't bother himself overly much with thinking.

"I've got her home address, too," Jojo said in his quiet voice. "It's an apartment building on the southside."

"Which floor is she on?"

Jojo gave him a greasy smile. "Ground floor, and it's one of those older buildings where the door opens outside. No internal hallway to deal with."

Jack nodded inside his helmet and looked back at the lab complex. Jojo looked like the kind of creep whose second nature was to notice how secure women's apartments were. "Okay, let's go see if she's home."

They left the facility and drove back into the city. Doctor Park's neighborhood was empty and the night was quiet as they pulled into the parking lot on her side of the building. Jojo pulled a telescopic device from a bag in the backseat and pointed it at the apartment.

"There's no one in there," he said. "What do you want to do?"

"We go in and wait."

Two hours later, the door to Susan Park's apartment opened and she walked in. Jojo stepped quickly from behind the door. He closed the door with one hand and clamped the other around her mouth. He pushed her roughly into the living room and dragged her down onto a sofa. Jack heard her struggling in the dim light, but Jojo was strong. Jack watched them wrestle for a moment before he turned on a lamp beside his chair.

"Stop it," Jack said, his voice amplified by a small speaker in his helmet. Parks froze mid-struggle and looked at him. Her eyes grew wide as she took in Jack's pressure suit. She'd stopped kicking, but Jojo kept a hand on her mouth.

"If you stay quiet, he'll take his hand off your mouth," Jack said. "If you make a sound, he'll make sure you stay quiet. Do you understand me?"

Her eyes were full of fear and she shot a glance at Jojo before nodding. Jojo took his hand off her mouth and stroked her cheek like she was a small pet he'd taken a fancy to. She looked like she was going to vomit, but she didn't say anything. In the lamplight, Jack could appreciate how young she was for such an accomplished scientist.

Jack's suit rustled as he shifted to leaned forward in his chair. "Just to confirm, you are Doctor Susan Park, correct?"

"Yes," she said with a small voice.

"We just need some information about your work. You tell us what we want to know and we'll leave. Do you understand?"

"Yes."

"What's your specialty? What do you study?"

She cleared her throat nervously. "I'm a Zoologist and my specialty is Teuthology. I study cephalopods." She paused and even in her terror, noted their marked confusion. "Like squids and octopuses."

Jack considered that and didn't understand how that fit in with his situation. He let it slide for now. "About a year ago, you sent samples to someone looking for genetic material from exotic animals. I need to know who that was."

Something crossed her eyes and Jack knew he had hit paydirt.

"I'm not sure exactly what you mean," she said. "Our lab collects and provides samples for many customers. Can you be more specific?"

"Look," he said, "I'm going to tell you how this plays out, because I've seen it all before. So listen to me, because I'm only going to say this once."

"I am listening," she said. "I want to help you—"

He held up a gloved hand. "That play is tired." He stood up from the chair and wandered into the center of the small living room, closing the distance on her. "You know what I'm talking about. I can read it on your face. There's no need to tell me I'm not giving you enough information, and without it you can't help. Save that story for your suspicious colleagues. What you want now is to help me help myself, so we'll leave, right? You don't want us hanging out here for a few hours, do you?"

Jack looked at Jojo and saw that the man was focused on her, maybe playing out some creepy fantasy. He wondered if he even realized Jack was still in the room. She swallowed hard and Jack knew he was getting through.

"Maybe you could tell me what the samples were?" Her voice was plaintive, hoping they would just accept her ignorance and leave. Jack didn't get the sense that she was frightened though, not of him and not of the person whose secrets she kept. It felt more like she'd just rather not spill the beans if it wasn't truly necessary. She was brave, he'd give her that.

Jack let out a sigh. "Put your hand over her mouth. I don't want her screaming."

Her eyes opened wide and she inhaled as Jojo's hand squeezed roughly over her jaw. Her panicked expression told Jack the story he'd heard a hundred times before; it was all real now, in a way she hadn't really thought they'd get to.

He knelt down, closing the remaining distance between them. He was close enough she could probably see her frightened face reflected in the glass of his faceplate.

He removed a glove and his hand burst into orange-tinged flames. Then he saw the look in her eyes, the one he'd been waiting for, the one they all got when they finally broke and decided to tell him what he wanted to know. Despite the pain he was feeling, he moved his hand closer so she could feel the heat and know this wasn't some holographic trick.

"Are you going to tell me what I want to know?" He asked. His heart rate was finally high enough that the suit injected him with painkillers.

She stared, entranced by the flaming hand only centimeters from her face. She tried to nod, but Jojo's other hand had drifted under her chin.

Jack slipped the glove back on, extinguishing the flames as the glove seal locked into place. The painkillers hit fast, dousing the screaming nerves in his hand. He returned to the chair he'd been sitting in. "Go sit in the car. I want to talk to her."

"Are you sure?" Jojo said with a perplexed look on his face.

Jack fiddled with his glove. He couldn't take his glove off again, not so soon, but the creepy little dude didn't know that. Jojo blanched then stood up and silently backed out of the apartment.

When he heard the door close, Jack turned his attention to Doctor Park, "See, I do you a favor and remove the sweaty pervert, now you're going to do me a favor and tell me everything about that shipment. Yes?"

"Yes."

"Okay then, get started."

She swallowed hard before speaking and tugged the hem of her shirt straight. "The tissue samples you're speaking about were for octopuses. We received the request, which isn't unusual, and filled it. That's all I know."

"Who did the samples go to?"

"Vibrant Passion," she said in a squeaky voice.

Jack stopped, taken aback. "The lifespan extension company?"

"Yes."

Jack looked at her, letting the silence build up. She still had more to say so he kept quiet.

"What made it unusual," she finally said, "was that they wanted samples from specific animals."

Now they were getting somewhere. "What was special about those animals?"

"Octopuses are some of the most intelligent animals on Earth," she said. "They are problem solvers. Hundreds of years ago they were observed doing things like opening jars to get their prey or boarding fishing boats to steal their crab catch. They even use tools to build shelters.

"Our lab has been experimenting with those capabilities with selective breeding. We test the animals and the ones that show the greatest ability are bred to pass those capabilities onto their offspring."

"And those offspring are smarter than their parents?" Jack asked.

"Sometimes, sometimes not, but we have had remarkable progress. Our current experiment has been going on for years and is thousands of generations long, so we've got some pretty bright octopuses. These are the samples that were requested."

"So, what made this request out of the routine?"

She looked away, clearly bothered by the question.

"The experiment is proprietary," she said. "It's not exactly secret but we haven't published our findings yet. I certainly never expected the director of the project to come to me and order me to fulfill the tissue samples request. As far as I know, we've never released samples from this particular experiment from the lab."

"Never?"

She shook her head. "I objected, but he was very convincing. I had to sign a non-disclosure agreement specific to this incident, which was weird because we already sign those annually for the lab work, and I was given a sizeable bonus. I got the feeling it was an incentive to maintain my silence."

Jack leaned back in the chair. Something Susan Park had told Doctor Charbonneau about this incident had made him believe it could relate to Jack's health crisis, but he couldn't see it yet.

"You know the samples went to Vibrant Passion?"

"I do."

"Do you know why?"

"I don't. Their whole business model is improving the lifestyle of wealthy customers. I don't know how octopus tissue samples relate to cosmetics and life lengthening. Especially samples from those particular animals." The words tumbled out as if she was confessing a long-kept secret to a friend.

He leaned forward, ending the false camaraderie between them. "You really have no idea?"

She shrank into the sofa. "No, none," she said in a small voice.

He was convinced she had nothing more to tell him. "Keep quiet about this. As you can imagine, my NDA has stricter penalties than any you've signed at work."

Her only answer was a curt nod.

He exited the apartment and got into the float car. Jojo pulled onto the highway and drove into the darkness.

"Did she tell you what you needed?"

"Yeah, and I want her left alone, understand? I may need more from her and I don't want your grubby hands on her."

"Sure, Jack. I understand."

Jack stared into the night, pondering his next move.

6.

The roar of four plasma thrusters split the air two-thousand meters over the small east-cost Florida town of Caroline. Nathan's co-pilot, Marla Jax, looked over at him. "Good thing this isn't a job that requires stealth," she said over the intercom. "I'm pretty sure people in Havana know we're coming."

"It's Florida," Marla's husband, Duncan, replied from his spot behind the cockpit in the cabin where the crew chief normally sat. "No one cares how much noise we make."

Marla was right about the noise, though. They were flying a rented AHL-30a "Dragonfly": a heavy-duty aircraft that had started life as a gunship four decades ago in the Protective Services. Now it was mostly used as a sky crane by anyone with enough credits to rent it. It wasn't his beloved *Blue Moon Bandit*, but it was just the machine they needed for Saji's job.

The ship dropped a few meters and then Marla leveled it out. She frowned. "Is that normal?"

Nathan grinned at her. "It's just a little crosswind. You'll have to compensate for it manually because they stripped out the good flight software when she was decommissioned." He rolled his wrists. "Just try and go with the flow."

"I think it's probably easier to do that when you have a few thousand hours in one of these. I'm not even sure I should have the stick right now."

He waved her off. "You're doing fine. The *Bandit* is a truck compared to this. Try and have a little fun with it."

Nathan had learned to fly one of these when he'd done his service in the Air Cavalry. The Dragonfly style of flight was quick and maneuverable, fun to fly — even when people had been shooting at him.

This particular ship was stripped of anything dangerous or classified. In addition to the high-end flight software being replaced with a clunky civilian version, there were no guns, and no military grade communication system. The ship bounced again.

"Plasma flow regulator to the second thruster is shit," Marla said. "It keeps fluctuating on me."

"Yeah, I know, but this piece of crap is all I could afford and your husband claims it will keep us in the air. Just—"

"Don't say 'go with the flow,' Nathan. This damn thing is going to drop us right down into one of those canals. We'll probably end up eaten by alligators."

Duncan's deep baritone broke in over the intercom again. "Don't worry, baby. She'll fly."

Marla shushed him, then said, "I'm certain that my good attitude and prayers are the only thing keeping us in the air at the moment."

Nathan checked the head's up display and pointed to the right. "Our staging area is right over there next to the river. See the empty parking lot?"

"Got it," Marla said.

She set the big airship down gently, despite the thruster flow issues. Nathan gave her a thumbs up. "Couldn't have done it better myself."

Before she could say anything, he stripped off his flight helmet and hustled back into the cabin where the rest of the crew were strapped in. Everyone unbuckled and stood up, holding onto the walls for support. Cole stood next to Duncan, and across the cabin their machinist, Richie Pearson, had Tricia at his side. If plan 'A' worked, Richie and Tricia would have a boring nice day in the Dragonfly with Marla.

Nathan slipped down the short set of stairs to the Dragonfly's larger cargo area and stepped around the pair of float bikes strapped to the deck. He pressed the red button mounted to the right of the rear ramp to release it but nothing happened. The ramp remained steadfastly locked in place. He gave the button a sharp smack and this time the heavy metal ramp released and slammed into the ground. Nathan looked at Duncan.

"I'll have a look at the hydraulics," Duncan said. "It shouldn't be doing that."

"Just make sure we can raise it back up so we can fly." Nathan said. Then he freed one of the hover bikes, mounted up, and started the anti-grav motor. Cole followed suit and they headed down the ramp into the humid Florida air. Nathan gave the river next to the parking lot a cursory look for gators and snakes. The area they were in was mostly deserted and wildlife had reclaimed much of it.

"Our target is about fifteen klicks away," Nathan said as he adjusted his helmet. Cole nodded and they raced off.

The highway was four lanes wide. Nathan hit the throttle and they approached the small town about five minutes after leaving their staging area. They crossed paths with few other vehicles as they approached the warehouses and shipping yards close to the river. The place they were looking for was here on the outskirts, close to the highway. Nathan spotted it and they pulled into the parking lot.

Nathan removed his helmet and took the joint in. It was nothing but a crappy little tourist trap. A giant animated-hologram sign overlooking the highway showed an old Saturn V rocket blasting off a launch pad and blazing a path into the afternoon sky before fading out and reading, "Wild Willie's Journey to the Stars Museum!" Nathan noticed that the holo-projectors must have been out of alignment, though, because the black and white colors of the rocket were out of sync and the resulting effect was of an all-white rocket shooting into the sky with an irregular black shadow chasing after it.

He looked over at Cole. "If I watch that enough times, I'm going to get a headache."

They looked the building over and things didn't get any better. The "museum" was a converted hangar. The gaudy paint had probably been bright and cheerful when it was fresh but now it was just faded and sad.

Cole pointed to a pair of glass doors. "Looks like that's our way in."

They walked across the parking lot and pulled on one of the doors. It opened into a dank vestibule with worn carpet and a kiosk in the middle of the space. Past the kiosk, there was another set of doors; Nathan gave each one a tug and then a push, but they were locked.

Cole paced back around to the front of the kiosk; the moment he was front and center a hologram popped to life and addressed them. "Hello, visitors! Welcome to the museum." It hiccupped on the last word. "You must purchase admission before entering the museum. You may do so at the kiosk."

Cole looked over at Nathan. "I was promised an all-expenses paid trip to Florida."

Nathan waved his mobi over the kiosk for payment. It offered him a combo package with lunch included but he turned the meal down. The doors opened with a soft click and the frames lit up, beckoning them through.

"After you," Nathan said with a wave. "Let's see if we can find what we came for."

Inside, the museum was a large, open space, with dim lighting and a series of space travel exhibits. Nathan pointed at a space capsule. "Check this out. It's a replica of a Soyuz capsule."

Cole glanced at the label explaining the exhibit. "People used this to go into space?"

"They sure did," Nathan said. "This was used by the Russians, although they were called Soviets back then."

"I've been in bigger bathrooms."

Nathan walked on through the exhibits, most of them life-sized replicas of famous crafts. He ran a hand over the rail surrounding them. It was dusty. "I don't think Wild Willie is cleaning very often."

"Well, I'm sure building these models and letting the lights burn out takes up a lot of his time. Do you see what we came for? All of it looks the same to me."

Nathan took a look around. "They really don't have things organized very well. The Soviet stuff is next to the American space shuttle replica and right here they've got the Mars exploratory rovers next to the Apollo gear. Man, who put this place together?"

"You're such a history nerd."

They walked past the chipped plastic dome that was Wild Willie's replica of the first permanent lunar settlement and Nathan pointed. "That's it over there."

The item they wanted was another life-sized capsule, this one painted dark gray with a small cylinder on top of the crew compartment. There were open spaces in the small craft where panels were missing. The words '*Liberty Bell 7*' were written on the hull in faded white paint.

"This is it?" Cole said. "It's even smaller than that Russian thing." He ducked under the metal railing and peeked inside. "There's one seat in this thing. What did they use it for?"

"You've got no appreciation for history, you know that? This was an orbital capsule. It was just supposed to go up and prove people could survive in space. As long as they made it back alive the mission was a success."

"Well, that's just stupid. There had to be easier ways of proving that then going up in this thing. It doesn't even have engines."

Nathan followed him under the railing and stroked the side of the capsule with his bare hands. He could feel the weight of history on it and a look inside convinced him of its authenticity. The surviving instruments looked worn and aged. This was definitely the real deal, not some plastic model or even a high-end replica.

"It was boosted into orbit with a Mercury Redstone rocket and then separated. It didn't have engines of its own."

Cole pointed at the open spaces. "This doesn't look airtight."

"A hatch is missing. There's a whole controversy, but basically, at splashdown this whole thing sank to the bottom of the ocean where it stayed for a few decades before it was recovered, one hatch door lighter."

Cole's eyes grew wide. "Wait a minute. This thing landed in the ocean? Not on land? It doesn't look like it floats."

"I'll explain it all to you later. Right now, we need to figure out how to get it out of here."

"And why would you want to do that?" someone said from behind them in a deep voice with a heavy southern accent. Most impressively, it seemed to come from slightly above them.

Nathan turned and looked at a thick torso clad in a dirty white t-shirt and denim overalls. He tipped his head back and looked up at the giant of a man looming over them. He had a wide face with deeply tanned skin and a bushy gray beard. Nathan backed up a few steps until he bumped up against the space capsule. The guy had to be damn near two meters tall.

"Geez, you gave me a scare," Nathan said.

"Well maybe that's not a bad thing considering I just heard you plotting to steal one of our attractions," the giant said.

Cole stepped up. "You're a big one."

"There's no reason to be rude."

"Okay," Nathan said. "Let me see if I can just straighten this out." He introduced himself and stepped back into the aisle. He held his hand out and the man shook it with a hand as big as a bear's paw.

"I'm Billy," the giant said and squeezed hard on Nathan's hand. "Now, why are you talking about stealing from us?"

Nathan flinched and pulled his hand loose. "Look, we're repo men here to collect this star … space capsule." He'd almost said 'starship,' but *Liberty Bell 7* didn't exactly qualify. He pulled a tablet from his jacket and held it out to Billy. "This paperwork from the court explains everything."

Billy took the tablet and looked at it, swiping through the pages. Nathan had his doubts as to whether he was actually reading it, but then he said, "This seems to be in order, but I can't let you take the exhibit."

Nathan kept his cool. "Sir, you need to realize this is happening. That capsule is now the property of Saji Vy. It was used as collateral on a business loan for this establishment and the loan was defaulted. The court ruled in favor of Mr. Vy."

Billy pointed at the tablet. "Well, Mr. Teller, what you need to realize is that this court date was last month on the tenth. See here?"

Nathan looked at the document. "Yeah. So?"

"So, this place was owned by my uncle William Pierce. He's the Wild Willie from the sign out front." He grinned. "I'm named after him. He was a great guy. Picked up his name when he was a firefighter. Apparently, he was very brave but also a bit of a risk taker."

"Uh-huh," Nathan said. "So what?"

"No need to be so impatient."

Feeling inexplicably chastised by the polite giant, Nathan said, "Of course. I apologize. Please, continue."

"Thank you. My momma always said there's no need to be rude when being polite only takes a little more effort. Anyway, Uncle Willie passed away on the third of last month, God rest his soul."

"Oh, how did it happen?"

"Taking a risk, of course. Uncle Willie was up on some scaffolding over there in the corner wiring up a light fixture and he stepped right off into thin air. Fell about ten meters to the concrete."

Nathan and Cole looked at the indicated corner as if Uncle Willie might still be splayed across the floor. Seeing that he wasn't, they looked back to Billy.

"Did he go fast?" Cole asked.

"No, sir. He was prone to working late into the night and as best we can tell he took his tumble around midnight. My momma came in to find him around nine o'clock the next morning. She's in her eighties herself but she's still spry and enjoys coming in to help out. Anyway, it was an awful mess with blood and everything all over the floor but he was still kicking. He lingered in the hospital for two days before going to his heavenly reward."

"You have my condolences," Nathan said. "But the ruling is still in effect."

Billy answered him with a deep sigh. "Sir, what you're not understanding is that Uncle Willie was unable to attend the court date, so the court automatically adjudicated in favor of Mr. Vy. However, the problem is the lawsuit was filed against Uncle Willie, and by the time the tenth rolled around he was deceased. Now, I'm no lawyer but I know enough about the law to understand that no court would expect a decedent to answer a summons."

It was a good argument, and more articulate than Nathan had expected. Usually, the guys he was repossessing from had more of a 'if I punch harder, I win' attitude. He decided to stick to his guns and barrel through. "Be that as it may, I have a lawful claim to the item, and I will be taking it."

"Sir, you're being a bit dim. I don't know if that's a personality trait or a lack of education in the applicable law, but this historical artifact is no longer the property of Uncle Willie, but rather an item included in his estate, as are this building and all the contents contained herein. The executor of the estate is getting things settled with the local court and as soon as that process is completed, we can see about determining ownership of this item. However, you may want to tell Mr. Vy that the court proceedings will likely start all over again." He handed the tablet back.

Nathan was starting to like Billy. But he needed the money from this job to buy back the *Bandit*. Cole gave him a look that said 'Please don't piss that guy off. If he decides to eat you, I won't be able to stop him.' Repossessing from the recently deceased wasn't pleasant business, but Nathan knew how to twist the rules at least as well as Billy.

Nathan felt his blood pressure rising but he smiled. "Billy, until your local courts and executor notify Mr. Vy and his team in Go City of Uncle Willie's untimely passing, and the courts there decide to reverse this ruling, then this order is valid. So, let's do this the easy way, huh? I take the capsule today, it's kept safe with Mr. Vy, then in another month or so there's a new ruling and bing-bang-boom you have your capsule back."

Billy looked down at him and for the first time Nathan saw something other than politeness on his face. He looked annoyed and Nathan didn't like it.

"Sorry, sir, but that just doesn't work for me. I'm afraid we'll be keeping the *Liberty Bell 7* right where she is."

"Well, that doesn't work for me," Nathan said. "So, call the local Protective Services if you want, but in the meantime, I'm going make preparations to leave with it."

Nathan prepared himself for a fight. This was usually when people got a little crazy in the process. If the big guy was going to swing, the time was approaching. Instead, Billy said, "I'm going to give my Cousin Earl a call. See if he can't straighten you out."

"Okay, you do that. Can't see where that will help, though. I'll just tell him the same thing."

A slow grin slid across Billy's face. "Oh, Earl is the local Chief of the Protective Services." Billy pulled out a mobi to make his call but stopped. "If you don't like what he has to say, my sister is the warden. Maybe they can persuade you."

"You don't say."

Billy nodded. "What with Uncle Willie working as a firefighter, I guess you could say our family has a long and storied tradition of public service."

"Yes, I suppose you could," Nathan said and then he turned to Cole. "Looks like we're leaving."

7.

A few hours later, Marla piloted the Dragonfly toward the museum. She was taking the long way around, approaching the building from out over the Atlantic Ocean. The low sun was in her eyes as it began sinking into the horizon. She lowered the shaded visor on her helmet and turned to Nathan.

"You're sure we've got enough room to set this thing down out back?"

"Yeah," he said. "I saw a landing pad and hangar door in the rear. It's probably how they get their exhibits in and out."

The ship bucked as the starboard side forward thruster coughed again. Marla made her adjustments without complaint this time, dropping altitude when they crossed over from the ocean to the beach and brought the Dragonfly in low enough that Nathan could make out individual people walking along the sidewalks. She double checked her coordinates and pulled a tight circle over the landing pad at the rear of museum, making sure there were no obstructions. Satisfied, she set the ship down so smoothly Nathan barely felt the landing gear make contact with the concrete.

He patted her on the shoulder and quickly exited the cockpit. When he got to the cargo bay, the ramp was already lowered and Cole and Duncan were at the museum's hangar door controls. Richie stood off to the side holding a black duffle bag and one end of a wire tow cable that trailed back into the Dragonfly. Duncan had a mobi in his hands connected to an auxiliary port. He tapped controls on the device's screen and after a few quiet seconds nothing happened.

"Is everything all right?" Nathan said with equal amounts of concern and impatience in his voice.

Duncan kept his attention focused on the screen. "Hang tight, I've almost got it."

Nathan scanned the area with his eyes, looking for trouble. If Billy the Giant was lurking around or a camera spotted them, the plan could be a bust. The scene was quiet, though. The sign at the

front of the building said the museum closed at five and it was
now six-thirty. Hopefully no one was inside working overtime.

"I think I've got it," Duncan said. He tapped the mobi's screen
and the hangar door started to slide open. The noise of the rollers
grinding against their track was immense but no lights popped
on from inside. Nathan and Cole stood in the opening as it grew
wider. If there was trouble, they would deal with it. When the
hangar door stopped, the light noise of traffic from the street out
front was the only sound.

Duncan tucked his mobi away and took the duffle bag and
cable from Richie. The machinist headed back to the Dragonfly
while the other three entered the museum and made their way up
the wide main aisle towards the *Liberty Bell 7*, which was about
halfway up on the right.

They moved quickly, keeping an eye out for robots or other
security measures but the building remained dark and quiet. When
they got to the exhibit, Nathan moved the metal railings out of the
way and Duncan set the duffel bag down. The engineer unzipped
it and removed two large anti-grav pallet jacks; the devices had a
lip that slipped under the capsule's base. Duncan and Nathan each
pushed one jack into place.

"Pass me the strap," Nathan said, hurrying Duncan along.

"Chill out, Nathan. I'm getting it," Duncan said in a harsh whisper.
Holding the anti-grav jack in place with one hand, he fished out a
wide yellow strap with a ratchet tie down on one end. They attached
the strap around the capsule and through the jacks. Duncan fed the
loose end into the ratchet and worked it back and forth quickly.

Nathan winced at the noise the ratchet made but there was
nothing to be done about it. The anti-grav pallet jacks usually held
on to large loads by generating a magnetic field, but the capsule's
titanium and aluminum hull rendered this less than useless.

As Duncan tightened the strap, Cole stood on alert, his head
on a swivel, looking for big Billy or anyone else who might be
creeping around. Duncan snapped his fingers and Cole jumped.

"We're good to go," Duncan said. "Turn it on."

They activated the jack units and stepped back. The capsule
floated off its display base and held altitude, hovering about ten
centimeters above the floor. Nathan grabbed hold of the open
hatchway. The capsule weighed about a ton and a half, but he was
able to move it with a single hand.

They threw another yellow strap, this one with a metal loop
affixed in the center, over the top of the capsule and tied it back
onto itself.

Nathan took a quick look around, wondering if their luck would hold. "It's time to go," he said.

Duncan tossed the duffel inside the capsule. Then the two of them grabbed the vertical strap and hauled the capsule into the aisle. It wobbled on the anti-grav units but stayed off the floor. Nathan spun the *Liberty Bell 7* so the metal loop faced the hangar door and attached the tow cable. They had to be careful; while the anti-grav jacks made the capsule easy to maneuver, it still weighed as much as a ground vehicle. If they moved it too fast, they wouldn't be able to stop it.

"Let's get gone," Nathan said. That's when their luck ran out.

Nathan saw movement from the corner of his eye but before he could say anything, a bolt of glowing blue energy shot out of the darkness and enveloped Cole. He went down hard on the concrete with a tight grunt.

"My sister didn't think you'd be dumb enough to come back, but I knew you weren't the kind of man to give up easily," Billy said as he crawled out of a replica of a deep space probe. The bruiser wore his coveralls and a harness for carrying tools. Nathan could read the exhibit's sign in the dim evening light and saw that one just like it had once been used to explore Jupiter's moon Io.

Nathan dropped low and scurried over to Cole. His eyes were open and he looked at Nathan with rage.

"Don't worry about him," Billy said. "It was just a little ol' jolt. Stealing that hunk of junk isn't worth killing anyone." He moved into the aisle and raised the short rifle at them. "Just stay nice and still until the law gets here."

"You didn't have to shoot anyone." Nathan stood up, having established that Cole was breathing and had a steady pulse; Tricia would need to look him over later though.

"Oh, I had to shoot him," Billy said. "You and the big fella were doing all the work so I figured he's your muscle. Since I'm all by my lonesome, taking him out first seemed like the best move."

Nathan was pissed. Not only had this giant country bumpkin got the drop on him, he was out-thinking him. "Well, aren't you the clever one."

Billy nodded. "I am. Some folks come around here and treat me like I'm an idiot because I got some size to me. They figure I'm only good for moving stuff around. Well, I can do more than that."

Cole rolled over and looked at Billy. "I know I won't make that mistake again." He rose to his knees and leaned against the capsule to steady himself, holding on to the loop on the vertical strap.

A slow grin crept over the giant's face. "No, I don't expect you will." He turned to Duncan. "You must be the smart one. Not many people could get by the encryption I have on the hangar door. You'll have to show me how you did that."

"Maybe next time," Duncan said.

Cole clambered to his feet and charged Billy. The giant swung the gun but Cole went low and slammed into his mid-section. Billy grunted and dropped his gun, but he only moved back a single step. Then he reached around Cole, picked him up, and heaved him across the aisle. Cole rolled and popped up with a grin on his face.

Nathan looked at Duncan and shouted, "Do it now!"

Duncan tapped the screen on his mobi and a whizzing sound filled the air. The cable jumped up from the floor, pulling taught against Billy's tool harness where Cole had clipped it. The giant shot down the aisle, tumbling ass over elbows toward the open hangar door.

Nathan let himself watch Billy bounce away for one more second, then he grabbed the capsule. "Now, let's get this thing out of here!"

Duncan and Cole each put hands on the capsule and they started pushing. The capsule moved easily. Within a few steps it had so much momentum they had to rush to keep up. When they got near the hangar door, they saw Billy untangling himself from their tow cable. Richie stood at the Dragonfly's cargo ramp with a bewildered look on his face.

"Richie," Nathan said, "help us get this thing loaded."

"Sis, they're getting away," Billy shouted.

Nathan turned and saw a woman easily as large as Billy jogging toward them from inside the building. She stopped, unharried, at the hangar door. "Well, I have to give you credit, Billy, you were right about them coming back, and here I didn't reckon they would."

"Daisy, they're getting away with the capsule!" Billy protested his sister's calm demeanor.

"I heard the ruckus and called Earl. He's on the way with Protective Services."

Nathan turned his head when he heard that and looked back toward his men. "Come on, we have to move this thing. I don't like our chances if cousin Earl and the law show up."

They pushed the capsule up the ramp just as Billy finished disentangling himself. Richie pulled the now Billy-free cable up and secured it to the capsule.

"Sir," the giant said, "This is barbarism. I could have been seriously harmed by your actions. There's no reason for further violence." He took a step toward Nathan and reached out with one huge hand.

Cole stepped between them. "We couldn't hurt you with a dump truck. Now, that's far enough."

Billy smiled. "Sir, I understand your need to prove your masculinity against a physically superior opponent and to do so in front of your employer, but this is just foolish."

"Try your luck if you want."

Billy charged the ramp. Nathan turned toward the cockpit and shouted, "Get us out of here, Marla!"

The Dragonfly lifted off with the ramp still extended and Nathan saw one of Billy's huge hands get a grip on the edge as they cycled into the air. Cole stomped on Billy's wide fingers until the giant let go. He fell about five meters to the ground and then stood up, seemingly unhurt. Nathan smiled; it may not have been their cleanest getaway, but they had the capsule and were in the air. Then he saw a blue flash from the museum's hangar door.

Daisy stood there with Billy's stun gun in her hands and she let loose another volley as he watched. The first shot went wide left but the second ball of sparking plasma scorched the air as it shot past him and impacted with the interior of the Dragonfly.

Nathan clambered up the ramp just as blue lightning jumped from panel to panel all through the heavy lifter. Smoke and the smell of burning electronics filled the air of the cargo bay. He looked toward the cockpit and shouted. "Marla? How are we?"

Before she could answer, the Dragonfly shot up into the air and Nathan found himself slammed to the deck. He recognized the effects of high g-forces pinning him but was powerless to do anything except try to catch his breath. Then the invisible force stopped; he floated free of the deck for a brief moment then slammed back down onto it. He reached over the wall mounted seat and grabbed a headset hanging from a hook above the seat. He fitted it over his ear and stole a look at the others.

Richie's face was bloody but he was pulling himself into a seat with the assistance of Cole, who was already strapped in. Nathan braced himself against the *Liberty Bell 7* for stability. He looked to his right and saw Duncan looking back at him from the cockpit.

"Are we still flying?" he said over the wireless intercom.

They shot up again and he tightened his grip on the capsule as he felt himself rise into the air of the cargo bay, then he dropped again, barely keeping his balance. He looked out the open cargo ramp and saw the dusky red sky shooting past. Duncan's voice came from the cockpit, not nearly as calm as it usually was.

"Nathan, we've got trouble up here. The throttle is jammed wide open and putting full power to the thrusters. Marla's keeping us level, but we can't move in any direction but up."

Even with the headphones on, Nathan could hear the roar of the four thrusters. It had been twenty years since he was checked out on these machines, but he still knew Dragonflies inside out. He keyed his mic and opened his mouth to speak, but the jarring sensation hit again, and this time the unsecured *Liberty Bell 7* shifted wildly. Nathan grabbed the edge of the open hatch with both hands and pulled himself inside the relic to keep from being smashed against the cargo bay bulkhead. Then he felt the small craft start to slide toward the back of the Dragonfly and he shot out into the open sky.

Nathan held onto the single seat in *Liberty Bell 7* for dear life. He was free falling, spiraling toward the waiting water of the Atlantic Ocean. He closed his eyes, prepared to die, because this splashdown would be without parachutes. It occurred to him that the last person to sit in this seat while the capsule was in the air was Gus Grissom returning from his suborbital flight. He desperately wanted a better outcome. There was a hard jolt as the tow cable caught and snapped taught.

He gritted his teeth and braced his feet against the control panel as the wind whistled through the missing hatch. The capsule spun in tight circles at the end of the tow line.

"Duncan! Can you hear me?"

"Nathan!" Duncan cried. "Are you alright?"

He closed his eyes before answering to keep from getting motion sickness. He might die in this capsule, but he wasn't going out vomiting. The Dragonfly lurched again and the movement was transmitted down the cable.

"Not dead yet. Marla, you have to listen to me."

"She's busy right now Nathan!" Duncan shouted.

Nathan ignored him. "Marla, can you hear me?"

It took a moment, but she finally answered. "I'm here."

She sounded frightened, and that wasn't something he'd ever heard from her before. He took a deep breath to calm himself, shut his eyes against the spinning of the capsule. "Marla, that shot we took caused a main bus overload and it's got the thruster control circuit stuck. You need to cycle it to break it loose. Give it at least five seconds in the off position."

There was silence and Nathan felt his jaw tighten under the strain of the g-forces, then she finally answered. "What if the thruster control system is fried and we can't regain control?"

Nathan shook his head. Between the g-forces from their ascension, the roar of the thrusters and the freezing wind whipping around him, he could feel consciousness becoming tenuous. "I promise you; it will work. You've got this. I have total faith in you."

He opened one eye and saw the sky and ocean trading places through the open hatch. Nothing happened and no one was speaking to him. He didn't blame her for hesitating. The Dragonfly wasn't something she was completely checked out on so all she had was his word that this would fix the problem. He bit his lip to keep from saying anything else. She either trusted him or she didn't and she was in control.

Then the capsule dropped again and the pressure from the g-forces stopped as he entered freefall. He figured Marla had thrown the switch. He did a silent count inside his head and shuddered as he saw the Dragonfly tip over on its port side through the hatch. The ocean rushed up at him, beckoning the capsule back to the watery grave where it had spent forty years. When his count got to five, nothing happened. The lights stayed off, the Dragonfly completed its roll to the left and he felt his blood rush to his head as they fell.

"Cycle it again," he said into his mic, but then he realized it was useless. Comms were down without power.

The Dragonfly shot past him with a roar of all four engines blazing mightily as it raced to gain altitude. He realized what was going to happen and braced his legs again. The tow cable snapped tight and Nathan lost consciousness.

He woke up when the capsule bumped hard against something solid. "Did it work?" he said. "Please let it have worked. We can't be the people that dropped the *Liberty Bell 7* in the ocean a second time."

His headset filled with static, then Duncan said, "Hang on, Nathan, it worked. We're reeling you in."

Nathan couldn't tell if anything was actually happening but then he felt the capsule tip as his crew hauled it inside the cargo bay of the Dragonfly. Once the capsule was properly inside and secured, Nathan squeezed himself through the hatch and into Tricia's sturdy arms. He hugged her and kissed her, grateful to be alive and able to do so. She helped steady him up the stairs toward the cockpit.

Nathan stuck his head in. "You're doing great, Marla. Just point us toward home."

She kept her eyes set on the controls. "Are you insane? I'm setting us down in the first open field I can find. This hunk of junk could drop us at any time."

"Trust me," he said, "we're fine. These things are over-engineered for warfare. They're meant to take shots like that and keep going."

"I'm landing."

Nathan knew it was useless to argue. The last time she'd flown had been in the *Bandit* when someone tried to crash it. She'd barely been able to set it down safely and save the crew. It had been enough to traumatize anyone, and today someone had tried to shoot her out of the air again.

He tapped Duncan on the shoulder. "Give me the seat."

He thought Duncan might want to argue and stay with his wife, but the big man unstrapped and squeezed past him without a word. Nathan gave Tricia's hand a quick squeeze and freed himself from her grip to drop into the seat and look at Marla. "I'll take the controls if you want, but let me say something first, okay?"

Marla finally looked at him, and then nodded.

He switched to a private channel. "This is the second time you've saved this crew," he said, "and you pulled that off because you are a fantastic pilot. That's the reason I hired you and that's the reason I keep flying with you.

"You're sitting there telling yourself that you just barely survived another close call, that you'd better get off the stick before something else happens and I'm telling you that's a load of horseshit." He waved a hand out at the sky. "You're flying straight and level, your gauges are green, and your crew is alive. If that's not enough for you, I'll take over, but I think you have to ask yourself what else you want."

The channel went silent and Nathan kept his mouth shut. He'd said everything he had to say. The rest was up to Marla.

She kept staring straight ahead, keeping on course. The silence lasted for five tense seconds and then she finally spoke. "ETA to home is sixty-four minutes."

"I'm going to rest my eyes," Nathan said, leaning back and smiling. "Let me know if you need anything."

8.

The next day, Nathan and Duncan drove a rented truck to a warehouse on the outskirts of Go City where companies like SajiCo manufactured and shipped flight components for starships. As they entered the property, a large door rolled up to let them in. The door closed behind them.

Nathan exited the truck expecting the building to be even hotter than the summer afternoon outside but was pleasantly surprised to feel cool air. A thin, tanned man stepped out of a small office near the door. He held out his hand as he approached.

"Captain Teller? My name is Norman Gassir. I'm the manager of this facility."

Nathan shook his hand. "Nice to meet you," he said. "Nice place you have here. It's very comfortable."

"This is a climate-controlled environment for the many antiques stored here," Gassir explained.

"You're here to accept delivery?"

"Well, I'm one of the people to do so." He gestured toward the opposite corner of the receiving area. Nathan saw a luxury float car and one of the rear doors opened. Saji Vy exited.

Duncan sidled up next to Nathan. "Did you know he would be here?"

"No."

The wizened old man walked with an unsettling alacrity. "Captain Teller," he said. "I understand you have something for me?"

Nathan grinned. "I certainly do."

Nathan opened the truck and Gassir operated a crab-like loader to remove the tarp covered shipment. The manager set it on the concrete floor and Nathan and Duncan unstrapped the covering. The recovered *Liberty Bell 7* sat on a plastic pallet in all its dilapidated glory.

"They didn't take very good care of it, did they?" Saji said.

"I wouldn't fly in it," Nathan said. "At least until Duncan here refurbishes it."

Saji reached out with a wrinkled hand and ran it over the capsule's hull. "We won't be restoring this, just cleaning it up and putting it on display. This is history. Every flight we take today is because of the small steps taken hundreds of years ago." He turned to Nathan and Duncan. "I'm glad you didn't drop it back into the ocean."

Nathan's brow furrowed. "You heard?"

Saji gave him a wry look. "There were social media drones in the air at the time. You were viral for about an hour. I shouldn't worry too much about it. As they say, any publicity is good publicity."

"Wow. I had no idea."

"You accomplished your task and that's all that matters."

Nathan pulled out his mobi and loaded up an invoice. "Speaking of that, I hate to ruin the moment with business, but I need someone's thumbprint to complete delivery."

Saji nodded at Gassir and the manager thumbed the document. Nathan forwarded it off for payment. "Thank you for doing business with Milky Way Repo, Mr. Vy. If you have further need of our services, just let me know."

"Well, I have nothing at the moment, but I've recently spoken with someone who may." The ancient billionaire pulled out a mobi from his colorful jacket and held it up. Nathan held his up and they chirped, transferring the data.

Nathan looked at his mobi and then glanced up at Saji. "Xandra Arili? The CEO of Vibrant Passion?"

"It's pronounced 'Cassandra,'" Saji said. "And yes, she's the very same."

"Do you know what she wants?"

"Given what you do, I imagine she wants you to find a starship."

Nathan nodded. "Right."

《》

Later that afternoon, Nathan and his crew took a pod share to Western Dune Shipyards and walked through the gate again. Cole flanked him on the right and Duncan was on his left. Nathan turned to the engineer. "I'm going to get the bill settled. You guys get the ship ready to fly."

"Can do."

"Oh, and check the flight system," Nathan said. "Bruce seems like the kind of guy to try something stupid, like a booby trap."

Duncan slapped him on the shoulder. "I'm on it." They peeled off and made for the *Blue Moon Bandit*.

Nathan walked across the shipyard to Bruce's office. The owner was standing outside talking to someone. He stood quietly until they were finished and the worker walked away. "Bruce, I'm here to get my ship."

"You have the credits?"

"I do," he said, holding up his mobi. "Fifty-five thousand. I just need your account information."

Bruce shook his head. "It's sixty thousand."

Rage boiled up inside Nathan. Every step forward seemed to lead him two steps backward. "Why would I pay you sixty thousand? I was just here and the figure was fifty-five thousand."

"Yeah, and then you didn't pay me and left your ship here, taking up all sorts of space for another week. It'll be sixty now. I told you storage fees run five grand a month. Today's the first. New month means another five thousand."

It took three full seconds for Bruce's words to register with Nathan. "You must be joking."

"I'm not. Read your contract."

Nathan stood still, staring at the greedy bastard. He bit his lower lip and made a decision. "I'll give you the fifty-five we agreed on last week for the repairs and three months storage, but I'm not paying you another five thousand for one day, you're overcharging as is."

Bruce puffed out his chest and crossed his arms. "Oh, is that right?"

Nathan turned and stalked toward the landing pad where his ship sat. He'd had enough and it was time to go.

Bruce paused for a moment and then chased after him. "You can't just take your ship. It's locked down to keep assholes like you from taking off without paying their bill." Nathan picked up the pace and Bruce huffed.

"I'm done talking to you," Nathan said. "If you want to be paid, give me your account info. Otherwise, keep talking."

Nathan approached the landing pad and saw the loading ramp open at the rear of his ship. He mounted the ramp and climbed up into the ship with Bruce behind him, breathing hard and struggling to keep up.

"Duncan, how we doing?"

The engineer stuck his head out of the cockpit. "We're just about ready to go. You take care of the bill?"

"I keep trying, but some people don't like to negotiate."

"You can't just leave," Bruce said again, his voice getting louder.

"Why not?" Cole said from behind him.

Bruce jumped and turned to face him. "Who are you?"

"He's with me, Bruce," Nathan said, "and he asks a good question. Why can't we leave?"

"The ship is locked down, idiot," Bruce said. "The flight computer won't boot until I give you the password. This isn't the first time someone has tried to skip out on me without paying."

Just then the engines roared to life. The steady hum of power was music to Nathan's ears. He looked at Bruce. "Uh-oh. Looks like your software is broken."

Duncan came out of the cockpit. "The software was working alright, but it was just some off-the-shelf crapware we've seen before." He held up a storage module. "We broke the encryption on a yacht we repossessed a couple years ago that used the same stuff." He looked at Bruce. "If you want it to be effective you really need to change the default codes."

Nathan looked at Bruce. "We repossess starships for a living. Did you think you could do anything to keep us from taking our own ship if we wanted it?"

Bruce shook his head. "I'll call Protective Services. You can't just leave."

"What are you going to tell them?" Nathan asked. "That I stole a ship that belongs to me? They'll laugh you out of the office. At best you can file a lawsuit and I'll be happy to see you in court. I'll have a good time explaining your business practices on the record. Now, do you want your fifty-five thousand credits or do you want to take me to court and wait a few years for a settlement?"

Bruce looked at the three of them and Nathan could see the moment he realized he'd lost.

"Fine, pay me." He gave Nathan his account info and confirmed payment.

"Cole," Nathan said, "why don't you see Bruce safely off the ship."

Cole swept an arm toward the rear of the ship. "After you."

Bruce stomped back down the corridor and stopped when he got to the top of the ramp, then he turned back. "We'll see what happens when the Syndicate catches up with you to collect that bounty on Nathan's head."

Cole grabbed a handful of Bruce's shirt. "If anyone comes after us now, I'll assume it was you and I'll make sure to come back here. Get me?"

Bruce swallowed. "You can't hide forever."

Cole laughed. "But we can try, now please get your feet safely on the ground before we take off."

Bruce scurried down the ramp and back to his office.

Shaking his head, Cole slapped the button and closed the ramp. "We're all secure back here."

Nathan moved his hands across the controls and pulled back on the yoke. The *Blue Moon Bandit* rose into the desert sky and Nathan pointed it away from the shipyard.

Cole walked up and poked his head into the cockpit. "That guy was an ass, but he had a point. The Syndicate still has a price on your head. How are you going to avoid it?"

"Isn't there something we can do?" Duncan said from the co-pilot's seat. "Like make some deal to get them off your back?"

Nathan shrugged. "I don't know. Today's problem was getting the ship back and we took care of that. Getting the Syndicate off my back is something we can take care of tomorrow."

"You need to be careful, Nathan," Cole said. "They aren't letting you go. They braced me a few times wanting to know where you were."

"Me too," Duncan said.

"They did?" Nathan said. "You guys never said anything. Did they threaten you?"

"No," Duncan said.

"Why would they?" Cole said. "They're watching us to see if we can lead them to you. I can guarantee after that job in Florida they know you're back in business. They'll come for you."

Nathan ran a hand over his mouth. "One thing at a time. I might have a new job for us, and if it takes us off planet, I won't have to worry about the Syndicate for a while."

9.

Xandra Ariti sat in the home office of her Go City house, it was one of a dozen homes she owned around the globe — she had three more out in the solar system: one on the Moon, one on Mars, and one at the largest settlement on Saturn's moon, Titan. That last was especially a favorite because she could observe Saturn in all its glory as it rose over the horizon. Watching the banded rings of the gas giant rise into the night sky proved that money could indeed buy happiness. Whoever said otherwise just didn't have enough.

She sat at a large desk made of smoked glass and leaned back in a comfortable chair, her feet propped up on one desk corner. Her eyes flicked to the clock on her mobi. The scheduled meeting time was approaching, but not yet here, and she was anxious. That simply wouldn't do. Business meetings were no place to feel out of sorts, especially when they were with someone she hadn't yet met in person.

She pulled her legs down from the desk and sat up straight in her chair. She closed her eyes and inhaled deeply through her nose, using a meditation technique she'd learned fifty years ago to center herself. After a few moments she felt her heartbeat slow and a looseness flowed through her limbs. She looked out the window at the only real view her sprawling Go City manor offered: the spaceships breaking free from gravity as they launched from Spaceport America.

Her mobi chimed softly and she saw it was her assistant. "Yes?"

"Mr. Teller is here for your meeting."

"Please show him in."

She stood and shook hands with the starship repo man and the young woman who accompanied him. They introduced themselves as Nathan Teller and Tricia Bergman. Her initial impression from the way he carried himself was that he was confident. She liked that, especially if she was hiring him for a sensitive job.

"Mr. Teller, I appreciate you coming to see me so quickly."

He gave her a friendly smile, one she recognized as a tool meant to set her at ease. "Not a problem Ms. Ariti. Saji Vy mentioned you were having an issue and since you set up this meeting so quickly, I assumed it was important." His expression changed to one of puzzlement. "I have to admit though, I didn't expect to meet with you personally. I assumed you have managers for this sort of thing."

She liked that he got down to the point. Most meetings were polluted with small talk that drove her crazy. She didn't care about the weather, people's kids or how much people enjoyed the services Vibrant Passion provided. Most people first wanted to ask her how old she really was; Xandra's age wasn't a secret, but people always stopped believing that she was ninety when they saw her in person. Despite entering her tenth decade, Xandra didn't look a day over thirty-five — a really good thirty-five. She had things to get done and even for her, time was short. She gestured to the chairs in front of her desk and they all sat down.

"You're very perceptive, Mr. Teller. Normally, you would meet with my Director of Operations, but this is a sensitive matter that I prefer to handle myself. Saji said that you've located and returned lost vessels to him on a number of occasions and that you are discreet. He also said you aren't afraid of dangerous situations."

Nathan turned and smiled at his companion. A shared joke passed between then, Xandra wondered what it was.

"We're very good at tracking down starships that people want to keep hidden," he said. "We've seen every trick under the sun and a few that were actually pretty clever, but there are only so many ways and places to hide."

"And the danger?"

He shrugged. "We weigh the risks and engage appropriately. Criminals often think they're smarter than they are and we like to think we're smarter. We examine what they've done and adapt our response. Can you give us some details? It will make it easier for us to make a decision about accepting the job."

Xandra smiled. There was no way he was going to reject the job. She admired that he was trying to negotiate by not accepting the job too quickly, but it was a worthless tactic. Saji had told her that Teller was available and needed cash.

"My company lost a research vessel about three years ago. The *Candlewax* represents a considerable investment in both equipment and intellectual property. We would like it returned."

"When you say it was 'lost,' how do you mean?" Nathan asked.

"There was a problem with the drive unit and the crew was evacuated," Xandra said. "The ship jumped to an unknown location."

"No one knows where?" Nathan said.

She shook her head. "The faster-than-light transit process requires two sets of coordinates, the starting point and the destination. It doesn't make sense that it just jumped into the void. We performed an extensive search for about a year. No trace of the ship was found. We assumed it was lost forever."

Nathan furrowed his brow, he knew she was holding back, but there were things he needed to know and things Xandra felt he didn't need to know. "What I've told you is what I know. It's a moot point anyhow. The ship has been found."

He smiled again. "Then what do you need us for?"

She returned the smile. He clearly knew there was more to come but was playing along with her. She could play too. She turned to Tricia and addressed her. "Ms. Bergman, why do you think I need Mr. Teller and his company?"

"Because you weren't the one who found it," Tricia said, without missing a beat.

Xandra nodded. "Correct. Someone else found it and they are attempting to blackmail me for its return."

"What kind of vessel are we talking about?"

"A class three research ship."

"Wow," Nathan said. "That's what, one hundred fifty meters? How much are they asking?"

"A million credits."

He nodded without being too surprised. "Time frame?"

"They've given us a week to make up our minds."

"That's irrelevant though, right?" Nathan said. "They have what you want, but more importantly you have the credits they want. You could stall them from now until doomsday."

She kept a well-practiced blank look on her face as she answered. "I suppose that's true, but I'd like to see this matter dealt with before the end of time. If it helps move things along, once you find the blackmailers, you can offer them a tenth of their asking price, as a finder's fee of sorts. I'll include that in my down-payment, yours to keep if you don't spend it."

His look intensified. "Unless there's something on the ship they can use to harm you. Is that what's going on here? You mentioned intellectual property earlier. Are they threatening to expose something about you or Vibrant Passion that you'd rather keep hidden?"

Xandra resisted the urge to lean back in her chair to give Nathan any indication that something was wrong. Her business was her business. "I'd like my ship back, Mr. Teller. Can you perform that task?"

He held up a hand. "Hold on. If you don't want to talk about what they're holding over your head, that's fine. It's your business and we're discreet. However, I need to know if my crew is going to be in danger, either from what's on your ship or from the people who are holding it. Did the communication from them indicate violence?"

"No."

"And whatever is on the ship? Is it a biological, toxic, or environmental hazard? I know it's been years, but nasty things can hang around."

Xandra drew in a deep breath. "As you say, it's been years. I have no idea what condition the ship is in. My engineers tell me it wasn't shutdown properly, so you should be extremely cautious upon boarding the ship."

Nathan drew in a deep breath. "Before we head out into the galaxy hunting for this ship, I just want to make sure the blackmailers provided proof that they actually found it."

Xandra was almost insulted at the question but she nodded. "Of course. They provided photos."

Nathan sat forward. "Exterior photos? If so, we may be able to use star positioning to determine a location."

"Unfortunately, not," Xandra said. "The photos were from the interior. I think they saw us coming with that one. However, we were able to verify the images were of our ship. What I can tell you is that the message from the blackmailers was transmitted from near Neptune, most likely its moon, Triton."

"How do you know that?"

"Metadata in the message itself," she said. "They didn't even bother to bounce it off any relays to obfuscate their position. They don't appear to be very bright."

"Well, most criminals aren't."

"So, are you accepting the offer?"

Nathan smiled and looked at Tricia, who nodded.

Xandra relaxed. "Thank you. This is a difficult assignment and I appreciate you tackling it."

"What information can you give us regarding the ship and the communication from the blackmailers?"

"Quite a bit, actually," Xandra said. She pulled open a desk drawer and removed a portable drive. She held it out to Nathan. "Once you board the *Candlewax*, plug this into any data port. It has an executable program that will give you control over the ship."

Nathan took it. "Thanks. Usually, we just get access codes and half the time they're wrong. Now, you're assuming the ship is in flying condition. What happens if I plug this in, but the engines are out? Do we get paid for coordinates?"

"There's no reason to suspect you won't be able to fly the *Candlewax* back. It jumped away, it can jump back. Are there any other questions?" Xandra said.

"Just one. Was anyone aboard the *Candlewax* when it jumped away? You mentioned the crew evacuating. Did everyone manage to get off? I'd rather not trip across any unexpected dead bodies."

She paused for a moment, despite her attempt not to. "Everyone got off. The ship should be empty."

Nathan stood and Tricia followed suit. "If you have nothing else to share, I think we can get started."

Xandra remained seated but held her hand out. "Thank you. I look forward to hearing from you." They took turns shaking her hand, before leaving the office.

Xandra listened to her assistant escort the couple from her property while she considered the meeting that had just concluded. Teller seemed competent and Saji had vouched for him, had in fact said that he and his crew had pulled off a couple difficult jobs for him.

She got up and walked to the sliding glass door overlooking the pool. It was a beautiful day and there wasn't a cloud in the bright blue sky. She slid the door open and walked out into the blistering heat but she soaked it up with every step. The dry warmth was one of the reasons she loved visiting Go City. It felt like the kind of day where nothing could go wrong.

In the distance, a shuttle raced up a kilometer-long ramp at the spaceport and was flung toward the heavens via a magnetic catapult. In almost a century of life she'd seen thousands of such launches, and while it was easy to think of the people aboard those shuttles taking the first step toward grand adventure, she knew that was just the romance people dressed up travel in. She knew those people were bound for colonies where they would work their asses off, often in dangerous conditions, all for a chance at living a life that was nowhere near as good as hers. If the shuttle occupants were lucky, one in a thousand would earn enough credits to pay for the life lengthening treatments Vibrant Passion provided. It might not be fair, but that was life.

She almost felt bad about setting up Teller, but honestly, he was a starship repo guy. Who was going to miss him?

10.

Later that night, Nathan and Tricia were back in bed in their room at Cole and Kimiyo's ranch, and Nathan felt almost at peace. A new, good-paying job on the table and Tricia's relaxed breathing at his side set him at ease. Then she said softly, "What was going on with you in that meeting today?"

"What do you mean?"

She shifted around to be able to see him better. "You were stiff around her, like something made you uncomfortable."

He was silent for a moment; the meeting with Xandra Ariti had bothered him, but he'd thought he had done a good job of hiding it. However, Tricia had a habit of seeing the things Nathan felt sure he had hidden. "You noticed that, huh?"

"I did," Tricia said. "I don't think she did."

He was quiet for another moment, maybe for too long because Tricia nudged him lightly with an elbow. "Come on, what's bugging you?"

"You saw that house? The whole estate? How big it was and the furnishings?"

She propped herself up on her elbows. "Her money bothers you? Isn't the whole point of having your own business to be wealthy?"

"Not exactly."

She raised an eyebrow. "You don't want to be wealthy? Are you sure? Because you quoted her an arm and a leg above our usual fees in up-front operating costs."

"I don't have anything against wealth or me having it, my issue is what people do with it." He looked at her in the dim light. "How many houses do you think she has like that around the world? How many safe, private homes where she has a staff maintaining things?"

"Back on Bad Rock you made a case for people being able to use whatever drugs they wanted. Now you have a problem with how some rich woman spends her credits?"

"What can I say? I'm a man with inconsistencies."

"So, what's the problem?"

"I grew up in the Great Lakes region and life's a little tougher there. The kind of money Xandra throws around every month on homes like the one we saw today could make things better for whole communities."

"Growing up there was that bad?"

He gave her a small, wry laugh. "You really don't see it until you're away from there. Growing up, it was just me and my mom. My mom earned enough to pay the rent, with a subsidy, which kept us out of a shelter. It was one of those small, plastic and concrete government places. It wasn't all bad, I mean, at least I had my own room.

"All the jobs and overtime Mom worked though, she never got paid a real living wage, and we stayed poor. It's just, I felt like I'd gotten out, then the way Xandra looked at me today in that meeting, like I was grubby and poor. Like she was doing me a favor just by hiring me."

Tricia ran a hand over his chest. "It's different, though. This time she needed you and you get to set the price. You get what you want for the job."

"I guess. What I really want is their respect. I'm a successful business owner and provide a service they can't get anywhere else. I shouldn't have to sit in meetings and be looked down on or condescended to." He paused for a minute, suddenly aware of how much he was speaking. "I'm sorry. We finally have some good things coming our way, I don't mean to spoil it."

She reached up and caressed his face. "You've got nothing to apologize for. I could tell something was bothering you. I just wanted to know what it was. Sometimes you can be closed off, so I like it when you open up with me. Never say you're sorry for that."

He swallowed hard, suddenly aware of how special she was and how much he cared for her. He kissed her softly on the forehead. "I love you."

She gave him smile. "Love you too."

11.

Xandra enjoyed traveling, especially off planet. Unfortunately, today's voyage to Europa, the ice-covered moon of Jupiter, was business and not pleasure.

Her private yacht, built with a range that allowed her to visit any point in the solar system she would wish for, was too large to land directly at the mining spaceport. She was dropping through Europa's thin atmosphere in a landing pod occupied by herself, her assistant Damian, and a pilot. Damian was in his mid-twenties and so still too young to avail himself of Vibrant Passion's life lengthening treatment. He was tall and lanky, as if the old Greek, Procrustes, had stretched him out, and Xandra enjoyed the way he looked in the dark business suits he wore. She didn't remember the pilot's name; pilots came and went so fast, it wasn't worth the hassle.

The pod slipped through an opening in the dome covering the facility and then touched down softly on the landing platform. Xandra unbuckled her safety harness and moved forward. She laid a hand on the pilot's shoulder and squeezed, just a small touch to provide him with the tiniest personal interaction.

"Thank you for such a smooth ride. I appreciate it very much."

"Thank you, ma'am," he said. "Do you know how long we'll be on station?"

Damian stepped forward, intercepting the question, and more importantly the interaction, as Xandra disembarked from the pod. "We're not sure how long we'll be here, so be ready for a quick turnaround or to spend considerable time here. Say, a few hours? Thank you."

Xandra glided across a short docking bridge to the facility's main corridor, where she was met by a stocky woman in a mining jumpsuit with the logo for Jupiter Mining Consortium stenciled across the right side of her chest and a name stitched on the left. Xandra didn't bother to read it. The miner kept her gaze down, avoiding eye contact with Xandra. It would be like that for her entire visit at the facility. She knew the crew had not only been instructed to be polite to her but to also avoid any unnecessary interaction.

Jupiter Mining Consortium was one of Vibrant Passion's largest clients, with dozens of operations across the home solar system and the Alpha Centauri system. Keeping them pleased was of the utmost importance to maintain cashflow.

She reached a wide window in the corridor and paused, looking out across the icy plains of the moon. Europa was known as the smoothest object in the solar system because there were no mountains to break up the surface features. The ice had a youthfulness compared to other planetary objects because no matter how often meteorites impacted or the surface cracked, the sea below refreshed it. Xandra thought it a fitting metaphor for how her life lengthening process gave the appearance of youth even into old age.

The mining facility was anchored to a relatively thin spot in the ice. The massive drill at the center of the complex burrowed through six kilometers of ice to reach the salt water ocean below her feet. From there, ore was extracted from the seabed another fifty kilometers beneath the ice sheet. They extracted minerals from the ocean water as well.

Damian cleared his throat. "The others are ready for you, ma'am."

"Of course," she said and followed him to the conference room. Damian held the door open, Xandra stepped through, and Damian closed it behind her. He would wait outside for her like a well-dressed statue.

Inside, Xandra took a seat between two older gentlemen and looked toward the head of the table where a man of about sixty sat. She nodded at him to begin and he cleared his throat.

"Thank you for traveling so far to join us, Ms. Ariti. As you've suggested, there are certain conversations that can only take place in person so what we say can't be overheard or intercepted. This is one of them."

Xandra didn't want to waste time being told things she already knew. "What's happened, Henry?"

He swallowed hard and his ruddy face flushed. "It's the Swimmers. The client has lost twenty-two percent of the latest batch."

Her eyes narrowed in concentration. "What do you mean 'lost'?"

"Batch J-five-thirty-one was shipped in two weeks ago and consisted of fifty subjects. Today, thirty-nine remain." He picked up a remote and activated a holographic projector at the opposite end of the room. "Some swam off beyond the scope of the mine, while others became highly aggressive."

He tapped the remote and a hologram appeared. It showed the dark saltwater sea beneath them teeming with creatures that resembled an Earth octopus, but these were larger and possessed only four tentacles, each ending with a white claw. They swam through the water with ease, their shiny, black bodies appeared almost gelatinous where the underwater work lights illuminated them.

The Swimmers moved independently of one another, performing tasks such as moving gear or operating machinery around the worksite. One carrying a container of some kind collided with another operating a piece of machinery and a fight broke out. Tools and the container were dropped into the murky depths as the two creatures circled each other. After a few seconds of sizing each other up, one dove at the other. They knotted around each other, hacking and slashing with their claws as the water around them turned a dark shade of blue. One of the Swimmers in the hologram went limp and the victor began consuming its opponent, then Henry turned off the hologram.

Xandra looked toward the head of the table. "How many incidents have there been?"

"Like that? Four."

"And all of them were instigated by subjects from the last batch?"

"Yes."

Xandra looked to her right where a woman sat across the table from her. She had short auburn hair and looked to be in her mid-forties, but Xandra knew she was in her mid-eighties. Those extra decades were necessary to learn the science needed to make Xandra's visions a reality. "Doctor Ebbers, do you have any thoughts on the behavior we're seeing?"

The doctor was quick to shake her head. "I have a team from the investigative group tasked with determining a cause. Currently, they are still collecting data."

"Doctor," Xandra said with a hint of menace in her voice, "they're fucking eating each other. Where is the cannibalism coming from? It wasn't an observed behavior in previous testing."

The doctor cleared her throat with a small cough before answering. It was the only indication that she felt any of the pressure directed at her. "Hopefully the cause for that behavior will be determined once the data is analyzed," she said. Then she sat back in her chair.

"You don't have any speculation?" Xandra pressed.

"Speculation would be counter-productive," Ebbers said. "It could lead us to waste time and resources. Give us a few days and I'll have an answer."

Xandra was fuming, but a tantrum had never solved anything; she had ninety years of experience reminding her that men could get angry and get results, but women who threw punches got sidelined. Under no circumstances would she give them a reason to doubt her.

Xandra looked back at Henry. "What's the impact if we suspend operations for two days?"

Henry sat up a little straighter in his chair. "It will be difficult but nothing the client can't handle. There is a shipment loading now and they have a sufficient quantity of ore, so that's not a problem, but there is a freighter arriving day after tomorrow. Every day we delay their operations pushes that shipment back another day and then the dominoes start falling. If it were to continue, eventually the client would have to begin missing shipment dates completely."

All eyes turned to Doctor Ebbers. "You have two days," Xandra said. "I need a cause and a solution. I will not have a client's operation interrupted because of us." She turned her gaze to a gray-haired man sitting farther down the opposite side of the table. "Reynolds, as long as we're all together, I'd like to discuss human capital stock acquisition."

He nodded politely. "Of course."

"We're almost one hundred units behind for the quarter," she said. "Why?"

Reynolds tried to sit up a little straighter, but only succeeded in making his chair grunt against the floor. "Our primary method of acquiring human capital stock has been to recruit human subjects and broker a deal between corporations and these new workers to facilitate those workers undergoing the transformative process. Those corporations require laborers to work in extremely dangerous environments, like mining."

"I understand how my company works, Reynolds," Xandra said.

Reynolds licked his plump lips before answering. "Ma'am, I'm trying to explain why we're seeing shortages. Recruits feel that our clients are not willing to pay labor rates commensurate with the risk involved in undergoing the transformative process."

Xandra sighed. "If that's true, then we're explaining the danger of the process in too much detail to the recruits. They shouldn't be demanding premium rates."

"It's for our protection, ma'am. Some of the recruits have legal representation."

"Then end the recruitment process the moment legal representation is mentioned," she said. "Our clients aren't hiring these workers for their intelligence."

Reynolds' face stiffened, like he had something to say, but he merely nodded. "I'll make the proper adjustments to the process."

"We have a backup program for filling in gaps in the recruitment process. Why is it also failing us?"

Reynolds swallowed hard. "The agents we employ are providing numbers we deemed as acceptable when we hired them."

Xandra leaned toward him. "Those numbers are evidently insufficient to make up for the shortfall recruiting is experiencing. Get the word out to them that we need an increase."

"That will be dangerous. Acquiring unwilling participants can lead to interference from authorities. Voluntary recruitment needs to remain our primary source."

Xandra inhaled deeply. The one thing she'd learned in her decades of running Vibrant Passion was that relying on other people to fulfill your vision could be the downfall of any endeavor. The men and women seated at this table were the most effective managers she could find, yet even they required near constant supervision to make sure things stayed on schedule.

"One of our more successful agents is that rainbow cult," she said.

"The Children of the Apocalyptic Rainbow," Reynolds offered.

"Yes. They collect people who are easily missed. Addicts, sex workers, and those who are estranged from their families. They have chapters all over the solar system, so their efforts are spread out, less conspicuous. I'm authorizing you to increase the bounty if they can increase their numbers."

"Understood."

She stood up and those around the table rose with her. "If that's all, we should adjourn and get to work. We have much to do and little time to accomplish it." No one said anything but their eyes followed her as she strode from the room. She exited through the doors and Damian fell in beside her.

They got to the landing pod and mounted the steps to board. The pilot looked at them expectantly. "Heading home?" he asked.

"Back to the ship, but we'll be staying for a few days"

"Yes, ma'am."

Damian looked surprised, but stayed silent.

As they strapped into their seats, Xandra looked over at Damian. "I want complete surveillance on Doctor Ebbers and her team."

Damian made a note on his mobi. "Is there anything in particular we're looking for? I can have the surveillance AI flag specific items."

Xandra gave it some thought as the pod lifted off from the surface and raced toward the yacht in orbit. "Ebbers knows more than she's telling. Up until this point in the project she has been on top of everything, but suddenly we're having a serious issue and it's a mystery? She's bought herself two days. Let's see what she does with that. As for what we're looking for specifically? I don't know. Anything that looks suspicious. Also, any contact that looks suspicious."

"I'll make sure we run background on any contacts she has," Damian said. "If she's in touch with anyone she shouldn't be we'll know. We have her workstations, both private and business, as well as her mobi. Nothing will get past us."

"Good."

12.

Two days later, Diane Ebbers sat on her bed, wrapped in a towel, gazing blankly at her mirror without realizing what she was looking for. Her eyes were hollow and her cheeks drawn. There had been a time when her face had been round and cheery, but now the excess weight was gone, and Diane felt as if the reflection were disconnected from her entirely. In the silence of her small room, she wished it were so. Her eighty-year-old mind examined her forty-year-old body, the result of Vibrant Passion's life lengthening process, and she suddenly wished that she was at the end of her life instead of in an interminable middle age.

Diane and the Swimmers, both transformed by Vibrant Passions. She'd never needed two days; her team had no samples to finish testing. But making Xandra wait just this once, was a reward all its own. The answer as to why the latest batch of Swimmers were behaving so poorly and being a danger to themselves and others was obvious; Diane had known it as soon as she saw the footage of their behavior. As malleable as the human body might be to the transformation process, the human mind was another story. She had explained as much to Xandra on multiple occasions, but the CEO either didn't want to hear her or had willfully ignored the danger.

What they were doing was the sort of thing there was no coming back from. When they'd started the research, she had been able to excuse the ethical breaches they were committing by thinking about the peaceful applications the process might yield. In a time when humanity was reaching out into the galaxy, her results could help them by transforming the basic stuff of who they were into bodies that could withstand harsh environments or space itself. On more than one occasion, after a bottle of wine, she convinced herself that she was carrying on the work of Almighty God himself, improving upon His work with her own brilliance.

Xandra and her vultures had taken a more overt interest in the program at the human trial stage; they locked down the intellectual properly, padded their bottom lines, and then there was the *Candlewax*: a mobile laboratory where prying eyes couldn't observe their actions, where peer review was non-existent, and where no one could hear the screams.

Ebbers had stayed the course, though. She refined the process, speeding it up, making it more efficient, and meeting the seemingly impossible deadlines imposed by Xandra. It was one of those shortcuts that was contributing to their current problems. Diane's mobi chimed, alerting her to the upcoming meeting with Xandra and the rest of the group gathered on Europa. Her forty-eight hours were up.

Ebbers selected a crystalline shard from a container on her small dresser. A designer amphetamine, the Diamond K would give her the enlightenment and confidence she needed to get through the meeting. She'd spent the last two days high in her quarters, so there was no need to change things now.

She dropped the shard into her mouth and ground it slowly with her back teeth, savoring the bitter taste. It wasn't possible to gain a tolerance to Diamond K, and the dopamine hit was nearly orgasmic. Ebbers got up, letting the towel fall to the floor, and dressed for her meeting with the devil.

———— «» ————

Ebbers made her way to the same conference room the group had met in two days ago. The others were already seated and looked more relaxed than she felt. Henry, the ops manager glanced up at her, nodded, and shifted his eyes back to the tablet in his hands. Reynolds, responsible for getting her test subjects, didn't even bother looking up, and why not? Both of them would be expected to have answers for Xandra today, but Ebbers would be the focus of Xandra's attention.

She settled into a chair and looked at her own notes, even though she knew exactly what she was going to say. She closed her eyes and enjoyed the tingling warmth Diamond K left on her skin. A minute later, the door to the room opened and Xandra swept in, her tunic flowing like a diva's cape. Ebbers almost giggled.

Xandra found her and held her gaze like a laser beam. The CEO lowered herself into a chair and from the annoyed look on her face, Ebbers could tell exactly how this was going to go. Xandra was like a child in the way she demanded results. Over their decades of collaboration, Ebbers had seen her be petulant more often than she hadn't. If a situation called for careful consideration, she was more likely to be rash, if a subordinate needed a reassuring hand, Xandra was more likely to metaphorically show them the back of hers, and if a problem became too complex to resolve quickly, she got the look on her face Ebbers saw right now.

"Doctor Ebbers," Xandra said. "It's been two days. Have you figured out what the problem is with this batch?"

Ebbers drew a deep breath to steady herself. "Ms. Ariti, I'm pleased to say we've found the problem with batch J-five-thirty-one. As you know, we've mastered the transformation process on the biological frame, but we've had less success dealing with the mental trauma of the human psyche awakening to find itself within a non-human body."

Xandra nodded, but Ebbers could see impatience cross her face.

"Are you saying that this continuing problem is the root cause of what we saw?"

And there it was. By framing the problem as a continuing one that fell into Ebbers' realm, Xandra was making it clear this wasn't a problem for the team to overcome. This wasn't something for Xandra to help resolve. This was an Ebbers problem and she'd better have a solution. She could feel her own patience growing short and gripped the arm of her chair to maintain her composure.

"That's exactly what I'm saying. We manage the problem by suppressing the original psyche and overlaying a replacement that is more pliable. After all, our product only needs limited knowledge from the original mind of the test subject, so it makes more sense to insert what we need."

"Doctor," Xandra said, "perhaps you could just skip to the part where you tell me what personnel and resources you need to resolve the problem?"

This time Ebbers shifted in her chair. What she wanted to do was stand and, in a calm voice, tell Xandra that this had only occurred because Xandra had repeatedly insisted on speed above good science, that she needed to take responsibility for her own lack of sound judgement, and that the only resource she, Doctor Ebbers, needed was independence; then she would exit the room. It would be fitting to leave Xandra like that, responsible for solving a problem on her own for once. Instead, Ebbers leveled her breathing and smiled.

"To prevent further problems of this nature, we will have to tailor individual imprints for each subject. We've been attempting a one size fits all solution and it's failing."

Xandra closed her eyes in a dramatic affectation of disappointment that Ebbers had seen many times. Ebbers felt a deep satisfaction that she had stung Xandra; Xandra wanted a solution and Ebbers had provided an inconvenient one.

"Doctor Ebbers," Xandra said in the tone of a teacher speaking to her most hopeless student, "this enterprise only works if the process is affordable. We supply labor stock to corporations with operations in hazardous environments. Currently they have two options. The first is to train humans to do the work and outfit them with the necessary protective equipment. The second is to use robots, which involves programming them for specific tasks and maintaining them. Both options are extremely expensive. For us to be competitive, we need to provide a cost-effective solution. If we have to provide every subject with a unique solution, costs rise and no one is going to buy from us."

Ebbers made sure her face remained placid. "As I see it, we have a long-term solution and a short-term solution. Would you like me to elaborate or do you have a solution of your own?"

Xandra's gaze hardened. "Please continue."

"There's no way around the problem of each subject requiring a unique solution. Human beings by their very nature are individuals and that doesn't change simply because we're breaking them down and rebuilding them." Ebbers paused for a drink of water; Diamond K had an irritating dehydration effect. "Therefore, we must make our solution more robust. I suggest an investment in artificial intelligence that can be used to take the workload off our transition team."

"We already use AI," Xandra said. The idea of unnecessary spending was abhorrent to Xandra.

"Only for the initial psyche mapping," Ebbers said. "The results of that process are used by our human engineers to overlay the new mapping. As you can see, pushing that kind of workload at them has resulted in a failure rate between ten and twenty percent. We need to do this properly; spend the credits to have our own development teams build and implement our own AI. I estimate the project can be completed within eighteen months for a cost of about one hundred million credits."

Xandra sat quietly, chewing on her lower lip. After a moment she said, "What's the short-term solution?"

"I actually see three options," Ebbers said. "One, we hire more engineers to assist in the overlay and hopefully reduce failure rates. Two, we continue with the current process and produce an inferior product. Three, we pull back from the market until our long-term solution is complete. One way or another, our costs go up or our revenues go down."

Ebbers knew that her solutions were well thought out. Her process could be perfected with the right investment in research.

It was why she had stayed after the *Candlewax* incident, and why she tolerated Xandra's involvement at all. Ebbers had warned against going to market before the process was perfected. It was Xandra who rushed things, so now it was her who had to choose a solution.

Xandra looked around the room, acknowledging the others for the first time with nothing more than a glance. Then she settled on Ebbers. "I'll be in touch."

She exited the room with a flourish, her white robes swirling about her. Her assistant had anticipated what was going to happen and held the door open for her. After she left the conference room, Ebbers looked around at the stunned faces of the management team. She stood, and deciding she owed them no explanation, walked out the door.

If she got the credits, she could complete her work. If Xandra was angry and decided to take it out on her, she had ways of protecting herself.

Ebbers opened an application on her mobi that was counting down. It was impossible to violate every ethical law known to humankind without leaving yourself exposed, no matter how wealthy you were. If anything ever happened to Ebbers, she had a data dump summarizing their activities to this point scheduled to go out to hundreds of journalists throughout the system. She pressed a button on the screen and the countdown started over.

As powerful as she was, Xandra wasn't omnipotent.

13.

Nathan braked the *Blue Moon Bandit* after it dropped loose from the light speed jump that brought it near Neptune. The azure-colored gas giant hung in space before him and he admired the majesty of it. One of the great things about working in space were the fantastic views, and he never tired of them.

He flipped a switch and contacted Triton air traffic control for a heading. As he spoke to them, Marla adjusted their course for Neptune's moon.

Half an hour later, Nathan dropped the *Bandit* into a landing bay of the moon's main port. After making sure the ship was secure, he moved back to the galley where the rest of the crew was gathered and poured himself a mug of coffee from the machine on the counter.

Nathan looked at Duncan first. The engineer sat at a table in the middle of the galley. He noted that when they were just a crew of four the table had been adequate. Now, with six, it was entirely too small. "How's our newly repaired ship doing? Everything looked alright from the cockpit."

Duncan set down his own mug of coffee. "Bruce and his guys back at the shipyard did a pretty good job, but I'm seeing a few things that need attention."

"Like what?"

"We ran a little hot on the trip out here from Earth," Duncan said. "I just need to tweak some settings on the goose. We can take care of it while you're doing your thing here."

Cole grunted. "I can handle most situations, but it sends shivers down my spine when you guys talk about tinkering with things that accelerate us past the speed of light like it's just a normal thing."

Duncan looked at Richie then back to Cole. "It is a normal thing. We do it all the time."

"I don't need to know about it," Cole said.

Richie smiled at him. "If you think that's bad, wait until you find out how often we have to monkey around with the life support system."

"What's wrong with life support?"

Richie shrugged. "Nothing. It just needs attention from time to time. You work in space, right? This can't be news to you."

"I don't need to know how you keep things working," Cole said. "I just need them to work." He turned to Nathan. "Speaking of which, are we going to do some work?"

"You have a name?"

"I do."

Nathan nodded. "Then let's get it done."

⟨⟩

Nathan, Cole, and Tricia exited their rented landing bay and headed for the dockmaster's office. From this vantage point, they could see how large the sprawling facility was. The bay they were using was tiny compared to the ones that held larger ore carriers and water tankers. Dozens of ships were docked in the bays around theirs. Tricia bounced a little on the deck as they made their way toward their destination.

"What's up with the gravity?" she said as she hopped a few meters down the wide corridor. "It's like walking on a trampoline."

"Triton's gravity is something like eight percent of Earth's, so they use artificial gravity," Nathan said. "Although this," he hopped a little himself, "feels pretty light. I'll bet they keep it this way to make it easier to load the ore ships."

"What do they mine?"

"Iron, nickel, and water," Nathan said, "all of which are useful for building starships and refueling them. This far out in the solar system it makes Triton a kind of oasis."

Cole nudged him and pointed down the corridor. "There's the dockmaster's office."

"How do you know this guy?" Nathan said.

"He embezzled half a million credits from a chain of jewelry stores back on Earth. When he got caught, he went on the run for over a year, ducking the local authorities. I arrested him at his mom's place during Thanksgiving dinner. He ended up doing eighteen months in a rehab facility."

"Thanksgiving dinner?" Tricia said.

Cole threw her a smirk. "These guys always run home to momma."

"And this is the only guy you know out here?" Nathan said.

Cole shrugged. "You're lucky I knew this guy. I looked over the public directory and his name was the only familiar one."

A long counter ran the length of the dockmaster's office. Clerks behind the counter moved slowly, like sloths in trees whiling away their workday. It took almost a full minute for someone to realize they were there.

"Can I help you?" the clerk who spoke was a young woman.

Nathan gestured to Cole. He stepped up and said, "We need to speak with Chester."

She looked them over, eyeballing them the way she probably looked over hundreds of freighter crew members to see if they needed some service the office actually provided or if they were going to be trouble. Satisfied they didn't look menacing, or if they did, they were Chester's problem, she turned and walked two rows back to a man sitting at a desk. He looked up at them and made an annoyed face. He rose from his chair and approached the counter.

"You asked for me?"

Cole leaned across the counter. "Hi Chester. You remember me?"

The blood drained from Chester's face as he recognized Cole and his eyes shifted from side-to-side at his co-workers.

"What are you doing here?" He said in a low voice. "I did my time and I'm caught up on restitution payments."

"Relax. I just need some information."

"What could I possibly know that you need?"

Cole glanced around the room. "Why are you here? I figured with your high-end tastes and talents you'd be living large somewhere instead of the ass end of nowhere."

Chester grimaced. "This is where you work when your record includes a stint in rehab for theft. It was impossible to get a job on Earth, so my cousin got me on here."

Cole nodded. "Oh, so your past indiscretions are a secret, huh?"

Chester nodded. "I'd like to keep it that way."

Cole held up his hands, palms out. "Hey, me too, and may I just say good on your cousin for looking out for you."

"What do you want?"

"I need to find a ship."

Chester pointed at a monitor mounted on the wall to their left. "The dock registry is right there. You don't need me to look at it for you."

Cole's eyes never shifted away from Chester. "The ship we're looking for isn't on the registry. It's parked somewhere the owners think is safe from prying eyes like ours. Know what I mean?"

He shook his head. "I don't know about anything like that."

"You sure about that, Chester? Someone flying something small, looking to hide out? Come on, requests like that must come your way once in a while. You know what I'm talking about?"

"I really don't."

"Maybe you could ask some of these other fine folks?" Then his voice rose, "Or hey, maybe I could?"

Several heads popped up and looked in their direction. Chester put a hand up. "Okay, just keep it down. Come back in a couple hours—"

Cole smiled and shook his head. "We need to know now, Chester. Come on, you know what we need. Go get it."

Chester swallowed and considered them for a moment, like he still had a choice in the matter. Then he nodded and walked away.

"Is he going to run out the back door?" Nathan said.

"Nah," Cole said. "He's already run to the end of solar system. There's nowhere left for him to go."

They made small talk for a few minutes while keeping an eye on Chester as he made his way through the office, stopping at certain desks to chat with clerks while skipping others. Eventually he returned to the counter. He pulled a pad of paper from under the counter and wrote something on a sheet, then he tore it loose and handed it across.

"Someone came in about a week ago asking about a place where a ship could be hidden." He tapped the paper. "This is that guy."

Cole opened the paper and Nathan and Tricia read it over his shoulder. "Who is Harold Melbourne?"

Chester shrugged. "All I know is he runs a small grocery in the shopping district. It's expensive stuff, so I never shop there."

"Where did your guy send him?" Nathan said. "Can't he just tell us that?"

"That's all he would tell me. I only had a hundred credits on me and all that bought was the name."

"We could probably give you more if that will loosen him up."

Chester looked back over his shoulder at the guy who had given him the name. "It won't. He's a prick. You'd better hurry, though. If I know him, he'll send a message warning Melbourne as soon as you walk out."

"You know, if this isn't right…"

Chester looked around, then his eyes came back to Cole. "This is all I know. Just go."

——— «» ———

Nathan followed signs on the walls that led them to the settlement's shopping area. The corridor emptied out into a wide space, exposing a couple dozen storefronts.

He pointed at a small place halfway down on the left. "It's over there."

They entered the store and saw that it was empty of customers, but the shelves were modestly stocked with high priced specialty foods. Nathan picked up a can and showed it to the other two.

"Why is anyone on Triton selling caviar? Is it possible workers down on the docks get a hankering for fish eggs?"

"People of all classes enjoy the finer things," a voice said from behind them.

Nathan turned and saw a small man wearing a white shirt and a red paisley vest standing near the checkout counter. Nathan referred to the slip of paper Chester had given them. "Are you Melbourne?"

He raised an eyebrow. "I am. Who might you be?"

Nathan advanced toward him. "I'm the guy who has some questions for you about a starship you have hidden around here."

The man smiled. "Sir, the docking bays are about a kilometer down the corridor to your right. That's where we keep the starships."

Nathan returned the smile. "Mr. Melbourne, I'm not in the mood for wise ass comments or lies. Last week, you contacted the dockmaster's office and bribed a clerk to help find you a place to hide a ship. I'd like you to tell me the name of that ship and its location."

"I'm sorry, but I just don't know what you're talking about." He held his arms out wide. "As you can see, I run a gourmet food store specializing in delicacies that can be hard to find this far from Earth. Now, is there something I can help you with?"

Nathan felt his frustration rise but kept it in check. Unlike the situation with Chester, he had little leverage over Melbourne. He opened his mouth to say something, but instead heard a glass jar break. He and Melbourne looked down an aisle and saw broken glass at Tricia's feet.

"Oops," she said. "I'm really sorry about that." She picked up a similar jar from the shelf and read the label. "Is ten-year-old balsamic vinegar very expensive?"

"Of course it is," Melbourne said, his voice rising with stress. "That's from Modena, Italy. It's insanely expensive to ship here. Please put it down."

"Oh," she said, "My mistake." She moved to set it back on the shelf, but missed and dropped it on the floor. Even in the low gravity the jar shattered on the floor next to its brother and the scent of vinegar filled the shop.

Melbourne put a hand over his mouth. "You did that on purpose! You're a vandal!" He pulled out his mobi and began to dial. "I'm calling Protective Services! You can't just break in here and steal my stock."

Nathan reached across the counter and slapped the mobi from his hands. It landed on the floor and skittered out of reach. "Look, tell us what we want to know, and we'll go away."

"But I don't know anything!"

"You do."

Cole started to reach for a vacuum pack with cursive writing and Nathan watched Melbourne's face dissolve into horror. "Don't you dare eat that," Melbourne said. "That's ten-month-old prosciutto! It goes for three-hundred credits a kilogram."

Nathan shrugged at Melbourne. "They are so clumsy, I wouldn't put it past those two to open enough stuff that you'll lose whatever profit you earned setting up that deal with the ship."

"Okay, okay, just stop!" Melbourne said, with panic in his voice. "It's the *Heartbreaker Amy*."

Nathan picked up a small package from the counter and looked at it. "Holy cow, is this real mozzarella? I love this stuff."

"I just told you what you wanted to know," Melbourne said. "Please go."

"You haven't told me where it is," Nathan said. "I need a location."

The shopkeeper looked at Cole and Tricia, both of whom were eyeing delicacies on the shelves, and surrendered. "There's an inactive iron mine near the north pole."

"No one else is there?"

He shook his head. "No, it's just sitting up there all by itself with nobody around. I don't know what they're up to, they just needed a place to lay low."

"And that's something you do? Arrange places to lay low?"

Melbourne nodded. "I introduce people with problems to people with solutions. It helps pay the bills."

"Good to know," Nathan said. "We're going to leave now, and I expect that you'll keep quiet about our visit. If I get up to the mine and that ship is gone, I'll come back in here with my whole clumsy crew, understand?"

"Yes, now please go."

Nathan held out the ball of mozzarella for Melbourne to take. "Thank you for your cooperation."

14.

The *Blue Moon Bandit* glided low over Triton's frozen nitrogen surface on a northerly heading. Nathan was at the controls with Marla in the co-pilot's seat. She kept a lookout for spying eyes that might detect their approach to Melbourne's abandoned mine.

The annealed surface of the moon indicated a history of melting, leaving it smooth without many ridges or mountains that let Nathan keep the *Bandit* low, hugging the deck to prevent their quarry from seeing them coming.

The sun's light was dimmer this far toward the edge of the solar system, so Nathan was relying on instruments to maintain safety. A head's up display projected above his flight controls gave him an enhanced view of the surface. Melbourne had been able to give them a rough heading but without a working landing beacon, the mining camp remained difficult to find.

"Hold up here," Duncan called from his engineering workstation in the large compartment behind the cockpit. "I've got them."

Nathan slowed the ship and set it to hover as he looked at a monitor to his left. The feed displayed there was from a whipper drone Duncan operated. In the sky ahead of the ship, the snake shaped drone was easily concealed in the sky over the target.

Nathan smiled. "Yeah, I see it." He turned to Marla on his right. "Not bad for a day's work."

She was looking at the feed on her monitor. "I only see one ship, looks like a little prospecting hopper."

The view from Duncan's whipper drone zoomed in, stenciled on the side of the small ship's hull was a registration number and the name, *Heartbreaker Amy*.

They'd already looked up the ship name Melbourne had provided on the registry. Owned by Grigory and Lake Ivanovich, a husband-and-wife duo who claimed to be prospectors. But given their current location, Nathan was guessing they were also Xandra's blackmailers.

Cole appeared in the cockpit doorway. "Are we going down?"

"Looks like it."

Cole squinted at the display on the monitor. "I'll break out the pressure suits. Looks like we're going to need them."

—— «» ——

Twenty minutes later, Nathan, Cole, and Duncan stood in a cramped airlock at the rear of the *Blue Moon Bandit*. All of them wore slim-fit pressure suits, but the compartment barely accommodated them. Nathan and Cole were armed for protection, Duncan had a tool bag in case technical problems. Tricia had her med kit ready, but would stay on the *Bandit*. Nathan hoped the people down below were content with blackmail and wouldn't resort to violence, but you never knew.

Nathan looked out the back window and saw the rear ramp lowering itself. He keyed his mic. "Alright folks, here we go." He touched a control and the air was pumped out of the lock.

He felt the ramp gently touch down on the large landing pad that also held the *Heartbreaker Amy*. Nathan slapped the button on the airlock and the outdoor doors opened. They hustled down the ramp as quickly as they could in the pressure suits. Nathan went left and Cole went right, bracketing the prospector's ship. He threw a look over his shoulder and saw Marla already lifting off again with the ramp closing up. They would keep a safe distance, ready to dip back down if Tricia was needed.

They moved quickly across the concrete landing pad and Nathan walked up to the prospecting ship and banged on the side of it. No one responded to Nathan's pounding, so he raised his hand and did it again. Cole came around the far side of the ship and stood looking across the landing pad to the mining camp main entrance about fifty paces away.

"What do you want?" a voice said with a Russian accent over the open radio. "Why are you here?"

Cole tapped Nathan on the shoulder pointed at the building. Nathan nodded and led his party across the landing pad toward the entrance. Through the airlock window, Nathan could see the blurred outline of a man. Nathan saw him get a little more animated and the voice popped in his ears again.

"Okay, you stay right there," he said. "Don't come any closer."

Nathan pulled up short of the building's airlock. "Open it up, Grigory." He guessed this man in the window was the owner of the prospecting ship and figured using his name would rattle him. People made mistakes when they were rattled.

Grigory looked back at him through the portal and shook his head. "You may not come in. This is our place."

Nathan shook his head. "I have a message from Xandra Ariti."

That caught his attention. He seemed to grow more suspicious as he eyed Nathan. "What is the message?"

"Open up or you don't get it."

Nathan could see him chewing it over, wondering if the risk of letting strangers in was worth it, but he'd already screwed up. Nathan and his crew were between him and his ship. Grigory had no cards left to play. Nathan saw him nod.

"You come in and there's no funny stuff, understand?"

"Don't worry, this is a no funny stuff type deal."

The outer door of the airlock slid open and Nathan switched to the private channel and spoke to Cole. "We good? No one else around?"

"I don't see anything."

"Look, I don't think this guy is going to try anything but, you know, keep an eye out."

"Of course."

The three of them stepped inside the airlock and the outer door sealed. He raised a gloved hand and indicated the inner door needed to be opened, but Grigory had already given the command. It opened, admitting them inside the complex.

Grigory stood alone in the complex, and he appeared nervous to Nathan. The man was unarmed and sweating in a way that Nathan thought was a little heavy considering they were all agreeing to be friends.

"You feeling okay over there, Grigory?" Nathan said. "Anything bothering you?"

He stood still without answering. The interior bay was huge, no doubt built to hold the digging machines that would have been used back when the complex was active. It was dimly lit, though, like the complex wasn't running on full power. Behind Grigory and to his right, there was a bare rectangular void on the floor, missing the dust that coated everything else.

"Scatter!" Nathan yelled, and he moved awkwardly to his right in the low gravity. He looked back and saw what would have been an effective trap if it had been sprung on Earth. As he watched, the missing shipping container dropped from an overhead hoist and floated silently toward the floor. It was eerie how something so deadly could make no noise as it drifted downward. He counted to three seconds before the metal container bumped against the concrete floor with a hollow noise like an ancient gong being struck by a mallet. The ludicrous noise rolled over Nathan and reverberated off the metal walls of the bay as a small cloud of dust rose up.

He bent knee and brought his pistol up. It felt awkward in the thick gloves of his hand but he could hit what he wanted; of that, he was sure. The problem was Grigory was long gone, vanishing back into the dimly lit bay.

Nathan keyed his mic. "Cole? Duncan? Are you okay?"

Cole emerged from the cloud of dust at a run, heading for the opposite end of the bay. Duncan followed him, moving more slowly while answering Nathan. "We're alright but that guy is getting away."

Nathan joined the chase, passing Duncan and finally catching up to Cole. Grigory was ahead of them, losing ground with every short step. Cole hefted his rifle like a bat and took a vicious swing at the man's legs. Grigory went down hard, skidding along the dusty concrete. He tried to roll over, but Nathan put a heavy boot between his shoulder blades, pinning him down.

He let loose with a string of Russian that Nathan didn't understand, so he just pressed harder with his boot while he caught his breath. Grigory got the message and fell silent.

Nathan looked up at Cole; he was breathing heavily but the fog-resistant coating on their helmets prevented any vision-obscuring condensation. "He wasn't holding the controls for the hoist, so he's not alone. Someone else is in here with us."

Cole nodded and bent, slipping restraints on Grigory, then he glanced up at the overhead hoist that had held the container that almost killed them. Something caught Cole's eye and he moved into the darkness.

Nathan looked at the sniffer built into his pressure suit's left gauntlet and it glowed green, indicating the atmosphere in the bay was fit for human life. He could have assumed as much from the way Grigory was running around without a suit of his own, but it never hurt to be sure. He removed his helmet and was met with musty, stale air.

There was a commotion from the direction where Cole had run off, and Nathan saw him returning from the shadows. He had a woman by the collar, half-shoving, half-dragging her toward the assembled group. When he got close, he pushed her down beside Grigory and wrapped restraints around her wrists as well.

"Found her over there," he said pointing back where he'd come from. "She was still holding the hoist controls."

Nathan nudged Grigory with the toe of a boot. "Why'd you do that, man? I thought we agreed to no funny stuff."

Grigory hung his head. "You're here to kill us. Killing you first only makes sense."

Duncan shined a light into the shadows. "Nathan, I don't see anyone else."

"Thanks, Duncan," Nathan said and turned his attention back to Grigory. "Look, is there somewhere we can talk comfortably?" He looked around at the empty bay. "Maybe a mess or something?"

Grigory nodded, clearly wary of Nathan's offer. "Through that door and down the corridor."

"Alright, let's go there."

——— 《》 ———

Aboard the *Heartbreaker Amy*, engineer Harmony Bettle looked out a small portal facing the mining complex; three figures in pressure suits had just entered the building. The crew of the *Amy* had been splitting time between the ship and the complex because the ship was in such poor shape that no one trusted it to maintain operations without someone aboard.

Unsure she would even pick up, Harmony grabbed her mobi and clicked on Lake's name.

"What do you want?" Lake spoke in a harsh whisper.

"What's going? Who are those people?"

"It doesn't matter," Lake replied in that same rough whisper. "In a minute they will be dead."

Harmony fumbled her mobi and almost dropped it. The blackmail scheme Grigory had talked her into was bad enough, but murder wasn't something she could be a part of, no matter how good the credits were.

She raised the mobi up again. "Lake, don't hurt anyone. Do you hear me? Don't do anything stupid."

The only reply was silence. She heard a noise behind her and turned to see Caster, one of the deckhands, looking at her. "Is something wrong?" he asked.

"There are people here and they've gone inside," Harmony said. "I don't know who they are and I'm afraid Grigory and Lake are going to do something stupid."

He bent and looked through the portal, but there was nothing to see. "Of course they'll do something stupid. I love Grigory like a brother, but he tends to blow things out of proportion."

Harmony considered the deckhand for a moment. If she decided to just take the *Amy* and fly off, would Caster back her up? Before leaving on this most recent trip out she'd already made up her mind to find another job. Maybe she could just scoot back to Triton's main port and contact Protective Services to come get her boss and his wife. They could deal with the consequences of their own actions while she shipped out with another crew. It was worth considering. Caster was so indebted to Grigory, though, he'd probably try and stop her. Was it worth a fight if it came to that?

"Let's see what happens here," she said. "I figure one of two things; they get their butts kicked and we leave, or they get paid and we leave."

Caster sat down in a chair and poured himself some vodka. "Twenty credits says Grigory can take them."

《》

The mess hall was small, a side-effect of automation — small human crew, small human facilities. Nathan had Cole remove Grigor and Lake's restraints and sit them at the sole, circular table. Cole remained behind them standing guard. Nathan selected the least grungy plastic chair and sat down facing the pair.

"You cannot hold us," Grigory said. "I will call Protective Services."

Nathan smiled. "You going to tell them you're blackmailing Xandra Ariti?" Grigory just glared at him from heavily lidded eyes. "I thought not," Nathan said.

"You weren't supposed to come here," Grigory said. "The message had account information and specified a credit transfer."

"Shockingly, Xandra Ariti didn't trust you and sent us instead. Next time you may want to consider obscuring the origin of your message. That's some free advice." Nathan leaned in a bit. "Now, where is the *Candlewax*?"

Grigory glanced at Lake, licked his lips, and looked back to Nathan. "The message had a credit figure we wanted for the location."

"You're not getting it."

"Then you cannot have the location."

Nathan smiled. "Here's what you can have. I've been authorized to give you ten percent of what you wanted as a finder's fee."

"The ship is worth more than that!" Grigory said. "I could salvage it and scrap it to make more."

"Well then, you probably should have done that," Nathan said. "Now it's too late."

To his credit, Grigory sat up straight and affected a pose of defiance. "This is where you torture us? Go ahead. I'll tell you nothing."

Nathan shook his head. "No, we don't do that."

"Because you are weak?"

"No, because I'm guessing the information we want is on your ship. I'm going to go search it. Then, when I find the location, I'm going to disable your ship and leave you here while I go retrieve it." He drummed his fingertips on the tabletop. "I saw your little prospector rig sitting outside on the landing pad and I'm familiar with that model. It may take us a few days to take it all apart, but we'll find the location eventually."

Grigory looked at Lake again, this time with less confidence. "He's lying," she said.

"I'm not," Nathan said. "I promise you I'm not."

Grigory turned back to him. "You would strand us here?"

Nathan turned to his engineer. "Duncan?"

The big man stepped closer. "Your ship is a LVT Expedition Special Model Nine-Six. It has a SajiCo X-three hydrogen fusion reactor. To disable it, I'll remove both the primary fuel pellet injectors and the secondaries. I assume, being prospectors, you have a limited machine shop aboard, correct?"

Grigory nodded, enraptured in Duncan's explanation.

"Right, well, if you have the correct alloy stock in your ship's stores, you'll be able to machine new ones, test them, and install them in about ten days."

Nathan smiled and maintained his gaze on Grigory. "Duncan, if we wanted to give Grigory a more dire problem, what else could we do?"

"I could spray parts cleaner inside the fusion reaction chamber, which would irreparably damage the laser emitters. Unless they have replacements in stock, they're stuck here until someone brings them new units."

Nathan zeroed in on Grigory and remained silent for a moment, just staring at him. "I want you to know, I won't hurt you, but I have no problem disabling your ship and leaving you here. The choice you have to make is whether I ask Duncan to do something you can fix, or something you can't. You tell me what I want to know, you're only temporarily stranded. If you don't, the situation will be more permanent."

Grigory dropped his head, resting his chin on his chest. Nathan couldn't tell what he was going to do. The guy looked like a tough little bastard, but looks could be deceiving. He'd seen tough guys crumble and meek dudes stand up to incredible pressure. Grigory chewed his lower lip, like he was trying to figure out which way to go.

Then he looked up at Nathan and locked eyes with him. "You don't have the balls to do what you're threatening," he motioned at the crew. "You're all soft."

Nathan wasn't all that surprised, but it was Grigory's choice to make. If this is what he wanted, then this is what he would get.

Nathan slapped his palms down on the table. "I understand, man," he said, then he stood up. "Why not make it tough on us, huh? I get that. Okay, I just want you to know I respect your decision, but right now I have to go search your ship."

"You'll find nothing."

Nathan turned back. "I think you're wrong. You went to the trouble of getting photos of the *Candlewax*, you didn't just commit the location to memory. It's in a database somewhere or written down on a sticky note. I'll find it."

He turned to Cole. "Think they'll be alright if we're gone for a while?"

Cole nodded and put the restraints back on the couple, this time in front of them. "They aren't going anywhere."

"Great, let's go check his ship."

They grabbed their pressure suit helmets and followed Nathan to the entrance at the mess. At the door, he stopped and looked back.

"You sure, Grigory? It's gonna be a couple hours before we check on you."

"Screw a goat."

Nathan pointed a finger at him. "You may be a tremendous pain in the ass, but I do admire your tenacity. Hang tight, we'll be back before you know it."

——— «» ———

"Oh, shit," Harmony said. "They're coming out to the ship." She could see three figures in pressure suits coming toward her, and none of them looked like Grigory or Lake. If they intended to board the *Heartbreaker Amy*, there wasn't much she could do.

The only other person on board was Caster and he had been drinking steadily for the last half hour. Harmony was pretty much on her own.

"Whoever found us was probably sent by Xandra," she said, talking to herself. It was something she did to work through problems when she was feeling overwhelmed. It had a tendency to drive other people nuts, but Caster had his head down on the table.

"I told Grigory that blackmailing her was an asinine idea. We could have just gone to her and asked for a reward, which I'm betting she would have paid."

She poked Caster. "Hey, wake up. We're going to be boarded."

Caster raised his head and blinked at her with heavy eyelids. "Well, that ain't good." He took a pull from his bottle, having eschewed a glass or cup. He looked pretty far gone. "We're probably all gonna die," he said, "just like poor Meatball."

"That's not going to happen to us."

He laughed, a short unhappy bark. "Whatever we ran into on that ship tore his head off. Remember me carrying his head? I sure as hell do."

"Caster, I need you to focus."

He took another swig and knocked over his empty glass with the bottle. "When we were back on that ship, and me and Meatball were making our way to the engineering compartment, I wasn't scared. I mean, I'd been on plenty of salvaged vessels and seen all kinds of stuff. If we'd tripped across fire damage or a dead fella, I'd have just thought it was expected." His face darkened as he spoke. "Then something grabbed Meatball. I heard him scream, but it was just a short one, like he didn't have time to even get all that fear out of him. Then something ripped his head off, Harmony."

"I know, Caster, but we have trouble coming at us."

He shook his head. "You don't know how right you are."

"What do you mean?"

"If the people coming at us were sent by the same monster who owns that damned ship, you can bet your ass they're here to kill us. They're just tying up loose ends."

"What do you think we should do?"

"Don't open the hatch. You and me aren't going to be any damn good at repelling boarders."

She rocked back and forth from foot to foot. "I didn't see Grigory or Lake with them. What if they're dead? Maybe we should just take off?"

Caster took another swig from the bottle. "I don't think we should do that. That would just piss Grigory off."

"If he's still alive."

"Right," Caster said. "If he's still alive."

"We need to do something!" she said, her voice rising with frustration. "How long do you think that stupid hatch will keep them out?"

"Oh, not long," he said, and took another swig.

Disgusted with his pessimism, she hurried to the narrow steps leading to the lower engineering deck. She hopped up so her feet were on the handrails and slid down, thumping to the metal deck when she got to the end.

Whatever the people coming at her wanted, maybe she could talk them out of busting in. She rounded the corner to the airlock and stopped in her tracks. Whatever she was going to do, it was too late. The inner airlock was cycling.

15.

Duncan used a device of his own design on the locking mechanism on the inner airlock hatch of the *Heartbreaker Amy*. The outer airlock hatch had opened almost immediately; the factory installed lock was designed to give up if a rescue was in progress and that's exactly what Duncan was able to trick the system into thinking. The inner lock was giving them a bigger problem.

"Think you can get through it?" Nathan said.

"I know I can," Duncan said. "Grigory thought he was being clever here by installing this after-market piece of trash but I've seen it before." Duncan had a lead from his device plugged into a jack on the control panel. He turned his head inside his helmet. "The manufacturer didn't want to be sued for locking out Protective Services in the case of an emergency, so there's a listener in here programmed to wait for a signal from rescuers. As soon as I hit this button all of them should be transmitted and the lock should pop. You guys ready?"

Nathan gave him a thumbs up. Cole moved forward, prepared to be the first one through the hatch.

"Here we go," Duncan said.

He jabbed a button and the device lit up. After a few seconds the airlock cycled and the hatch popped open. Cole charged through, and Nathan followed him. They spotted a woman in the corridor to their right. Cole advanced on her, hand on his holstered weapon and told her to get her hands up on a bulkhead. Nathan turned and looked down the other end of the corridor but saw nothing. Duncan cycled the airlock and the inner hatch closed, sealing them inside.

Nathan broke the seal on his helmet and took it off to address the woman Cole had pinned to the bulkhead.

"Miss, we're not here to harm anyone. I just need your help to find some information."

She looked at him and Duncan behind him. "Where are Grigory and Lake? What did you do to them?"

"Cole, let her go," Nathan said. The security man released her and stepped back. "Your crewmates are inside the complex, safe and sound. However, he's a stubborn cuss and wouldn't tell me what I need to know. Hell, he didn't even tell me you were on board."

"Speaking of," Cole said. "Who else is here?"

The woman glanced at the three of them and a look of resignation crossed her face. "Why don't we go down to the galley? There's just another deckhand aboard and that's where he is. There's no need to hurt us."

"As long as everyone behaves," Nathan said, "we'll just have a nice chat."

—— ⟨⟩ ——

A few minutes later, Nathan and Duncan sat on one side of a table while Harmony and Caster sat on another. After they'd all been introduced, Caster had his put head down on the table and Nathan wasn't sure if he was awake or not. Cole was somewhere in the ship, searching for anyone Harmony hadn't mentioned.

"I'm getting tired and it's been a long day," Nathan said, "so I'm going to get right to the point. Your crew stumbled on a lost ship and your idiot of a captain decided to blackmail one of the wealthiest people in the solar system with the location. You know what I'm talking about, right? The *Candlewax*?"

Harmony nodded. "That's right."

Nathan blew out a deep breath. "Thank you for being honest with me." He leaned back in his chair. "It should come as no shock to you that when wealthy people are the victims of a crime, they don't take it well. Having gobs of credits gives them options folks like you and me don't have. I mean, someone tries these shenanigans with you or me, we either pay up or call Protective Services." He pointed at himself and Duncan. "Xandra calls people like us."

Harmony swallowed hard, clearly worried about the situation. "And who are you?"

He grinned. "We find lost ships. Now, I only need one thing from you and we'll be on our way. After that, you can do whatever you want. If you feel like heading over to the mine complex to help your boss, that's fine, or you could just take his ship and leave, which is probably what I would do."

She raised a water bottle to take a sip and Nathan noticed the water inside the bottle shook. Harmony was clearly rattled.

"What do you want to know?" she asked.

"That's easy. Where is the *Candlewax*?"

Her eyes flicking between Nathan and Duncan. "If I tell you that, how do I know you won't kill us? For all I know Grigory and Lake are dead over there."

"That's an excellent question and one I would ask were I in your position." Nathan pointed at her utility pockets. "You still have your mobi?"

She nodded.

"Then give them a call. I'll wait."

She looked at them like she didn't believe him, but then pulled her mobi out and tapped the screen, keeping one eye on Nathan, like he might change his mind. She seemed like the kind of person he might be able to cut a deal with. Exposing her to Grigory's anger one more time might help push her over the edge.

"Grigory?" she said. "Are you and Lake alright? I'm here with Captain Teller."

The angry prospector's voice exploded from the mobi's speaker. "Don't you tell that *Svolach* anything. Just come and get us!"

"Are you alright? Are you hurt?"

"We're fine, just keep your damn mouth shut!"

"Heard enough?" Nathan said.

Harmony nodded and dropped the call. "That's pretty much what he's like whenever the smallest thing makes him angry."

"All the more reason to go your own way," Nathan said. "Tell me what I need to know and you can take off."

"Just like that?" She pushed back from the table, clearly upset. She paused for a moment and ran a hand through her hair. "There's a reason I'm here with these people. I need a job. Right now, I've got nothing except the gear in my quarters and a few credits. If I just fly away, where would I go? How would I support myself?"

"A finder's fee," he said. Harmony looked up at this. Nathan continued, "Grigory was trying to get a million credits from Xandra. I'm authorized to pay a finder's fee to whoever coughs up the location."

"Did you explain this to Grigory?"

Nathan shrugged. "He told me go screw a goat. Some people, once greed digs its claws in, can't see any other way to go. Your boss is one of those guys."

She shook her head. "How much did he turn down?"

"Hundred thousand."

Harmony blinked and looked at Caster. "Do I have to share?"

Nathan glanced at the slumbering drunk. "They're your credits. Do whatever you want with them. So, can you tell me where the *Candlewax* is?"

She leaned across the table. "Yeah, I can do that."

"Good, now, there is one more thing," Nathan said.

She eyed him with distrust. "What?"

"You get half now, but you have to come with us until we confirm the ship's location. Is that a problem?"

She hesitated and looked at all three of the people seated across the table from her. Nathan thought she might back out of the deal, but then she said something odd. "There's someone else who needs to come with us. But it's a little complicated."

Harmony led them down to a storage compartment on the lower deck. In addition to the racks holding the tools and suits used for prospecting and sample drilling, a medical stasis pod was mounted to one bulkhead. It was white, with dark scuff marks where equipment had banged into it, and greasy handprints around the latches that held the lid closed.

Nathan looked at Duncan. "Call the *Bandit* back down, we're in Tricia's court now."

———— «» ————

Half an hour later, Tricia was through the airlock and caught up on Harmony's willingness to turn against Grigory. She handed Nathan her helmet and approached the stasis pod with confidence. She ran a hand over the clear polymer of the lid and studied the man within. He was middle-aged, with light brown skin. His face seemed restful, as if he were merely sleeping instead of being in a medically induced stasis waiting for someone to rescue him. The room was silent as the others waited for her to finish her examination. Vital signs displayed on a screen as she scrolled through them.

"What happened to him?" Tricia eventually asked.

"We found him when we were on the *Candlewax* and he collapsed," Harmony said. "There was some trouble and while we were running, he dropped."

"What kind of trouble?" Cole had finished his search of the *Amy* and rejoined the crew.

Tricia held a hand up to him. "Deal with that later. He was living on the *Candlewax*? What can you tell me about the conditions he was living in? Did you see any of that?"

Harmony nodded and swallowed. "We met him in small quarters and there were stacks of crated provisions everywhere. I got the feeling he didn't get out of there much."

Tricia narrowed her eyes. "Boxes of rations, you're saying? Nothing fresh? No vegetables or fruits?"

Harmony shook her head. "No, nothing like that. Just the boxed stuff."

Tricia ran a gloved hand across her chin, considering Harmony's information. "When you ran, was it sudden, like a big burst of energy?"

"Yeah, you could say that. We had to go quite a ways down a corridor and then another one to get back to the *Amy*."

Tricia turned back to the stasis pod and looked over the readings again; the EKG showed clear waves forms and a steady heartbeat, and his blood oxygen was clicking between ninety-eight and one hundred. The pod was administering drugs to keep him stable, though, which accounted for his good condition. Tricia looked around the storage compartment they were all crowded into and frowned. "If I'm going to treat him, I'd rather do it over on the *Bandit*. Can we haul this thing over there?"

"Do we really need to?" Nathan said. "He looks fine here." Everyone turned to look at him at once with puzzled looks. He got the hint. "On the other hand, moving this thing shouldn't be a big deal."

"I saw an anti-grav lifter back there," Duncan said. "I can use that to transfer him over. Cole, give me a hand."

"I'll get my gear," Harmony said.

"Better get it all," Nathan said. "I don't think you'll be back."

"Suits me fine," she said.

16.

An hour later, Duncan crawled out from under the stasis pod and grunted as he stood. "You're all set, Tricia. The pod is hooked into the *Bandit's* power supply and things look good. Any problems on your end?"

Tricia looked at the screen on the pod and swiped through the diagnostics screen. "Looks okay to me, Duncan. Thanks for the help."

"No problem."

Nathan, Duncan, and Tricia were in a cargo hold on the lower deck where it had been easiest to move the pod after Cole muscled it up the cargo ramp with the anti-grav lifter from Grigory's ship. Nathan had returned the anti-grav lifter to the *Amy,* placing it on the table beside Caster, who was still sleeping off his afternoon of drinking, and returned to the *Bandit.* Then Marla cleared them from Neptune airspace.

"What are you going to do with him?" Nathan asked.

Tricia was sitting on a beat-up chair that Duncan usually kept across the corridor in his fabricating compartment. She scrolled through the data on the screen with her index finger, going up and down to check it again and again. "I think I'm going to wake him up."

"Did something serious happen to him, like a heart attack or stroke?"

She shook her head. "No, his stats look good and the pod injected him with microscopic internal scanners. There's no arterial blockage and no signs of a stroke."

She called up a menu and started the process to revive him. "I can understand why Harmony and the others were concerned when he collapsed, but I think what we're seeing here is the result of malnutrition, dehydration, and years of inactivity. The pod has been pumping him full of fluids and nutritional supplements since they put him in there, so I think he's going to be alright."

The latches on the pod released with loud clicks and the lid made a hiss as it depressurized and slid open. Tricia bent over her patient. "Can you hear me?"

Nathan saw his eyes blink rapidly and he looked up at the strangers staring down at him. A look of concern crossed his face and Tricia turned around. "Okay, this may take a while. Why don't you leave him with me and I'll let you know when he's up and around."

Duncan gave her a quick salute and left the compartment while Nathan slipped an arm around Tricia. "I should relieve Marla up in the cockpit. Are you sure you don't need help?"

She smiled and kissed him lightly. "No, tell everyone to get some rest. I've got this. If I need anything, I'll give you a call."

"We don't know anything about this guy except that he was alone on a derelict ship for three years. Who knows what his mental state is?"

Tricia placed a hand on his chest and softly pushed Nathan back toward the door. "I don't try and help you with the flying, you don't need to help me with the medicine. Go find that ship so we can get paid."

He looked at the pod and then down at her. "Okay, sorry, I just get concerned with strangers on the ship."

Tricia had slowly maneuvered him out into the corridor. She waved with a cheeky smile and shut the door.

———— «» ————

Nathan ascended one deck and made his way to the cockpit. Marla was in her usual right-hand seat while Harmony occupied his pilot's seat on the left. "How are we doing?"

"Harmony gave me the coordinates," Marla said. "The Neptune warpgate doesn't have an outlet near where we want to go, so I'm prepping for the jump. It's going to take us to a red dwarf system, Barnard's Star, which is roughly six light years away."

Nathan sighed. It was cheaper if you could use a warpgate. Jumps like the one Marla had set up burned their own fuel. "Alright. Harmony, do you know where we're going once we get into the system?"

"I should be able to find the ship. It was adrift and without power, so the drift from where we left it should be predicable enough."

"Can I ask you a question?" Nathan said.

"Sure."

"What made you hook up with Grigory? You seem too well adjusted to be working for a blackmailing prospector."

She sat back in the seat and swiveled toward him. "It's a tough job market out there. When I got that job, I was one of three people to apply, so I felt lucky. Unfortunately, Grigory sucks at prospecting. I shipped out with him twice and we didn't find anything. He paid a minimum rate and we were all supposed to get a cut of the profits, but that never happened."

Nathan considered her for a moment and bit his lower lip. She seemed smart enough to do better. "Where did you stand on the blackmail? Were you supposed to get a cut of that too?"

She blew out a deep breath. "Come on, what was I supposed to do?" She pointed out the canopy at the darkness and stars. "I was stuck out there with him and Lake and they were calling the shots. It's not like I could just walk away from them."

"You didn't have an opportunity when you were docked on Triton? Just gather up your stuff and take a hike?"

Anger flashed across her face, but she kept her voice low. "With what? A duffle bag full of clothes? Because that's all I had. If I would have walked into the local Protective Services office and told them what went down, Grigory would never have paid me." She stood up in the cramped cockpit, eyes all afire with anger and her voice full of indignation. "I appreciate you have your own ship, and an expense account that lets you hand out credits like they're candy, but if I walked out on them, I literally didn't know where my next meal was coming from." Her chest heaved and her voice hitched. "I'm not proud of what I did, but I needed the money. Have you ever found yourself in a position like that? Where you'd do anything just because you needed some credits to get by?"

Nathan thought back to the night he took a bag of drugs and tried to sell them off, just to save his ship and his business.

"Yeah, I've been there," he said, his voice quiet. "Speaking of credits I can hand out like candy, I believe I owe you fifty-thousand." Nathan transferred Xandra's money to the Harmony, "You just get us to the *Candlewax* and you'll get paid the other half of the finder's fee." He looked to his right. "Marla, are we ready to jump?"

"As soon as you give the word."

"Let's do it in five minutes. I'll let the crew know" Then he rolled around the corner and left the cockpit.

He made his way back to the galley to find Duncan, Cole, and Richie sitting at the table. They looked cramped there, like the ship was too small for everyone on board. He shook off the feeling. It wasn't like he could do anything about it anyway.

"What are you bums doing?"

"We heard you talking about making the jump," Cole said, "so we were getting comfortable."

"You could hear all that?"

"Oh, yeah," Cole said. "You certainly have a way with making new friends."

Nathan shrugged. "Whatever. She's on board until we get back to Earth, so I just wanted to know what her story was."

"She did seem to overreact, didn't she?"

"You thought so too?" Nathan said as he sat down and buckled in. He dropped a text message to Tricia about the jump and got a thumbs up back.

Cole nodded. "Maybe there's something else there, maybe not. People get funny when they're desperate."

Marla's voice came over the intercom. "I've got green lights. Here we go."

The ship jumped and Nathan felt the familiar inside-out folding feeling that accompanied the process. He opened his eyes and saw Duncan and Richie were fine, but Cole looked nauseous. The poor guy had never gotten used to it.

Then Tricia screamed, high and loud from the deck below.

17.

Nathan burst through the door into Tricia's makeshift med-bay with Cole, Duncan, and Richie in tow. He saw Tricia standing at the head of the stasis pod and the stranger looked up at them with a puzzled look on his face.

Nathan ran to Tricia. "What happened? Did he do something to you?"

"No," she said. "I just got shook up when I looked in the auxiliary storage compartment." She took a deep breath and let it out slowly, centering herself. "Sorry, I shouldn't have screamed like that. It just took me by surprise."

Nathan motioned for Cole to look in the compartment. Cole, Duncan, and Richie moved toward the pod in unison and looked inside. A grimace crossed Cole's face. Duncan jumped back in shock. "Oh, hell no! What is that doing in there?" He looked at the recovering stranger. "It's definitely not his."

Richie just shook his head. "That is nasty."

Nathan moved past them to take a look himself and pulled back when he got a good look. A decapitated head with long red hair lay on its side, blank eyes staring out from inside of the storage bin. Its mouth was agape in rigor. Nathan slammed the compartment door shut.

"Why the hell is someone's head in this?"

They all looked at the stranger, but he still seemed unaware of what was happening around him.

"Revival is going a little slow," Tricia said in answer to Nathan's unspoken question about the stranger. "But that's to be expected. It's like coming out of anesthesia, some people wake right up and others need a little time. He's doing fine, though. He said his name is Doctor Izad Mir." She looked down at the storage bin. "The question we should be asking is, whose head is that?"

Nathan sighed. "I think we need to ask Harmony for a few more details."

⸺ ⟨⟩ ⸺

Richie stayed behind to help Tricia deal with the head and the other three made their way back up to the galley. Nathan called Harmony to join them from the cockpit. She made her way down and Nathan indicated a chair at the table. "Have a seat."

She looked around with a concerned expression on her face. "Is something wrong?"

"Yeah," Nathan said. "Our nurse just found someone's head in the statis pod storage bin. What can you tell us about that?"

Harmony's face went blank for a moment, like she was trying to remember where she'd put her mobi. "Oh yeah, that's where we put Meatball."

"Meatball?"

"He was a deckhand on the *Heartbreaker Amy*, one of Grigory's charity cases who needed a job and worked cheap."

"Did Grigory decapitate him?"

She shook her head. "No, he has a temper, but nothing like that."

Nathan tried to keep his own temper down, but having a decapitated head on his vessel wasn't something he wanted to deal with. The last thing he needed was an inquest from Protective Services.

"Harmony, why is his head in the pod and not attached to the rest of him?"

Despite keeping his voice calm, he could see Harmony getting defensive. "It happened on the *Candlewax*," she said. "I don't know how exactly."

"Why not?"

"When we boarded the ship, we split up. Lake and I went toward operations and Caster and Meatball headed for engineering. We weren't expecting to find anyone and were just checking the condition of the ship."

"And seeing if anything on board was worth stealing?" Cole said.

She looked at him. "You know, I don't have to tell you a damn thing." She sat back in the chair and crossed her arms.

"Shut up, Cole," Nathan said then looked back to Harmony. "So, what did you find?"

"Well, the man in the pod, obviously."

"Tricia said his name is Doctor Mir," Duncan chimed in.

"Right." Nathan nodded. "What else?"

Harmony threw her hands up. "I don't know. I really don't. The guy — Mir or whatever— freaked out when he learned Meatball and Caster were down in engineering. That's when all hell broke loose. We ran, Caster came running with Meatball's head and then Mir collapsed. We just picked them up and got off the damn ship." She looked down at the table and scratched at the pitted surface with a thumbnail. "I just wanted to keep the crew safe and it was a total cluster."

"You didn't see anything else?"

"I heard something growl," she said. "It sounded animalistic, and angry. I know that sounds ridiculous, but that's what I heard. A really angry animal."

Nathan looked at Cole and Duncan and both men shrugged. No one had an answer. "What about Caster? He had to have seen something."

"He told us he didn't see anything. They went into a compartment with no lights and something attacked Meatball. Caster said he just grabbed the head and brought it with him, which was the decent thing to do, I guess."

"Why put Meatball in the stasis pod?"

"Oh, the pod has that extra bin to store severed limbs so they can be reattached. I just figured that was the best place. I mean, I don't know if he had a family, but they deserved to get his remains."

Nathan didn't know what else to say, so he just said, "Yeah, that sounds decent."

"If you want answers, you need to speak with Mir," Harmony said. "He survived three years on that ship with whatever killed Meatball. Hell, he may even know why it was adrift and beat to hell. All I can tell you is how to find it."

"Nathan," Cole said, "we're going to need those answers before we board it. I need to know what we're dealing with to keep us safe."

"Me too," Duncan said. "Maybe Mir can tell us if there's anything wrong with the ship I need to know about. If he was fighting something for three years, the last thing I want to do is walk around a ship that's booby trapped."

Nathan nodded his agreement. "Okay, Let's see if he's in any shape to give us some answers."

18.

It took two more hours, but Tricia was able to fully revive Doctor Mir, and they all crammed into the galley. Even Marla was there, leaving the ship's AI to complete the faster-than-light jump. Izad Mir sat at the table with a bottle of water in his hand, looking like he wanted to be anywhere else in the galaxy. Tricia had put him in the shower and gotten him dressed in fresh clothes, but he still looked disturbed. His long gray hair hung limply and his cheeks were drawn in. His eyes were set in dark hollows. Careful of the doctor's fragile state, Nathan decided to gently break the ice. "Hello, Doctor. My name is Captain Nathan Teller and this is my crew."

They went around the group, slowly introducing themselves so as not to overwhelm him and explained their jobs on the *Bandit*. Nathan was sure the doctor wouldn't be able to remember anyone until after they'd spent some time together, but for now he needed him to understand he was safe and among friends.

"Doctor, my crew and I have been hired by Xandra Ariti of Vibrant Passion to locate the *Candlewax* and make arrangements to return the vessel to Earth. Harmony here has given us the location of the ship, which is what we need, but she also told us there is something dangerous on board which has already resulted in a death. What we need to know from you is, what is it?"

Doctor Mir took a swig of water from his bottle before he answered in a shaky voice. "You don't want to go to that ship, you don't want to board that ship, and you certainly don't want to fly that ship back home." He paused and the room was quiet. "I don't suppose that's enough of a story for you?"

Nathan gave him a small smile. "I'm afraid not. There's a large payday on the line. If there's something too dangerous, we'll let Xandra deal with it. After all, it's her ship."

"Xandra and her love of credits is why I stole the damn thing, Nathan. Hell, my love of credits is what led me to work for her." He took a deep breath and looked at the all the curious faces surrounding him. Nathan saw fear in his eyes when he turned his way. "Maybe if I tell you the story of how it ended up out there, it will keep you from doing this insanely stupid thing."

Nathan nodded. "We'll see."

⸻ ⟨⟩ ⸻

Izad Mir was lying on his bunk aboard the *Candlewax*. According to his mobi, today was his second anniversary on the research vessel. He rolled to his left and checked the view outside through a small portal. Space was as dark as ever, with only small pinpricks of distant stars breaking up the blackness. He stared into the void for a few minutes, until his mobi chimed. It was a message from one of his lab assistants, requesting his presence in the lab.

He had been with Vibrant Passion for almost ten years, working first on the life lengthening project and then moving over to the transformation team after his work with telomeres had been noticed. The idea of not only expanding the lifetime of a person, but being able to change their very physical structure into a specific form had caught his attention and dominated his thoughts from the first moment Xandra Ariti explained the project to him and Diane Ebbers. They had both accepted Xandra's offer of a position on the development team.

This was something more than just giving people a longer lifespan. It was giving them a chance to overcome congenital defects, heal more thoroughly from devastating injuries, or even give doctors another option to treat patients with psychological issues like body dysmorphia. If they could just master the process, this kind of research could help millions of people. The work they'd accomplished so far had been fantastic, they just needed to get across the finish line. Subjects One through Fourteen-Alpha would be the first to help Izad Mir and his team make that final leap.

He walked the length of the large ship down Main Street, the long corridor that ran through the center of the vessel. Security checkpoints logged his movement down the ship. Some checkpoints were automated, like the one that let him pass from the personnel cabins to the common areas housing the recreation module, mess, and the storage area for crew consumables. The next module had an unarmed guard standing by a hatch with a thick steel door. The guard was friendly enough, with a wave and smile for everyone who passed through.

Here, Main Street split left and right. To the right were the engineering compartments holding the reactor room, environmental support, and everything else needed to run and power the ship. To the left was his domain; research and development.

Inside the corridor ran a series of chambers; the first was large, with a guard on the locked door. This guard was armed; a stun baton, chemical irritants, and a pistol hung from her belt. He glanced over and she waved, as friendly as the first guard, and he nodded in return. Through the window on the door, he could see the large compartment outfitted as a dormitory, with twenty bunks lining each side of the room. Currently, about half those bunks were occupied by test subjects.

He continued on, past a series of life sciences labs and then he came to the process chamber. It was here that the real work began on the test subjects. The locked hatch swung wide for him as the biometric reader built into the frame recognized him. His lab assistant, Teri, was standing beside a specially modified medical pod

"What's going on, Teri?"

She held a tablet out to him and launched right into her explanation. "Subject One-Alpha had an adverse reaction to treatment one thirty-seven."

Izad looked over the data on the tablet and scrolled through it. "This all looked fine, what's the problem?"

Teri pointed at the pod. "Total disincorporation to a liquified state. I'm going to call this one a failure, but I wanted your opinion."

Izad looked into the pod and saw that it was full of a gray sludge shot through with rivulets of a pink substance.

"I don't understand. Nothing in the new mixture should have caused this." He looked at her. "None of our test models indicated this kind of reaction was even a possibility."

She moved closer and glanced around to ensure they had their privacy. "It occurred thirty-two minutes after the introduction of the stage one fluid. Once the immersion of the subject was complete, I heard a muffled noise and checked on her. She, uh, melted in front of me. Rapidly."

Izad moved to the pod's control panel and began running a scan of the contents. The transformation process had three stages. The first one, this immersion, was carried out on a sedated subject. The stage one fluid prepared the subject for stage two, which instigated the actual change. Stage three, completing transformation, took the most time. Alpha group, if all went as predicted, would be the first human test group to go through all three stages. Nothing was readily apparent that would explain such a catastrophic outcome.

"We have no reason to believe that this will happen again. Yes, we lost a valuable test subject, wasted an experimental cycle. But each subject is different, something in her own system is the most likely cause of this reaction. I'll discuss this with Doctor Ebbers. In the meantime, shut the pod down, run a full clean and disinfect, we'll lose some time but nothing else."

She nodded, hurriedly making notes on her tablet. "Right away, sir." She turned to go but he put a hand on her shoulder.

"Teri, sooner would be better than later. I don't want this downtime impacting my schedule."

"Of course."

He watched her scurry off, eager to be anywhere else.

《 》

Izad walked back through the ship, toward the crew's mess for a late breakfast, but was surprised as he walked in to see the test subjects seated at tables. A staff member in dark green overalls approached him before he could make it too far. Green was the color worn by the tests subject and their support staff: pale green for subjects, dark green for staff.

"Sir, if you'd care to wait about thirty minutes, this area will be crew only once again."

Izad glanced at the subjects. "Why are they in the crew's mess at all?"

"There was a plumbing problem in their mess that resulted in it being flooded and the maintenance staff is currently repairing it. Rather than making them wait, we thought it was better to bring them here."

Izad nodded. "Good initiative. Disrupting their routine can be counterproductive. I'll keep to myself."

"Thank you, sir." The handler walked back to the group and rejoined his comrades at a round table.

Izad picked out a breakfast consisting of a fresh fruit medley and scrambled egg whites. Then he found a table and started to eat. As he chewed his first bite, someone joined him at the table. Her pale green jumpsuit marked her as a test subject. She smiled when he looked up.

"I hope you don't mind," she said, "but I thought it would be nice to spend time with someone new. I know all the other volunteers and I've heard all their stories."

Izad saw a handler start to get up from their table, but he shook his head and waved him off with a hand under the table. There was something familiar about this woman, something that reminded him of someone else.

"Of course," he said. "No problem at all." He looked down at her tray and saw it was loaded with pancakes, eggs and sausage.

"You must think I'm a total pig, but I have to tell you this is the best food I've had in a long time. I mean, this food is actually cooked aboard the ship, not just warmed up from frozen meals prepared somewhere else or reconstituted from a powder pouch."

"It sounds like you're enjoying your time here."

She shrugged. "Compared to some of the other places I've worked recently, this isn't bad at all." She forked a wad of pancake into her mouth and kept talking. "My last job was on an ore freighter. I shipped out with them twice, hauling precious metals from the asteroid belt between Jupiter and Mars to a refinery on Luna." She washed down the pancakes with some coffee. "The food sucked. I mean, mealtimes we'd just pop a food pouch on the heater and eat right out of it. Can you imagine? We didn't even use plates."

"It sounds like this is quite an improvement."

"You can say that again. I mean look at what you've got on your plate. Is that an orange?"

"A grapefruit."

"We would never have gotten those unless we snagged one in port on our own because they are way too expensive to provision a ship with." She reached over, took a fat round grape from his plate, and popped it in her mouth. "See, now I love these. I mean, I could just eat these all day."

Bemused, he gave her a small smile. "Please help yourself."

"Oh, I'm so sorry," she said, suddenly aware of what she'd done. "You must think I was raised by barbarians."

"No really, it's fine," he said. "Do you mind if I ask you a question?"

"I'm eating the food off your plate, so I suppose it's alright," she said with a smile.

"Are you enjoying your time here? Is everything working out for you?"

She swallowed another bite of pancakes and nodded. "I can honestly say it's the best job I've ever had. I mean, this ship is clean, the food's great, and there isn't that sense of gloom that you feel on most freighters."

"You've spent a lot of time working in space?"

"Oh yeah, ever since I graduated from school. I grew up back on Earth and it was hard to find a job, so I just started shipping out as a deckhand. From there, I worked my way up to environmental technician, but even with my credentials the pay wasn't great. I hate to admit it, but that's what got me on board. You guys are offering me more credits for this gig than I've made in the last two years."

Something tickled the back of his mind again, but he couldn't figure out what was so familiar about her. It didn't sound like they had ever met or worked with one another. He looked down at his tray and saw that he'd finished off breakfast.

"Well, it's been lovely speaking with you, but I have to get back to work." He stood to leave and she held out her hand.

"I'm Mindy."

He shook it lightly. "Izad. Nice to meet you."

Later on, after his work was caught up and he'd made his way back to his cabin, he laid down on his bunk. There in the darkness, as his mind cleared and he started to drift off to sleep, it finally occurred to him what was so familiar about the woman he'd eaten breakfast with. It was her eyes.

She had his mother's eyes.

《》

Up until the time he was fourteen years old, Izad enjoyed a privileged childhood in Qom, Iran — a city so bustling that Izad felt like he could discover something new every day. His mother and father both worked in a hospital in the ancient metropolis, her as a pathologist, and him as an administrator.

"It's easy to accept the first solution that resolves a dilemma," his mother would say as she helped Izad with schoolwork, "but often, if we keep looking, we find there may be more than one, and they may be better. Remember, curiosity is our most valuable gift from Allah." Izad took that to heart and made sure to always look at problems the way a jeweler might examine the many facets of a diamond before deciding on a way to cut it.

His father was responsible for the culture and work environment for thousands of hospital workers. He taught Izad that sometimes it was necessary to lock away his feelings to do the things expected of him rather than the things he would like to do. Resolving disputes between workers, investigating accusations, and resolving incidents rarely left everyone involved happy, but that was the job.

"It's impossible to make everyone happy," he'd told Izad more than once. "So don't even try. Just do the job you agreed to do and leave your feelings at the door." That lesson was lost on young Izad, but as he grew older, he thought about it more and more.

When he was fourteen, his life changed forever. He returned to his empty house from school, as he did every day, grabbed a snack, and used his mobi to connect with Soraya, the prettiest girl in his Trigonometry class. He was having trouble keeping his grades up and Soraya was tutoring him. These sessions were his favorite hours of the week. He didn't care if he ever learned trig, so long as she kept trying to teach him.

They were thirty minutes into the study session, their hologram-selves much closer than they had ever been in real life, when the door chimed. He looked up in annoyance, hoping whoever it was would go away. Then the chime sounded again. Izad excused himself and opened the door to find two Protective Services officers standing on the front steps.

Izad didn't remember ending the call with Soraya, didn't remember the exact words the officers used to tell him his parents were both dead, and didn't remember when his aunt arrived at the house. It had been a monorail accident on their way home from the hospital. A misaligned magnet had dropped the train a few centimeters too far and the speeding conveyance had dug into the concrete structure, throwing all ten cars free of the track and onto a neighborhood surface street. Seventy-eight people had died, but Izad only cared about two of them.

Aunt Cyra stayed with him in his family's house for two weeks and settled his parent's estate. Then she helped Izad pack up his things and he went to live with her, on her farm.

His aunt's farm was small, only about eight hectares, and situated hundreds of kilometers northwest of Qom in a rural area. For someone used to grabbing a monorail or share-pod and being able to go anywhere or do anything, Izad found himself bored and lonely. He mastered schoolwork that his new classmates struggled with, and he blew off as many farm chores as he could, angering Aunt Cyra, but Izad knew he was destined for more than farming.

One early morning, after a year had gone by, Aunt Cyra snapped on the light in his room. "Come with me," she said. "I need your help."

Izad, annoyed and blinded by the sudden brightness, glanced out the window and saw it was still dark outside. A quick look at his mobi told him it was a little after four in the morning. "Aunt, it's too early. Turn off the light and let me sleep."

"No," she said. "Get dressed. Jasmine needs us. Now hurry."

She walked away from the door and left the light burning. His head swam and it took a minute for what she'd said to register. "Jasmine needs us? She's a cow! What could she want from us?"

There was no answer, though, and he heard the door to the house close. Reluctantly, he threw off his warm blankets and got dressed. He wrapped a jacket around himself and followed the path from the house to the barn.

Inside, the barn was lit with one dimmed lantern. Izad heard a loud moan from the pen where they kept three dairy cows. He approached slowly and saw his aunt in a stall with Jasmine. The cow was clearly very pregnant and lay on her side. His aunt looked up at him. She was wearing a disposable apron and gloves that went all the way up to her shoulders.

"It's her time to give birth."

"I don't know anything about this," Izad said, completely befuddled at the situation unfolding before him.

His aunt was at the business end of the black and white cow. "Just stay up near her head and soothe her. Everything looks fine."

He moved as she instructed and reluctantly ran a hand over the cow's head. He patted her, running his hand over her rough fur, but the animal seemed calm. Behind Aunt Cyra was a collection of towels, ropes, and chains. Izad didn't want to know what had to go wrong for the chains to be needed. "Shouldn't the veterinarian be here? I mean, don't we need a doctor?"

"For this? No. I've done this many times."

The cow mooed loudly.

"Oh, good, the head is out," his aunt said. Izad rose up on his knees and looked over Jasmine's belly. He could see long front legs and the calf's black and white head emerging. He watched, amazed, as the calf, still in an alien looking sac, tumbled free of the mother and lay still on the straw.

Aunt Cyra split the membrane that wrapped the newborn, cut the umbilical cord and sprayed it with a brownish fluid, then she checked the calf's mouth and nose, pulling back the lips to look at its gums. She frowned. "Now you help me, Izad."

Aunt Cyra had him take the calf's back legs and swing it in a wide circle until he felt dizzy. Then, with the calf's airways cleared of fluid, Izad set the calf back on the ground. Aunt Cyra handed him a towel and showed him how to rub the calf's chest vigorously to stimulate breathing.

They rubbed for so long that Izad's arms ached. Aunt Cyra stopped every few minutes to listen for a breath. Each time she did this, she breathed into the calf's nose.

Eventually, Aunt Cyra looked up at him with disappointment on her face. "You can stop now." She waved a hand at him ushering him out of the stall. Jasmine stood up and sniffed at the calf, then he watched as she went to work cleaning the small animal. Her large tongue mimicked the stimulating towel rub that Izad and Aunt Cyra had given up on.

His aunt smiled at him, holding back tears. "You did good, Izad."

He shook his head. "But the calf is dead."

Aunt Cyra shuffled away from the calf and assessed Jasmine's hind end. Appearing satisfied with her cow's condition, she stood up and stripped off her apron and gloves and dropped them in a plastic bin. "It's not your fault the calf died. That's just nature."

He stood still, amazed by what he had just seen. He'd had biology classes in school, but the concepts there were academic, whereas what he'd just witnessed was visceral. This was what he'd learned in a classroom put into practice. He reached into the stall and stroked Jasmine as she continued to clean her calf.

A hand squeezed his shoulder and his aunt said, "You can go back to the house now."

"What about Jasmine and the calf?"

"Jasmine has already smelled that something is wrong. If we had an orphaned calf for her, things would be different." Aunt Cyra took a large bag from a box on the storage shelf. "You don't have to stay for this part."

Izad stayed and watched his aunt prepare the small body for disposal. Then he followed her back up the house in silence, still enraptured by what he'd seen.

After the birth of the calf, Izad consumed everything he could about biology. It was amazing to him, that he could learn how something was supposed to work and then go actually see it on his aunt's farm.

After a few years, he left the farm and went away to university, using the small trust his parents had left him. During his third year, he was studying in his dorm room when his resident advisor came to his door with a Protective Services officer. Before the officer spoke, Izad knew what he was going to say.

There hadn't been a train crash this time; Aunt Cyra had suffered a fatal heart attack. Once again, the capricious duo of human error and nature had left Izad Mir alone.

———— «⟩ ————

Three weeks after the accident that liquified a test subject, Phase Eleven had nearly concluded. This phase had called for fourteen subjects to undergo the transformation process, and although one had died, the next dozen had encountered no problem. With one last subject to push through the first step, Izad would be able to relax for the next few weeks as the transformation proceeded. He stood in the process chamber with Teri and Ebbers. Ebbers had reviewed the materials and agreed: one melted test subject meant very little to their dataset. The specially modified pod was between them, awaiting their last test subject, Fourteen-Alpha.

The door to the compartment opened and Izad saw a gurney being wheeled in. The test subject was already drowsy, having received a sedative a few minutes earlier.

She smiled groggily as she noticed Izad. "Hey you," she said with slurred words. "Today's the big day." Fourteen-Alpha was Mindy, the breakfast thief.

He returned her smile and took her hand, giving it a gentle squeeze. "All ready?"

"Yep," she said. "Time to earn the big credits."

"Yes." He tried to release her hand, but she squeezed harder.

"Izad, I'm going to be alright, aren't I? It's safe?"

His lips pressed together as he struggled to hide his emotions. He reached out with his other hand and lightly brushed a strand of hair away from her eyes, and for a moment, he saw his mother's eyes again. His voiced hitched as he said, "it is." He gained confidence with one lie leading to another. "You'll be fine."

Her hand slipped from his and her eyes closed as the sedative took hold. Izad stood still for a moment looking down at her, as though he might change his mind. Then he stepped back and nodded to the two technicians who had wheeled her in. They picked her up, the sheet slipping from her naked body, and set her inside the pod. Teri closed the lid and tapped a command into the control panel. He watched as the transformative fluid rushed in from the holding tanks, immersing her. He touched the transparent panel and after a moment let his hand slip off. Whatever she was, whatever she would have been in this life, she was now on her way to becoming something new.

He looked up at Teri. "Have her moved to the holding area so we can continue."

——— «» ———

It took two weeks for the subjects to work their way through stage one. The fluid they were immersed in was hard at work re-writing the DNA of each subject, improving the plasticity of their cells. They were each being reprogrammed for their final form. This change was necessary for stage two.

Izad spent those two weeks troubled by what he'd said to Mindy. He'd promised her everything would be alright and nothing could be further from the truth. She would never be okay, never be who she was. Once transformed, there was no going back.

He wandered down to the compartment where stage two was scheduled to take place and saw that the staff were already moving the pods out of the stage one compartment. All thirteen were lined up against the far bulkhead. This compartment was sterile, clean and white so that contaminates could be easily seen. He stepped into an entry chamber and dressed in a clean room suit, complete with an air filtration helmet. He walked past all of the pods, giving them nothing more than a cursory glance. Their readouts were all in the green, indicating the process was working as expected. Then he came to Mindy's pod.

He reached out and stroked the lid, looking at the test subject within. Mindy was still humanoid in shape, but no longer recognizable as the woman he knew. Her hair was gone, her skin was unnaturally smooth, and the features of her face were blunted.

"Doctor Mir?" A voice said from behind him.

He turned slowly and saw Teri standing nearby, similarly dressed in a clean suit, and holding a tablet. "Hello."

"We're prepared to begin stage two."

Behind Teri stood a half-dozen technicians and lab techs, all lined up and prepared to move ahead with the work.

"Of course," he said to Teri. "Please begin."

He gave Mindy one last look then moved back toward the entrance to the room and watched as Teri directed the technicians. In teams of two, they moved from pod to pod, programming each to begin the transformative process. The test subjects were essentially blank slates at this point, waiting for a final form to be imprinted upon them. The teams were efficient and well-practiced in their work. It took less than half an hour for them to begin the process that would completely remake thirteen human beings into something else. Nowhere to go but forward; inertia had overtaken them all.

As stage two progressed, Izad kept picturing his mother's eyes looking out of Mindy's trusting face. What would his mother say now about the gift of insatiable curiosity? Would his father still advocate for silently getting the job done?

The third and final stage began on schedule, and this time he watched from the corridor outside the compartment through an observation window. Teri was inside, directing the team. She was efficient and carried out his plan without deviation from any step. He watched as each pod was rolled into the stage three compartment and hooked back into the ship's power supply.

What emerged from the pods in twenty days would not resemble the human beings who had started the process. They would be transformed, and he would be seen as a success. For the first time he wondered if his parents would be proud.

———— «» ————

After twenty days Izad stood in the stage three compartment, dressed in a clean suit and anxious to start. When Teri the team arrived, they seemed surprised to see him there already.

"Doctor Mir," Teri said. "Is everything alright?"

He gave her a smile from inside the helmet. "Of course." He pointed at Mindy's pod. "I'd like to start with this one."

Teri checked her tablet. "That would be out of protocol, sir. That pod should be last."

"It's an acceptable change," he said. "Please start here."

Teri frowned but directed the team to the pod and they set to work, running the revival sequence. Izad looked over their shoulders, double checking the results on the pod's control pad and the tablets each member carried. From what he could see, the test had been a success. Mindy appeared to be healthy.

He moved to the head of the pod and looked inside. From a purely aesthetic standpoint, Mindy was now hideous. Then her eyes opened.

They were the same soft, warm eyes that reminded him of his mother. Then her eyelids squeezed shut in pain. He tapped the lid and the eyes opened again, focusing on him this time. They pleaded silently with him, begging for solace he could not provide and help he was powerless to give.

"Doctor Mir," Teri said, "it looks like we were successful. Congratulations."

19.

The crew of the *Blue Moon Bandit* was silent, soaking in Izad Mir's story. Then Nathan spoke. "Do you know what kind of crimes you just confessed to?"

Izad nodded. "I do. Can I get some more water?" Richie was closest to the dispenser so he filled the doctor's bottle and passed it forward. Izad took a long pull. "I know what I've done. As soon as I looked into Mindy's eyes, I could see that her mind wasn't wiped the way it should have been. Not completely."

"That's part of the process then?" Nathan said. "Taking away their minds as well as changing their bodies?"

"Yes, it is. You see, for our purposes, we needed what their minds were capable of, not who they were. Everyone has the capacity to learn. That's what was important. No one cared what they knew." He sipped more water. "You understand? Their personalities, the things they'd learned and experienced up until that point in their lives? It was useless to us."

Tricia stood up. "That's monstrous! You lied to those people. They were desperate and you took what little they had away from them."

"These are crimes against humanity," Nathan said. He looked at Izad and felt like chucking him out an airlock. The man sat across the table from him, as calm as if he'd just explained a recipe for baking a cake instead of confessing to the casual murder of a more than a dozen people. "I don't understand how you could do that. How anyone could do that."

"It was the credit and the credits," Izad said. "We were a bunch of brilliant people who were curious. If you put a problem in front of us, we couldn't help but pick at it until we'd come up with a solution."

"You're a doctor," Tricia said with revulsion in her voice. "How could you go against your oath, against everything you were taught in your ethics classes? You did these horrific things for money? For accolades?"

He nodded slowly. "I did. That's exactly why I did it." He rubbed a hand over his face and took a deep breath, as if unburdening his soul had tired him out. "You have to understand, Xandra Ariti came up with this idea to transform people who weren't productive into something that could be. Humanity is spreading out into the galaxy. We're in more star systems now than we've ever been in before and the corporations paying for that exploration need labor."

"Then why don't they just hire people," Nathan said. "It solves the problem of unemployment and gives companies the labor they need."

Izad shrugged his shoulders. "Why pay for labor when you can have slaves?"

"That's heinous." Tricia looked as if she regretted waking up the doctor.

"It is," Izad said, "but there's precedent for it. Everywhere you look in our history, humanity has enslaved those who were weaker. Even today, people are trafficked on Earth and on planets and moons far from Earth. Xandra Ariti is in charge of a business that earns an enormous sum of credits, but you have to understand, it's not the same as what you do with the credits you earn. I mean you and I, we earn credits and we save it, invest it, or give it away if we're feeling generous. What Xandra does is hunt out new opportunities to develop, either meeting the needs of an existing market or creating a new market from scratch. That's what she did with the life lengthening process she sells. Everyone wants to live longer but no one knew how to make that happen. She actually unlocked the genetic code that controls aging and slowed it down. I'm a geneticist, and it's the single most impressive thing I'd ever seen until she had her next big idea."

"Slavery is not a new idea." Nathan prompted.

"In a manner of speaking this is," Izad continued. "Corporations are fueling the exploration of new systems and they aren't just doing it for the riches they can discover. The farther they get from Earth, the less laws matter to them. If some company is light years from the governments of the home world, they effectively become their own entities."

Nathan considered this for a moment. "The East India Trading Company."

"How's that?" Cole asked.

"This idea that you're giving Xandra Ariti credit for isn't new," Nathan said. He got up and poured himself some coffee. "It was something the British did back in the seventeenth century. The government and private companies teamed up to seize control of

India and parts of Asia. They were effectively the law and could do whatever they wanted with little oversight. Slavery became common practice then, too."

"That sounds about right," Izad said. "These corporations are committed to earning large returns and their stockholders don't pay much attention to how they do it as long as the dividends keep coming in."

"Why go to all this trouble of changing them?" Nathan asked. It made no sense to him, from a business standpoint. Why dump all this cash into something that was more expensive than other solutions?

"The worlds these corporations explore are hostile to human life." Izad said. "If they hire workers, they have to feed them, house them, and provide for their safety while working. That means a lot of life support and personal protective equipment to ensure the workers can be productive in hazardous environments, not to mention unions."

"Hostile to *human* life." Tricia said. "What exactly does the transformation do, Doctor Mir?"

Before Izad could answer Tricia, Marla's mobi chimed.

"Alert from the AI, we're about to arrive," Marla said. "Everyone may want to strap in."

"Cole, make sure the doc stays here," Nathan said. "I'll be right back."

He followed Marla up to the cockpit and belted in to his chair. She watched the clock and when the countdown reached zero, dropped them back into normal space. Nathan started working the scanner, trying to find the *Candlewax*. After a few minutes he slid the readout on his monitor to Marla's.

"Harmony did a good job," he said. "Her coordinates were dead on. The ship is about a hundred klicks to starboard on a twenty-degree downward angle."

Marla adjusted their course so they were aimed directly at the flying lab. Nathan adjusted the telescope to zoom in. The ship's exterior looked as rough as Harmony had described. He could see the bulges in the hull where explosions had taken place along the port side. The bridge looked like it was exposed to open space with whole pieces of the canopy missing.

"Are we going to return this thing to Earth?" Marla said.

"I'm not sure yet."

She looked over at him. "It's a death ship, all the horrors that sonovabitch perpetrated there. We should set the reactor to overload and atomize it."

He met her gaze. "Don't tempt me. You got this?"

"Yeah, I don't want to hear anything else he has to say."

"Let me know if you need anything."

He went back to the galley, where everyone was silent once more. Nathan took his time, got more coffee, and took his seat at the table.

"We've arrived at our destination," he announced to everyone, then he bored in on Izad. "Judging from the damage I just saw, I assume you have more to tell us?"

Izad's face still looked blank, like what he was reciting didn't really bother him. "I do."

"Well then, please, Doctor Mir. Go on."

"It was her eyes," he said. "Every time I looked at her, I saw my mother's eyes, and eventually I knew I couldn't go on any longer. I needed to stop the experiment." He swallowed hard. "I realized that speaking to Xandra was worthless; she'd pumped hundreds of millions of credits into the research. The rest of the research team was like me, just there for the credits and the credit of being first to solve the problem. Among the scientists, I was all alone in my concerns. But the *Candlewax* had a large crew."

20.

It had been several months since Izad Mir and his team had started waking up Alpha group and testing their genetic alteration. Now, Izad sat in his cabin with Hassana Bamba, the chief engineer of the *Candlewax*. She was still in her work coveralls and looked out of place swirling the crystal glass of bourbon he'd poured her.

Izad laid the whole thing out, told her everything he was supposed to keep secret, which was a breach of protocol. Xandra had done an excellent job of keeping Hassana and her crew in the dark. They ran the engines, kept the lights on, and the air pumping. They had no idea what was being done in the sections of the ship that were off-limits to them. If there was any reason for them to enter those compartments, they were escorted and the work paused.

She sipped her drink, the ice clinking in her glass the only sound in the cabin. Then she drained it and held the glass out. "I'm going to need more of that."

He got up and poured her another, this time leaving the capped bottle on the desk she sat at. She shook her head. "Security won't budge. They're armed and we aren't."

"Look, I'm not asking for an armed insurrection here. I don't want a mutiny. All I want is some way to get everyone off the ship. You could do that couldn't you? Fake some accident that requires us to evacuate?"

"What about Captain Wull. Why aren't you talking to him?"

"He's a functionary. All he does is steer the ship in an elliptical orbit. I need someone who actually works for a living, down where things happen. Wull is useless. My team won't help either. If I go to them with this, there's a fifty-fifty chance they'll put me in one of those damn pods and run me through the process."

"Really?" Hassana said. "That's what you're afraid of? What do you think they'll do to me and my crew if they figure out I helped you pull off something like this?" She leaned toward him. "Do you think one of the richest people in the world will just blow it off or do you think she'll arrange it so none of us ever work again? And that's if we're lucky. You just said she'll put you in one of those pods. Why wouldn't she do that with us? I manage a dozen people and my job is to get them paid, not killed."

She drank more. "My job and the job of my crew is to make sure this ship runs. Xandra clearly doesn't want my crew learning about your monster-making. I can't justify endangering my team with that knowledge. I get what you want, but you're making your problem my problem and I don't want any part of it."

Izad put his head down in his hands. "These people are enslaved. Surely you understand—"

Hassana slammed her glass down. "I dare you to keep implying that all Black women, by their very nature, must do more to end slavery than the person doing the enslaving. Which in this case, is you!"

Izad poured himself another drink, then moved to the portal, gazing out at the void. He was alone, no one was going to help him, and the experiments were going to go on. He threw back the bourbon.

With it still burning his throat he turned to Hassana. "It would be a shame if Xandra found out that you know what's happening here."

"Oh, no. That's on you. You're not dragging me into this."

He moved closer to her. "You know. There's no going back."

"You told me."

He moved even closer, his presence forcing her back into the chair. "That's irrelevant. All I have to do is let Xandra know and she'll take care of it, one way or the other. If you tell her it was me, I'll just tell her you found out some other way. Who do you think she'll believe? The lead researcher on a top secret, highly illegal project or some lower decks flunky who learned something she shouldn't know." His head bumped hers. "I could send her a message the minute you walk out of here and get permission to make you disappear."

Hassana looked up at him with hate filled eyes. "You are no better than Xandra."

He backed away, giving her some space. "I don't want anyone hurt. I just want everyone off the ship."

She grimaced. "I could maybe do something like that, but it would be temporary. The ship would still be here for Xandra to repair."

He sat back down on his bunk, nodding his head slowly. "You can do it though, right?

"You're still not getting it. I told you already, she'll just recover the ship. You aren't ending anything. At the very most you're just endangering me and putting this shitstorm on pause. What does that accomplish?"

"How can we make the ship disappear?"

She threw her hands up, a look of shock on her face. "Are you kidding me? You come up with some half-assed plan and now not only do you expect me to be your accomplice, I have to come up with a way to pull it off?"

"What do I know about ships or engines?"

"I think it's pretty clear you don't know shit about anything."

Izad studied her for a moment, watching as she mulled over the problems he'd thrown into her lap.

"Just so we're clear, you want everyone off the ship, unharmed, and the data on the ship unrecoverable."

"Yes."

"We could just blow it up. Force a reactor accident; the *Candlewax* would be like an orange in a microwave." She mimed a balloon popping with her hands.

He considered it, then shook his head. "That won't work. An accident gets the authorities involved and they'll recover the wreckage. There could be enough left over for them to figure out what we've been doing out here. Is there a way to make the ship vanish? Make it go somewhere it can't be found?"

"I'm an engineer, not a magician."

"Even with your own life on the line?"

"You're a bastard." Hassana poured herself another drink. "What about the test subjects? What do we do with them?"

"They're too far gone. I don't know how we would explain them if they were recovered with the crew."

"Then I know how to do it."

——— «» ———

A week later, Izad stood nervously in Hassana's office; he had access to this section of the ship but little reason to be here if he were questioned.

"You're absolutely sure about this?" Hassana said. "Once you walk out that door back to your clean rooms and experiments, there's no going back."

If the experiments continued, Xandra would be happy, they would all be paid, and he would have the credit he desired. His work would have merit. Then he thought of Mindy's eyes again and knew it needed to end.

He looked at Hassana, his mind made up. "Let's do it."

"Alright," she said. "Now get the hell out of my office."

He walked back to his section of the ship and donned a clean suit. The test subjects from Alpha group were back in their pods recovering from the day's tests. Mindy's was the last in line and when he got to it, he stalled, checking her vital signs. She was still healthy, just as expected. Then the alarm went off.

He looked up, surprised that Hassana was starting so early. Their plan wasn't supposed to kick off for another hour.

"Sir," Teri cried from the compartment hatch. "What's going on?"

"I don't know. Check the status board."

Teri ran to the monitor mounted next to the hatch. "It's an airborne chlorine leak in water treatment." She turned to him for guidance. "Do we need to do anything?"

"Secure the test subjects," Izad said. "I'll see what's happening."

Izad peered through the window into the corridor and looked in both directions. His people were reacting as they were trained, calmly, moving to their emergency stations. Then, explosions rocked the vessel, knocking Izad off his feet. He landed hard on the metal deck, banging his head, and lost consciousness for a moment. As his senses returned to him, blood seeped from a cut on his forehead and drops pooled inside his clean suit helmet. A pair of hands gripped him.

"Are you alright, Doctor Mir?" Teri leaned over him.

"I think I'm alright."

Teri was struggling to lift him from the deck. He waved her away, rolling to a sitting position and scooted back against the bulkhead. "What about the test subjects? Are they safe?"

"The pods are in lockdown mode, totally secured." Teri put a hand on his shoulder to steady herself as the ship rumbled again.

"I heard an explosion," he said. "What happened?" He grabbed a pipe and pulled himself to a standing position.

"I'm not sure, but it sounded terrible."

Vibrations came again in waves, moving through the deck and bulkheads forward and backward. Izad found it difficult to keep steady on his feet and braced himself against the bulkhead with one hand while Teri led him out of the lab to another chamber. They stripped off their clean suits and he was about to give Teri more instructions when the original alarm was replaced with a louder, more obnoxious klaxon. The lights dimmed and switched over from white to their red emergency setting. Then a recorded voice sounded over the intercom.

"All personnel, an emergency has occurred. Proceed to lifeboats and abandon ship. This is not a drill. Evacuation protocol is now in effect."

A look of fear shot across Teri's face. "What are we going to do? The experiment is running. We can't leave."

Izad pressed a bandage against his forehead. "You heard the announcement, we can't stay." She started to object again but he held a hand up. "You said it yourself, the pods are in lockdown mode, so they're safe." He stood up and a wave of dizziness rolled through him but he kept his balance. "We have to go."

Teri put a hand on his chest. "There's too much at stake. If we lose the data cores, everything we've accomplished will be lost. Just let me download them. I can do it quickly."

He brushed her hand away. "You try that and you'll be the only one left on board. The cores are backed up to servers on one of the lifeboats, remember? We won't lose anything." Of course, that was a lie. He'd reformatted the servers last night before bed and severed the lines leading to them. Everything they'd learned during this deployment would be lost with the *Candlewax*.

She pointed back at the pods. "But what about them?"

He pushed her toward the hatch. "As long as the reactor doesn't melt the damn ship, the pods will keep them safe. Now move! We have to go. I can't afford to lose brilliant personnel."

They rushed from the lab to the corridor outside. Research personnel moved through the space and Izad put Teri in charge of counting heads. He wanted no one left behind that could scuttle his plan. There were three lifeboat stations spaced evenly along the hull of the *Candlewax*. His people were boarding number two in the center of the vessel, he watched Diane Ebbers lower herself in behind one of his lab techs.

"That's everyone, Doctor Mir," Teri said. She had her mobi in her hand and had scanned everyone as they passed through the hatch to the lifeboat.

He checked her list. "Looks good. Now get yourself down the hole."

Teri dropped down the ladder into the lifeboat. Izad took one last look around, confident that everyone he was responsible for was gone. He crouched down to enter the hatch. Hassana's plan was on schedule; in a just a few minutes, they would all be off the ship and the second step would run. Before he could climb down and join his team, the hatch at the end of the corridor opened and Hassana came running through, tools bouncing on her belt. He stood up. "Is something wrong?"

"No," she said, out of breath. "I just wanted to make sure everything up here was alright. You good?"

He nodded. "I am. How much time do we have?"

"Not long. You better get going."

He grabbed her hand. "Thank you. Good luck."

"Don't worry, I won't need it." Her other hand came up fast, swinging at him. He saw the wrench she was holding a second before it connected with his head. He hit the deck for the second time in fifteen minutes. This time his brain was scrambled. His vision blacked out and he couldn't determine which way was up. His head jerked around as Hassana grabbed him by the collar.

"I'm really sorry about this," she said, "but you aren't coming along."

"Wha-?" he mumbled, unable to form words.

"Xandra is about to lose a ship worth millions of credits and research worth even more," she said. "You blackmailed me, and you played God. You're the only person who can hang me up, so you get to stay here."

Izad's head buzzed with so much pain he couldn't even sit up. He looked at Hassana. "Don't do this, please."

She jerked him up by the collar. "If anyone ever finds you maybe you'll treat them better than you did me and your test subjects." She released him and he fell back to the deck. "I'm not going to kill you, but you're on your own from here out. Besides, an incident like this has to be blamed on someone, so it may as well be you."

He saw her stand up and walk away, not even sparing him a look back as she slammed the hatch closed leading to the lifeboat. He held out a hand, but she didn't see him.

He rolled over to pull himself toward the lifeboat, but every movement drove another dagger of pain into his head. He took a deep breath, gritted his teeth, and managed to crawl slowly toward the hatch. There was a roar and the lifeboats launched.

21.

Nathan's crew and Harmony sat in the galley, a little war council figuring out how to assault enemy territory. Before shutting Izad Mir in a cabin so no one had to look at him and think about what he'd done, Nathan had asked him one last question the *Candlewax*.

"What I need to know is can my crew and I safely board the ship?"

"Do you have guns?"

Nathan studied him, wondering what he was up to. It was clear they couldn't trust anything he had to say. "We do."

Izad looked Nathan right in the eyes. "Good. You're going to need them."

Now, without the doctor, the crew was focused their next steps. One of Duncan's drones flew a programmed path around the *Candlewax*, mapping the damaged hull of the modified freighter. The data was relayed to the *Bandit* and used to create a hologram projected over the table.

"Izad said there's pressure and atmosphere throughout most of the ship," Nathan said to Harmony. "Is that what you found?"

She sat with a lidded mug of coffee in front of her and nodded. "In the areas we explored, yes. However, we couldn't get into the flight deck because it was exposed to vacuum." She seemed happy being an engineer again.

Duncan reached out to the hologram and gave it a spin so they could see the exterior of the bow in greater detail. "The canopy blew out here," he said gesturing at the damaged section. "There's a coolant line running here that was affected by whatever happened back in engineering. Looks like that cracked the canopy. Do we need to access the flight deck?"

Nathan nodded. "I'd prefer it. The ship can probably be operated from other work stations, but it's easier from there. There's no airlock on the damaged compartment, so if the hatch fails, we'll lose all our air. After three years of it being closed off like that, I'd rather not take a chance. Can you seal it up?"

Duncan grunted. "We can. It means Richie will have to fab a patch for the busted canopy and we'll need to go EVA to install it."

Richie grinned. "Oh good, we get to go outside." He pulled out his mobi. "The drone is giving us good data, so I can spin up the printer and have the patch done in about an hour."

"That's great," Nathan said. He was proud of Richie. The kid had come a long way since they found him being chased by Syndicate thugs looking to collect on gambling debts. "While you guys are outside, me, Cole, and Tricia will head inside with Harmony and Doctor Mir."

"Do we really need that guy?" Cole said. "I'd just as soon leave him locked in his cabin. That way I know where he is."

"He spent three years over there," Nathan said, eyeing the hologram. "It won't hurt to have a guide along."

"I assume we'll be armed?"

"You, me, and Tricia will be." He turned to Harmony. "Sorry, guns are only for crew."

"No problem," she said. "I don't know how to shoot anyway."

"With Duncan and Richie outside, can you help us in engineering if we need anything?"

She nodded. "Sure thing. The sooner I get home with my credits, the better."

"Tricia," Nathan said. "Bring whatever you'll need to keep us in one piece if something gets after us. As always, we'll try not to need you."

"After Florida? I'll be ready."

He nudged Marla. "You going to be alright over here by yourself?"

"I'll be fine," she said. "Just make sure you bring my husband home."

"You sure?" Cole asked with a smirk, "If we lock him out, we could take the opportunity to run off together."

She eyed Duncan and smiled. "No, I'm still happy with him. And Kimiyo would hunt us down."

"Anyone have anything else?" Nathan asked. He looked around the table and everyone shook their heads. "Okay, gear up, suit up, and we'll go in two hours."

—— ‹‹›› ——

Two hours later, Marla maneuvered the *Blue Moon Bandit* into position over the bow of the *Candlewax*. Nathan stood behind her in the hatch leading into the cockpit. He was already in his pressure suit. He keyed his mic. "Duncan, you guys ready?"

"All set," Duncan replied.

"Okay, you're go for EVA. Good luck."

He watched on a monitor as the ship's cameras tracked Duncan and Richie. They used the jets on their suits to leave the airlock. A trio of small drones carrying the patch Richie had fabbed followed them. Behind all of them was a safety drone that could help rescue them in an emergency. Everything looked good so he told Marla, "Swing us around to the main airlock and we'll get inside."

"Will do," she said.

Nathan moved down to the airlock and saw the rest of his crew waiting in their pressure suits. Cole and Tricia each held a kit bag; though Tricia's kit favored pressure bandages over weaponry. Harmony and Izad stood on the opposite side of the corridor. Izad, closest to the airlock, looked at Nathan with annoyance.

"I really don't see why I have to go back aboard," he said. "I spent three years there by myself."

"That makes you the most qualified to lead us around," Nathan said. "Now put on your helmet."

"There's air over there," he said. "What's the point?"

Nathan approached him and the doctor backed up until his butt bumped the hatch. Nathan took Izad's helmet from his hands and held it up. "The point is, I don't entirely trust you. Are you putting this on, or am I putting it on you?"

Izad swallowed hard and his eyes darted around. Finding no support among those gathered, he took the helmet back. "I can do it."

"That's the winning attitude we're looking for," Nathan said with a smile. "All you have to do is show us around and hang back while we do all the work. I'm sure you can handle that."

Izad nodded and sealed his suit.

Through the airlock portal, Nathan could see the *Candlewax* approaching as Marla steered them into position. There was a small bump as they docked. The automated sequence ran and he heard the locks synchronize. The gauge beside the hatch showed green.

"We're heading in, Marla," Nathan said over his mic. "Keep everything locked up until you hear from us."

"Will do," she replied.

Nathan turned and Cole handed him a rifle and bag. He hoisted the bag over his shoulder and checked the rifle. "I'll go first," he said. "Then Tricia, Harmony, Izad and Cole." He pointed at Harmony and Izad. "If anything jumps off, just stay down and let us handle it."

They walked through the hatch on their ship and Nathan peered through the portal in the hatch leading to the *Candlewax*. The dimly lit corridor beyond looked empty, but Nathan still felt uneasy. Doctor Mir may have changed his mind about the experiments he was performing here, but the remnants of his evil still lurked in this abandoned vessel. With Tricia on his right and slightly behind, Nathan and his crew stepped through the hatch onto the *Candlewax*.

Cole secured the hatch behind them. It closed with an ominous, dull thud, sealing them in. Nathan checked the atmo gauge built into his suit and saw it glowed green. They all opened their face shields, now that they knew the hull was still pressurized and the air was good.

They moved slowly up the corridor toward the T-junction. Harmony leaned forward and whispered, "Left goes to engineering and right goes to the living quarters and flight deck."

Izad crammed close. "Left also goes to the labs. We should check them."

Nathan nodded and took a quick look down both directions, careful to keep his body behind the corner. Some lights were out, making it dim. He drew back. "I can't see anything."

Cole bunched up. "We can't get to the flight deck until Duncan and Richie are ready for us. We should secure this juncture in that direction and move toward the labs and engineering."

"Okay," Nathan said. "Tricia, you look left, I'll go right and cover Cole while he secures it. Remember, there's nothing friendly in here."

They rolled around the corner, each according to their assignments. Bright lights mounted on their rifles beat back the darkness. Tricia spoke first. "Nothing over here."

Nathan stepped forward to give Cole room to work. The corridor to the right was empty and dimly lit. He heard something scrape against the deck in the distance. He shined the light toward the sound, but saw nothing.

"I'm good, Nathan," Cole said in a quiet voice. "You can step back."

He moved backward, careful to step around Cole. He put the light on either side of the corridor and saw the anti-personnel mines Cole had rigged to the bulkheads. They were offset, one about three meters down from the other, secured waist high, and shaped to blow into the empty space of the corridor leading to the flight deck. A magnetic field generated by the mines would keep the ball bearings within a specific range and out of the walls. Richie had been quite proud when he'd design the mines: "Anti-personnel, but not anti-ship," he'd said.

Cole flipped a switch on each. "They're armed now," he said loudly enough for the whole group to hear. "No one goes past this point. If you do, you'll catch a couple kilograms of ball bearings. Understood?"

The group softly murmured their understanding and they set off in the opposite direction, toward the labs. Nathan keyed his mic. "Duncan, we're in. How's the repair coming?"

He heard the channel open with Duncan breathing hard. "We're getting there. The shape of the patch is good, so now we just have to secure it with the adhesive. I'll let you know when we've got it."

"Copy that," Nathan said. They continued moving slowly through the dark corridor, their lights bouncing from side to side. He turned Izad. "Where should we check first?"

The doctor pointed at an opening on the left. "That's the first stage lab. If we go in there we can move through the other labs and get out of the confines of this corridor."

"Okay, let's go."

They moved slowly through the lab. Most of equipment was incomprehensible to Nathan, so he just kept an eye out for movement. The air was stale and the tables dusty, showing their neglect. "Can we get some lights on?"

"I usually kept things dark," Izad said. "Lights and sounds attracted the one that was loose."

"Well, we're not all that stealthy," Nathan said, "and the lights on our guns are hard to miss."

"The lights used to work with motion sensors but I shut them off. Just use the switches near the doors. They should work."

They moved into the stage two lab and Nathan felt for the switches. The sterile, bluish-white lights came on and lit up the space. It was even creepier now that he could see everything. This lab held tanks of chemicals and a track in the deck led to the next lab. There were closed doors blocking their access. He nodded toward it. "What's in there?"

"That's the stage three lab," Izad said. "That's where we're going to find the test subjects in their pods. We should definitely check on them."

"What's with the locked doors?"

"I wanted to limit access to the lab," Doctor Mir said. "I didn't know what Mindy would do if she ever had access. I didn't want her or anyone else hurt."

"Cole, why don't you and Harmony stay here and keep an eye on things?"

They moved as quietly as possible to the doorway between the labs. Doctor Mir entered a code in the pad next to the doors and they slid open. Nathan took the lead and reached a hand in, fumbling for the light switch. The lights snapped on and they moved into the stage three lab.

Izad froze up. Nathan followed his line of sight and saw a dozen or so pods secured to the far bulkhead. All of them were secure. "Are your test subjects in those?"

It took Izad a moment to find his voice. "Yes, they are."

They approached the pods and Nathan looked inside. Tricia came up beside him and accessed the built-in status monitor. He watched as she flipped through the menus, collecting data for her diagnosis. "This subject looks like he's successfully in stasis. All his vitals look good."

Nathan didn't answer her. He was staring through the transparent lid of the pod. The man inside was barely recognizable as a human being. At first, Nathan thought his head was enclosed in a thick bandage, but then he realized the man's skull and skin tissues must have been transformed, because the shape was inhuman. He could see what had once been, and what existed now.

Tricia put a hand on him. "Are you alright?"

He replied in a soft voice. "I thought I was prepared to see it, after Doctor Mir explained what was happening, but this is terrible."

"If it means anything," she said, "he's in stasis and probably unaware of what's happened to him." She waved a hand at the other pods. "I'm going to take a look at all of them, make sure no one needs help."

"Good idea."

"I can help," Izad said, and he moved toward the pods.

Nathan put a hand in his chest and stopped him. "You just hang out right there. Tricia will let us know what she finds."

"But she's just a nurse," Izad objected. "I was in charge of this experiment."

Nathan pushed him back, getting him away from the stasis pods. "You just stay over here." He left Izad in the center of the compartment and joined Tricia as she rounded on the stasis pods. "And for the record, I'll believe Tricia over you anytime."

They stayed like that for the time it took Tricia to check each pod. The moments were tense as she sounded off after each one, letting them know each test subject was healthy and successfully in stasis. Nathan stayed close, ever mindful they had a test subject loose, and that it had killed one man already.

After looking at a few of the subjects, he had to stop. Each one he examined looked different from the one before. Some looked like unchanged people while others were inhuman, appearing beyond the scope of what could be recognized. The last one he looked at resembled an inky black octopus, just a rounded head at the top of the pod with tentacles trailing down below it. Nathan looked away from the tentacled subject and glared at Doctor Mir. Izad looked away, with fear and shame crossing his face.

"They're all as well as can be expected," Tricia said from behind him. "Twelve patients, all in stasis. The last pod is empty, as we expected."

"Okay," Nathan said. "I'll check with Duncan and see if we can get into the flight deck yet." He put a hand to his mic but was interrupted by a roar from out in the corridor. It was a howl that wasn't human, yet it didn't sound like any animal he'd ever heard.

Nathan shouldered his rifle and started looking around. "Cole, you see anything?"

"Nothing over here," Cole said from the hatch leading out into the main corridor. He swung it closed and locked it down. "What are we doing?"

Nathan moved closer to Doctor Mir. "Is there a section of the ship where that thing hangs out?"

"I set up a nutrition station in a storage compartment near the number one engine room," Izad said. "I had hoped that would keep the creature as far away from me as possible and let me move around. Still, it can roam freely, so we shouldn't stay here." Another roar echoed from the direction of the first. "Maybe we should get off this ship."

"Duncan," Nathan said into his mic. "What's your status?"

"The patch is in place," the engineer said. "The adhesive needs about ten minutes to cure, then we can try re-pressurizing."

"Copy that," Nathan said. "Let me know as soon as you're ready." He pointed back toward the labs they come through. "Back this way."

They moved quickly, but carefully, with Nathan keeping an eye behind them. He turned out the lights as they moved through each compartment in order to eliminate signs of their presence.

Something scraped against the deck behind them and they turned as one, all five searching the darkness of the corridor. Then a roar erupted and Nathan could hear something approaching quickly, heavy sounds like hoofbeats rushed toward them, the sound echoing off the bare metal of the deck. Nathan looked at Cole and Harmony, then Tricia. "Okay, back to the *Bandit*. Hustle up."

They gave up on stealth and broke out in a run, rushing toward the T-junction where they could get back to the relative safety of their ship. Cole lead the way this time while Nathan kept an eye on the direction where they'd heard the growl. Then it came again, louder this time, almost continuous now, clearly pursuing them.

"How much danger are we in, Doctor Mir?" Nathan said. "What can this thing do?"

"I should never have come back aboard," Izad said, his voice cracking with fear. "You can't keep me safe. Nothing can keep us safe here."

Nathan grabbed him and dragged him along the wall as they kept moving. "What will it do?"

"Eat us!" Izad screamed, his voice tinged with madness. "Every time I left my cabin, I had to be careful because she chased me. For three years she just wanted to kill me."

They got to the junction and Nathan glanced back into the darkness. The thing was still coming. "She? The one that's loose is Mindy? The lady you told us about?"

Izad slapped at Nathan's hands, trying to free himself. "I thought I could revive her and change her back. I thought I could save her! Don't you see?" He shoved Nathan away. "I thought I had it figured out and but she went mad. There's nothing left of her but hatred. She just wants to kill me."

"Nathan, we have to go," Cole said. "She's getting closer."

Nathan glanced down the corridor and Izad shoved him hard from behind, sending him stumbling back across the corridor into the opposite bulkhead. When Nathan regained his balance, he saw Doctor Mir running off past the corridor that would lead him back to the *Bandit,* and toward the corridor leading to the crew cabins and the flight deck.

Nathan chased after him, desperate to stop him. "Doctor Mir, stop! Don't go that way!"

Izad made it three large steps past the junction before the mine secured to the bulkhead exploded. Then the second one went off and they were all thrown to the deck by the pressure wave as it washed over them.

Nathan groaned and rolled onto his side with his head spinning, unsure of which direction he was facing. It felt like he'd been stung by bees all up his left side, from his thighs, to his arm, to his head. He couldn't hear anything but ringing in his ears. Then the distant chatter of a rifle broke through.

Hands rolled him over onto his back and pain shot through him. Tricia was there above his face, talking to him but he was having trouble hearing her. Lights flashed to his right and he shifted his head, looking back down the direction of the corridor they had come from. He saw Cole bent on a knee, rifle tight in his shoulder, firing at something in the darkness. Even in his dazed condition he could see his chief of security drop a magazine from his rifle, insert another and go back to firing. Cole shouted something in Nathan's direction and Tricia appeared to answer him, but Nathan still couldn't make out individual words.

A huge arm swept out of the darkness and caught Cole on his left side, slamming him against the corridor bulkhead. Tricia shouted something at Harmony and the engineer ran past them, out of Nathan's eyeline. Then he felt himself being dragged away from the action and he knew Harmony had grabbed his ankles. His head lolled and he saw the blood and gore that had been Izad Mir slide past. Tricia was up now, leaning into her own rifle as she fired short bursts at the thing attacking Cole.

Cole was still down on the deck, but now he had his sidearm out, firing up into the torso of the thing attacking him. It was squat and wide, actually twisting its body to keep from scraping the sides of the corridor. Its skin was heavy and thick, like a rhinoceros. It looked back and forth between Cole and Tricia, both of whom were firing at it. Through the buzzing in his head, Nathan heard it roar. He didn't know if it was in pain or anger.

Tricia moved forward, firing as she did so and ducked a swing from the creature. She reached down, grabbed Cole by the collar of his pressure suit and tugged at him. Nathan could tell the man wanted to hold his ground and fight. Finally, he gave up and rolled away, causing the creature to miss with a blow that dented the wall of the corridor. Then, with Tricia still pulling at him, Cole was up and moving.

Nathan rolled, trying to stand, but as soon as he got to his knees his head swam again, making him dizzy and causing him to lose focus. He still couldn't hear anything but a dull roar, but he could see Tricia and Cole moving toward him and Harmony, catching up as the raging monster followed. Tricia grabbed hold of Nathan and together with Harmony, they dragged him down the corridor.

He fell back down to the deck as Harmony dropped him. Tricia knelt beside him, not to check on him, but to get a better angle on firing down the corridor. Nathan pulled himself up to a sitting position and fumbled for his sidearm. If they were going to go down, he was definitely not going to have ammo left in his gun.

The wall behind him vanished and he fell backwards into another compartment. Harmony reappeared, getting a good grip on his collar and dragged him inside. The last thing he saw in the corridor was Cole firing into the darkness.

Tricia ran into the compartment and then Cole leapt in, slammed the door closed, and locked it. The three of them stood while Nathan lay there, trying to catch his breath.

Tricia bent over Nathan, waving a medical scanner over his body. He looked at her, feeling silly in love with her at that moment. He smiled and raised an arm that looked like it was entirely too long. It stretched out toward her face like she was moving away from him. Then his vision tunneled with blackness at the edges. As the darkness closed in, the last thing he saw was her beautiful face, shouting at him.

———— «» ————

He woke up later to loud, arguing voices, and had no idea where he was. The couch he was laying on wasn't familiar and the cabin definitely wasn't one aboard the *Blue Moon Bandit*. Cole sat in a chair with his shirt off. Tricia was treating wounds he had on both arms. Bandages were wrapped around his left bicep and his right forearm. Nathan sat up, which caused his head to swim, but it passed quickly.

"How are you feeling?" Harmony said from a chair on his left.

"My head hurts."

"Well, be careful," she said. "Your girlfriend closed up three holes and you were bleeding pretty good."

Tricia looked over at him as she secured another bandage on Cole's hand. "Don't move. I don't want to have to patch you again."

Pain swept over his left side. "How bad is it?"

"You were too close to Mir when he set off Cole's explosives; took two hits in your thigh and one in your arm, above the elbow," she said. "Luckily your suit slowed down the projectiles, so they didn't penetrate too deep. Just stay still and let the tissue regeneration gel do its thing. You also have a mild concussion."

He nodded and leaned back on the couch. "Okay, thank you." He looked around the cabin. "Where are we?"

Tricia jerked her head at Harmony. "Ask her."

"It's Doctor Mir's cabin," Harmony said. She waved a hand at the small space. "This is where he hid out for three years while he dodged whatever the hell that thing is outside."

Everything that happened came rushing back to Nathan. "Mir's dead."

"He sure is," Cole said, wincing as he pulled his shirt back on. "His ass is smeared all over the corridor outside."

"Why aren't we aboard the *Bandit?*"

"That thing pushed us past the junction leading back to the airlock, so we holed up here," Tricia said.

"We could have made it back to the ship," Cole said. "That's what I was trying to do."

"Well, you almost died doing that, didn't you?" Tricia said.

"Maybe."

It was clear what they were arguing about, Nathan realized. "Alright, knock it off. Whatever happened is done and fighting about it won't accomplish anything. We need a new plan." There was a roar from the corridor outside, pulling his attention to the cabin door. "What's our situation?"

Cole stood up and moved to the door. He put a hand flat against it, like he was checking its durability. "We're trapped in here while that thing is roaming around out there. I don't know what its hide is made of, but it's damn near bulletproof. We probably hit it a hundred times and all we did was make it angry."

"It's a person," Tricia said, "not a thing."

"You weren't making that distinction when you were shooting at it."

"That was self-defense," she said. "There's no reason to kill anyone unless we absolutely have to."

"So, we're stuck here for now," Nathan said. He pointed at the door. "Will that hold or do we have to worry about that thing getting in?"

"It appears to be strong enough," Cole said. "We've been in here for about two hours and it hasn't been able to beat it's way through. Believe me, when we first got in here, it was plenty mad. Besides, Doctor Mir stayed alive for three years, right? I think we're good."

"What about Duncan and Richie? Did they get the flight deck repaired?"

Cole nodded. "They think so. Can't be sure until we repressurize it."

"Right." Nathan wondered about that. They couldn't do anything stuck in Izad Mir's old room. "Is Marla alright?"

"Yeah," Cole said. "I had her break the *Bandit* loose just to be sure that thing couldn't get aboard. I know it seems improbable, but better safe than sorry. She picked up Duncan and Richie and they're floating alongside, all safe."

"Good call," Nathan said. "We need a new plan to get to the flight deck. I need to be there to fly this heap home."

Tricia looked at him with narrow eyes. "Are you serious? You still want to repo this thing?"

He grimaced with pain as he adjusted himself to be more comfortable. "That's the job we were hired to do."

"So?"

"So, I'd at least like to get paid after this."

Tricia held her hands up in frustration. "Fine. We jump back home, the victims can be treated, and we can blow the whistle on Xandra. Let her explain to Protective Services why she's running experiments on people that are really crimes against humanity."

"She won't pay us if we turn her in." Nathan said.

"Then we just fly home and send the authorities out here?" Tricia said. "We'd be safe and they can deal with it."

"If you trust them to deal with her," Nathan said. "The only reason this happened at all is because Xandra was able to do all this in secret at the ass end of nowhere. Even when Doctor Mir came to his senses and tried to stop it, the ship and the evidence aboard it was just hidden."

"That's true," Cole said. "For all we know, it's still going on right now somewhere else. If Xandra could cover it up and make herself look good, she will."

Nathan shifted forward. "We sort out the details later. I'd like to get paid if we can. For now, we jump this thing home and park it in Earth orbit, we'll have all kind of eyes on us. It won't just be Protective Services, it will also be journalists and the media. We'll be able to control how the message gets out." He pointed toward the rear of the ship. "If you want those people back there to get help, we need to get their story out."

"Plus, we'll be able to slam dunk Xandra Ariti," Cole said. "You know that's going to feel good."

Tricia thought about it, and nodded at Nathan. "Okay, I'm in."

Nathan looked around the cabin and saw his duffle bag on the floor near the couch. He grunted in pain and stretched for it, grabbing a strap. He unzipped it, dug through inside and pulled out the module Xandra had given them during their meeting with her. He examined it, rolling it over in his hands. "It looks like this thing is still in one piece."

"That's the doohickey that gives us control over the ship?" Cole said.

"Right. We should just have to get to the flight deck and plug it in. As long as we have power from at least one reactor, we can jump home. Marla can follow in the *Bandit* with Duncan and Richie."

"But we have to get to the flight deck, right?" Harmony asked. "How will we do that with that thing outside?"

"That's a good point," Cole said. "Shooting it just makes it mad and I don't have anything more powerful than my rifle."

Tricia glared at him. "And we don't want to kill that person anyway."

"Right."

"I think her hide is just keratin," Tricia said, "the same stuff that makes up your nails and hair. In bigger mammals, like bears, it's what their claws are made of. If they wanted Mindy to work in a harsh environment, they could use keratin to thicken her hide. It's probably why bullets aren't hurting her."

Cole smiled. "That gives me an idea."

22.

"Couldn't Mir have created some smaller creatures? Why did Mindy have to be almost as big as a rhino?" Cole said from his side of the cabin door. He was on the right with Harmony while Nathan and Tricia were on the left.

"Shush, I'm trying to listen." Nathan had an ear pressed to the door, eyes closed tight in concentration. It had been almost four hours since they'd locked themselves in Izad Mir's old cabin to escape from Mindy.

Tricia was hunched lower, with an ear to the door as well. "I haven't heard anything for a while. I don't think she's out there."

He stepped away from the door. "Look, I think she's gone to feed. Doctor Mir said he had a nutrition station set up at the other end of the ship to keep her away from him when he was living here. I think she got bored with us and took off. We should be able to get to the flight deck and repressurize it. Once we do that, we own the ship. We'll be able to jump home and dump all this on Protective Services." He looked at Cole, expecting to hear grumbling. He wasn't disappointed.

"What if we get there and the compartment isn't air tight?"

"It's air tight," came Duncan's voice over their ear pieces. "The adhesive has had plenty of time to set up and Richie's patch was perfect."

"I notice you're not the one over here running the test," Cole said.

"Well, someone had to do the dangerous work in space."

Nathan put a hand on the door handle and moved it slowly to minimize noise. The last thing he wanted was for a squeaky hinge to give them away. He braced himself against the door and pulled it open carefully. Cole pointed his rifle into the small gap between the door and its casing.

"It's clear," Cole whispered.

Nathan pulled the door wider, and peered into the corridor. It was empty and he heard nothing. He looked toward the flight deck and saw nothing but empty space. A look to his right revealed nothing but the blasted remains of Doctor Mir spread all over the walls near the junction.

The corridor was dark the farther he looked toward engineering. "I think we're good."

Cole shouldered his rifle and picked up a tank with a spray attachment from Doctor Mir's stockpile of stuff. "You ready to go?"

"Yeah," Nathan said. "Everyone clear on what they're doing?" There were head nods all around. "Okay, let's do it."

They exited the cabin, with Nathan and Tricia moving toward the flight deck while Cole and Harmony headed in the opposite direction. Nathan concentrated on his job, not sparing a look over his shoulder. Cole knew what to do, he reminded himself.

The flight deck was about fifty meters from the cabins where the research team was quartered. They hustled and Nathan was breathing heavily by the time they got to the thick door blocking their entrance. His arm was sore and his leg was on fire where the mine pellets had penetrated. "I thought that gel was supposed to heal me."

"It will," Tricia said, "but only if you rest." She faced the opposite direction from him, looking back toward where Cole and Harmony had gone.

Nathan studied the control panel for the hatch. It was undamaged and had power, so he was happy. The air pressure gauge was still in the red, indicating vacuum on the other side, and like most ships, the built-in safety mechanisms prevented a hatch from being opened if there was a pressure imbalance. They couldn't just swing it open and hope for the best. He tapped the screen and was able to walk through the menus to the environmental controls.

"I'm releasing atmosphere into the compartment now," he said to Tricia and the rest of the crew on comms. "Pressure is building."

He stole a look down the corridor now that the first part of his job was underway. He could see Cole and Harmony doing their thing and decided to leave them alone. They looked safe for the moment and that's all that mattered.

A quick look at the gauge showed the pressure building slowly. "Duncan, are you sure your patch is good?"

"Be patient," Duncan said. "It's a big compartment. It's going to take some time."

《 》

When they got to the junction where Izad Mir had turned himself into the world's worst paint job, Cole, set down the tank he'd taken from Izad's possessions, and turned back to Harmony.

The engineer stood in the corridor just shy of the junction with her eyes closed. Cole was impressed that she hadn't run away screaming.

"Keep an eye in that direction, alright?" He pointed down the corridor toward the lab spaces. "If Mindy comes up here to eat us, we're going to have to move fast."

Harmony opened her eyes to see where he was pointing. She nodded and moved past him, hiding herself in the offshoot corridor leading to the airlock where they had first entered the *Candlewax*. "I don't see anything yet."

"Good," Cole said. He knelt down and opened a pressure valve on the tank. There was a hose attached with a spray nozzle and he unclipped it. "It would be a good idea to stay back," he said to Harmony. "You don't want this crap on you."

He aimed the spray wand down the corridor and let loose a stream of fluid from the tank. It shot down the deck about ten meters, leaving the metal coated with an oily sheen. He played the wand up and down the walls, painting them with the industrial lubricant Izad Mir had stored in his cabin.

"Is this normal for you guys?" Harmony said, keeping a nervous eye toward the darkness of the labs. "Fighting monsters with lube?"

"Not for other people, but it is for this crew," he said. He bent and picked up the tank. "Alright, I think we've done as much damage as we can here. Let's start heading back toward Nathan."

The roar came at them like a thunderclap in the enclosed space of the corridor, loud and unending. A bolt of fear shot through Cole, producing a shiver that raced up his back. He dropped the tank of lubricant and got the rifle off his shoulder, aiming it into the darkness.

Mindy came out of the lab nearest to them, caught sight of them, and howled again. Her roar found the essence of frustration and anger and let them loose. "Run," he said to Harmony. "We need to get to Nathan."

She stood frozen for a second, staring at the monstrosity coming toward them. Cole reached out, grabbed her arm, and yelled. "Come on, we have to go!"

She nodded and said, "Right." Then she sprinted up the corridor toward Nathan.

Cole stood his ground, letting the wave of fear wash out of him. "Nathan," he said over his mic, "that thing is pissed and coming fast. You'll see Harmony first, so be careful."

"The pressurization is almost done," Nathan answered back. "Start heading this way."

"You got it," Cole answered. He took a look at Mindy and she was moving quickly now, bouncing off the corridor walls as she came. She reached the edge of the deck covered in lube and immediately fell down.

He watched with rapt attention as she attempted to stand, slipped on the lubricant, and fell down again. It looked like the oil was working as expected. Designed to reduce friction in the moving parts of engines, Mindy's limbs had trouble getting a grip. She rolled on the decking, trying to brace herself, but the slick substance prevented her from exerting any force.

He keyed his comms. "Hey, the lube is working. She's having trouble getting past it."

"Good," Nathan said. "Get up here. We're getting close to opening the door."

Cole turned to run, but he was uneasy about turning his back on Mindy. Then he heard a second roar. He spun back around and looked past Mindy's fumbling form. Something was moving behind her, farther down the corridor near the stage three lab entrance. Cole watched as the shape moved quickly toward him.

When it finally broke into the light, Cole saw that this being was nothing like Mindy. It was inky black, with a central mass that served as a hub for four long tentacles, each tipped with a jagged white claw. The new creature reached the area where Mindy squirmed. Cole watched as it reached out carefully with a tentacle, touched the deck, and drew back as it failed to gain purchase. The creature raised its body, and Cole saw a single red eye lock onto him with an alien gaze.

"Holy shit." He swallowed and got on comms again. "Guys, Mindy isn't alone anymore."

A confused chorus of voices came back, asking questions he didn't want to answer. He started backing away, aware that he had about eighty meters to sprint in order to reach the flight deck. As he watched, the newcomer stretched a tentacle above the decking to Mindy and pressed down, getting a grip on her hide. Another tentacle reached for an air vent in the ceiling and pushed the small grill aside. It steadied itself with two points of contact and then hurled itself across the lubricant trap.

Cole raised the rifle and fired controlled bursts at the creature. It howled in pain and backed away, sliding in a puddle of the lubricant as its claws failed to grip the deck. Cole ran up the corridor, keeping an eye over his shoulder. The new creature started after him, but Mindy howled, a high plaintive wail that gave the octopus-like being pause. It turned, looked at her, and whimpered back. Mindy raised an arm and the octopus-like creature seemed to understand. It reached back with a tentacle, stretching across the distance far enough for Mindy to grab hold. Then it braced itself against the junction walls with its other three tentacles. Pulling mightily, Mindy slid easily against the frictionless floor until she was clear of the area Cole had coated.

He stopped for a moment and his mouth dropped open. "No way," he whispered to himself. Both creatures rose and looked at him, then Mindy howled. Cole fired again and his bullets seemed to have no effect except to make the creatures angry. They stood at the junction, as if they were considering what to do.

He knew that wouldn't last. "Nathan, get that door open. They're coming for us."

"We're not ready. Can you buy us some time?"

"Sure," he said, sarcasm dripping off his words. "No problem." He had plenty of ammunition but it was ineffective. Then he spotted the lubricant tank near the two creatures. Sighting carefully in the dim light, he loosed a three round burst at it. The bullets opened holes in the metal casing and it took off like a rocket as the pressurized fluid inside escaped. It banged into a wall, ricocheted, and caught the octopus squarely in its bulk. The creature screamed in pain, dropped to the deck and curled into a protective ball. The lubricant tank shot out of sight down the corridor leading to the airlock. He watched, hoping the creatures would be frightened enough to limp back to the labs, but it didn't happen. The octopus uncurled, zeroed in on him from thirty meters away and launched itself at Cole, tentacles taking advantage of the deck, ceiling and walls to close the distance between them.

Cole's heart dropped and he turned to run as fast as he could. "I've done all I can," he shouted into his comms, "and they're still coming. You'd better get that door open."

23.

Nathan watched the pressure gauge rise slowly, still in the red zone. "Duncan," he shouted into his comms, "when will this damn lockout release?"

"It doesn't have to be one hundred percent," the engineer said. "It just has to be about two-thirds. Once the door pops, the pressure will equalize with the ship's atmosphere."

Nathan could hear footsteps rushing toward them. He looked and saw Harmony running flat out, like the devil was behind her. "We're at five hundred millibars. There's an indicator line at six hundred. Is that it?"

"Six hundred should be fine," Duncan said. "Your ears may pop from the pressure change, but the door should release."

Nathan watched as the indicator line rose incrementally toward the line indicating the minimum pressure necessary for opening the door. Harmony reached them, breathing heavily with wide eyes ripe with fear.

"There's more than one," she whispered hoarsely through a heavy exhale. "They're coming."

"We know," Nathan said, unslinging his rifle from his shoulder.

Tricia put a hand on his chest. "Nathan, please, I don't think the test subjects know what they're doing."

He looked at her and took her hand. "They'll kill us if we can't get away from them. I'm not letting anything hurt you just so it can keep living." He heard Cole coming, his steps heavier and quicker than Harmony's.

Tricia nodded at him. "I don't have a death wish, but I want to save them if we can."

Nathan hugged her. "I promise." He felt her arms around his back pulling him in tight and he held in her the same way; both knowing that when they let go it might be for the last time. Then Cole was only a few steps away. Nathan spun Tricia away from the danger and toward the door to the flight deck. "Open the door as soon as you can. We'll buy you as much time as possible."

Cole stopped about five meters away and turned to face what was following him. He dropped to one knee to present a smaller target and Nathan joined him. "How many?"

"Two, and bullets don't do dick." Cole's opinion didn't stop him from firing several short bursts down the corridor.

Nathan sighted on what was coming at them and put his finger on the trigger. What he saw gave him pause, though. It looked like an inky black octopus was racing toward them followed by a what could best be described as an armored rhino.

"Come on, man! Fire!" Cole said from beside him as he changed magazines.

"Right." Nathan concentrated his fire on the octopus creature, which seemed to be much faster than its companion. There was something inherently frightening about the way it moved, slithering along the walls and ceiling as well as the deck. It was quick, but their bullets seemed to affect it more than they did Mindy.

The octopus collapsed to the deck, opening a maw lined with brilliant white teeth that looked like they could bite through steel if they had to. Mindy gathered the octopus into her powerful arms and shielded it with her body. Nathan looked back toward the door as he swapped magazines. The gauge was still crawling up, not quite where they needed it to be.

"Look out," Cole said and he pushed Nathan out of the way. A thick black tentacle whipped through the air where his head had been and the claw impacted the wall next to him, leaving a scratch in the metal. Nathan ripped off short bursts at the octopus creature. Mindy howled again, the sound like a physical punch at this close of a range. Then a third rifle joined them and Nathan looked up and behind him. Tricia stood there, a look of rage on her face, spraying rounds into both creatures. The creatures were close enough now that Nathan could hear the deflecting bullets bouncing from the walls and decking.

"It's open," Harmony screamed. "The door is open. Get inside."

He saw the hatch slide open and his ears popped when the air pressure in the corridor dropped to feed the flight deck. He stood, careful to avoid Tricia's gunfire, and pulled her toward the now open compartment while firing his rifle one handed.

"Cole, let's go. I'll cover you."

Cole backed up, firing the whole time, then he turned and dove for the doorway. The octopus reached for him with a pair of tentacles. A claw swiped across his back and Cole fell to the deck, writhing and screaming in pain.

"Help him," Nathan yelled as he continued firing down the corridor. Tricia grabbed hold of Cole and pulled him clear of the doorway, leaving a wide smear of blood. Nathan jumped over them to push against the hatch. The door started to close but two tentacles shot through the opening, flailing as they hunted for prey.

Nathan fired his rifle until it was empty. Instead of retreating, the tentacles struck in his direction, clawing at him. He ducked them, backed away, and pushed against the door again. He reached down to Cole's belt even as Tricia worked on his wound. Cole kept a knife there, and Nathan pulled it free from its sheath. Cole had told him more than once it was his last-ditch defensive tool and Nathan figured this situation qualified. The knife was large, about twenty-five centimeters long and heavier than he expected. The handle was some sort of black composite material that felt indestructible and the blade was a matte gray, except for the sharpened edge which gleaned when it caught the overhead lights.

Harmony leapt towards the hatch and helped Nathan keep pressure on the door. The door rebounded under their shoulders, and they shoved it back, pinning the tentacles against the frame of the doorway. Before it could bounce back again, Nathan stabbed at them, slicing the inky flesh deep, over and over. Blue blood oozed over him, but he continued hacking until the tentacles finally retreated into the corridor. Harmony pushed the door closed.

Nathan slid down with his back against the metal of the door, spent from the action and his wounds. The door vibrated against his back as the creatures hammered it, but the steel appeared to be holding. His head ached from the earlier blast and he felt wetness down the left side of his suit, like he was bleeding from the wounds where the mine's ball bearings had perforated him.

The banging on the door got to be too much so he rolled onto his back and stared up at the ceiling. "How's Cole doing?"

"It's a bad laceration," Tricia said.

"I saw a lot of blood." He rolled his head to watch as she worked on him. Cole lay on his side, unconscious. Tricia was on her knees and had Cole's pressure suit and shirt cut open so she could access the wound to his back. She already had him sedated and had an IV line in his arm, a bag of fluids dripped into him, the rate controlled by a small machine. What Nathan saw frightened him. Cole's lower right back was sliced open, and Nathan could see the flaps of skin part as Tricia reached between them with gloved hands. She wore scanning goggles from her kit to give her a better view of what was happening internally. As he watched, she injected syringe after syringe of lidocaine into the open wound, then tore open sterile packets of surgical foam and shoved the sponge-like material into the gash. Nathan backed himself out of her way and remained silent as she worked. Harmony sat in a chair at the flight controls, watching intently, but helpless to do anything. Finally, Tricia sat back on the deck and stripped off her gloves and goggles.

"I've got the bleeding under control," she said, "I've sprayed it down with an anti-septic sealant, and pressure wrapped it. That should hold him together until we get him back on the *Bandit*. I numbed the area as much as I could with lidocaine, but it's not enough and it won't last."

She dug into her kit and came out with an emergency blanket that she unfolded and spread across Cole's still unconscious body. She pinched the corner of the blanket and slid herself back across the floor; the blanket self-warmed and kept her patient out of shock. Standing up, she fiddled with the fluid line, adjusting the rate. "Right now, he need rest and fluids."

The nurse turned to Nathan. "How about you? Everything okay? You look a little gray."

He swallowed, not wanting to tell her how much pain he was in, but he'd learned there was no fooling her. "My head hurts again and I feel awfully wet in my suit."

She worked quickly, directing Harmony to help her, and stripped his damaged pressure suit and blood-soaked clothes from him. "Yeah, you opened up your wounds."

He rested while she went to work, cleaning his wounds again and re-bandaging them. He looked down and pointed at the bandages. "What do those do? They feel damp."

She threw him a smile, one of those gorgeous ones that made him want to sit up a little straighter. "You mean besides the obvious?"

"Yes, besides the obvious."

"They're impregnated with a solution that speeds up healing. If you give them a few hours to work, they'll knit the tissue back together. They're especially effective on small wounds like this."

He glanced at Cole. "What about something larger like his?"

"They'll keep him together until I get him back on the *Bandit*." She gave him a more serious look. "Any idea when that will be?"

He listened to the door vibrating in its casing. The creatures hadn't lost interest in them yet. "Yeah, not sure about that. We're trapped in here with them outside and there's no other exit."

"Can Duncan and Richie do anything if Marla gets them back on board?"

He shook his head. "Neither of them is much good in a fight. Besides, I don't have any ordnance aboard that would be any more effective than what we just used, and that barely slowed them down."

"I noticed that," she said. "I know I hit them but Mindy's hide is just too thick."

"That octopus thing is even scarier."

"What do you mean?"

"I hit it, too," Nathan said, "but my rounds seemed to just pass through it without doing much damage. If it doesn't have internal organs susceptible to damage, we could be in trouble."

"It feels pain," Cole said from his spot on the floor, his face ashen and sweaty. "I saw it curl up into a ball, wrapping its tentacles around itself twice. Each time I'd really done something brutal to it, then it jumped back up and came after me again."

Tricia settled on her knees beside her patient, "First off, how're you feeling, hero?"

"Sore as hell, can I get in a more comfortable position?" He tried to push himself up, but Tricia put a hand on his shoulder, keeping him on the floor.

"I'm afraid not. I don't want anything moving around inside until I've had a better look at all your organs." She looked puzzled for a moment. "You know, cephalopods have a distributed nervous system rather than a central one, like mammals. Maybe the scientists here took that idea and applied it to other bodily systems." She got quiet and Nathan stayed the same way, letting her think. "You said your bullets just seemed to pass through it?"

"That's right."

"If that thing has distributed systems, you were probably hurting it, but not hitting anything vital." She looked at the door where the pounding continued. "It may be out there right now, healing up."

Nathan leaned his head back against the bulkhead. He'd wanted to get in the flight deck and they'd accomplished that, but they'd almost died doing it, and Cole couldn't stay here indefinitely. Was it worth it? Xandra was evil for building this hidden laboratory and funding Doctor Mir's experiments, but was he much better? Sure, he wanted to deliver the evidence so no one could cover it up, but he had almost killed Cole just getting this far, and he wasn't in great shape himself.

There was also Tricia to consider. Without her, he and Cole would probably be laying here bleeding to death. She was here of her own accord, but he was still the captain, and getting everyone home safely was his job.

Tricia moved next to him and gave him a nudge. "What are you thinking about?"

"We may have to go a long way to get some help."

Her eyes narrowed. "What do you mean?"

He ran a hand over his face and felt beard growth, meaning it had been a couple days since he'd shaved. "I think we stick with the plan. I use Xandra's module to control the ship and we jump back home. We get into Earth orbit, yell for help and let Protective Services get us out of here."

"What's our travel time?"

"We'll need to calculate it out, but not too much longer than it took us to get here; five hours at most. Can you keep us alive that long?"

"I'm not dying here," Cole said from across the way. "No way do I get taken out by an octopus in space. That's a stupid obituary."

Tricia nodded. "I can keep you two in stable condition, but you have to take it easy and do what I say." Her attention turned to Cole. "Especially you. One of your kidneys is bad and I'd be happier if I could get some fresh red cells into you. You try and jump up and start running around, you'll start bleeding again and there may not be anything I can do. You understand?"

Cheek smooshed into the floor, he gave her a thumbs up. "Got it."

She leaned close to Nathan, and in a whisper said, "Sooner is better."

"Yeah, okay," he said and she helped him up. He made his way to the flight controls and collapsed into a chair. Xandra had spent some decent credits outfitting the ship; the padded chair folded itself around him, adjusting to the shape of his body. "I've got to get one of these for the *Bandit*."

He winced as he reached into his pocket and came up with the module Xandra had provided during their meeting. It looked like every other external drive he'd ever seen and he laid it on the console in front of him. Then he pulled out his mobi and called Marla.

It took a few minutes but he relayed what had happened to her, Duncan, and Richie and gave them the plan. "So, we just jump home, and yell for help. Protective Services can rescue us and deal with Xandra."

"Are you sure there's nothing we can do?" Marla said, with concern evident in her voice.

"Believe me, I'd feel better if we were with you, but we're stuck in here and our pressure suits are shredded, so we can't even spacewalk to you." He stole a glance back at Cole and caught the worry on Tricia's face. "Let's just roll and reconvene in Earth orbit."

"Sounds good," Marla said, in the most unconvincing tone he'd ever heard. "Let us know when you're ready and you go first. Then we'll follow."

"Will do," he put his mobi down but left the line open. Then he picked up the module and looked over the console. "Harmony, you're an engineer, right?"

She slid her chair over to his. "Yes, do you need help?"

"This ship has been cold soaking out here for three years. Since we have lights and heat, I assume our power situation is nominal."

He picked up Xandra's module and inserted it into a port on the console. As promised, an executable program ran, displaying root code on his main monitor. It ran quickly, streaming top to bottom and then the screen cleared. He touched the controls and set up the transit back to Earth.

"That should give control of everything. Can you run some diagnostics from here on the engines and power systems to see if we can actually perform a jump?"

"Will do," she said. "Thanks, I was feeling kind of useless while Tricia was stitching you two up." She checked her board. "This ship has three reactors, one of which is still running and doing quite well. Saji Vy really builds some good reactors."

"That's good. If we get home alive, I'll introduce you to him." He checked the readout she moved to his console. "What about the engines?"

"As far as I can tell, we can move with no problem. They were shut down, but I initiated the startup sequence and plasma pressure is building nicely."

He scratched his cheek, flaking off dried octopus blood. "If we have power and engines, why didn't Doctor Mir ever make his way home?"

"He was a geneticist and it looked like he spent most of his time in his cabin or the labs, areas where he felt comfortable," she said. "I got the feeling he didn't know beans about operating a starship. I also noticed the ship's AI was off-line. I think that engineer he told us he teamed up with scuttled it, so he couldn't utilize it to run the ship and get home."

"Well, we don't need that to fly," he said, "but we do need a nav system." He pulled up the navigation controls and studied them. "I think we can do this," he said, hope rising in his voice. "It looks like we can set a destination for the jump."

A notification pinged and Harmony looked at her console. "Plasma pressure is good and the reactor is ready. We can move on your command."

"Thank you," Nathan said. He took a deep breath. The dull ache in his head was still there, fuzzing out the edges of his thoughts. More than anything he just wanted to lay down to go to sleep. He couldn't believe how much he craved rest.

"Marla," he said into his mobi, "We're looking good here so I'm going to send you our destination coordinates. We'll see you on the other side. When you get there, yell for help in case we have some problems."

"Copy that, *Candlewax*," she said. "Good luck."

"Harmony, I'm going to need you to keep an eye on our engines and reactors," he said. "I don't trust systems that haven't been properly maintained for three years."

"No problem," she said. "I'm going to be stuck here for a few hours, so I may as well keep busy. My board is green, by the way."

"Okay then, let's go home." He called up the drive controls and clicked the button. Space folded around them and for the first time in three years, the *Candlewax* moved under her own power, leaving the solar system where she had been abandoned.

Nathan slumped in his chair, closing his eyes, as the ship moved faster than light toward home.

⸺ «» ⸺

Nathan woke a couple hours later to see Tricia hovering about him with her diagnostic goggles on. She wore a clean pair of gloves and was touching the wound on his head, which he felt as pressure rather than her actual hands. "What's happening?"

"It looks like your head wound may have been a little more serious than I initially thought," she said. "You drifted off after we jumped, so I took a closer look and your concussion is worse than I thought. There's no bleeding in your brain, so I've been monitoring your vital signs and letting you rest."

He reached up and his fingers brushed the wound. "Why can't I feel this?"

"I gave you a local anesthetic so I could treat the wound." She raised her goggles and spritzed his scalp with something cool. "I cleaned it again to fend off any infection and closed it properly. When we get home you and Cole both need proper treatment in a hospital."

"Okay. I may want to talk to the authorities first."

She shook her head and leaned back against the console. "No, I've done all that I can but if you want those wounds to heal right, I think you both need proper surgeons as soon as possible. The rest of us can handle Protective Services and Xandra." She put a foot up on his chair and swiveled it toward her, making sure he had her attention. "In this case, you do what I say. Got it?"

He nodded. "I do." He glanced over his shoulder and saw that Tricia had moved Cole onto a makeshift gurney made of cushions ripped from five flight seats, tied him face down with seatbelts, and kept him wrapped up in his blanket. "What about him?"

Tricia followed his gaze. "He's still stable, but that's all I can do. The bleeding is under control and I'm still pumping fluids into him." She bit her lower lip and held up her goggles. "These are pretty good, but the scanners in a hospital are way better. The claw may have penetrated deeper than I think and nicked his liver. He needs a surgeon."

Nathan looked at the flight controls. "Looks like we're almost home."

"That's what Harmony said, so we woke you up."

"Engines and the reactor did great," Harmony said after hearing her name. "The ship held up just fine."

"Just under a minute until we reach our destination," Nathan said, noticing a timer. "You probably want to strap in."

"Aye-aye captain," Tricia said and kissed him lightly. "Don't worry about Cole, either. He's strapped to the bulkhead. I didn't want to move him any more than necessary."

"Good idea," he said as he strapped himself in and watched the countdown on the monitor. When it reached double zero, space unfolded and stars reappeared through the remaining canopy.

As he watched, a line of code quickly shot across a small window at the bottom of the monitor, then vanished. He tried to pull up the nav controls, but all that opened was a blank window.

Tricia stood and leaned over the console, looking through the canopy. "Shouldn't I see Earth?"

Nathan worked the controls furiously, his heart rate increasing as he didn't see what he expected. "Harmony, I can't get a reading on where we are," he said, his voice calm. "The nav controls aren't showing me anything. Can you take a look?"

Tricia looked at him with concern on her face. "Somethings wrong, isn't it? Where are we?"

He called up the ship's telescopes and scanned the space around him, looking for the brightest light source. "I'm not sure anything is wrong yet. Faster-than-light jumps are tricky things, so occasionally you wind up a little off course."

The image on the monitor from the telescope whizzed through space, orienting itself with the brightest object it could see. It finally settled and focused, showing them an image. Nathan stared at it for a moment, silent and disbelieving. Then he turned to Harmony. "What's up with the nav database?"

She turned to him, her face ashen and grim. "It's not there," she said. "The entire database has been wiped."

All Nathan could think to say was, "Sonovabitch." He stared back at the monitor, looking at a red giant star rather than the familiar yellow sun that had risen every day of his life. "Where the hell are we?"

24.

The *Blue Moon Bandit* popped free of folded space like a cork from a champagne bottle. Marla oriented the ship so the Moon filled a large portion of the canopy. "How we doing, honey?" she said to Duncan.

The engineer sat in the pilot's seat, occupying the empty chair normally used by Nathan. Marla was in her usual position in the co-pilot's seat. He checked the information streaming from the sensors on the monitor in front of him while she made sure their immediate area was clear. "Looks like we're half a million klicks from Luna. That's where we want to be, right?"

"Yep," she said while running a systems check. "Looks like we're right where we're supposed to be. Clear of the shipping lanes, but close enough to get home and grab some help."

Duncan glanced at the sensors sweeping space around them. "So, where's Nathan and the *Candlewax*?"

Marla looked at his monitor. "They aren't here?"

"Don't see them."

Marla hit Nathan's number on her mobi, it flashed for a minute then dropped and gave a 'no connection' message. Wherever the *Candlewax* was, it was too far away for a mobi signal. She considered it for a moment. "It's not unusual for ships jumping together to have different transit times."

"But they jumped before us. Shouldn't they have arrived before us?"

She looked at the monitor and then at him, quiet for a few seconds. "You'd think so. Are you sure the sensors are working correctly?"

He pulled up the settings to examine them. "We just got this thing back from the shipyard. Everything should be fine."

"You calibrated the sensors?"

He gave her a raised eyebrow. "Why would you even ask that? You think I'd let you fly around without calibrating the sensors and a hundred other systems?"

She held up a hand. "Don't get defensive, I'm just brainstorming here!"

"It's not the sensors," he said. "Diagnostics checked out. I'm not reading anything around us."

Richie appeared in the cockpit doorway, eating an apple. "Did I hear you right? Did we lose the boss?"

"We didn't lose anyone," Marla said. "They're just not where they're supposed to be yet."

"Oh. Do we know where they are?"

"Not exactly."

"Sounds like they're lost."

She turned her head. "Do you have anything else to do?"

"Right now?" he said. "Not really. The ship's like brand new." He chewed another bite and swallowed. "Hey, you don't think the patch gave out, do you? The one we put over the canopy?"

Duncan shook his head. "It was printed from transparent carbon. No way did that thing fail."

"Yeah, but it was only glued on."

Duncan shrugged. "That's how you affix in space. It's not like it can be welded."

"Besides," Marla said, "Even if it did pop loose, the *Candlewax* would still be here. They'd just have a hole in the front of the ship."

"Man, I hope I didn't kill them," Richie said.

Duncan stood up and put a hand on his shoulder. "They're not dead. For all we know the nav system on that thing was jacked to hell and back. They might be on the other side of Earth." He was silent for a moment. "Maybe it was the nav system on the *Candlewax* that needed calibration."

"Wouldn't they know to do that?" Marla said. "I mean I would do it."

"Then I'm sure Nathan did," Duncan said. "This isn't his first flight."

"But we saw them leave," Marla said. "The ship was spaceworthy and the jump looked fine. Where did they go?"

Duncan turned back to her and sat back down in the pilot's seat. "How long do you think we should wait here for them?"

She sat back, contemplating the situation. She didn't want to worry Duncan and Richie, but Nathan should have been here waiting for them. Their transponder wasn't squawking, and that really concerned her. No matter where in the solar system the *Candlewax* was, her transponder should have been picked up and displayed in her search results when she requested a position from the system. Instead, every other ship she didn't want to see filled her screen. She smiled at Duncan. "Let's do a couple orbits around Earth, make sure they aren't just somewhere we can't see, and if they don't show up, we'll report them missing."

Duncan nodded. "Sounds like a plan."

«»

Nathan kept staring at the nav system database, unable to believe his eyes. It was empty, wiped clean of any location records. It had been an hour since they arrived wherever they were and he was no closer to figuring out the problem than he had been when he started.

Behind him, Tricia sat with Cole, checking his wound and doing what she could to keep him stable. Harmony was hard at work at another flight deck station. He focused on her screen and said, "what are you up to?"

"I'm looking at the server logs for the nav system," she said, pointing at one record. "You see this here? Whatever wiped the database did it recently, like in the last few hours. Do you have any idea what that could be?"

His eyes fell to the command module Xandra had given him and he gestured to it. "When I plugged that thing in, it executed a command. I thought it was just getting us into the system so we could take control of the ship."

Harmony's eyes narrowed. "Hold on." She called up Xandra's module in the operating system and examined its contents. Nathan watched as she scrolled through the code, going back and forth as she read it.

He sat quietly for about twenty minutes before she turned to him. "We're fucked."

He shifted on his feet, very uncomfortable at the confidence with which Harmony had made her pronouncement. "What did you find?"

"The program in this module gives you the control you expect, but it also has a couple more commands that we don't need. The first is to override any destination coordinates entered."

"But the coordinates for home that I selected showed up in the display," he said. "I double checked it."

"That's what you were meant to see," she said. "Whatever you selected was going to display in the user interface. Behind the scenes though, there was a randomizer running and that seems to be a real piece of work."

He moved in closer. "How so?"

"The randomizer selected a destination while filtering out any inhabited systems. See this?" She said pointing to a table. "This is a list of every inhabited system I've ever heard of, and these insert dates are recent, which means it's definitely not three years old. So, the randomizer runs, and as long as the destination is not an inhabited system in this table, it is acceptable to the program and that's where we got sent."

"Are there coordinates in that list of destinations?" he said. "Can we use that to formulate a jump?"

She shook her head. "The coordinates are wiped, it's just a text list of labels."

"Damn."

"The second part of this is pretty diabolical," she said. "Once the jump is initiated and the program doesn't need the list any longer, it wipes the database. The minute we popped back into normal space, it finished up its job and stranded us."

Nathan slumped down in his chair, defeated. He glanced over at Tricia. "How are you making out with your patient?"

"He's asleep right now," she said, "getting some badly needed rest." She stood up and walked over to him. "Even if we could get him back on the *Bandit*, he needs more help than I can give him."

"Yeah?"

"Yeah."

"Harmony," he said, "how is everything else we need? Is our life support alright? Engines? Is the goose still able to operate so we can initiate another faster-than-light jump?"

She pointed at a secondary monitor with multiple tabs open. "I started diagnostics on everything while I was looking at the program. So far, everything looks okay. The trouble is, without navigation data, the hardware isn't much use."

"What I don't understand is, why strand us?" Tricia said. "If they wanted to do something that would keep us from getting home and ratting them out, why not just set the reactors to overload and blow us up?"

"I think I can answer that," Nathan said. "Xandra never wanted us to bring the *Candlewax* home. She wants it lost. It's like Mir said, an explosion could lead to an investigation. He and Xandra had the same plan, the best place for this ship is intact but unfindable. She knew we'd get it in flying shape, Saji Vy told her all about Duncan and Richie before she offered us the job. We were never supposed to get back home."

Tricia nodded, understanding.

"She really covered her bases," Nathan said.

"Can you get a fix using stars?" Tricia asked. "Figure out where we are so we can point ourselves home?

Nathan shook his head. "I need data to match our findings to, and it's all gone."

"It even wiped the backups," Harmony said. "There's a back up copy stored here on the flight deck and another in the engineering compartment. The program sent wipe commands to all of them."

Nathan looked back Cole, resting on the floor. He'd received the message loud and clear from Tricia; get home and do it quickly. He just had no idea how.

———— «» ————

The *Blue Moon Bandit* completed its third orbit of Earth, this one on a route that took them over the poles, just in case something had happened that prevented Nathan from getting into an orbit over the equator.

"Anything?" Duncan asked.

"No," Marla said. "It's been hours and now I'm worried. It's been long enough that if they jumped anywhere into the solar system, we'd have gotten a message from Nathan. I don't know where they are."

"We saw them leave," Duncan said, "so if they're not here, where did they go?"

Marla shrugged. "They could literally be anywhere. There's no way to mount a search because we don't know where to begin looking."

"We need help," Richie said from the doorway. "Should we call Protective Services?"

Marla though about it. Was it possible this wasn't an accident? With what they'd found on the *Candlewax*, was it possible she meant for them to never come home? She felt a chill run up her spine.

"I don't know if we can trust them," Marla said.

"Why not?" Duncan said.

She turned to him with wide eyes. "We saw them jump away, but what if Xandra boobytrapped the ship somehow? What if she just pushed them farther out?"

"Or jumped them into a star?" Richie said. "Oh God."

"We can't call Protective Services," Marla said. "Xandra's one of the wealthiest people in the system. Billions of credits buys a lot of access to politicians and authorities. If we call them, somebody may contact her and fill her in and we don't have the *Candlewax* as leverage."

"You can bet that will happen," Duncan said. "She sent us out there to find that ship of horrors without telling us what we'd find. No way is she conducting experiments like that without paying off someone in power. We need to keep this down low."

"So, who can we call?" Marla said. "We need someone in a position to help us, which means credits and resources, but someone who will keep things quiet."

They sat in silence, and Marla looked out the canopy into the vastness of space. She'd spent a good deal of her adult life here, moving cargo and people from place to place. Once you got past the thrill of actually working in space, it became routine and even boring. Working for Nathan wasn't like that, though. Their jobs were exciting, and she never knew what the day would bring. This, though, was different. Xandra Ariti had clearly done something to sabotage them. She couldn't prove it yet, but Marla had that feeling that they were being played and now her friend's lives were in danger.

She grinned and looked at her husband and Richie. "Dibs on not being the one to call Kimiyo."

25.

Atomic Jack stood in a dark warehouse. The only light came from a work light mounted on a tripod. It illuminated a man hanging upside down from a forklift. That guy was Lou Datello, head of the lab where Susan Park worked.

He'd actually been hard to nab. Jack and Jojo watched him for almost a week and all the guy did was work twelve-hour days before leaving the office. Then the guy usually stopped for take-out before heading home. They never saw him stop anywhere or meet anyone. He lived alone in a pricey condo on the third floor of a secure building.

They nabbed him one night after work when he exited a rideshare pod carrying his dinner. Jojo threw a bag over his head, grabbed him by his collar and belt and shoved him into another pod parked along the curb. He was hefty guy, probably tipping the scales at a hundred and fifty kilos, but Jojo managed. Now, Lou Datello was hanging with one ankle bound to each fork with a ratchet strap. His hands were tied to his waist with a third one. They'd taken the bag off his head because it could be hard to hear someone talk when they had one on. He seemed to understand that he should stay quiet, so he wasn't screaming. He was whimpering, though, and that was getting on Jack's nerves.

Jack had the light setup so Lou was staring right into it and couldn't see anything past it. Jack was sitting on a folding chair. Ever since his last appointment with Doctor Charbonneau, he'd been having more bad days than good ones. Taking his glove off to light up his hand so he could scare Susan Park had really wiped him out. It was taking him longer to recover when he pulled stunts like that. He certainly didn't have it in him tonight, but he needed to move ahead if he had a chance of living much longer. So, he and Jojo were going old school.

"Lou, I need you to shut the hell up, okay? Cut out that whining and just answer my questions. You do that and you'll be home in a little bit to eat your dim sum."

"Who are you?" Lou said.

Jack raised a hand and Jojo shook the mast of the forklift, giving Lou a little shake.

"You answer my questions. Do you understand that? Tell me you understand."

Lou moved his head to see who was talking, but the light blinded him. He squeezed his eyes shut. "I understand."

"Good," Jack said. "Tell me about a shipment of octopus tissue samples that went out last year. The special samples. You know the one I'm talking about?"

Lou was quiet for a moment, like he was turning something over in his mind. "I don't know what you mean."

Jack sighed. "Lou, do you know why you're hanging from your legs and not your arms?"

Lou whimpered again. "No."

"I was afraid your bulk would pull your arms out of your sockets, then you'd be screaming from the pain and not answering my questions. The hips are stronger. I could leave you there all day and not do any real harm."

Jack raised a hand up and twirled a finger so Jojo could see him. The hydraulics on the forklift hissed as the pressure released and the guy lowered toward the ground. He looked down and noticed for the first time a five-gallon bucket full of water. He took in a breath to yell and was dunked before he could get the sound out.

Jack counted to ten and then gave Jojo a thumbs up. Lou rose up slowly, exiting the bucket sputtering for air.

"Did you like that?"

The guy gulped air, coughing and spitting, but he didn't answer.

"He's not answering," Jack said to Jojo, "so he must have liked it. Give it to him one more time."

Lou started to say something but Jojo dunked him again. This time Jack counted to fifteen. Kind of give the guy the impression that he may not be coming out.

Jojo raised him up again and Lou found his voice as water spilled on the concrete floor. "Okay! Okay! I know what you're talking about. I'm not supposed to say anything. You're putting me in a bad position."

"I don't have to tell anyone what you tell me, Lou. This is between me and you."

"Yeah?"

"Yeah, you can trust me," Jack said. "Now, I know the tissue samples went to Vibrant Passion. What does a beauty company want with octopus tissue samples?"

Lou paused like he was considering his answer. Jack was prepared to dunk him again, but the guy finally started to speak.

"Look, this is going to take a while and I'm getting a headache from the blood rushing to my head. Can I sit down?"

"Sounds like you should talk fast."

"Alright. Look, I had the same questions you did. I know someone over there, someone I went to school with. Back in the day we used to party, so I called her up and we got together. One thing led to another and she told me Xandra Ariti isn't satisfied with just living a longer life, she wants to live forever."

"Are you serious?"

"Please, let me down and I'll explain it."

"Keep talking."

Lou took a deep breath and nodded. "She wants to be able to build new bodies from people's old bodies."

"Can't she clone people?"

He shook his head. "She wants to keep her mind. Can't do that with a cloned body."

"So, what's with the octopus tissue samples?"

"She needs money. What she's trying to accomplish is incredibly expensive. If she can mix human DNA with specialized animal DNA to create custom bodies, she thinks that will raise the money she needs."

Jack sat back in his chair and considered that answer. Something didn't make sense to him. "Who would want to be turned into some kind of human-octopus mash up?"

"At the level she's playing at, she'll sell it to the corporations that explore space. They'll transform workers to operate in hostile environments." He coughed again. "Come on, let me down. I don't know anything else."

Jack considered him for a moment. If this is what Charbonneau knew, no wonder he kept it quiet. "Can she do it?"

"What?"

"You're a smart guy, right? You run a lab, know all about animals and stuff. Tell me if she can do it."

Lou looked around the darkened warehouse. "Yeah. Yeah, she can do it. People tell you that with enough time and money you can do anything. Well, she figured out how to make people live longer and earned a mountain of money doing it. I definitely think she can."

"Okay, there's one more thing I need and you're going to get it. I want copies of everything. Orders, invoices, everything that proves the transaction took place."

"How am I supposed to get that?"

"Don't be stupid. You already have it and you keep it somewhere safe."

"How do you know that?"

"You're too smart to have done anything else. After your friend spilled her secrets, she sobered up and made with some threats. You decided the only way to protect yourself was to keep a copy of everything for leverage. Since then, you've kept your mouth shut and you've been safe."

Lou blinked in the bright light. "Okay, then I give it to you. What happens to me?"

"What do I care? Go to work tomorrow. Go on vacation. Do whatever you want. Just get me those documents."

26.

Nathan sat in the pilot's seat of the *Candlewax*, staring out at the stars. The ship was adrift at the moment because they had no idea which direction to travel. In the day since finding themselves stranded, Harmony had run diagnostics on all ship's systems. For the moment, at least, they had no other problems than being lost in space and trapped on the flight deck.

His attention was drawn to the patch Richie had printed. The transparent carbon seemed secure enough, but he wasn't crazy about the fact that it was basically glued into the canopy. Like everything else, it was just good enough, but who knew how it would stand up to any real stress?

He leaned forward toward Tricia who occupied the seat next to his and whispered. "How is Cole doing?"

"We need to do something," she said. "His temperature is rising, I ran a bacteria sensor over him and sure enough, he's got an infection. I gave him a dose of long-lasting antibiotics, but whatever he has seems to be resistant, which is not surprising given that we're in a ship that hasn't been cleaned in three years."

"Can you do anything more for him?"

She let out a small sigh. "I don't have very much in my kit. I can treat him for another day or so and then things are going to get bad."

They'd been through a lot together and she was usually as cool as anyone he'd ever met, but this was clearly bothering her. He realized that she was doing everything she could, and he was sitting on his ass.

What he knew for sure was that without a navigation database, he couldn't find their way home. So, he decided to work with what they did have. "The equipment in the lab, could that help you? I mean, could you treat him better or even throw him in one of those stasis tubes?"

She pointed at the door. "How do we open that without getting eaten?"

"Speaking of eating," Harmony chimed in, "we don't even have emergency rations in here. If we're staging a prison break, we need to swing by and grab some grub from Izad's cabin."

Nathan sat back in his chair and let out a breath. "Look, Doctor Mir survived three years on this ship with just one of those things on the loose, and he didn't know beans about how a starship works. There's no way the four of us can be trapped in here. It's a matter of pride at this point."

"He told us he rigged up a nutrition station in the engineering compartment to lure Mindy away," Harmony said. "If we could get her and the octopus in there, it would give us access to more of the ship."

"We need more than a few minutes, though," Tricia said. "I need time to treat Cole."

Nathan turned and pulled up the ship's surveillance system. He scrolled through the cameras until he found one that looked like it was pointed at the engine compartment.

"Can we shut the doors remotely?" Nathan asked.

"No, the door systems are manual," Harmony said.

"I wonder why they did that?"

"I've seen similar systems on prisoner transport ships," she said. "It's a failsafe to prevent users from gaining control of the ship from a workstation. Maybe Xandra didn't trust her crew?"

"That could be," Nathan said. He chewed his lower lip, trying to come up with a way to pull off his idea remotely, when a system didn't exist that allowed him to do so. "Hold on, this whole section is built to be isolated in the case of a fire, right?"

Harmony nodded. "For sure. It's got safety doors that will fall and a chemical drop system to replace the oxygen to help extinguish any fire. I wonder why Izad never did that?"

"Start a fire? Because he didn't know how to stop it," Nathan said.

"Still," Harmony said, "I don't think a fire is going to help us. Those things tend to get out of hand when a full crew is available to fight them. There's just three of us still standing."

"Yeah, but two of us are a pilot and an engineer." He threw her a smile. "We can make this work."

———— «◊» ————

An hour later, Nathan and Harmony were bent over the surveillance system, watching the two creatures outside in the main corridor. Mindy and the octopus rarely moved together. Whether by design or bad luck, one would wander away toward the engineering and lab modules, while the other remained close enough to the flight deck that they couldn't exit. Currently, Mindy was wandering the labs, and Nathan was worried. She must have had some of her mental faculties in place, because she kept attempting to work with the stasis pods holding the other experiment subjects. She'd managed to free her octopus pal, and if she released another, things could quickly turn from bad to worse. The octopus seemed angry, sitting on the deck in the corridor outside Doctor Mir's cabin.

"You ready?" Nathan asked Harmony.

She pulled up another set of controls at the work station. "I am."

"Hit it."

Harmony leaned in close to a microphone and said, "Come and get us, you assholes!"

Nathan watched as both creatures raised their heads. They didn't rush toward the sound though, as he'd expected. "The only speakers active are those in the engineering section, right? That's all we're broadcasting to?"

"That's right."

"Try again, but try to be serious. I think Mindy may have more of her marbles than we're giving her credit for."

Harmony nodded and pressed down on the mic button again. "I've reached the engineering section and I'm making my way to the reactor room. Once there I can—"

That did it. Nathan watched as both creatures rose in their different locations and moved toward the rear of the ship. The octopus had a difficult time navigating the area Cole had coated with lubricant, but it made its way through and followed Mindy toward the engineering section. As he watched, they both moved deep into the machinery running the ship.

He pulled up a different set of controls and felt Tricia squeeze his shoulder in support. He smiled up at her and hoped his nervousness was hidden. "I really hope this works."

On the surveillance array, nothing much changed at first, but then flashing lights lit up every compartment and a siren sounded, high pitched and screaming. That sound was interrupted by a recorded message stating that carbon dioxide levels were rising. Then the siren sounded again.

He turned his attention back to the cameras, and Harmony pointed at a small window on the monitor. "The engineering doors fell, just like we wanted," she said, with excitement in her voice. "They're trapped in there."

"And it should stay that way until we turn off the safety drill program," Nathan said.

"I hope so," Harmony said. "I really think we should get down there and lock them in, though. If what you think about Mindy still having some level of intelligence is true, she may realize they were fooled. There's no reason she can't just open that door if she remembers how."

"Okay," Nathan said, "let's move."

They pulled the flight deck hatch open and stepped into the corridor. Cole was on a portable anti-grav litter from Tricia's kit, held between himself and Harmony. The unit was small, though, and the power wasn't going to last forever. It was really just a stiffened blanket that hovered a meter or so off the deck.

Nathan guided the litter with one hand while the other held his rifle. Tricia walked beside him, a rifle in her hand. They didn't need to discuss it anymore; Tricia wanted to keep everyone alive, but if push came to shove, if it was their lives or the creatures, they both knew who they were going to choose.

They passed by Doctor Mir's cabin and Nathan shook his head at Harmony. As hungry as they were, they had to secure a position before they could eat. They moved farther down the corridor, passing the remains of Doctor Mir himself. They stepped carefully, went past the intersection leading to the airlock where they had entered, and came to the area Cole had coated with lubricant. Nathan stopped short and looked at the stained deck and walls.

"This stuff is really slick," he said and looked at Harmony. "The last thing we want is it on the soles of our boots. Can you hand me the towels?"

She passed him a handful of shop towels and he laid them down on the deck in pairs, one for each of them. "Everyone ready to skate?"

Each of them placed a boot on a towel and slid across the slippery deck plates. Harmony balanced herself against the litter. When they got to the other side, they kicked the towels away in a pile against a wall.

The siren had stopped sounding but the flashing amber lights continued to light up the corridor. When they came to the lab complex, he ducked in first, clearing the area. He couldn't be sure Mindy hadn't managed to release more test subjects.

He checked the area thoroughly, but the only change was the stasis pod that used to hold the octopus was open. The other eleven remained sealed.

"It's clear," he called back to the women. They pulled the litter in and Harmony sealed the hatch behind them. If nothing else, he thought, at least they were off the flight deck and in a different compartment.

Tricia moved to an empty stasis pod and powered it up. The control panel came online and she ran through it.

"How's it looking?" he said. "Can we use it?"

Her hands moved across the screen in a flurry of practiced motion. "We're good. I just need to get him in."

Nathan hurried over to the hovering litter and pulled it closer to the pod. "How does this work? Do we just toss him in or what?"

She looked up at him. "You're worried about the monsters getting loose?"

"Very much."

"Go, Harmony can help me."

"You're sure?"

She kissed him lightly on the cheek. "You're slowing me down and he needs treatment, so come on, do your thing. We've got this."

He nodded, hefted his rifle and ran to the door.

———— «‹›» ————

Nathan raced down the corridor toward the engineering section. The big fire door was still down in the safety position. His pace slowed and then something moved behind one of the thick windows in the door. As he approached, he saw bright human eyes looking back at him through the small window. Normally, rescue crews could use the small portal to ascertain the condition of the compartment in an emergency. Now, it was just Mindy glaring at him. He understood now what had bothered Doctor Mir so much. Her warm, brown eyes were all too human, but right now they were also extremely angry.

He looked at the controls mounted on the bulkhead next to the door. The carbon dioxide drill program was only going to run a few minutes longer and at the conclusion of it, the safety doors would pop open. The drill was meant to simulate a high carbon dioxide level in the atmosphere, putting each compartment on its own internal air supply until the situation was resolved. They were closing in on the end of that, so he had to find a way to secure the door and keep Doctor Mir's experiments contained.

He ran through the door control menus and jumped when the big door beside him vibrated from a loud shock. If Mindy still had some of her faculties, she might understand what he was up to. Or maybe she just wanted to kill him in a rage. It was hard to tell.

There was no locking mechanism on the door menu that he could see. He examined the door itself as Mindy continued hammering against it from the interior. It was thick steel, and set into a track to help make it airtight when it dropped from the ceiling. Times like these were when he missed Duncan the most.

If he were here, Nathan knew he'd cobble together some way of securing the door and tell him a story about how he'd done this a few years ago on some other ship. Thinking like his friend, he started to look around at what he had.

Mounted on the bulkhead next to the door was a first-aid kit in a metal box. He opened it and saw nothing that would help him. Next to it was a slightly larger maintenance toolbox. He opened this with more enthusiasm, and was rewarded with a selection of tools. Most of them were hand tools, meant to be used in an emergency or if someone didn't have something specific in their kit to maintain the machinery at this station. He took a screwdriver with a wide flat blade out and looked at it in the flashing amber light. The track the door was set into was a tight fit, but it wasn't perfect. He pushed the wide blade into the track near the top, where the top angled toward the side. He gave it a couple good jabs with the heel of his hand and it stuck there, seemingly secure. If the door rose back into ceiling, it should jam in even tighter. Then Mindy clobbered the door with an especially hard blow and the screwdriver fell out, clanging off the metal deck.

"That is not something Duncan would do," he said to himself. "He'd be clever."

He stepped back, looking above the door, bolted to the slim bit of door frame between the top of the door and the ceiling was the hydraulic pump that did the heavy lifting.

He glanced back at the tool kit and removed a set of hex wrenches. The pump was higher than he could reach, so he grabbed the first-aid kit and threw it down on the deck in front of the door. He stepped on it and gained just enough height to reach the pump. Mindy continued her assault on the door and it vibrated in its frame.

He found a hex keyway on the pump that seemed to be the head of a valve and rotated through the wrenches until he found the one that matched. He twisted on it, tightening the valve until he couldn't move it any further. He returned to the tool box and pulled out a pair of pliers. He was able to use these to remove the spring clamps holding the hydraulic fluid hoses in place on either side of the pump. The little bit of fluid in the disconnected hoses dribbled out and ran down the door.

He stepped back into the corridor and looked at his handiwork. With the pump valve closed and the hoses disconnected, there was nothing mechanical left to lift the door. Hefting his rifle, he moved to the control panel and pushed the open command. Machinery whined, trying to lift the door but it went nowhere without the assistance of the hydraulics and the control panel lit up with error messages.

Mindy continued to wail on the door in violent rage, but nothing he had done would help her. The door hadn't budged at all, so there was nothing for her to get a grip on. He stood silently until he was sure the door really wouldn't raise and release the beasts. As angry as Mindy was, at least she was safe. He turned and started walking back to the lab complex to check on Tricia and Harmony. Hopefully they had Cole stabilized and protected in one of Xandra's fancy stasis pods. The door was one problem solved and he only had a hundred more to go.

<h1 style="text-align:center">27.</h1>

Xandra sat at the conference table on Europa with Doctor Ebbers and the rest of the staff gathered around. They all seemed uncomfortable, and that was understandable because the topic of the meeting was as bad as could be imagined. The room was heavy with silence because no one wanted to be the first to speak and therefore the first to say the wrong thing.

She had taken a couple days to consider Ebbers's options for getting the program back on track. The urge to move quickly and get something done had a strong allure, but it meant finding, vetting, and hiring new personnel. That increased the risk of exposing the entire project to the authorities. In the end, after great contemplation and working off her frustration in a frenzy of zero-G coupling with Damian, Xandra had made a decision.

"Doctor Ebbers," she began, "I considered your options and I've made up my mind to increase the investment in artificial intelligence to resolve the issue of creating a unique psyche overlay for each unit of labor stock." Addressing everyone, she said, "As you all know, this will require time and considerable capital investment." She narrowed her eyes and looked at each in turn. "I expect all of you to work diligently toward this goal. That means holding costs down, finding new ways to increase revenues from existing streams, and meeting deadlines." Her voice caught an edge as she projected her expectations. "This eighteen-month timeline will not be blown, stretched, or reconsidered for any reason. If you cannot perform your job, you will be replaced. I need to know that all of you understand what I'm saying."

The silence continued for a moment with everyone too unsure of their voices to answer even this direct question, but then Ebbers spoke up. "I believe this is the correct path to take and believe we can meet our goal." After that, the others nodded their approval and spoke up with small, constricted voices that were much less confident.

Ebbers spoke up again. "Will we have further access to the subjects from batch J-five-thirty-one? I believe we have more to learn from them."

"It's funny you should mention that," Xandra said. She took her seat at the end of the table and gestured at the monitor mounted against the far wall. Damian tapped his mobi and the monitor lit up. The video feed was of the current batch of Swimmers in metal fencing underwater. "As you can see, this is the pen we use to hold the labor stock when they are not working. We've conducted a census and all of the remaining units from the batch are present."

As she watched, it became clear which Swimmers were behaving as expected and which were in the throes of some kind of episode. Most were swimming calmly within the cage, lazily making their way around the underwater paddock. The others would surge violently at the fencing, banging their bodies into the screening. When it became clear that wouldn't work to get them free, they tore at the metal with their tentacles, but even their claws wouldn't cut them loose.

The project staff around the table turned away from the violence and stared at the table or found something less disturbing to look at on their tablets. Xandra looked at the things costing her a small fortune. She realized she had rushed things, putting subjects into the field without enough testing, but it had seemed like the right decision at the time. Now, though, she understood that she should have followed Ebbers's advice and tested more. However, she hadn't built one of the largest fortunes in the solar system by being timid. Sometimes you just had to go with your gut and that's what she'd done.

"Jupiter Mining Consortium has had their entire fee refunded," she told the group. "That makes them whole and keeps them quiet." She picked up her mobi and composed a text message. On the screen, the view shifted and the Swimmers were all pushed to the bottom of the paddock. Something was clearly lifting the structure up through the water of Europa's moonwide ocean.

"Doctor Ebbers," she said, "you'll remain in charge of the project and you now have final say over all decisions." Xandra cast her gaze at everyone seated around the table, finally settling on Ebbers. "No matter the subject, no matter the question, your word is law."

"Of course," Ebbers said. She was doing well hiding the shock she felt at having the whole operation suddenly thrust upon her, but Xandra knew her well enough to see the small signs on her face. "Thank you. I'm sure we won't have any problems."

On the monitor, the paddock broke the surface of the water and rose through a hollow tube of ice toward the surface. When it got there, the container swung out over the Europa ice sheet. The cracked, frozen surface of the moon zoomed past quickly as the crane moved to the right. It dropped suddenly, jittering across the ice until it settled.

The Swimmers were clearly in distress. Removed from the relative warmth of the ocean to the whisper thin atmosphere of the moon, the inky black creatures writhed in pain as the cold overwhelmed them. Xandra noted that the Swimmers that had been trying to escape previously were still trying to do so. Whereas the others flopped and squirmed against the ice, these others climbed to the top of the pile of bodies and futilely struck the sides of the paddock with their white claws. She looked around the table and saw that no one was ignoring the images of the freezing bodies on the monitor now. The scene held their attention until the last Swimmer stopped moving. Their bodies crusted with thin ice as their last dregs of heat fled into the void.

Xandra stood and turned to Damian. "Please make sure those remains are delivered to the ship Doctor Ebbers and her team are using to get home."

"I'll take care of it," he said.

She left the room without another word. If the message hadn't gotten through, she didn't know what else she could do.

——— «» ———

Once Xandra and Damian were back aboard her yacht and the ship on its way to Earth, she lay down on a couch in her cabin. Seeing the Swimmers writhing in their death throes on the ice reminded her of an incident when she was a young woman with her father, a chicken farmer back in Greece. As the excitement of the day faded, her eyes grew heavy and she allowed herself to drift off, thinking of chickens and octopuses thrashing in cages.

"Xandra," her father called from across the yard, his voice booming under the bright blue Mediterranean sky. "Come here. I need your help."

The poultry farm they owned was located thirty kilometers outside Athens, and had been in their family for generations. Her father stood near the large barn where their chickens were kept in long rows of small cages. Thirteen-year-old Xandra hurried across the yard, dodging birds who were enjoying the good weather and sending them flapping into the light breeze. As she approached, she saw the van of the veterinarian her father used hovering near the entrance. That wasn't a good sign. She knew her father was concerned about illness in their flock.

She rounded the van and saw him standing there, speaking to the doctor. He was agitated, swinging his arms wide while they spoke. She hesitated at approaching any closer. Her father's temper was legendary and the doctor seemed to be bearing the brunt of it.

"You can't be serious," Vassilis Ariti bellowed at the doctor. Her father was a large man, the kind who just cleared doorways without bumping his head and he was wide enough that shirts stretched over him. "Culling the flock is too expensive."

"That's only one option," the doctor said in an exasperated voice. "We have a treatment for this version of the avian flu. Simply add it to the flock's feed and wait a week. Efficacy rates are high so you shouldn't lose more than twenty percent of your birds."

"You say that like it is nothing!" Xandra didn't like how loud her father was becoming. She'd heard him get like this before and over situations that were less dire than losing a fifth of their chicken flock. What if he struck the doctor? He'd been violent in front of her before. "How much is the medication?"

The doctor gave him a figure and Xandra was shocked. She helped do the books for the farm and the cost quoted by the doctor was more than the profit for an entire quarter of production. Her father grew red in the face.

"That is outrageous," he said. "Who is making all the money from this treatment?" he pointed at Xandra. "They are stealing the food from the mouths of my children."

"Those are your choices," the doctor said, tucking his tablet under an arm. "The infection is here and I can't allow your birds to be sold at market until it's cleared up, one way or the other."

As the doctor went to leave, her father stepped in front, blocking the gate. "This is you making the decision. It would be cheaper to kill all these birds and start over than treat them. How is that fair? Tell me, how is that fair to farmers like me who could lose everything?"

"Vassilis, stand aside," the doctor demanded. "I have three more farms to visit today and you have a decision to make."

Xandra held her breath. She had never heard anyone speak to her father this way. He normally got what he wanted, either by cajoling them with the easy charm he could bring to play, or by bullying his opponents with his massive bulk and attitude. If the men were going to brawl, she didn't want to be anywhere close to them. She turned a foot toward the barn door, prepared to flee if they came to blows.

After a short pause her father threw up his hands and stepped aside. "Leave then, go to your masters after you collect more money for them." The doctor walked past him, eyeing him with suspicion, but eventually he reached his van and drove off.

Vassilis turned and looked at the barn full of squawking chickens. There were immense rows of cages, each holding thousands of birds. Xandra stood still, looking out over the chickens just as her father did. She felt sorry for him, understanding that no matter what decision he made, it was going to be difficult. When she got within arm's reach of him, he lashed out with a hand and grabbed ahold of her arm.

"You heard that despicable gasbag? He gives us a choice of losing our flock or keeping them by spending most of our savings."

"You're hurting me, Papa."

He jerked her to the big door at the entrance of the large metal building and pointed out into the yard. "Go round up all of those chickens in the yard and get them inside." He released her and the pain in her arm stopped as warm blood flowed to the spot, but she could tell there would be a bruise there later. "Do it now! I want every chicken in this barn. Come on, come on."

She moved through the yard, chasing chickens back into the barn and she wished her mother was still around to comfort her. She had left last year with Xandra's brother Stavros. Their parents hadn't yet divorced, but her mother lived in town with her brother while Xandra remained with her father. As mean as he was, she could not bear to think of him alone on this farm.

When the yard was clear of chickens, she went into the barn and saw her father closing up all the openings using the controls on the wall. It grew dark inside the building as the sunlight was closed off by metal shutters. She looked up at her bear of a father. "What are you doing?"

He pulled a lever and the fans kicked on even as the vents to the outside closed. "You heard the doctor. We can't sell them and the medicine costs too much. It will be cheaper to buy a new flock and start over."

It finally dawned on her what he meant to do. "You're going to kill them?"

He answered without looking at her. His eyes had a faraway look that frightened her in its intensity. "They're just birds, Xandra. If you are going to be good in business you can't hesitate to make the hard decisions. You can't be afraid to wipe the slate clean and start all over. We can do that. We'll just begin again with clean birds."

She followed as he walked to the fire suppression system and keyed in the code that let him override the system. "It's the most cost-effective way, you understand? They are only birds. It means nothing."

He pulled a lever and the array of valves in the ceiling of the barn opened up, venting a cloud of gas into the vast space. She felt him grab her arm again, pulling her through a small door near the controls. As she watched, the fog descended and quickly dispersed across the whole space.

The chickens were trapped in their cages and seemed to sense their impending doom. They reacted as one, raising a cacophony as the fire suppression gas replaced the oxygen in the air. They made horrible, strangling noises as they struggled to breathe, then her father closed the door.

"They're just birds," he said again. "Don't give them a second thought."

She could still hear them through the steel door, squirming and fighting for life as the poisoned air did its work. Then she realized her father was speaking. "I'm sorry, what did you say?"

"Make a note, we'll need that Turkish fellow from Athens out here to recharge the fire system after we dispose of the chickens. The last thing we want is to lose the barn. Bad enough we've lost the flock."

"I will, Papa," she said as he walked off. She followed him with her eyes until he rounded the corner toward the house and then she cracked the door open. The chickens were mostly dead, she saw, except for a few that squirmed as the process finished. After another minute the great building was silent. Sometimes it had been so loud inside that she couldn't hear when someone spoke to her, but now all was quiet. The sensation of ruthlessness excited her. This was how you got things done. This was how you accomplished what others thought was impossible.

———— «⟩⟩ ————

Ebbers numbly made her way back to the cabin she was calling home on the mining station. She closed the door, crawled under the covers of her bed, and sat back against the plain metal headboard, hugging her knees.

What she had just witnessed was the callous mass murder of dozens of people. True, they had been changed by her process into Swimmers that more closely resembled octopuses from the oceans of Earth, but they were still people. Slicing off a tissue sample would reveal radically altered human DNA.

It wasn't that she had illusions about the kind of lives the test subjects lived or how they could be cut short if something went wrong. After all, Xandra's presence here was due to some of them attacking and eating one another. Given the fact that they had no way to reverse the process and transform the subjects back into human form meant they were doomed to a life that was not of their choosing. But to watch Xandra cold-bloodedly murder them as if they were nothing more than lab mice disturbed her.

Xandra had been alive a long time, and they were in unchartered territory for understanding how those extra years affected someone's mental faculties and emotional well-being. What if Xandra, in her nineties and looking forward to her next century of life, was losing any semblance of the compassion or empathy people needed to function in a society?

There was also her wealth to consider. The credits she'd amassed formed a barrier around her that was as thick and effective as any physical wall. It bought her isolation that removed her from random encounters and allowed her to set up arcane rules about who she interacted with. Everyone close to her was an employee by design. Even the people she was intimate with, like Damian, worked for her. While there were other wealthy people who had partaken of the life-lengthening process Vibrant Passion was built on, she didn't have access to how they lived their lives. For Ebbers's purposes of determining her state of mind, Xandra was a dataset of one.

That frightened Ebbers immensely. If Xandra would end an experiment with little consideration for who she was murdering, Ebbers and her team could be next. Fear gripped her and her breath hitched as she realized the danger she was in. With the life-lengthening treatments already under her skin, Ebbers had years to live however she wanted. Xandra could take it all away, though.

Ebbers closed her eyes as the frustration of her situation made tears flow. She curled under the covers, hiding fully from the responsibility that had been thrust upon her. It was just all too much.

28.

Nathan made his way back to the laboratory, satisfied that Mindy and the octopus-like creature were secured in the engineering section. He was breathing hard and felt exhausted. The wounds he'd received when Doctor Mir was killed still felt sore despite Tricia's attention. He needed sleep and a decent meal more than anything.

He rounded the wide doorway into the lab and said, "I've got them secured—", then he stopped. Inside the lab, Tricia and Harmony stood in front of Cole's pod, shoulder to shoulder, facing a man.

"Who the hell is that?" Nathan said. The man was slight and stood no taller than Tricia. He was bald, and wore a gray jumpsuit bearing the name and logo of the *Candlewax.*

"We don't know," Tricia said.

The man spoke with a deep voice that belied his slight stature. "My name is Thomas."

Nathan looked past him and saw one of the stasis pods was open. "I'm Nathan, and this is Tricia and Harmony." He pointed to the pod. "Did you come out of there, Thomas? Were you in that pod?"

The man turned slowly to look at the pod behind him, like he was as puzzled as Nathan and his crew. "I did," he said finally, like things had clicked into place for him.

Nathan took a good look at him and noticed that he didn't just look small, he seemed diminished. Thomas's arms looked thin where they stuck out of the rolled-up sleeves of the jumpsuit. His neck was so thin it looked like holding up his head was an effort. His remaining hair was wispy across his balding head.

Rather than treating him as an opponent he decided to go another way. "Are you alright? Do you need help?"

Thomas gave him a puzzled look. "Are you part of the crew here?"

"No, the ship has been lost for many years and we were hired to find it."

Thomas turned and gestured at the row of pods. "But you know what they did here."

Nathan gave him a small nod. "We're learning. We came aboard and were ambushed." He pointed at Cole's pod. "One of my crew was harmed by someone who came out of a pod, like you."

Thomas looked at the pod holding Cole. "They experimented on us."

Nathan stepped around the women. "We know, and we're sorry about that. If we can help you, we will."

"I'd like to go home," Thomas said.

"So would we, but we're having a problem with that right now. The ship was sabotaged. We tried to jump home but we got lost instead."

Thomas looked at them with lost, sunken eyes that were stained with red lines, like the effort of conversing was too much.

"Would you like to rest? We can find you a bed. You wouldn't have to go back in one of those pods."

Thomas didn't answer at first. He looked at each of them in turn, and he must have decided they were trustworthy. "I'm hungry. Do you have anything to eat?"

"I'm feeling that way, too," Nathan said. "I think we can find something."

Thirty minutes later they were in the ship's mess hall, eating a selection of meals they'd found in a storage pantry, and which Tricia had deemed safe to eat.

Nathan took a bite of processed turkey. "For being three years old, this isn't bad."

"I miss our chow," Tricia said and turned to Harmony. "We always stock up on fresh food before we leave."

Harmony moved something claiming to be beef stroganoff across a pocket of her tray. "This is about as good as the food was on Grigory's ship. I can't wait to get someplace with real fresh fruits and vegetables."

They all looked at Thomas and saw him shoveling some kind of chicken casserole into his mouth as fast as possible. Nathan was amazed at how quickly he was making the meal disappear.

He wiped a small dinner roll through the greasy remains and popped it into his mouth. "Does anyone care if I get another?"

Nathan shook his head. "Knock yourself out. Being asleep for so long probably gave you a hell of an appetite."

Thomas was gone before he finished speaking and loaded another meal into the oven. Nathan was quite sure he hadn't looked to see what it was, just grabbed the first one he saw.

Harmony pushed her dinner away. "If you guys don't mind, I'm going back to the flight deck to see if I can do anything with the nav system. There's got to be some way to get back home."

"You have your mobi?" Nathan asked.

She nodded. "I'll holler if I need help."

"Be careful. It looks like everyone is accounted for, but people keep popping up anyway."

Harmony moved off, passing Thomas as he was on his way back to the table. This time he had lasagna, and he dug in just as hard.

"Thomas," Nathan said, "can you tell us how you came to be on this ship? Do you remember?"

Thomas started to say something and put his hand to his head. He grimaced in pain and groaned.

Tricia moved around the table, putting a hand on his shoulder. "Are you okay? Does something hurt?"

"Yeah," he said. "My head is killing me because Richie just hit me with a wrench."

Nathan and Tricia looked at each other and then Nathan turned back to him. "What did you say?"

"Richie's mad at me and he wants to know where you are. He keeps asking, 'Where's Nathan?' but I don't know what to say to him."

Nathan sat there, stunned into silence.

———— «◊» ————

The *Blue Moon Bandit* orbited Earth at a distance of about two-hundred thousand kilometers, or about half the distance to the Moon. Marla was frustrated and alternated her attention between the flight controls and the communications system, hoping to either see the *Candlewax* appear on her scope or receive a message from Nathan. In the time they'd spent hiding in the darkness, neither had happened.

They'd been successful in contacting Kimiyo, and she'd been as outraged as Marla imagined at the prospect of Cole being put in danger by Xandra Ariti. The problem, as Kimiyo regarded it, was, all they had were suspicions. There was no hard evidence that Xandra had done anything nefarious. Space was big and dangerous, and there were a thousand ways for things to go wrong in something as routine as traveling faster-than-light speed. Doing it every day didn't mean things couldn't go wrong.

What worried them was the fact that the *Candlewax* had been cold soaking for three years. Who knew what affect that could have on complex systems? Sure, Duncan had given the ship the all-clear, but really, without getting his hands deep in the machinery, he couldn't be one-hundred percent sure.

Marla wished there was something else she could do than sit and wait. It seemed like a colossal waste of time if Nathan and the others were in danger. She heard footsteps behind and looked up to see Duncan in the cockpit doorway leaning against the frame.

"What's wrong?" he asked.

She sighed. "We should be doing something."

He rested a strong hand on her shoulder.

She gave him a side eye. "What are you and Richie up to?"

He grunted, and it felt tinged with exasperation. "The shipyard put the *Bandit* back together, but things aren't quite the way I like, so we're just getting things put back right."

"I haven't noticed any problems."

"No, you wouldn't, but flightworthy isn't the same as me being happy with the way things are running. Bruce Corbin and his crew at the yard did a great job getting her all straightened out and installing the new engine, but I like things my way. I can eek out a few more points for thrust efficiency and it means we burn less fuel, which puts more credits in our pocket. We also run with a lean crew, so we have to automate more systems. Don't worry, it's all behind the scenes stuff that won't impact you."

"How's Richie holding up?"

"Sitting around is making him a little squirrely, but I just keep giving him things to do. The busier he is, the less he whines."

Marla gave him a little laugh and then they heard screams from below. "Was that Richie? Is he hurt?"

Duncan came off the door frame and started moving toward the rear of the ship. "He was working on life support. There shouldn't have been anything to hurt him."

They rushed through the galley and Duncan slid down the stairway with practiced ease. Marla followed him, keeping close. Richie yelled again, but Marla couldn't make out what he was saying. She entered the starboard engine room prepared to see Richie lying injured on the deck. Instead, she pulled up short and stared in amazement.

"Who is that?" she said.

A small, slightly built bald man lay on the deck, bleeding from a head wound. Richie stood over him with both hands wrapped around a large adjustable pipe wrench he held shoulder high. There was a small bloodstain on the head of the wrench.

"What's going on in here?" Marla demanded.

Richie pointed at the man on the deck and lowered the wrench. "He's a stowaway. I found him hiding in the tool cage and he scared the hell out of me."

"Did he hit you?" Duncan asked.

"Well, no, but I wasn't about to give him the chance." He raised the wrench again. "You know he had to have gotten on board when we were docked with the *Candlewax*." He turned back to the prone man. "Where's Nathan? What did you do to him and the rest of our crew?"

Duncan grabbed Richie by the collar and yanked him away from the man. "Come on, you've been hanging around with Cole too much. Get off the guy."

"What if he's dangerous?" Richie said, breathing heavily.

"What if he's just a stowaway looking for a ride?" Duncan said. "Do you remember when we found you that way on the *Martha Tooey* a few years ago? Would you have liked one of us to smack you with a wrench?"

Richie dropped his head in embarrassment. "No, of course not."

"Alright then," Duncan said. "Why don't you go up to the cockpit and keep an eye on things?"

Richie nodded. "Yeah, okay." He turned to the man. "Sorry about that."

The man nodded from the deck and Richie left Duncan and Marla to deal with him.

Duncan held out his hand to help him up. "What's your name?"

"Thomas," he said, taking Duncan's hand and stood up.

Duncan handed him a clean shop towel. "We can help you, but I want to know who you are and where you came from."

"Why was that other guy so angry?" Thomas said as pressed the towel to his head.

"Some of our crew are missing. We're trying figure out where they are and get them back." They walked into the small room that served as a sickbay. Duncan directed Thomas to lay down on the lone exam table.

He opened a cabinet and took out a medical scanner. "Look, I'm not a doctor. A nurse is normally part of our crew, but right now she's lost. So, be quiet and hold still."

He ran the scanner over Thomas's head. "I hope I'm reading this correctly. Normally I take care of reactors and engines."

"Thank you, I'm sure it will be fine."

"Just hold still," Duncan said.

Marla looked over his shoulder and stared at the device. "I don't see a concussion or any neck trauma. He just needs that cut patched up." She opened a drawer and removed some first aid supplies. She cleaned the wound on his head and placed a bandage on it. "That dressing has medication on it that should heal the cut in about a day. Just keep it dry." Next, she dug into a cabinet and came out with a fluid bag. "I'm going to give you this, as well. The scanner says you're dehydrated." She hung the bag and attached a small device to his wrist. "This will insert an IV catheter for the fluids, which is way safer than me trying to find a vein."

Thomas grimaced as the catheter was inserted. "Thank you."

"Okay," Duncan said. "Now that we've fixed up the damage Richie did, I need you to tell me how you got onboard."

Thomas looked at them, as if he was making his mind up about whether he could trust them. "I was on board the *Candlewax.*"

"And you came aboard then?" Duncan said. "How? We secured the door."

Thomas gave him a knowing grin. "I've always been good with locks. I was able to get in and I just found a place to hide down below."

"What were you hiding from?" Marla said.

"They were doing awful things to us. Experimenting on us and changing our bodies to suit their needs. When I woke up, I knew I had to escape."

"We know they were up to some shady stuff," Duncan said. "We ran into a doctor named Izad Mir who warned us that we would find some dangers when we docked. The rest of our crew was attacked by a pair of test subjects who trapped them. Obviously, you aren't one of them. We were supposed to join up here to get them help, but something went wrong."

"Can you tell us anything about the *Candlewax?*" Marla said. "Like where it might be?

Thomas's face fell and he stared at them before answering. "No, it feels better now."

Duncan glanced at Marla before turning back to Thomas with a puzzled look. "What feels better?"

"My head," he said. "Nathan wanted to know if I felt better."

Duncan was very confused and faced Marla. "Did we read that scanner right? I mean, are we sure he doesn't have a concussion?"

She picked it up and looked at the readout again. "I don't see anything."

"Sure," Thomas said, "I can tell them that."

"Tell us what?" Duncan said.

"Nathan wants you to know that they're all fine and for right now, they're safe on the other ship."

"You're talking to Nathan right now?" Duncan said.

"I'm sorry," Thomas said. "It's difficult to have divergent conversations at once."

"What do you mean?" Marla asked.

"I'm both here on your ship and on the *Candlewax* with the rest of your crew," Thomas said. "They seem to be very far away."

"Just so we're clear, you're talking to Nathan right now," Duncan said. "Like, you can hear him and speak to him at the same time you're speaking to us?"

"That's right."

"How can that be?" Duncan said. "Are you telepathic?"

"Not as far as I know," Thomas said. "I'm here and I'm there and I can see and hear everything on both ships." He put a hand on his head. "I'm trying to explain but it's hard when you both ask questions at the same time." He squeezed his head. "Please, just be quiet and I'll explain." He fell silent for a moment and looked up at Duncan and Marla, who stood silently in front of him.

"This was the experiment they conducted on me. I'm able to split my body, but I only have one mind. It's very difficult to process all the sensory input. We can have a conversation, but you all need to speak slowly. I get headaches when there's too much input." Thomas lay back on the exam table, raising it up to get comfortable. "Okay, Duncan, why don't you and Marla go first?"

"Can Nathan hear us?" Duncan asked.

"No, I have to tell him what I hear."

"Sure," Duncan said. He was worried about that. What if Thomas didn't pass something on correctly? This was like that game they used to play as children, passing messages around a circle and seeing how twisted it was by the time it got to the recipient. "It's not that I don't trust you, but I'm going to need to test this."

Thomas closed his eyes. "That's fine."

Duncan nodded to Marla and they stepped out of the small room, closing the door behind them. "Do you believe this?" he asked.

She shrugged. "I guess we'll know if he can pass a message. Is this any stranger than being chased by a Syndicate leg-breaker who can burst into flames? I mean, we've seen some stuff that's pretty weird."

"Yeah, you got that right. What do we ask him?"

"Something personal."

"Right." He thought for a moment. "I think I have it."

They re-entered the room and Thomas remained on the exam table. He looked thin and exhausted. Duncan felt bad for him. Whatever had happened, it had obviously been against his will and now they were using the consequences of those experiments to help themselves. Duncan grabbed a blanket from the first aid kit and settled it over Thomas' insubstantial legs.

"Thomas," Duncan said. "Can you ask Nathan about the last time he saw his ex-wife?"

Marla punched him on the arm. "Really? You're going to bring up Celeste in front of Tricia? What's wrong with you?"

"What? We decided on something personal."

"You could have just asked him about our last job," she said. "Honestly, why do I have to explain this to you?"

Thomas cleared his throat. "He wants me to tell you that he hasn't seen her since that day in the bar on the Moon. He thinks she's still a pilot working for Saji Vy's company."

Duncan looked at Marla. "Well, there's no way he could know that."

"For sure," she said, and turned to Thomas. "Can Nathan tell us where he is? If he can, we can come get him."

Thomas shook his head. "He thinks Xandra set them up to fail." He went on for some time, explaining what had happened to Nathan and the rest of their crew. At the end of it, Thomas was sweating and his skin looked grey.

"We need to think about this," Duncan said, "and you need some rest. Tell him we're going to sign off for now and give you some time to get your strength back. Say, about four hours? Would that be alright?"

Thomas was curled up under the blanket and still had his eyes closed. "That would be great. I appreciate that." He was quiet for a moment. "Nathan agrees. He says everyone should get some rest."

Marla moved beside the bed and said, "Are you hungry? You look like you could use a good meal."

"I am," Thomas said, "but I think I need some sleep first. Maybe when I wake up."

"That's fine," she said. "We'll make some dinner and put some aside for when you wake up. Just let the IV line get your fluids back up to where they should be." She raised a siderail on the exam table. "If you need anything, press the red button and someone will check on you."

"Thank you," he said. "You've been very kind."

She patted his hand and left the room. Duncan locked the door and followed her up the corridor. "That was really weird."

Marla started pulling things from the fridge. "As strange as this all is, I'm not sure it helps us."

"What do you mean?"

She started boiling water for pasta and Duncan pulled a loaf of garlic bread from the freezer. Cooking dinner together was something they did to give themselves a sense of normalcy while they were on a job.

"If Nathan doesn't have access to an operating nav system, we may not be able to help him. I mean, he can't just look out the window and tell us which stars he sees." She stopped for a moment and wiped away a tear. "It's great we can communicate with them, but now we know that bitch Xandra did all this on purpose. I mean, she planned to strand us all out there in the middle of nowhere. If it wasn't for Thomas, we would never have known what happened. They'd just be another ship that vanished. A story that people tell in spacer bars when they've had a few drinks."

Duncan moved behind her and slipped his arms around her waist. "We've been in tight spots before. We'll figure it out."

She leaned back into him. "You really think so?"

He kissed the top of her head. "I do. I've got no idea how right now, but that's okay. Let's eat, get some rest and see what kind of ideas we can come up with. Ideas are attracted to full bellies."

29.

Three hours later Duncan was dozing when he awoke to someone screaming. He listened for it again and sure enough, the noise repeated. It didn't sound like rage, though or pain, but terror. He rolled off the couch in the galley where he had been stretched out and ran toward the sick bay compartment. He unlocked the door and Marla rushed in behind him. They entered the room together to see Thomas thrashing around on the exam table. The blanket was on the floor where he'd thrown it, but his eyes were still closed and he was drenched in sweat.

Duncan put his hands on him and used his bulk to restrain him. "Hey, man, wake up. Thomas, can you hear me? Are you alright?"

His eyes popped open and at first he looked dazed. He looked at Duncan and Marla with wide, fearful eyes. She was on the opposite side of the table and put a reassuring hand on his shoulder as she checked the IV bracelet to ensure the line was still flowing.

"It's okay," she said. "You're safe. You have nothing to worry about."

He swallowed hard and sat up suddenly, like he was preparing to bolt from the compartment. Duncan gripped him tighter.

"You're safe," he said to Thomas. "No one here is going to hurt you."

Thomas looked around the compartment with wild eyes set deep with fear. Marla stroked his shoulder with one hand. His breathing slowed and he eventually shifted around so his legs hung over the side of the bed.

"I'm sorry," he said. "I think I was dreaming that I was back on the *Candlewax* and they were killing me again."

Duncan stole a look at Marla. "What do you mean?"

"Before being put in stasis, Doctor Mir and his staff discovered my 'gift,' namely that I can split myself in two."

Marla took one of his hands in hers. "If you don't want to talk about it, you don't have to. You don't owe us an explanation."

Thomas swallowed hard, considering what she said. "Thank you for that, but I want someone to know in case anything happens to me. Mir and the others were brutal to us and if I don't live to tell the tale, he'll just get away with it."

Marla squeezed his hand. "If you want to talk, we'll listen. You don't have to suffer alone."

"Okay, but can I get something stronger than this fluid bag?" Thomas said. "I need to brace myself."

Duncan clapped him on the shoulder. "We can definitely do that."

They unhooked Thomas from his fluids and moved to the galley. Duncan pulled a bottle from the cabinet. He set it and a glass on the table. "I hope whiskey is alright. We just got the ship back and there isn't anything else on board." Marla and Duncan weren't drinking.

Thomas unscrewed the cap and poured himself a drink. "That will do just fine." He shot it down and smiled. "Hey that's pretty good." He grabbed the bottle and poured another. "I hope you don't mind, but your friends on the other ship are sitting in with us. I thought it would be easier to do this once."

"You're going to talk to them at the same time, both bodies?" Duncan said.

"That's right," Thomas said. "Anyway, if you're ready, I can tell you what happened aboard the *Candlewax*."

Duncan set his mobi on the tabletop to record and nodded at Thomas. "We're all ready."

"Only what you're comfortable with, okay?" Marla said. "You don't owe us anything."

"I know," Thomas said. "I want this out there, though. People need to hear this." He took a deep breath. "I was homeless and living on whatever work I could find...

———— «» ————

Thomas Meer stepped off a shuttle and looked around at the only spaceport on Saturn's moon of Rhea. The passenger complex was large, with high walls painted a stark white that reflected the bright lights hanging from the ceiling. Some of the lights were out, though, and the remaining ones illuminated a dingy floor badly in need of cleaning. The other passengers from the flight moved toward a door about ten meters away so he hefted his single bag to his shoulder and followed the crowd.

The crowd of passengers moved through a short corridor that emptied out into a larger waiting area. Thomas collapsed into the first hard plastic chair he saw. A large window was set into the wall facing him and he stared out at Saturn. Satisfied that no one was watching him, he relaxed into the chair to contemplate his next move.

Thomas was a life support technician by training but he'd had three jobs in the last year and had been fired from all of them. It wasn't that he was bad at his job, he just wasn't good at working. Managers expected him to be on time for every shift and that really wasn't the kind of worker he was. The way he looked at it, as long as the work got done, who cared when he clocked in? This wasn't a view shared by most supervisors, so he tended to move around frequently. His last position had been on an agricultural freighter and the crew had been so fed up with him they'd dropped him at their last port of call on Triton. He'd had just enough credits to travel as far as Rhea and now he was stuck here.

The small moon was frozen and airless, just another cold rock at the tail end of the solar system. Since the surface ice could be cracked into its chemical components of hydrogen and oxygen, the small outpost's economy was reliant on being a refueling station. Thomas figured he'd be safe as long as he kept a low profile.

He yawned, suddenly aware that he hadn't slept more than a few hours over the last few days. He settled deeper into the chair and his heavy eyelids closed.

The prodding of a heavy stick woke him and he looked up into the face of a Protective Services officer. He had a stun wand in his hand that he used to nudge Thomas. Saturn had moved beyond the window. Thomas wasn't sure how long he'd slept but it must have been hours.

"You can't sleep here," the officer said. "Do you have someplace to go?"

Thomas looked at him in panic, suddenly aware that being identified as a vagrant could get him arrested. He didn't want his name popping up on any official reports because it would make it more difficult to find work.

He gripped his bag and sat up straight. "I do have somewhere to go, officer. I apologize for sleeping here. My flight must have taken more out of me than I realized."

"Where are you staying?"

Thomas froze. Coming up with a lie to satisfy the officer might be something the protagonist of a spy holovid could do on a moment's notice, but he drew a blank. As he opened his mouth to say something, he was interrupted by a voice from behind.

"Cousin! What are you doing here? I've been waiting for you at the café for the last hour."

Thomas rose from his chair and looked at the man speaking. He was tall and lean, with no hair. He smiled at Thomas and held out a hand.

"Can I take your bag? You must be tired from your journey," he said. Then he looked to the Protective Services officer. "My cousin has come a long way and I'm sure he must be hungry. If you're all finished here?"

The officer eyed them suspiciously but as tired as Thomas was, he wasn't stupid. He handed his bag across the chair to the man and grinned. "Thank you for finding me. I only sat down for a moment to enjoy the view of Saturn and I must have drifted off. Sorry I kept you waiting."

Thomas took a deep breath and followed his 'cousin' out of the waiting area to a line of shops. When he stole a look behind, the officer had moved on.

"Thank you," he said to his mysterious benefactor.

The tall man handed his bag back to him. "No problem. You have to be careful around here. The officers will roust you for sleeping in public. They don't have a sense of humor about that at all." He was dressed in dark trousers and a blue shirt that had a wide white stripe running from the neck to the bottom. It gave the appearance of a casual uniform, like he might be a clerk in a shop somewhere.

Not knowing what else to do, Thomas followed the man along the line of shops. "Do you work around here?"

The man looked over and gave him a wry smile. "Not exactly. Tell me the truth, do you have anywhere to go?"

Thomas considered his predicament. A week ago, the wad of credit vouchers in his pocket after payday had felt huge but now it was gone. "I'm sort of just kicking around without a plan. Is there a hostel around here?"

"There is, but I believe I can do better." He offered his hand. "My name is Marcus."

Thomas took the man's hand. "I'm Thomas. Nice to meet you."

"Thomas, I belong to an organization that helps people in need, and I have to tell you, you strike me as a man who is in need at the moment. Would you like to join us for dinner?"

Thomas had heard stories of travelers disappearing out here at the far end of the solar system. No one knew where he was or why he was traveling. No one was expecting him because he had no destination. Right now, his only plan was to find another job. If he went with this man and he had a nefarious plan, Thomas would certainly fall victim to it. On the other hand, he hadn't eaten properly for the last two days. He looked at Marcus and decided the man looked as trustworthy as anyone else.

"If it's not an imposition, I'll accept your offer. You're certain it will be alright?"

Marcus smiled again, this time more warmly, and put a hand on Thomas's shoulder. "My new friend, don't worry about it. We have plenty and we're happy to share. Now come, our place is just down this corridor."

Marcus led him to a storefront in the shopping district of Rhea's only settlement. They entered through a double glass door and Thomas saw a group of about a dozen people sitting at a long table. The space was neat but he could see it was being repurposed from its former life as a small grocery store. There were large decorative labels on the walls describing where vegetables, meat analogs, and dairy products had been stored. A counter ran along the opposite wall from the large table.

When they closed the door, a short, matronly woman looked up and smiled when she noticed Thomas. Excusing herself from the conversation she made her way over. She extended her arms wide and hugged Marcus before settling her gaze on Thomas.

"Who have you brought home, dear?"

Marcus handled the introductions. The woman was his wife, Arlene. While they spoke, Thomas's stomach rumbled at the scent of something delicious cooking nearby. He shook her hand and cast an involuntary glance at the back room where he assumed the kitchen was.

Arlene smiled at him. "If the two of you are hungry, take a seat. Dinner is just about ready."

Marcus led him to one end of the long table and they sat down. He poured them cold water from a sweating pitcher.

"Are you a religious man, Thomas?"

Thomas drank half his glass of water on a single pull before he answered. "Not really, no. My family left Earth three generations ago and my grandmother on my mother's side was the last one to worship."

"So, you don't believe in God?"

Thomas paused the glass he was raising back to his lips and noticed the other people at the table staring at him; they all seemed to be waiting on an answer. He wondered what he had stumbled into and decided to play it safe. "I wouldn't say that I'm not a believer. It's more like I just don't have religion in my life." He swallowed hard as the others continued staring at him. "Is that what this is? Some kind of church, or temple?"

Arlene and a couple other women arrived and set down bowls and platters on the table. The food smelled even more delicious close up. Thomas looked at them and saw one bowl full of red beans and rice, mixed with onions, green peppers and celery. The platters held grilled portobello mushrooms with the scent of soy sauce.

Arlene fixed a plate and handed it to him. "Guests first," she said.

Thomas took it and had to restrain himself from gobbling it down. He realized that it had not only been a long time since he'd had enough to eat, but even longer since he'd eaten a meal prepared so well.

"Thank you," he said. "I can't describe how good this looks."

The bowls were passed along the table and Marcus nodded to him. "Well, dig in."

Thomas nodded and practically attacked his plate. Everything tasted as good as he imagined. The beans and rice were savory and the mushroom had just the right texture.

"We're a group called the Children of the Apocalyptic Rainbow," Marcus said, answering his question. "We help people who are left behind by society, who need a second chance," he gripped Arlene's hand as he said this, "or who have no one else to turn to. We're not a church in the traditional sense, but we do have tenants of worship, one of which is charity. If you'd like to hear more, you're welcome to stay the night. If there is a problem with Protective Services or other authorities, we don't care as long as you're not a danger to yourself or others. We have room to spare."

Thomas paused for a moment and looked at Marcus. He seemed honest enough and so far, he and his friends had been nothing but kind. There was also nowhere else for him to go.

"I appreciate your offer very much, Marcus. I think I'd like that."

Marcus smiled. "Good."

"You'll have to let me help clean up after dinner, though. It's the least I can do."

Arlene smiled. "I certainly won't stop you." She glanced at Marcus. "It will be nice to have some help for a change."

After they finished cleaning up in the kitchen, Marcus showed him down a hallway and led Thomas into a cramped room, containing a bed and a small desk with a chair.

"It's a little small," Marcus said. "Sorry about that."

Thomas grinned. "It beats the hell out of a bench in the spaceport."

Marcus pointed to a narrow closet door. "There are clean sheets and blankets in there. The bathroom is just down the hall on the right. Our room is two doors past that if you need anything."

"Thanks, I'm sure I'll be fine."

"We wake up early," Marcus said. "There's work to do and I hope you'll help us."

"Sure, no problem."

Marcus left and Thomas went to the closet to grab the bedding. He made up the single bed and the worn foam mattress compressed a little too far under his weight, but Thomas didn't care. It was the first bed he'd had in a week. He collapsed into it and was fast asleep a few moments later.

— ‹‹›› —

Two hours later, Marcus and Arlene snuck into the room. Marcus shook Thomas' shoulder, but he kept sleeping. Arlene was getting good at dosing the water. They moved quickly; Arlene took a roll of tape from the kit bag slung over her shoulder and together, they wrapped the blankets around Thomas, cocooning him. Then they strapped Thomas and the blankets together with tape. They were careful to leave them loose enough for him to breathe but tight enough that he wouldn't be able to escape if he woke up. That never happened, though.

Marcus moved to the head of the small bed and pressed a hidden switch. The bed rose to float waist high in mid-air and the legs folded neatly beneath it. Then they maneuvered the cocooned Thomas out into the hall, past the bathroom, and through a wider doorway at the end of the hall. A quiet buzzing noise filled the air in the room.

Arlene let the door slip shut and she helped Marcus push the floating bed toward a wall lined with metal racks. They positioned the bed over a pair of steel arms. It settled onto the arms when Marcus flicked the switch near the headboard. He tapped another control on the rack and the low hum of a stasis field joined the buzzing noise of the room.

They stood back and looked at the wall. The steel racking held a total of five beds, all of them occupied with a slumbering occupant. Two men, two women, and one small girl.

"That's a full load," Arlene said as she slipped an arm around Marcus's waist. "You'd better give Caleb a call and tell him we need a pickup. We can't keep them in stasis forever and a couple have already been here a week."

"Yep, I'll do it in the morning," he said. "I'm beat right now."

"Make sure he doesn't screw us on the payment, either," she said. "Last time he tried to give us two thousand each instead of three. I know he's getting four apiece so he's trying to skim off the top."

Marcus yawned and nodded. "Yeah, I'll make sure."

They turned off the lights and draped the room in darkness.

———— «» ————

The next time Thomas woke up, it was to a soft chime gently ringing through the air. He looked around and saw that he was in a compartment he didn't recognize, surrounded by people he didn't know. His head buzzed and ached dully, like he had a hangover. He blinked rapidly, trying to get his eyes to adjust to the bright lights and white walls. There were men and women lying on the bunks around him. Everyone was dressed in a similar pale green outfit. He turned to the red headed woman next to him.

"Do you know where we are?"

"This isn't a place," she said, pointing toward a wall with a window. "It's a ship and I don't know where in the galaxy we are. I was never very good at recognizing stars. I'm Mindy, by the way."

Thomas followed her outstretched finger and saw the darkness of space punctuated with a few bright pinholes of light.

He put a hand to his aching head. "Oh man, I knew those people were too good to be true."

"Whatever they told you, this job pays really well. The contract I signed will pay me what I made in my best year for six months of work here." She waved a hand around. "I was broke, but now I've got a place to sleep, it's safe, and the food is great. I can deal with a little mystery for a deal like that."

The prospect of good pay caught his attention. "We get paid? Who do we see about that?"

"They'll probably talk to you after breakfast." She pointed to the opposite end of the room. "The bathroom is over there, and you should have a locker with clothes. There isn't much variety, but they are clean and comfortable."

Thomas felt a rumble in his stomach. "I could eat. I feel like I'm starving."

Mindy smiled. "Well, let's go."

Over the next week Thomas fell into a routine. He followed the rest of the people in his group. Mindy was right about the food, clothing, and sleeping arrangements. He thought he might have trouble adjusting to dorm life, but the dull routine of the testing helped him. He took tests for a few hours each day and the rest of his time was his own. He slept, ate, played games, watched holovids and sank into a deep satisfaction that for the first time in years, he didn't have to worry about being fired. It didn't escape his attention that he'd essentially been kidnapped and pressed into service, but after years of living rough he found it difficult to care. Whatever else was happening aboard this ship, no one expected very much of him and he was fine with that.

After a month, Thomas was called into a meeting with Doctor Izad Mir. He'd met the doctor a few times and always found him to be aloof, but friendly. He'd had bosses like him before and learned the best way to get along with them was to do what they asked and stay out of their way. The doctor pointed to a chair on the opposite side of his desk in the small office and Thomas sat down. Then he got right into it.

"Thomas, I'd like to thank you for helping us with our little project," Doctor Mir said. "I don't know if it's been made clear to you, but we've all noticed how diligently you've worked on your testing."

It hadn't occurred to Thomas that his contribution was anything special. Everyone in the testing group seemed to work as he did and it didn't seem to be that difficult.

"Well, I'm glad I could be of use," Thomas said, with a little nervous stammer in his voice. "I'm still not sure what I'm doing here."

Doctor Mir waved his hand, as if that dealt with all his concerns. "I'm sure Human Resources can help you with all that." He leaned closer to the desk. "What I'd like to talk to you about today is a very valuable opportunity for you to advance the work we're performing. Doesn't that sound exciting?"

"I suppose so." Thomas said, very confused about the conversation, but Doctor Mir's enthusiasm was contagious. "What do I have to do? Is it more tests?"

"No, those tests were preliminary, to give us an idea of how you think, how your particular brain works at problem solving, and I have to tell you, you're tops in the group." Doctor Mir held his hands up. "What we're talking about here is the next step. I won't lie to you, there's a little risk, but there is such an opportunity to do something absolutely breathtaking." His gaze focused intensely on Thomas. "You are just the person we've been looking for."

"I am?"

"You are, and I'd like to start tomorrow if that's alright with you."

"I suppose so," Thomas said. "Will it be painful?"

"You won't feel a thing," Doctor Mir said. He rose from his chair. "Let me congratulate you on your achievement, Thomas." He held his hand out and Thomas took it, surprised by the strong grip. "We're going to do great things together."

Before Thomas went to sleep that night, he made a note to get more information tomorrow. The last thing he wanted to be was unprepared.

———— «◊» ————

Thomas awoke groggy and not in the dorm where he had fallen asleep. With bleary eyes he realized he wasn't even in the same bed. Instead of the cot he had been using since arriving aboard the ship, he was sunk down in a pod of some kind. The lid of the apparatus was raised up, and he noticed a half dozen eager faces looking down at him.

"What's going on?" he said, with a hoarse voice.

Doctor Mir smiled down at him. While he may have intended it as a comforting gesture, Thomas was taken aback by it. It seemed more like the grin a mouse might see right before a cat settled in to playing with its prey.

"Thomas?" Doctor Mir said. "How do you feel?"

Thomas blinked and considered his question. He let his attention drift from his core to his extremities. His fingers wiggled and his toes curled, so he cleared his throat and answered in a croaky voice.

"I feel alright, I guess. Did something happen? I feel like my head is full of cotton."

Doctor Mir gave him that toothy smile again. "I'm not surprised. You've been in stasis for three months. I imagine you're a little confused."

Two orderlies reached into the pod and gripped him by the shoulders. They lifted him like he was a child and placed him in a wheelchair. Thomas's head swam from the sudden movement and his stomach tightened, hitting the reverse gear faster than he could compensate and he regurgitated. An orderly with gloved hands had a plastic kidney shaped tray under him, preventing the need for a mop. He coughed hard, expelling dark green bile. The orderly kept the tray steady until he was reduced to dry heaves, then gave him a small cup of water to rinse his mouth.

"Thank you," Thomas said. "Sorry about that."

"Don't worry about it," Doctor Mir said. "It happens after extended stasis. Now, let's get you into bed, so you can rest up. We have more work to get started on."

"I don't understand," Thomas said.

Doctor Mir put a hand on his shoulder. Thomas thought it was meant to be comforting, but he recoiled from it.

"Remember, you agreed to help us." Doctor Mir said. "Do you feel any different?"

"Not really."

"Then all is well. Don't worry so much, Thomas. You are in very good hands."

The orderly wheeled Thomas from the lab to another compartment with a few hospital beds set up. The orderlies helped him out of the chair and got him set up in bed. When they were completed, Doctor Mir approached his bedside.

"Feeling better? Hopefully, you're getting your strength back."

Thomas put his hand on his abdomen. "I know it sounds funny, but I'm actually kind of hungry. Should I be?"

Doctor Mir gave him that smile again, making him feel like something to be used. "After all your time in the pod, I imagine you feel ravenous." He turned to one of the orderlies. "Let's get Thomas a lunch tray."

"Can you make it two?" Thomas said. "I'm really hungry."

The orderly looked at Doctor Mir for confirmation and he nodded. "Of course."

Over the next week, Thomas ate more than he ever had in his life. Instead of three meals with a couple snacks, he was up to nine full meals per day with constant snacking in between. Doctor Mir said it was alright and just a side-effect of his stasis. Thomas wasn't so sure. He could feel a pressure building within him that wasn't painful, but it was uncomfortable, like persistent indigestion. Still, nothing stopped the hunger.

Ten days after exiting stasis, something happened. Thomas finished his second breakfast tray and he started sweating. He reached for the call button that would summon a nurse, but several people entered his room before he could press it. One of them was Doctor Mir.

"Thomas, I need you to stay calm for me, okay?" Doctor Mir said.

Like every other patient who has ever been told that by a physician, Thomas's blood pressure immediately shot up and he became very worried.

"What's wrong with me? Everything hurts."

Doctor Mir was too busy giving orders to the rest of the staff to answer him immediately but once he had them scurrying around, he turned his attention to his patient.

"Thomas, something wonderful is about to happen. I know it's difficult, but you must remain calm."

Thomas was sweating harder now and he could feel his temperature rising. Pain ripped through his chest and shot into his abdomen. His muscles cramped and he moaned with pain.

"What's happening to me?"

It dawned on Thomas that Doctor Mir knew exactly what was happening because he'd planned it. Desperate and angry he reached for Doctor Mir and got a grip on his collar.

"What did you do to me?" he screamed. "I'm dying!"

A large orderly removed Thomas's hands from Doctor Mir. Then he scooped Thomas up like he was an infant and moved him to a double wide gurney. The doctor kept his concentration on a tablet, intensely studying some readout. He stepped back and waved his hands at the medical staff.

"Back up everyone. This is it."

Thomas felt a pain like nothing that had ever hurt him before, even the time his left hand had been crushed when an air compressor had fallen on it. Then he closed his eyes and screamed, long and loud, but he never lost consciousness. He felt something tear down the center of his torso. Every muscle in his body tensed and then, mercifully, the pain trailed off to a less intense version of itself. He opened his eyes, looked down at his ripped open chest cavity, then turned his head and saw another body on the gurney, identical to his own.

The new thing was bloody and it looked up at him with questioning eyes. Orderlies moved quickly, taking away the new thing to its own bed. Nurses attended to Thomas but he barely felt what they were doing. All of his energy had been expended in whatever had just happened.

His torso healed remarkably quickly. Once he was cleaned up and in a new gown, Doctor Mir came to his bed and squeezed his hand. "How are you feeling, Thomas?"

He pulled his hand free of the doctor's. "You said it wouldn't hurt," he said with a weak voice. "I almost died."

"Nonsense," Doctor Mir said. He didn't seem to notice Thomas's discomfort. "You were never in any danger. Everything went according to plan."

"What was that? What did you do to me?"

"Tell me, Thomas. Have you ever wanted to be in two places at once?"

"What?"

"You know, to get a lot of work done?"

"I guess?"

"Well, now you can," Doctor Mir said. "Your contribution to our experiments was to be able to split yourself in two. It's absolutely incredible. All those extra calories you consumed was your body storing up additional mass and then, when you had enough, you split yourself. It all occurred just as we predicted. This is an amazing achievement, and you should be very proud."

Thomas recoiled. "Why would you do such a thing?"

Doctor Mir leaned in close. "A very wealthy woman wanted to see if it could be done and it was a challenge. What other reason would we need?"

⸺ «◊» ⸺

Thomas faced Nathan aboard the *Candlewax* and Duncan aboard the *Blue Moon Bandit*. The crews on each ship centered around them, enraptured with their story. He spoke with one voice, informing them what happened next.

"As you can imagine, Doctor Mir was thrilled with his success. In the months I'd been undergoing my transformation, everyone I bunked with had been drawn into their own set of experiments. As they led me from the lab, I could see Mindy's name on a pod, but I couldn't see what was happening to her. I certainly never envisioned anything like what she would become."

Thomas paused for a moment, dipping his head down. Duncan put a hand on his shoulder. "It's okay. You don't have to tell us anymore if you don't want to."

Thomas looked up and smiled. "It's alright. It just all came flooding back at once." He gripped Duncan's hand. "I can finish."

He coughed, cleared his throat and went on. "Anyway, Doctor Mir played it pretty low key, but I think his expectation would be that I could multiply myself. After a few months of experimentation, he figured out that I could only replicate one body at a time. It was a complete shock to him that I maintained a single consciousness across both bodies. It became clear that what he expected and what Xandra Ariti wanted, was a way to create workers cheaply and easily. I imagine that appealed to them and their clients. I was a failure in that respect, but then Doctor Mir discovered that my brains seemed to be connected over distance, which thrilled him to no end."

Duncan spoke up. "It's some kind of quantum entanglement, isn't it? Your brains are essentially connected on a quantum level."

Thomas took a moment and repeated Duncan's statement to Nathan and the crew on the other ship. "Yes, that's correct. Well, that was his theory anyway. He used a shuttle to take one of me farther and farther away to experiment and never did find a limit." He gave a wry smile to his audiences. "In fact, I've never been so distantly separated as I am now and it seems to make no difference."

"Incredible," Duncan said.

"You'd think such a discovery would be enough, right?" Thomas said. "Of course, Doctor Mir needed to know something else. One night he woke me up and walked me down a corridor to the airlock where your ship was docked. He was kind the whole way, apologizing for waking me up, telling me that it was another experiment. I just wanted to make him happy. I mean, it had finally dawned on me fully that these people could do anything they wanted to me. I just did what they said because it made no sense to make them angry. They had complete control over me.

"Anyway, Doctor Mir opened the airlock and I stepped in, thinking we were going to do another distance test. Then the door closed behind me with him on the other side. I turned, looked out the space-facing door and saw there was nothing docked there. It was just open space."

Thomas's voice hitched at that. Duncan and Nathan, light years apart, each put a hand on his shoulders to comfort him. "Doctor Mir cycled the airlock and the small amount of air and heat in there with me rushed out. It's not fast like you'd think it would be, freezing and suffocating. You're aware of what's happening to you. I remember every second of it."

Duncan shook his head. "I'm so sorry."

"It was only the first time," Thomas continued. "I've also been electrocuted and shot from behind without any forehand knowledge. In case you're wondering, that's the way to go. As long as the shooter has decent aim, you won't feel a thing."

"And you remember each of these incidents?" Nathan said.

"I do," Thomas answered. "I don't know what else they had in store for me, but Doctor Mir put me back in a pair of pods. I think my pod was set differently from the others because I was still relatively human. When I woke up, I saw the nutrient tank was on empty. It could be that reviving me was a failsafe so I didn't starve.

"Before I went under, I'd seen what they did to Mindy and Earl. He's the octopus looking fella. I figured it was a good idea to take a chance and escape, so I snuck aboard your ship. That way, no matter what happened, I'd have a better chance of surviving."

"I'm glad we could help," Nathan said.

"I'm glad you're not some lunatics who want to experiment on a guy." He was quiet for a moment. "If it's alright with everyone, I'd like to lay down for a bit."

"Of course," Duncan said. "Take all the time you need.

Duncan looked at Marla and shook his head as Thomas walked away. "We have to stop this. Xandra can't get away with experimenting on people for profit."

"If we're going to expose Xandra, we'll need proof," Marla said. "We believe Thomas because of everything we saw, but no one else is going to. What can you do to get Nathan and Tricia back to us?"

Duncan sat back in his chair. "I've worked on ship's remotely before, but never over a distance of who knows how many light years."

"What about Harmony? She's an engineer."

Duncan shrugged. "If she could get them home, I'm sure she would have already. We need to know where they are before we can get them back here. Xandra really screwed us by wiping the navigation database on that ship. Nathan said they have engines, but they have no way to figure out where they are. That's the problem to beat. You can't go from 'A' to 'B' unless you where 'A' is."

Marla stood up and kissed him on the forehead. "I have faith in you and so does Nathan. You'll figure something out. I'm going back up to the cockpit to make sure Richie hasn't steered us toward the moon or anything."

"Thanks, babe. Love you."

"Love you, too."

30.

Jack swallowed hard. He'd gotten to Doctor Susan Park by breaking into her apartment. Xandra Ariti was an entirely different matter. There was no way to break into one of her many homes. Hell, it had taken almost a week just to figure out if she was in town.

The office complex he was looking at now was similarly off-limits. It was easily twice as large as the place where Doctor Park worked. Like that facility, Vibrant Passion's main office was on the outskirts of town, albeit on the west side with nothing but the Jornada del Muerto desert facing it. There were no landscaping tricks disguised as security here. The place was a fortress. It was a dozen buildings surrounded by a high wall with guardhouses on the gates. He had a contact in the city planning office and she'd gotten him a copy of the blueprints. After examining them for a couple days he'd come up with a plan.

He tapped Jojo on the shoulder and had him advance toward the main gate. The float car glided up to the guardhouse and a large armed man in a black and gray uniform stepped to the car and leaned in as Jojo rolled the window down. Jojo winced at the mid-day desert sun, but Jack felt nothing inside his pressure suit. In his hands he held the folder of printed evidence that Lou Datello had kindly provided.

"Can I help you?" the guard asked. The tone of his voice was anything but helpful. If you weren't here with a purpose, he was going to send you on your way.

"Jack Murphy for Xandra Ariti," Jack said from the passenger side. The guard's eyes lingered on his appearance for longer than most people. It was normal for people to see him and steal a glance before looking away embarrassed. This guy lingered, not giving a shit if Jack was uncomfortable with it. Then the guard consulted the tablet in his hand.

"Arrangements have been made for your visit, Mr. Murphy," the guard said. "You will be escorted to your meeting location and you will follow the directions of your escort, Failure to do so will result in your eviction from the premises. Do you understand?"

"I do," Jack said.

The guard nodded at his companion inside the guardhouse and the heavy metal gate rolled aside. A car was waiting on the other side.

The escort pulled ahead and Jojo followed them. Another car fell in behind them.

"They're being a little dramatic, aren't they?" Jojo said.

"That's how we know we have the upper hand," Jack answered. "The two of us just got here and we've already got four guys on us."

The cars traveled past the large buildings trimmed out in glass and chrome to a dull looking warehouse at the back of the property that backed up against the security wall. The small procession stopped and Jack exited the vehicle. Before he closed the door, he told Jojo to stay put.

The four guards walked up to him and surrounded him. One of them took out a hand-held scanner and stared at him through it, looking for anything amiss.

"Guys, come on," Jack said. "I don't carry guns. I don't need them."

They didn't respond. The guard finished the scan and pointed at the door to the warehouse. "In there."

One of the guards held the door open and Jack walked through. It wasn't until it closed behind him that he realized he was alone.

"Walk forward," a male voice said from the darkness.

Jack moved forward, aware this could be a trap, but what choice did he have? For the first time in a long time, he was at the mercy of someone else.

A light clicked on and he saw a cheap metal desk. Xandra Ariti stood behind it in all her glory with three guards flanking her. She was the kind of woman Jack coveted, when he allowed himself to have those feelings. It wasn't just that she was attractive, it was that she'd achieved her success by being a total hardass. That was what he needed right now.

"Okay, Mr. Murphy," she said, "you got your meeting. Did you bring my property?"

"Yeah, I have it." He held up a folder.

"Printed copies?" Xandra said.

"That's how they came to me, that's how I'm giving them to you."

One of her men moved forward to take it, but Jack pulled the file away. "Not until we come to an agreement."

"How much do you want?"

Jack shook his head inside his helmet. "I don't want money."

Xandra blinked and looked for a moment like she might laugh. "Do you understand how blackmail works? This isn't your first time, is it?"

Jack lifted out a sheet of paper from the file and handed it to the man nearest him. "Take a look at that. I want you to understand I have the real deal."

The man took it and handed it across the table. Xandra didn't take it, though, so he laid it on the desk.

"I know what you have," she said. "If I didn't, I wouldn't be here meeting you. The scans you sent were deemed authentic by my accounting department. So, what do you want?"

Jack realized he was correct in his assessment of her. He'd been in some rough spots over the years, but this was the first time in a long time where he wasn't the one in control.

"I know what you're up to," he said. "How you're transforming people, giving them new bodies. I need one. I want you to build me a new body."

It annoyed him to ask anyone for help. Usually it was the other way around. People in need came to him for what they needed. Now, Atomic Jack needed something and the woman standing in front of him was the only person who could help.

Xandra took her time before answering. "You're in that suit because why?"

"I'm radioactive. It's down deep inside and so is the cancer it gave me. The suit keeps me alive with regenerators, skeletal stabilization, and meds."

Her focus narrowed. "Why else? I've heard rumors about you. Show me."

He took a deep breath. This wasn't the way he used what he could do. He wasn't a freak in a sideshow entertaining an audience. When the gloves came off, it was because someone had screwed up and was going to find out what the consequences of that were.

She stepped forward. "Show me. I want to see it."

He swallowed, feeling degradation rise up from his gullet. Her and all her men, staring at him like he was an attraction. What was he going to do, though? He needed what she had.

Without saying a word, he snapped the glove free on his left hand and pulled it off. The flesh burst into flame as soon as it was exposed to the air. He looked around at the mix of pity and fascination on their faces. Neither was acceptable.

He pulled his glove back on and tightened it down. He hadn't felt shame in a long time and now it was spilling over him in waves.

"That's quite something," Xandra said.

The suit pumped him full of painkillers. "It's killing me. Can you help or not?"

She gave him a small nod. "I think I can. You're abilities weren't gained by design, correct? Your condition is the result of an accident?"

"That's right."

"Then you have much to teach us," she said. "Do you have objections to us learning from your condition?"

"Why would you want to do that?"

"Why wouldn't I?"

Jack could see it then, as he'd seen it in so many other people like her. That drive to gain whatever she wanted, no matter the cost. If he wasn't careful, she'd tear him apart looking for what she wanted.

"What you're asking isn't something we've fully achieved yet," she said. "Do you understand that?"

Jack threw the file on the desk and papers fanned out across the top of it. "Just do what you can."

"Okay. We'll start now. Come with me."

Jack wasn't expecting that, but it didn't matter. He used his mobi to send a message to Jojo. He didn't need him anymore.

31.

Duncan lay on the bench in the galley near the table, staring at the ceiling as he considered their dilemma. It was great that they were in communication with Nathan, but what they really needed was a way for the stranded crew to determine where they were. Marla walked into the galley with a stainless-steel coffee mug, obviously looking for a refill.

"What are you thinking about?" she said.

"How to get the crew home," he said. "Any ideas?"

She removed the lid from her mug and poured in more coffee. "If we can't figure out a way for them to get a fix on their location, we've got no way to point them home. I'm worried about Cole, too. I know Tricia has him in stasis, but that's just a stop gap measure. He needs a doctor."

Duncan blew out a breath, suddenly remembering that the stakes were even higher than he'd been thinking about. "You're right. We've got to solve this."

"Have you thought about what you'd do if you were there?"

He swung his legs to the floor and grunted into a sitting position. "Thomas relayed everything they've tried so far. Nathan and Harmony were pretty thorough."

Marla moved closer and sat down at one of the chairs. "That's what they did. Forget about Nathan and Harmony. What would you do?"

Duncan rubbed his eyes to chase away the fatigue he was feeling. He checked the time on his mobi. It had been about two hours since Thomas told his story. "Let me get Thomas and see what he says."

Twenty minutes later, Duncan, Richie, and Thomas were seated around the table while Marla watched things remotely from the cockpit via a videoconference on their mobis. When he'd suggested they do a deep dive, Thomas had been very receptive. Whether he was driven by revenge on Xandra or the opportunity to be reunited with himself seemed to be a fifty-fifty split.

"Are you comfortable?" Duncan asked.

"I am," Thomas answered.

"Okay, here's how I want to do this. You're my eyes on the *Candlewax*. Your background as a life support technician will come in handy, but Nathan and Harmony will help you locate things if you have trouble. I need you to describe what you're seeing to me. A lot of my questions will seem redundant, but we need to be extremely thorough. You understand?"

"I do. We can do this."

"Alright, let's get started."

Duncan had Thomas start on the flight deck and they ran through the workflow for calling up the navigation system and confirmed what Nathan reported earlier, that while the system was still active, the database had been wiped clean. He then had them try different methods for recalling the data, just in case Xandra had tried to be clever and merely hide the data instead of deleting it, but they found nothing. In one painstaking hour, he walked Thomas and Harmony through the steps needed to purge Xandra's code from the system so it couldn't delete anything further.

From there, he directed them to different areas of the starship where data backups could be located. There were two drives on the flight deck and both were non-responsive. They moved back through the ship, and found two more data storage locations; one in the lab and one in a small compartment right outside the locked engineering compartment where Nathan had secured Mindy and Earl. The beasts heard them working and pounded on the door, but it was thick enough to contain them. Neither location gave them what they needed.

Duncan noticed Thomas was sweating and looked at his mobi. They'd been at it for five hours with no joy. "Let's take a break. Everyone get something to eat and then we'll get back to it."

He grabbed a couple sandwiches from the fridge along with a pair of cold drinks and headed for the cockpit. Marla took one of each from him and he flopped into the seat Nathan normally occupied. They dug in and half of his sandwich disappeared in three bites.

"It sounds like she was pretty thorough in her sabotage," Marla said.

"Yeah, which kind of pisses me off. I really thought we could out-think her but she did a good job."

"What about that one backup drive in the array on the flight deck? The one that was broken? Can you do anything with that?"

Duncan looked at her with a half-chewed bite in his mouth. "Fix a drive from who knows how many light years away? Not likely.

That would be almost impossible here under the best conditions. That things been drifting for three years without maintenance. I'm surprised more things aren't broken."

"But the data could be on it, right?"

He shrugged and kept eating. "Could be, but it didn't respond at all."

She leaned in close. "I know it seems like a longshot, but I think those are all we have now."

He nodded. "Okay, I'll see what I can do."

He walked back to the galley and patted Thomas on the shoulder. "We're going to try something. Can you go back up to the flight deck?"

"Sure."

It was too weird to think of the other Thomas walking on the *Candlewax* while this one sat still in the *Bandit's* galley. After a few moments he nodded at Duncan.

"I'm here and Nathan and Harmony are with me."

"Tell Harmony I want to remove a drive from the rack. It's the one that was dead when we tested it."

Thomas repeated the message and nodded. "She says we can do that."

Duncan waited as Harmony did her bit. It was frustrating as hell to sit idly by while others did the work. As helpful as they were, it wasn't the same as getting his hands in there and doing it himself. No matter how fast they worked, he was always convinced he could do it faster.

"Duncan?"

"Yes?"

"Harmony says the drive is reading as dead because its disconnected."

"What?" He grimaced with concentration, not understanding.

"She says the drive was unplugged. Should she plug it in?"

"No, don't do that. Give me a minute." Duncan smirked; people as smart as Nathan and Harmony never remembered to check the simple stuff.

Duncan thought about Xandra's code. All their equipment was with him on the *Bandit*. All Nathan had with him was his mobi. "Tell Harmony to plug it into Nathan's mobi. She might need to power it up externally, but his mobi should have the correct port to accept it."

Thomas repeated everything and nodded. "She's trying that."

Duncan sat quietly while they worked. Normally he might have chatted with Thomas but he didn't want to distract Nathan and

Harmony from their work by hearing one side of a conversation. After ten interminable minutes, Thomas smiled.

"They have it connected and it's powering up. Harmony says the drive looks fine and is going through the boot cycle."

The next minute crawled by and then Thomas pounded on the table. "It's there, the nav database is on the drive!"

Duncan let out a deep breath. "Hold on, Thomas, we want to be careful here. Tell Harmony to back it up to Nathan's mobi before we do anything else. That's the only copy we have and who knows how old that drive is."

Thomas repeated the message. "She says she's already doing that." He paused for a moment, clearly listening to someone on the other ship. "It's done. Nathan has a copy and she's disconnected the drive."

"Good, that gives us some breathing room," Duncan said. "Now, plug that drive back into the array and let's see if it can be read."

"Harmony wants to know if you're sure the malware was purged?"

"I hope so," Duncan said. "We did everything I know how to do."

"Okay, she's getting to work."

Duncan rested his head on the table so his impatience wouldn't show. Finally, when he could stand it no more, Thomas spoke.

"It's in," he said. Then his voice rose. "Nathan says it's in and reading! The ship is scanning stars looking for their location."

"That can take a while, but tell Nathan not to jump when they get a result. We'll come to them."

Thomas relayed the message even though he looked puzzled. "Why?"

Duncan stood up and walked around the galley, trying to burn off his pent-up nervous energy. "Because the last time we tried to jump that ship her malware re-directed them and wiped the nav database. I don't want to risk that happening again. We'll come get them."

Thomas repeated what he said even before he was finished saying it.

"Nathan says that will eat up a lot of expensive fuel."

Duncan spun, incredulous that his captain was worried about costs at a time like this. "Tell him this is how we're doing it."

Thomas was blank faced for a moment. "Tricia and Harmony threatened to lock him in a stasis pod if he brought up credits again, so he's fine with that."

〈〉

It took almost a day for the *Candlewax's* nav system to identify its position. After that, Thomas passed word and Marla got them there as quickly as she could. Xandra had pushed them all the way out to 61 Cygni, a relatively unexplored binary star system almost twelve light years from Earth.

The airlock opened after the two ships docked for the second time. Nathan greeted his crew with a wide smile. He hugged Duncan. "Thanks for coming back, man."

"We were thinking about just taking the ship and business for ourselves," Duncan said, "but Marla said you owed us too much back pay, and Kimiyo threated to kill us all if we didn't bring Cole home."

"She probably would, too."

The two groups merged and they walked down the corridor into the *Candlewax*. Duncan and Richie both carried bags of tools and equipment. Marla stayed behind on the *Blue Moon Bandit*, unwilling to leave it completely empty. They walked into the lab and took a look around.

"Thomas said you secured Mindy and Earl in the engineering compartment?" Duncan said.

"Yeah, we're safe for the moment," Nathan said. "I think I speak for all of us when I say we'd like to get out of here as soon as possible, especially with Cole needing medical attention. But first I want to gather enough data to burn Xandra's ass. No way does she get away with this."

Tricia spoke up. "It's going to take Harmony, Richie, and me about a half hour to get Cole's pod situated on the *Bandit*. After we're done, we need to go."

Nathan nodded. "That should be enough time. Let me know if you need help."

While the other group went to work on moving Cole, Nathan, and Duncan moved through the lab, recording everything they could see. Duncan grabbed servers from their racks rather than trying to download the information. They had no idea what was on them, but they could always look later.

They rushed down the corridor to Doctor Mir's quarters, aware of the limited time they had. The cabin looked as bad as Nathan remembered.

"Mir was here alone for three years," Nathan said, "and he felt screwed over by Xandra and her crew. He must have recorded what happened to him somewhere. Look for anything he could have used."

They hit the space like a tornado, throwing boxes aside, looking for mobis, computers, or anything else that Mir may have used to record his thoughts. Nathan ducked into the cramped sleeping space. The tiny space had a bunk, a small side table, and a closet. He tossed the bed and saw nothing amongst the sheets. They smelled like they hadn't been cleaned in months.

There was nothing in the bunk, so he moved onto the side table. There was a metal water bottle there that sounded half full when he shook it. Nathan hit paydirt in the top drawer of the side table. He reached in and pulled out a bright orange notebook with a pen stuck in the wire rings. Nathan flipped it open and saw the book was full of messy handwriting. He didn't know anyone who still wrote by hand on paper. He put the notebook in his pocket and moved on.

The bottom two drawers were empty except for some protein bars so he moved onto the closet. Several jumpsuits bearing the ship's logo hung inside. There were extra pairs of boots lined up on the floor of the closet. The only other thing was a small box full of personal items: old coins from five or six currencies, a university acceptance letter, and a folded photo of a young Izad Mir, bottle feeding a newborn cow, grinning wildly. Nathan put it back on the shelf.

He went back to the living quarters to find Duncan waiting for him. The big man held up two tablets and a mobi. "I don't know what's on them, but we can take a look later."

Nathan glanced at his own mobi and was surprised to see their allotted time was almost up. "I don't think Mir spent much time anywhere other than here. Let's go see how the others are making out."

When they returned, Nathan pulled the airlock hatch closed on the *Candlewax*. Tricia hadn't wanted to leave Mindy and Earl locked up in the engineering section, but they didn't have a choice. He hoped the nutrition station Doctor Mir had set up was well stocked. He gigged the hatch for his own ship and made his way inside the *Bandit*.

The others were gathered in a spare cabin with Cole's stasis pod. Richie lay on the deck below it, securing it for flight. Tricia stood beside it running through the menus.

"How's he doing?" Nathan asked.

Tricia answered without looking up. "He's stable for now, but I don't like his vital signs."

"I thought stasis meant keeping him in some kind of suspended animation," Nathan said. "How can he be getting worse?"

"The claw sliced one of his kidneys open and punctured his liver," she said. "He needs that kidney removed and I'm good, but I am not a surgeon. The pod's doing what it can, but it can't heal his injuries, only slow down the resulting damage."

Nathan placed a hand on the pod, aware that Cole's injuries were due to him protecting everyone else. It was his job, but it didn't make it any easier for Nathan to deal with. Someone as close as a brother had been harmed because of decisions he'd made.

"We'll be home in under twelve hours. He just has to make it for a little bit longer." He said.

"I did everything I could." She stepped closer to Nathan and their arms slipped around each other. His around her shoulders and hers around his waist. "Just get us back as soon as possible."

"There's a large settlement on Titan," he said. "I know it's got the best trauma center in the outer gas giants. And we need a plan before we head back to Earth." He leaned down and kissed the top of her head. "Do what you can. I'll get us there."

Nathan moved quickly through the ship, heading straight for the cockpit. He entered and dropped into his chair.

"How's Cole?" Marla said.

"Not good," he said. "We have to go." Nathan pulled up the docking controls and kicked the *Bandit* loose from the *Candlewax*.

Marla got the picture and keyed the intercom. "Everyone strap in. We're moving quickly."

Nathan oriented the ship toward home. It took a moment for the navigation system to work through the calculations but he was already accelerating, burning hard in the rough direction they needed to travel.

"Easy," Marla said. "We've got crew in the back."

"Are they strapped in?"

She checked the board. "I've got confirmation on all of them."

"Good," he said. He switched to the intercom. "Duncan, we're doing a hard burn. We'll probably get to max on the reactor and the engines will be around the red line. Keep us flying."

His voice came back, solid and dependable as ever. "We're on it."

Nathan reached out, slammed the goose control forward, and the ship leapt past the speed of light as starlight smeared across the canopy.

32.

Nathan poured two cups of coffee from the courtesy pot in the hospital waiting room. They'd arrived at Titan fourteen hours ago and landed on a nearby pad. One short ambulance ride later, Cole and his pod had been ushered into the great machinery of the trauma center. Nathan made his way back to the hard plastic chairs and slumped into one beside Tricia. He handed her one of the coffees.

"Two milk and two sugars," he said.

"Thanks," she said and took a sip. "Perfect."

He and Tricia were the only ones in the waiting room. Marla, Duncan, Richie, and Harmony were still aboard the *Bandit*, going through the items they'd taken from the *Candlewax*.

"I'm glad you were with us," he said to her. "I mean, not that you had to face down those things that attacked us, but Cole would be dead without you."

She nodded and patted his leg. "I'm glad I was there too. But I'm not going to lie to you, I was worried."

"You didn't let it show." It was true, too. Tricia had been able to calmly and succinctly give the doctors on staff a detailed explanation of what happened and what she'd done. To see them react to her as another professional had made his heart swell with pride. Doctors always intimidated him, but she just treated them as equals and they treated her the same way. This woman, who had saved the life of his best friend, chose to love him.

She sipped more coffee. "Just a regular day for the *Bandit* emergency nurse. What matters now is the outcome of the surgery."

As if summoned by her statement, a doctor entered the waiting room. He was still sporting scrubs, but they looked remarkably clean for someone who had been in surgery for hours. The doctor stood so still that Nathan felt like he had been standing there when they'd chosen the site for the hospital and they just constructed it around him. He looked exhausted, though. Nathan saw the same weariness he encountered when Duncan put in overtime fixing something on the ship. He hoped that meant good news. The doctor sat down on a chair in the row opposite them, and Nathan watched the doctor's wispy white hair dance around like a fluffy halo.

"I'm Doctor Ray Starling," he began. "We've just closed-up your crewmember. He's still waking up, but you can relax for the moment, everything went well."

A wave of relief washed over Nathan. He hadn't understood how much anxiety he'd been holding in, wondering if Cole was going to die. He breathed out and the next one he took in was sweeter, like the air in the room had the gloom filtered out of it.

"His kidney?" Tricia asked.

"Oh, that's gone," the doctor said, and Nathan's gut tightened. "Whatever hit him trashed it. The docs in the ER told me a nurse brought him in. Is that you?"

"Yes," she said.

"Okay, well, you did a really good job treating him. I want you to know that. There was no saving that kidney, whatever hit him just decimated it."

"What about his liver?" Tricia asked.

"That we saved, no problem. Yeah, we were able to suture it and it will heal with the drug therapy we have him on."

"But the kidney? He lost it?" Nathan said.

Doctor Starling and Tricia shared a laugh at Nathan's expense. Then the doctor explained what was evidently common medical practice; "You can live with one kidney, but your friend won't have to, we used cultures from the old organ to print a new one. We stabilized him and started the blood transfusion and antibiotics while the organ printer did its thing, then we put the new one in and closed him up."

"And that's it?" Nathan said. "You just built him a new kidney and transplanted it? It's that easy?"

The doctor slumped back in his chair and looked at Tricia with a knowing smile, which she returned. "Yeah, it was just that easy."

Nathan felt his face go red with embarrassment. "Sorry, I didn't mean it like that." He leaned forward and put his elbows on his knees.

"Ah, that's okay, son," Doctor Starling said. "I understand."

"When can we see him?" Nathan asked.

The doctor glanced at the clock on the wall. "He should be awake by now, if you want to sit with him, you can. Just don't expect any coherent conversation for a while, he's on some fairly substantial pain meds." He stood and looked at Nathan. "When's the last time you slept?"

Nathan shrugged. "I honestly don't remember."

"Well, my advice is to go bunk down for a few hours," Doctor Starling said. "You've done everything you can for your friend and he's in the best hands possible. Go take care of yourself."

"That's a good idea," Tricia said and she stood up to shake Doctor Starling's hand. "I'll see he gets some rest."

The doctor left and Tricia tugged on Nathan's arm. "Come on, let's go back to the *Bandit* and sleep in our own bunk instead of these chairs."

"I want to stay," Nathan said. "I should be here for him."

"That's just stupid," she said. "You can't do anything and the staff here is good. All you can do is freak out and get in their way if something happens. They'll call us if they need us. Besides, you have to call Kimiyo. She needs to know what's going on with Cole. Come on."

Reluctantly, he rose and followed her. Tricia was right. Kimiyo needed to know. He would do that and get some sleep.

《 》

They slept for almost twelve hours. Nathan didn't remember waking even once. When he finally came to, he hit the head and crawled back under the covers in the cabin he shared with Tricia. She passed him on her own journey to relieve herself. When they were back under the covers, she kissed him and they spent some time getting reacquainted.

When they were done, he wrapped his arms around her, taking in the strawberry scent of the shampoo she'd used before bed. She turned her head and said, "You okay?"

He squeezed her tight, enjoying the warmth of her skin on his. "I don't understand why Xandra did this," he said. "I mean, I can understand her being angry with Grigory for trying to blackmail her, but she was willing to vanish our entire crew to prevent the *Candlewax* being near Earth."

Tricia pulled back a little. "She doesn't see us as people, not in the way she thinks of herself as one. We're just resources to be used for whatever she needs."

Tricia's tone stunned him. Nathan wasn't sure he'd ever heard actual hate in her voice before. "What makes you say that?"

"It's those billions of credits," she said, with contempt in her voice. "She's sitting on a stack of cash that couldn't be spent in ten lifetimes, except now she's figured out a way to give herself at least two lifetimes. All that life expectancy has combined with the credits to make her into something new."

She was angry, Nathan could see, and he thought he understood why. Tricia fought death every time she did her job, losing as often as she won, and Xandra purchased a way out of the war, but only for herself.

Tricia pulled the sheet around herself and sat up, her back against the headboard. "She could do so much good, and she chooses not. It's always like that: the old European monarchs, the First Gilded Age, the Second Gilded Age with the tech billionaires of the twenty-first century. It's just rich people fucking with working people. Look at what she had Mir do to Mindy and Thomas.

"Think of all she could accomplish, Nathan. Xandra could spend billions of credits on anything she wants and still have billions left. She could just pick a problem and solve it. Heart disease. Cancer. Instead, she just keeps coming up with new ways to put credits in her account."

Tricia had strangled a corner of the sheet. "Other people are literally just a revenue stream to her. That's why she's comfortable hiring us to go find her ship and double crossing us. We're nothing to her."

Nathan didn't know how to respond. Tricia was right. Xandra knew absolutely nothing about him and his crew except that Saji recommended them, and she was fine with sending them out to be lost in the darkness of space. She gave him no more thought than something she might wipe off her shoe.

Nathan tugged the suffocating sheet out of Tricia's hands. "She won't get away with this. We're going to tell everyone. That was the plan. That's still the plan. We have the drives from the *Candlewax* and Mir's notebook."

She stood up and started pulling on clothes. "Then we'd better go see what's on those drives."

———— «» ————

The whole crew sat in the galley because it was the only compartment large enough to hold everyone. All six of them, Nathan, Tricia, Duncan, Marla, Richie, and Harmony had tablets out, searching through the data they'd taken from the *Candlewax*. Thomas was still recovering in the cabin he shared with himself. Tricia, the most familiar with medical databases, directed their effort; she was able to roll through directories quickly and point out where the others should look and explain what to keep an eye out for.

It was still a slog, though, and they took turns making fresh pots of coffee. Tricia had the engineers looking at the reports from the lab where they'd found Thomas and the stasis pods. Marla looked at the mobis they'd found stored in Doctor Mir's cabin, and Nathan reviewed his hand-written journals.

After almost eight hours they had little to show for their efforts. Every time someone thought they'd found something, Tricia would examine it and shake her head no. Much of the data was corrupted, as if someone had attempted to scrub it during the crew evacuation Doctor Mir had orchestrated, but the job had been poorly done. There were still patient records, but the data was mundane and what one would expect. It may prove that individuals were aboard the ship, but it didn't explain what was being done to them. The database administrators at Vibrant Passion had done an excellent job of compartmentalizing their information.

Nathan sat up straight and pointed to the journal he was reading. "Hey, I just found the reason why the backup nav hard drive on the flight deck was disconnected."

Duncan looked at him, finally happy to have something to discuss that involved his expertise. "What happened?"

"Doctor Mir didn't know anything about flying a ship," Nathan said, "but he was willing to try after he'd been stranded for a few months and realized help wasn't coming. In addition to being angry at that engineer who left him behind, he has notes about what he was doing to get the ship up and running. None of it would have worked, by the way. As smart as he may have been, he was never going to teach himself how to pilot a ship.

"He was thorough and careful, though. In this entry he talks about how he disconnected the backup nav hard drive so that if he made a mistake, the backup system wouldn't be compromised." Nathan closed the notebook on his finger to hold the place. "That little bit of caution ended up saving our asses. We'd probably still be trying to figure out where we were if not for him doing that."

"Yeah, we would," Duncan said, "because I had no idea how to get you back."

"I think I have something," Tricia said. She'd finished up the written journals and grabbed a tablet off the stack on the table. She flicked a file from her tablet so the hologram hung in the air above the galley table. It was Doctor Mir, looking disheveled. His hair and beard were unkempt, with wiry hairs poking in all directions. Tricia hit the 'Play' button.

Izad Mir was seated on the small couch in his cabin; empty alcohol bottles were strewn around the room. Mir was silent for a few moments and then he spoke.

"It's been a year since I was abandoned," he said, and held up a mostly empty fifth of whiskey. "So, happy anniversary!" He swallowed a mouthful and wiped his mouth with the back of his hand. "I'd like to take this time to thank the following people for leaving me stranded out here at the ass end of nowhere. First, Chief Engineer Hassana Bamba, for orchestrating my being left behind during the evacuation. That kind of underhandedness should be applauded."

He coughed hard, clearing his throat before he went on. "I never saw it coming, Hassana. If we are ever reunited, I'll be sure to buy you a drink. Secondly, Captain Wull. You were never any damn good at your job and the fact that someone was able to steal your ship from you proves it. Oh, and thanks for not doing a

headcount before taking off. That worked out really great for me."
Mir belched and took another swig from the bottle. Then he looked
directly into the camera.

"I know what I'm guilty of. I ruined lives by performing
horrible experiments on unwitting subjects, but I also know that
I wasn't alone." He grew silent for a moment. "Diane Ebbers was
right there, doing all of this right beside me. Sorry to sell you out
Diane, but there's no reason for me to go down alone.

"Finally, let's raise a glass to Xandra Ariti. The soulless harpy
who made all of this possible."

He scoffed at the camera. "Of course, I can't forget myself.
Xandra couldn't have accomplished any of this without me. This
whole thing is possible because I took her idea and rudimentary
work and turned it into something heinous and vile. Oh, Xandra, I
wish I'd told you this before but you're really a piss poor scientist.
You're good at having ideas and selling them, but without people
like me you'd just be an ordinary huckster hawking beauty
products, rather than one of the biggest criminals in history."

He raised the bottle again. "So, here's to me, the enabler who
sold out humanity for a few million credits and some points on the
back end of the deal. I guess I got what I deserved." He reached
forward and the recording stopped.

Tricia spoke first. "Does that help us? I mean he mentions
Xandra."

"Yeah, but he doesn't say specifically what they were doing,"
Nathan said, "or mention anyone they harmed in particular. I
think it works to give context to things, but it's not like he admitted
to specific crimes he committed or that Xandra enabled. I can't
imagine what some lawyer on her staff could do with this. We'd be
lucky if it made it into court."

Duncan tossed a tablet onto the stack on the table. "Well, that
may be all we have." He waved a hand over the pile before them.
"Some forensic team might be able to find something, but we're
not going to. That recording is the only thing that ties Xandra and
Doctor Mir to the ship."

"What about the people he mentions in the recording?" Nathan
said. The captain of the *Candlewax*, that engineer or the other doctor?
Maybe we can find them and convince them to give us testimony."

Tricia bit her lower lip. "It could be worth a shot. I mean, we
have the ship and his recording. Even if they don't want to give
us any evidence, we may be able to force the issue. No one wants
to be on the wrong side of a criminal case where they could be
charged with crimes against humanity."

Duncan grabbed his personal mobi and started a search. His face fell as results were returned. "This doesn't look good. The former captain, Roger Wull, died when his boat sank during a fishing trip near Florida two years ago."

Nathan didn't look shocked at all. "Did they find a body?"

Duncan scanned down the news article. "They did, in fact they found him and two of his companions. Let me check on the engineer." He typed and his face fell after a few seconds. "She died too."

"How?" Nathan said

"Oh, this isn't suspicious at all," Duncan said. "She was learning how to fly and during the final test for her pilot's license, both her and her instructor were killed when their plane crashed. That was also two years ago."

Nathan looked at Tricia and she returned his wary glance. Xandra was very good at tying up loose ends. "We could be in trouble if she finds out we're still around and know what she's been up to. What about the third name he mentioned, Doctor Ebbers?"

This time Duncan didn't have bad news. "I don't see any death notices or stories about her having a mysterious accident. She has an entry on a professional networking site with an active contact code. It says she still works as a researcher at Vibrant Passion."

"I wonder if we can get to her?" Nathan said.

"If we do, I wonder if she'll help us?" Tricia said. "Xandra kept her alive after the *Candlewax* debacle, she's probably being paid well to keep her mouth shut."

"We need to find her," Nathan said. "How soon until Cole is turned loose from the hospital?"

"At least a few more days," Tricia said. "He just got a new kidney."

———— «》 ————

It turned out to be a week before they discharged Cole. Conscious of the fact that Xandra didn't expect them to ever return, they waited on the *Bandit* until Cole was healed and ready to work. It was slow going, but after three days of searching on various networks and reaching out to old acquaintances, Cole updated the crew in the galley over a lunch of tacos, rice, and beans.

"I found her," Cole said. "She was working on Europa where a mining consortium has an operation. My contact said that assignment ended recently and the doctor is back on Earth overseeing a new project."

"Does your contact know what it is?" Nathan said.

"No, but whatever happened on Europa was a failure. He told me a whole group came back at once, and Doctor Ebbers immediately started this new deal. My contact is in their accounting department and told me Xandra moved a ton of credits from other projects to this new one that Ebbers is heading up. There's a lot of grumbling in the organization and a lot of unhappy people. We may be able to use that for gathering more intelligence if we need to."

"Was getting this information expensive?" Nathan said.

Cole smiled. "Nothing's free." He leaned forward and crunched into a taco. After chewing for a moment, he said, "You have a plan?"

Tricia looked at Nathan, steel in her eyes. She knew he wanted to find a way to expose Xandra and still get paid. They'd discussed it before Cole was discharged and come to the conclusion that if they tried to trade the coordinates of the *Candlewax* for the promised credits, Xandra wouldn't let them leave the office breathing.

Nathan drew his hand down over his face and leaned against the back of the booth. Despite everything they'd found out about Xandra and having the location of the ship, he still felt like their back was against the wall. He couldn't prove it, but he strongly suspected she'd killed the captain and engineer from the *Candlewax*, and she'd definitely set him and his own crew up for failure. Was it worth putting everyone in danger?

"You all want to do this? Knowing that Xandra will turn all of her considerable resources against us, knowing that a lot of people will want us dead, does everyone want in?" Nathan surveyed the room.

"We have Xandra's ship, we have her data, and we have living specimens." Cole said. "Let's get Ebbers, and then just tell the press and blow this thing wide open. Let Xandra fight it out in public."

Trica and Richie nodded in agreement.

Nathan turned to Marla. "What do you think?"

Marla looked at Duncan, then Tricia. "Once her secrets are out in the public, we're beneath her notice. I know you want to keep everyone safe, but the way to do that is to hit her hard."

Duncan held up his hands. "If I've learned anything being married, it's to trust my wife. What she's saying makes sense."

Lastly, Nathan looked at Harmony. She'd already been paid half her finder's fee. The engineer could ask for the rest of what Nathan owed her, hop off the *Bandit* free and clear; Xandra none the wiser about her involvement.

"Stop stalling and tell us the plan." Harmony said, grabbing the last taco before Duncan could reach it.

"Okay, then it's got to be big and loud, I think you'll all like it."

33.

Three days later, Nathan was returning from a supply run to the *Bandit* where it was parked at a rented docking facility on the outskirts of Go City. The street was deserted, and the sun was dipping toward the horizon. The crew had a 'last supper' of sorts planned at Cole and Kimiyo's and Nathan was headed there next. Thomas had vanished the moment they'd touched down; somehow hiding his two bodies better than most people could hide their own one.

He crossed the broken sidewalk and tapped a control on his mobi to open the black metal gate. Just as the gate motors started to whine, Nathan heard a scrape on the concrete behind him. He turned, smelled something like burning metal, and lost consciousness.

⸺ 《 》 ⸺

Nathan raised his head and it felt heavy enough that he thought he might need a crane to complete the effort. The last thing he remembered was being at the docking pad. Now he was in a dimly lit room. He tried to move his arms and legs but found them tied securely to the chair he was sitting in. This realization caused him to panic and he coughed, expelling a metallic odor. That brought on a whole bout of coughing. His chest seized up with the effort and for one terrible moment it felt like he may not catch his breath. Then his lungs opened and air flooded in.

After a moment he realized he could hear a low hissing noise, like the rebreather on an environmental suit. He looked around the room, snapping his head right and left. His eyes got wide when he saw a figure seated at a desk on his left.

"Hi, Teller," Atomic Jack said, raising a hand. "You are so screwed."

Jack was seated backwards on an office chair, leaning over the back of it. As usual, he was dressed in a pressure suit, but not the one Nathan had seen the previous times they'd met. This suit was sleeker and less bulky. It was also cleaner. On the earlier occasions,

Jack's suit had been stained with dirt and grease. This gray suit had white piping leading to black joints at the elbows and knees. Through the helmet his face still had a thin, sallow quality to it and a hint of orange emanated from beneath the surface. A flunky stood behind him. Nathan dropped his head because, yeah, he was screwed.

Jack stood up and approached him slowly, dragging out the moment. Nathan broke eye contact with Jack's fiery orange gaze and looked around the room. There were shelves with restaurant supplies. It seemed to be a combination storeroom/office.

Jack slapped Nathan's face with a gloved hand. "I know you're still a little groggy from the crap we dosed you with, but don't bother looking for a way out. Once you're here, there's no escape."

Nathan had no problem imagining terrible things taking place in this room. "Jack, come on. You can't still be holding a grudge about what happened on Bad Rock." He knew the Syndicate damn well could, but he had no other play here except to talk.

"Come on, what?" Jack said. He smiled and it was just as horrible as Nathan remembered. Just a couple rows of orange gravel. "You can't blow up one of our Diamond K labs and think you're just going to get away with it."

Nathan shook his head to clear the effects of whatever they'd used on him at the docking pad and to convey how much he disagreed with Jack's statement. "First, I didn't blow up your lab. I imploded it." He smiled, remembering how good it felt to bring down the building housing the lab. "Second, that whole mess happened because you put an addict in charge of your Diamond K operation."

"Who? Dodger? You talking about that skid mark? Let me show you something." Jack held up his mobi so Nathan could see the screen. It displayed the dealer he'd known as Dodger from Bad Rock, but he was clearly dead. It looked like someone had beat him to death. Jack pointed at the screen. "Did you think we just let him walk away because he was our boy? We took care of him a week after you clobbered our operation."

Nathan took a deep breath. If the Syndicate were willing to sacrifice Dodger, if that lunatic was already buried in some unmarked grave, he was definitely toast. "I don't care about Dodger. I didn't seek him out. He found me and tried to force me into delivering your crap and when I refused, he crashed my ship. Was I just supposed to let that slide? He could have killed my crew. Everything that happened after that was on him."

Jack smiled and leaned in. "So what? If that's all true, and I really don't care if it is, you should have taken the deal Dodger offered you. If you had, you'd be on our team, earning tall stacks of credits. Now, you're in the last room you'll ever see."

"I didn't want to run drugs."

Jack held his hands up, palms out. "I don't care. It was Dodger's job to make and move the stuff. Pulling you in was in his job description. I mean, you understand the best way to move illegal stuff is by using legitimate means, right? If your excuse for destroying our lab is to blame Dodger, you're out of luck. You should have taken his offer."

Atomic Jack held out his hand and the stooge behind him put an aluminum baseball bat in it. "This is what I used to kill Dodger," Jack said as he twirled it in one hand. He had surprising dexterity for someone wearing gloves. "Remember that time in Port Haven when your ex-wife and that conman took off with millions of Syndicate credits?"

Nathan closed his eyes, remembering how Jack and his psychos had shot Cole and almost killed the rest of them. He'd barely been able to talk his way out of that mess. "I remember. That was another time that had nothing to do with me."

Jack laughed and it sounded hollow, coming from inside his helmet. "You know, it really is crazy how often you stick your dick where it doesn't belong. I mean, you show up, we lose millions of credits, and it's never your fault."

Nathan glanced around the room again. It looked like the backroom of some business. A bar maybe? There was a desk and two doors, but he had no idea where either of them led. His hands were tied to the arms of a chair and his feet were tied to the legs. His military pilot escape and evasion training course had taught him how to get loose in different situations, but this one would be tough. He wasn't about to let this asshole beat him to death, though.

"Maybe you guys are just really bad at being criminals," he said. "You ever think of that?"

Jack pointed the bat at him. "You think that's what it might be? Maybe we just suck at our jobs? I mean, you're the one tied to a chair, so your opinion may not count for much."

Nathan tugged at the restraints. They weren't reinforced handcuffs or anything Protective Services would use to restrain someone. They were just plastic wire ties for bundling cables together. He flexed hard, the way he'd been taught, trying to stretch them out.

"Let me ask you something," Nathan said. He had to keep Jack talking and distracted.

Jack kept strutting, so sure things were going to go his way here. The bat kept spinning. "Go on, I've got all day."

Nathan lurched forward, tugging on his wrist restraints but covering it like he was angry with Jack. "You mentioned that time on Port Haven. If I recall correctly, Montario Dawson took you guys for millions and you were right there as he escaped. Did you ever catch him?"

That stopped Jack strutting across the small room. "No."

Nathan leaned forward again, putting all his weight against the plastic bands. "That's because you don't just suck at your job, you're absolutely terrible at it. How the hell did some con man lose you when you were right there?"

Jack shook his head. "Do you know where he is? Are you trying to barter for your life with his?"

Nathan tugged again. The ties weren't giving. Panic rose up and he felt his heartrate jump but he tried to fight it down. He'd been trained in escape and evasion courses to keep it together in difficult situations, to make the most of any small chance for success. It didn't matter if he was in a cockpit or here, freaking out wasn't going to help. He let Jack see a little smile cross his face, a pitiful act of defiance but it was all he could muster.

"I don't know where Montario is. You know why?"

Jack shook his dumbass pumpkin head inside his helmet. "No, why?"

Nathan licked his lips. Whatever they'd used on him made him thirsty. "Because he didn't steal my money. If those millions of credits were mine, I'd have hunted him across the solar system and any colony where he thought he could hole up. I'd never let him make me look like a chump."

Jack exhaled so hard the clear faceplate of his helmet fogged. "You're just asking for it to be worse, and believe me, it was already going to be hard."

Nathan pulled so hard the ties bit into his skin but they wouldn't give. The only move he had was to play for time. He dropped his gaze to the lower half of Jack's pressure suit. "Oh, I bet it's plenty hard. This is what you like, right? Beating on people? Burning them with your bare hands. I figure there must be some reason you break legs for the Syndicate." His gaze rose to meet Jack's. "What's the matter? Can't get off any other way?"

Jack looked at the stooge behind him, seeming to suddenly remember that he and Nathan weren't the only two people in the room. The underling found a reason to be looking at the blank wall beside him. Jack turned back to Nathan and dropped the bat on the ground. It landed on the concrete and made a sharp sound like a ringing bell. Then Jack unbuckled the right glove on his pressure suit. He pulled it off and the bare skin ignited, orange flames licking across the hand. Jack winced but kept control of himself.

He stared at Nathan. "I was just going to use the bat, but now you're getting the full treatment. I hope it was worth it."

Nathan felt a calm flow over him and he steeled himself for what was coming. "You trying to talk me to death?"

Jack came at him ferociously, crossing the distance between them in just two long strides, arm cocked in a flaming fist. The first blow struck him on the left side of his head, rattling his brain. Then he grabbed Nathan's face with his open palm and when he tried to pull away, Jack put his left hand on the back of his head to steady him.

Nathan couldn't hold back a guttural cry as the flaming hand encompassed him from cheek to cheek and his skin began to burn. It was like having a hot clothes iron pressed against his face. Jack squeezed his hand tight and screamed with rage as Nathan twisted, trying to break loose, but the mob enforcer was too strong, too determined to do some real damage.

Jack dragged a thumb across Nathan's right eye and the fierce heat trailed a crisp blister. Nathan kicked back as hard as he could, throwing his weight to the left. The chair tipped to the floor and he landed hard. His injuries from the mine aboard the *Candlewax* sent agonizing jolts of pain to his brain and he screamed again. Tricia had warned him repeatedly that he needed rest for the muscles to finish healing. He was never going to ignore her advice again. He kicked hard with his good leg, desperate to escape.

"Oh no you don't," Jack said, reaching for him. "Get back here."

Nathan rolled the chair and put his face against the cool, hard floor in a desperate bid to keep the mob enforcer away from it. He tugged at his bonds again, but the straps held tight. This was it; this was how it would end. Panic rose again and he flailed with all his trembling limbs, trying to get away.

Then the stooge stepped forward from his place in the shadows and grabbed the chair, setting Nathan upright again. Jack stood before him like a real-life ghoul coming for his flesh. He grinned again and his face transformed into a horror show of paper-thin skin lit from within with an unearthly orange glow.

"Not so mouthy now, are you?"

Nathan swallowed and decided that if this was it, if this was really how he was going out, then it would be legendary. He glanced at the stooge and imagined the stories he would tell about what happened here.

"No matter what you do to me, you'll always be someone's flaming little bitch."

Jack raised his fist again, all fury and noise as he launched himself at Nathan, then a burst of gunfire stopped him. Jack and the stooge both looked toward one of the heavy steel doors set into the wall, then they looked at each other.

"What the hell was that?" Jack said.

Nathan smiled. "Unless I'm wrong, that's the cavalry come to save my dumb ass." Another burst of gunfire sounded through the wall. "I hope that's Cole out there killing every asshole who works for you."

Jack put his glove back on and the flames were extinguished. He jerked his head at his underling. "Go check that out and tell me what's going on." Jack picked up the bat from the floor. "I'm going to keep him entertained."

Nathan studied him for a moment and realized how much pain Jack must be in. There's no way he could do the things he did and not pay a price. The suit must deliver painkillers but even the best pharmaceuticals had a limit.

Over Jack's shoulder Nathan could see the stooge open the door and heard a gunshot. He bucked against the doorframe but managed to push the door shut and lock it.

Jack looked back at him. "What did you see?"

The stooge slid down the wall to a sitting position on the floor, leaving a trail of blood on the wall. He had a gun in his hand but hadn't managed to get a shot off. "It's not his friends."

Jack's head moved slightly inside the helmet. "Who is it?" The answer didn't come fast enough and Jack's voice rose. "Jojo! Who the hell is it?"

Jojo was breathing heavily. "Banger Stoltz"

Jack dropped the baseball bat and hustled over to the desk. "Oh, no." Then he looked back at Jojo. "Did you get that door locked?"

"It's locked, man, but I'm bleeding here. You have to help me." Jojo had a hand over a chest wound, but blood soaked his shirt and pooled in his lap.

Jack pulled open a drawer and yanked a gun out. "We have to get out of here."

Someone banged on the door, heavy knocks that echoed through the small storeroom with an urgency. "Jack? You in there? I need to talk to you."

Jack looked at the door and Nathan saw real fear cross his face. He aimed the gun at the door like a talisman that could ward off the evil spirit on the other side. Pain stung Nathan's face like the worst sunburn he'd ever had and it just kept doubling. He needed a little hit of whatever Jack had in his suit.

"Who'd you piss off, Jack?" He had trouble forming the words through the thickness of his burned lips.

Jack pointed the gun at him. "You'll shut that mouth if you know what's good for you. The guy on the other side of that door? He's death. That's all you need to know. If he gets in here, we're all dead."

Jack walked over to a closet and yanked the door open. He reached in and pulled a large bag out. Then he walked over to where Jojo was sitting on the floor.

Jojo looked up at his boss. The stooge was holding his hand tight against his stomach but blood kept pushing past the pressure. "You have to help me. I can't get the bleeding to stop."

Jack looked at him, at the wound in his chest. "Sorry, man." He raised his pistol and put one right between his eyes. Jojo went limp and his head hit the ground. Blood pooled from the exit wound and seeped into the smooth concrete floor.

"Oh my God!" Nathan said. "What is wrong with you?"

"He would have talked," Jack said. "I can't have that."

Someone banged on the door again. "Jack, you can't hide in there. I need to talk to you. If I have to blow up this door, I will."

"Talk to him," Nathan said, still shaking from seeing Jojo murdered. "Maybe show him your flaming fingers trick. I bet that will impress him."

Jack ignored him and put his back against the wall. He closed his eyes like he was contemplating which was the best from a bad bunch of options.

"Come on," Nathan said. "What's he want?"

Jack started to respond, but the voice came through the door and cut him off. "Jack, if you don't answer me, I'm going to blow the door, and I'm going to do it right now."

Jack sagged inside his pressure suit and his shoulders slumped. "Just hold on, Banger, I need a minute."

"For what, Jack?" Banger said. "There's no way out. I've got guys on your back door and I'm out here."

Jack's face flared orange. "Just give me a minute!" He turned to Nathan and grabbed a paring knife from a box of bar supplies on a shelf. He held it up. "I can let you go, but I need your help to escape."

Nathan looked at him, his face burning with pain. He could feel scorched skin crinkling with every movement. "What are you talking about?"

Jack held the knife up again. "I will cut you loose, but only if you help me escape."

"From the bar?"

"From the planet," Jack said. "When we grabbed you, you were heading for your ship, right? Will it fly?"

Nathan licked his lips, tasting burnt flesh on his tongue. "It will fly, but I'm not in the business of helping psychopaths. If that guy wants to come in here and murder you, I'll open the door for him."

Jack dropped the bag and bent down on one knee. "If that psycho gets into this room, he'll kill us both. You still have a price a price on your head."

Nathan's eyes narrowed in concentration. "Why does he want you, Jack? Whoever that guy is, he's Syndicate, right?" He took a moment and paused so he could think. His eyes drifted to the bag on ground beside Jack, the one he'd pulled from the closet. "What have you been up to? Why did they send him to find you?"

"I can pay you," Jack said. "I can get us out of here, but I don't have a way off planet that they can't track. All I need from you is a ride."

"Tell me what you did," Nathan said. "I want to know why they're after you."

"What's it matter?"

"I'm already in deep," Nathan said, "over what happened on Bad Rock. Now you're asking me to dig that hole deeper. I need a way out. Your credits are useless to me if the Syndicate still wants me dead."

"I can give you a quarter million credits. With that much you can start over with a new life. Take that pretty little nurse to some colony and do whatever you want. Eventually they'll stop looking for you."

Nathan glared at him. He was frustrated that the Syndicate knew so much about him, let alone Tricia. What Jack was proposing was just another way to run. It didn't resolve anything. He would still have to look over his shoulder everywhere he went. "I want this price off my head. You need a ride? Make that happen."

Jack snorted. "I can't do that. I'm done with these jackals. The fact that Banger is on the other side of that door and already killing people means they know what I've been up to. I can't save you anymore than I can save myself. All I can do is get us out of this room and then you need to get us the rest of the way."

"Can't you just give them the credits back?"

Jack shook his head inside the helmet. "You think this is over me stealing from the Syndicate? That's not it. My sin is mortal. I'm quitting."

"What are you talking about?" Nathan said. Up to that moment he'd been sure that Bruce had gone and tattled to the Syndicate about Nathan and his crew lifting the *Bandit* from his shipyard without full payment.

"I'm dying," Jack said, his voice hitching. "Been dying of fucking cancer for years, ever since the accident that did this to me. I just found out that I'm near the end now and nothing's going to save me. No more suits or medicine. I'm done."

"So why are you wasting time with me?" Nathan said. "Why aren't you somewhere enjoying the little time you have left?"

Jack swallowed hard. "Because my doctor put me on to someone who can fix me. Someone who can remake me and let me start over in a new body." There was another hard knock at the door but Jack ignored it. "You hear what I'm saying? I get a fresh start and I'm not going to waste it working with these assholes."

Realization dawned on Nathan and he tugged against the restraints. "This isn't about Bad Rock or the price on my head. You're killing me for Xandra. My death is the price of your fancy new body. You sonovabitch. You're working with her."

Jack nodded his head inside the helmet. "You thought you'd been so quiet coming back to Earth. Xandra knew you were here days ago. Do you have any idea how many times your little *Blue Moon Bandit* circled the planet before jumping away and back again? Did you think you could re-enter this atmosphere without being picked up on a satellite owned by someone who knows someone who gets paid to tell Xandra what she wants?"

Nathan shook his head at the revelation. "I could give her the coordinates of her ship, get paid, and walk away. You don't have to kill me."

Jack laughed. "I know about the *Candlewax*. In fact, I know all about what Xandra has been up to and how she's going to brand it as job creation, a solution for homelessness. Take all the people who aren't participating in society and help them to help themselves! Anything untoward that may have happened, well that was the nasty Doctor Mir acting outside her authority. She's good, Teller, she's very good. And we agree that you are just too stupid to keep your mouth shut."

Something heavier than a fist slammed against the door. "Jack! Come out now or I blow it."

"In or out," Jack said. "That door is reinforced but he's got a boner for blowing things up. It's how he got his nickname. I have to go, and I'm not leaving you behind to tell him anything."

Nathan nodded. He needed out of this chair and out of this room. There was nothing here for him but death. "Cut me loose, you freak."

Jack put the blade against the plastic ties and snipped him loose. "We're all, freaks, Teller. Some of us are just more comfortable with it."

Nathan stood up and rubbed his wrists. He kicked the bag on the floor. "Is that full of credits?"

Jack shoved the desk aside. Nathan saw a trap door set into the floor. "That's my go bag and I earned every credit in it." He pointed at the trapdoor. "It's an old delivery tunnel for the bar, so you could bring stuff in without bothering customers. It runs about twenty meters to the street next to the bar. That door," he pointed at the other door, "goes to an alley between the bar and the building next door. That's where Banger will have someone. By the time he figures out what happened, we'll be airborne."

Jack knelt and turned his back to Nathan as he pulled up a ring on the steel trapdoor. "Can you give me a hand with this?"

"Sure thing," Nathan said, and bent to the floor, picking up the baseball bat. He swung it down as hard as he could on Jack's hand. He heard bones break and the enforcer screamed, his skin flaring orange inside his helmet. Then Nathan swung again, and again, and again, hammering him as hard and fast as he could swing the aluminum bat. He hit him in the head, moved down his back and finished up on his legs, concentrating on his joints. He got a solid lick on one of his knees and Nathan heard it pop even as Jack howled.

"You murdering psycho!" Nathan screamed. "You think I'd ever let you near me, my crew or my ship? You're insane."

Jack lay on the floor rolled up in the fetal position, moaning. The pressure suit had provided him some protection from the beating, but not nearly enough. "You shithead," he said between groans. "We had a deal."

Nathan spit blood on the floor. "You have this coming. It's like you told me years ago, 'you owe, you pay.'" He grabbed the duffle bag Jack had been so eager to take with him and unzipped it. It was full of credit vouchers, untraceable and banded together in bundles of ten thousand. There was too much to count in the bag. It was everything he needed to start his life over. He hesitated. The last time he'd picked up a bag that didn't belong to him, he'd started down a path that led him here.

"Screw it," he said. "Maybe this time will be different."

Banger hollered from the bar. "You should stand away from the door," he said. "We're wiring it now."

Nathan kept his mouth shut. There was no reason to advertise his presence and Jojo was dead. As far as Banger knew, no one else was here.

"Maybe I can buy my way out of here," he said. "Trade you and a bag full of money for my freedom?"

Jack pushed himself up on one elbow. "Don't be a fool, Teller. If you open that door, they're going to kill both of us."

Nathan gripped the bat and looked at the trap door in the floor. If he moved as fast as he could, he'd probably give himself a few minutes head start. Then an idea came to him.

He reached down and rolled Jack onto his stomach, looking over his pressure suit, and found what he was looking for. There was a zipper running down the back of it. Nathan grabbed a ratchet strap from a nearby shelf and clipped it to the zipper. Then he knocked on Jack's helmet with the bat. "Stand up."

"You broke my knee, asshole."

"You want me to break the other one?"

Jack grimaced and his face glowed deep orange with the effort it took to rise up. He leaned against a shelf. "Okay, now what? You taking me with you?"

Nathan twisted him so his back was to the door. "Just stand there and don't move."

He dropped the duffle but he kept hold of the strap. He tightened it down to shorten up the distance between the two ends. When he judged it short enough that Jack wouldn't be able to reach it, he hooked the loose end to the door handle.

Nathan picked up the bag and the bat. He tapped on Jack's helmet. "This is where we part ways, asshole. I've got you tied to the door, so if you take a step, you'll pull down the zipper and open your suit."

Fear seized Jack's face. "He's going to blow the door, Teller."

Nathan shrugged. "You'd better come up with some way to stop him then."

As Nathan crossed the floor and headed into the tunnel, he heard Jack call out, "I've been dying for years, Teller. One big boom is nothing."

Nathan ran through the delivery tunnel and when he got to the other end, he climbed up a ladder to street level. He blew out a deep breath and hoped no one was on the other side. He pushed the steel hatch open and emerged on the sidewalk. There was no one waiting for him, just as Jack had predicted.

He closed the metal trapdoor softly and looked at the street. There was some light traffic but no one noticed him. He raced across the street to the line of shops on the other side. He made it ten steps up the opposite sidewalk before he heard the explosion.

It was a muffled sound and he turned to stare at the bar he'd just escaped from. A small fireball rose into the evening sky. He didn't know if Banger was overenthusiastic with his explosives or if Jack's unique physiology had contributed to the explosion, but the bar was in flames.

People watched as thick black smoke rose into the sky. All at once, exhaustion and pain overcame Nathan and he almost collapsed on the sidewalk. He leaned against a closed shop to catch his breath.

"Goodbye, Jack. I hope it was all worth it."

34.

Nathan barely remembered getting into the rideshare-pod and directing it to Cole and Kimiyo's house. He passed out from the pain of his torture across one of the curved bench seats that lined the interior of the little bubble shaped conveyance and awakened only when Cole banged on the door.

"What are you doing?" Cole said. "Are you drunk in there? Is that why you didn't make it to dinner?"

The door lifted and Nathan managed to get out but he stood unsteadily in the darkness of the evening. "Had a little trouble in town," he said and then stumbled. Cole got an arm around him to keep him from falling over.

Cole helped him into the house and finally got a good look at him under the lights of the living room. "Oh my God, Nathan. What happened to you?"

Nathan collapsed onto a couch without a word.

"Kimiyo!" Cole shouted. "Can you and Tricia come here? Nathan's hurt!"

The women came rushing into the room from opposite directions. Tricia got there first and took control. She checked Nathan's eyes and looked at Cole. "Get my kit from my room. It's at the foot of the bed."

She was all business. Cole returned and she dug into the kit, pulling on a pair of gloves. "Nathan can you hear me? What happened to you? Did someone do that to your face?"

He was still groggy but nodded. "Atomic Jack. He caught me out at the landing pad. Worked me over." His head lolled over so he could see Tricia. "My face hurts."

"I'll bet." She ran her hands over his chest and abdomen, probing for more injuries. "Does any of that hurt?"

"Just my face," he said. "That's all he hurt. Just my face."

"Do we need an ambulance?" Kimiyo said, breaking her silence. "They can fly one out here in no time."

"No ambulance," Nathan said.

"Hush," Tricia said. "I'll be the judge of that." She went to work on him and everyone backed away. She started by checking his vital signs and, not seeing anything that troubled her, she used a scanner from her kit to determine how deep the burns went in his face. They were at least second degree because blisters were forming.

"It hurts," Nathan said.

"Lay still," she commanded. "I'll give you something for the pain in a moment." Tricia reached into her kit and pulled out an injector. She loaded it with something from a vial and pressed it against his bicep. There was a slight sting as the medicine passed through his skin.

"What was that?" he said.

"Wide spectrum anti-biotic, and it was the expensive stuff too, so you owe me." She readied another injection and held it against his arm.

He looked at her. "Painkillers?"

"Something like that," she said. "Goodnight."

He felt the injection and for the second time that day, darkness took him.

——— «》 ———

The next morning, Nathan's eyes fluttered open and his mouth felt dry. He tried to swallow but his tongue was thick and seemed to be in the way. He blinked rapidly, adjusting his eyes to the dawning sunlight streaming through a window. "Window, lower opacity by fifty percent."

The window dimmed to block some of the light and he was able to open his eyes. The room was the spare bedroom at Cole and Kimiyo's place, so at least he knew where he was.

He sat up in and swung his feet off the bed so his bare feet touched the rough carpet. Blood rushed to his face in an unfamiliar way, setting off waves of pain from his burned skin. He touched his face lightly, because no matter how much something hurts, human instinct is to touch it and see if the pain can be made worse. It could and he winced. His fingers came away greasy.

"Don't touch that," Tricia said from the doorway. She looked lovely in the dim light of the room and he smiled.

"What did you do to me?"

She came in and sat beside him on the bed, throwing him a small smile and then took his hands in hers. "You were exhausted last night and you'd clearly been through some stuff."

"That's putting it mildly."

"I needed to treat you and you seemed agitated, so I knocked you out."

He shifted and looked at her. "Not sure how I feel about that."

She sighed and shrugged her shoulders. "You can be mad if you want, but you needed rest and fluids, and the dermal regeneration salve works better if your pulse rate is low. That's the stuff on your face, by the way. Besides, I had to debride the damaged tissue and believe me, it's better for you to be out while I do that."

He nodded, not really understanding everything she'd said but trusting her to do what was right. "How long will I have to wear this stuff?"

She checked the time on her mobi. "Another twelve hours or so should do it. The healed skin will be a little pink and sore for a while."

"That's not so bad."

She swallowed. "It looks better now. Harmony saw it while I was debriding and she's out, says she'll take the rest of finder's fee that you owe her, but then she's heading off on her own."

Nathan nodded again. He didn't blame the kid; she was the only one that Xandra didn't know about; she could actually start fresh.

"Was it that guy you told me about? Atomic Jack?"

"Yeah."

"I could see what he'd done," she said and her fingers traced the air in front of his face. "There's a handprint and one of your eyelids was really bad. Are you seeing alright?"

He blinked and looked around the room. "I seem to be." He put an arm around her. "You shouldn't have been so quick to get me unconscious. What if Jack had followed me? You guys didn't know what was going on."

"Cole's been up all night keeping watch. If Jack or his goons had followed you, he would have dropped them before they got close to the house."

"Oh yeah?"

She nodded. "Really. He had some drones up watching the perimeter and he was on the roof with a rifle." She reached behind her back and came up with a pistol that she laid on the bed. "He even insisted that Kimiyo and I carry."

Nathan grinned and then winced because it hurt to pull the skin tight near his mouth. "That's why I like him." He swallowed and his stomach rumbled. "Can I eat? I feel like I'm starving."

"Yeah, that's the regeneration kicking your system into high gear. Come on out to the kitchen and we'll get you something."

She led the way to the main part of the house and he was surprised to feel dizzy from hunger. He put a hand on the wall in the hallway and steadied himself, hoping Tricia wouldn't notice. Then he crossed the living room to the kitchen without falling over and fell onto a stool at the counter.

"Want anything in particular?" Tricia asked.

He shook his head. "No, just lots of it. I feel like I could eat for days."

She turned to the cooker and programmed it. "You're getting a sausage omelet and pancakes. The protein will be good for you."

"Thank you."

The backdoor opened and Cole came in carrying a rifle. He had one of his armored vests on with an equipment harness that had extra magazines hanging from it. He opened the fridge and pulled out a pitcher of orange juice. He looked at Nathan and Nathan nodded, accepting the offer. Cole poured three glasses, gave one to Tricia, and sat down at the counter.

Nathan took several long sips from it and got an instant rush from the sugar. "Thanks, you don't know how good that tastes." Then he waved a hand at Cole's gear. "You don't need all that crap. Jack's dead."

"What do you mean?" Cole said and Tricia turned to look at him from the cooker.

Nathan laid it out for them, explaining what happened in the backroom of the bar and how he'd gotten away.

Cole sat back in his chair. "I've heard of this Banger Stoltz guy. He's supposed to be a heavy-duty cleaner for the Syndicate."

"What's a cleaner?" Tricia said as she set a plate in front of Nathan.

Cole rubbed his tired looking eyes. "Someone they call in to clean up a mess that someone else made. Cleaners know how to make problems go away. If Jack really was quitting and they didn't want him to go, Banger is the kind of guy they'd send to take care of it."

"Well, he was scary as hell," Nathan said. Then he looked down at his plate and dug into breakfast without coming up for air. Everything tasted incredible and before he believed it, he was chasing the last bite of pancakes through the remaining pool of maple syrup. "That was delicious."

Tricia nodded. "That's good. Let it settle and if you're still hungry in ten minutes we'll get you more."

"Now that your stomach is full," Cole said, "tell me about the bag of credits you had with you."

Nathan had nearly forgotten the money he'd stolen from Atomic Jack. "Where is it?"

Cole pointed toward the living room where the bag sat on the coffee table in front of the sectional sofa.

"I searched it for tracking devices and didn't see any," Cole said. "I also counted it. There's a little more than half-a-million credits in that bag." He grinned. "Nathan, have you been picking up bags that don't belong to you again?"

"It was Jack's life savings," Nathan said. "I figured he didn't need it anymore and I was due a little something for pain and suffering."

"Well, I can't argue that. What are you going to do with it?"

Nathan thought it over. It wasn't just him who had his life turned upside down by running from the Syndicate, not to mention what Xandra had put them through. What the hell? He could afford to be generous with someone else's money.

"Split it up," he said. "Give all of us and Thomas an equal share. We all deserve a bonus and Thomas needs a little seed money to get his life started again."

Cole raised an eyebrow. "Really? Just split it up?"

"Yeah, equal shares to all of us."

"What about Harmony?"

Nathan thought it over. There was no reason to be too generous. "She has more than we will from her finder's fee, so she's okay. Just us and Thomas if we ever find him again."

Cole nodded in agreement.

"So where do we stand with our plans for Xandra?" Tricia asked.

"Everything stays the same. She knows we're back and according to Jack she suspects we're going to try and expose her. Nothing changes."

Tricia looked at him with concern. "You have serious injuries! You need rest."

"I can't hang out here because I'm feeling a little punky. She'll figure out Jack failed when he doesn't get back to her."

Tricia looked at Cole. "Talk some sense into him. He needs rest for the dermal regeneration to work."

Cole shrugged. "He's a grown man who just got Atomic Jack blown up. He can do what he wants. Besides, off-planet might be a good place to be."

Tricia threw her hands up. "You're not helping."

Cole shrugged.

She turned back to Nathan. "This is ridiculous. You're going to lose half your face to scar tissue if you don't care for yourself."

Nathan stood up and put his plate and glass in the sink. "I've always heard chicks dig scars."

"And we'll all be laughing when you can't speak or eat properly because you reopened your burnt off face and I have to bandage your mouth shut," Tricia said. "This is your health. You can't just be so cavalier with it."

He smiled at her. "I'm not being cavalier. I've got a fantastic nurse on my crew who will give me excellent care. Besides, I can rest while we fly. Marla and the ship will handle the piloting. See? It all works out." He looked at Cole. "I want to be in the air as soon as we can. Let Richie know I didn't finish my supply drop, kidnapped and all that, so we still need our meals restocked. Oh, and can someone tell Harmony I need to speak with her." He turned back to Tricia. "You want anything special? Maybe that chicken parm you like?"

She shook her head and walked out of the kitchen.

Cole put his arm around Nathan's shoulders. "Your success with women continues to baffle me. Now excuse me while I make my calls."

35.

A van dropped them off at the landing pad where the *Bandit* was stored. The crew headed toward the ship, but Nathan and Tricia lingered behind with Harmony.

Nathan reached out a hand and Harmony shook it. "Thanks for everything, Harmony. You really helped us out."

She held up her mobi. "Well, thank you for the finder's fee. Believe me when I say that will help me."

"You're sure the other half was deposited in your account? I keep thinking Xandra will find a way to take it back."

She glanced down again at the device's screen. "It's all there. I know that Xandra is a terrible person, but I'm still going to spend her money."

"Believe me, you earned every bit of it. Look, I just wanted to touch base with you before we left. Xandra shouldn't know about you, but we also didn't think she'd know we'd landed, so look over your shoulder for the next few days."

Harmony nodded, then looked uncertain. "Are you sure it's okay that I go? You'll be able to make it work with one less engineer?"

"You'll be right back in the thick of it when you're called up to testify," Nathan said. "For now, why don't you just go enjoy your credits?"

She nodded and hugged them both. "Thank you both for everything. If it wasn't for you, I might still be on Grigory's ship looking for asteroids to mine."

"Good luck," Tricia said.

They watched as she entered the van and it drove away.

The crew gathered in the galley, regrouped and resupplied.

"If we're to have any chance of making it through this alive," Nathan said, "we have to put so much heat on Xandra that she'll be too afraid to even look in our direction, let alone touch us. I mean every eye in the world has to be on her. We can't give her the chance to claim that we are the bad guys or to try and shift the blame.

"Xandra and the oligarchs like her think they rule the world, but they don't. We can't just be disposable labor for her. We matter beyond what we can do for her. We're worth more than what she can use us for. She can't just kill us with impunity. Our lives are our own. Nobody owns us."

He looked at Cole. "You ready to talk to Doctor Ebbers?"

"Can I take Tricia with me?" Cole said. "I think this will work better if we can get her to talk without kidnapping her."

Tricia nodded. "I can help."

"Once we have her on the record, it's go time," Nathan said.

———— «⟩⟩ ————

An hour later, Cole and Tricia left in a rideshare. They both sat up front, Cole in the driver's seat and Tricia in the passenger, but it didn't really matter. The float car did all the driving.

"How do you think we should play this?" Cole said.

"Do we know anything about her?" Tricia said. "Aside from the fact that she's comfortable performing experiments that are probably crimes against humanity?"

Cole looked her over, concerned that being a nurse was going to interfere with what he needed to accomplish. "Is that going to be a problem for you?"

"Isn't it for you?"

"Of course, but I need you here for your expertise," he said. "You know how to be calm when dealing with people who are upset." He shifted in his seat so he could focus on her. "She's a means to an end, that's all."

"These people, Xandra and her little mad scientists, they all deserve to be locked up forever."

He smiled, they hadn't spent a lot of time together since Tricia had joined the crew, leastwise not while Cole was conscious. "I agree, but for now, we need to find something we can use to drive a wedge between her and Xandra. My contacts said she may have some kind of drug problem. I'll do the talking. Finding a crack in her relationship with Xandra is something I was trained to do. I've got that. I just need you observing her, and if she starts to veer into any kind of medical dialogue I don't understand, you can help me out. Think you can do that?"

"I can save your life on a murderous space vessel with almost no supplies, so yeah, I can do that."

"For which I am very thankful, by the way. I don't think I've said that yet."

"It was my pleasure," she said. "Thanks for fighting Mindy and Earl long enough for us to get to safety."

"Yeah, well, that's my job." The car slowed and settled to the pavement in front of a townhouse in an upscale part of the city. "I guess this is it. You ready?"

Tricia was already out of the car and stepping to the sidewalk, so he followed. He set his mobi to record the interaction. They moved up the walk to the front door quickly, and Tricia knocked on the door.

It opened and a woman who appeared to be middle aged looked at them. She had watery red eyes, as if she'd been crying. "Can I help you?"

"Diane Ebbers?" Cole said.

"Who is asking?"

Tricia stepped closer. "We need to speak with you about Xandra Ariti."

Ebbers's face became icy. "I'm sorry, I have nothing to say about her. Please leave."

She moved to close the door and Cole wedged his foot between it and the jamb. "We're going to talk."

"Leave or I'll call the authorities."

Tricia pointed a finger at her. "We're doing you a favor. If we leave without speaking to you, I'll be calling the state board of medicine, medical professional to medical professional, we both know they'll take a dim view of illegal human experimentation. Now open the door."

Cole kept his face outwardly calm, but inside he was stunned. Tricia was full of surprises today. Clearly, he was not running the show.

"I don't know what you're talking about," Ebbers said, but Cole could see her icy façade crack. There was fear creeping in her red-rimmed eyes.

Tricia held up her mobi and a holographic slide show appeared in the air above it. "Maybe this will jog your memory."

Images flipped by displaying the interior of the *Candlewax*. They all watched silently as photos of the lab went by. The pods were there, as were high resolution photos of the lab equipment. Finally, they saw the thick-hided Mindy and the octopus-like Earl. Tricia paused the slide show.

"This one right here?" she said, pointing at the inky black creature and then Cole. "It almost killed him. If I hadn't been aboard, he'd be dead. Your boss sent us out there and this is what we found. Now you let us in and we discuss some things, or I make a call about your license."

Cole's gaze shifted to Ebbers. There was terror on her face now that she knew they weren't bluffing. She looked them over again, trying to decide what her options were. He knew this look because he'd seen it on the faces of hundreds of felons. He knew that she was going to talk before she did.

She pulled the door open. "Turn that off before someone sees it and come inside."

Cole went first in case Ebbers was prepared to pull something. Tricia followed and Ebbers shut the door behind them.

The townhouse was decorated exactly like Cole expected. It was tasteful, but boring. Hardwood floors flowed throughout with expensive looking area rugs in the living room sitting area. The furniture was all deep brown leather. The coffee and end tables were real oak, polished to a high gloss.

What he wasn't expecting was for the place to look like a drug den. The air was stale and stunk of old food. Take-out containers littered the tables. Empty glasses and wine bottles were everywhere. There wasn't a clean flat surface in the room.

"Are you high right now?" Cole asked.

Ebbers walked past them and dropped onto the leather sofa. "I'm never not high." She waved a hand. "Clear a spot and sit down."

Tricia sat down on the other end of the couch. Cole remained standing, making a circuit of the room.

"Are you here alone?" he said.

Ebbers laughed hollowly. "Look around. Who would want to be here with me?"

Cole walked across the room and looked in the kitchen. It was more disgusting than the living room. Flies buzzed over garbage strewn across the floor. He held his breath and moved to the staircase. It was silent upstairs. It seemed like they really were alone. He did a quick circuit of the second floor and found it to be as empty as Ebbers claimed. He returned to the women in the living room and heard them talking.

"You were really on board the *Candlewax*?" Ebbers asked Tricia.

"We were."

Ebbers swallowed. "When you were there, did you see anyone? I was close to a doctor named Izad Mir. He didn't make it off with the rest of us; I've always wondered what happened to him."

Cole leaned against the entryway to the living room, glad that he didn't have to answer the question. He felt guilty enough for setting the mines that had killed Mir.

"We did find him," Tricia said. She paused for a moment. "He's dead. It looked like he'd been alive for some time, but eventually was killed as a result of an encounter with one of the experiments. I'm sorry."

Tears rolled down Ebbers' already sad face. "I had a feeling, but you hope when you don't know for sure." She pulled a wad of napkins from near an old take-out meal on the coffee table and wiped her eyes.

Cole was uncomfortable, but they still had some things to learn. He started to say something, but he heard Tricia say, "Your boss is in a lot of trouble. We know what she's been doing. We know that you were a big part of it."

"She'll kill you, you know," Ebbers said, her voice quivering with grief. "What you showed me outside is enough to get her attention. You do that and you'll just disappear. Take my advice, just walk away and save yourselves."

"We can't," Cole said. "She's already onto us. That's why we're here."

"Then you're already dead," Ebbers said.

"Hey!" Tricia said. "She isn't going to kill us because you're going to help us."

"I can't do that," she said. "She's starting a new program and I'm running it. There's no way I can just disappear."

"There's no way you like working for her," Tricia said.

Ebbers's eyes narrowed. "What do you want?"

Cole started to get an itch at the back of his neck. If Ebbers wasn't lying, if she really was as important to Xandra as she claimed, there could be drones circling the townhouse right now. If they were under surveillance, trouble could be heading right at them. Tricia was doing a good job of working her, though, so he just kept an eye open out the windows.

"Xandra sent us out to find the *Candlewax* because someone else had found it," Tricia said. "They were blackmailing her with what they found on the ship. We managed to shut that down, but then your boss double crossed us. Her plan was to keep the ship lost and us with it. So, what is she up to? Is it just turning people into slaves for corporations or is there more?"

Ebbers looked tired, like she'd been awake for weeks. Whatever weight she was carrying, it was too much to bear. Cole had seen this before, too. People leaned on so hard they broke under the strain.

She sank back into the deep leather of the sofa and stretched her legs so she could rest them on the coffee table. "Xandra wants to live forever. All this other bullshit she does serves that goal."

"You mean the life lengthening process she sells?" Tricia said. "I thought that just extended someone's lifespan. Are you saying it's more than that?"

"No," Ebbers said. "I'm saying it has the potential to be more than that. Xandra takes the long view of everything. Most of us think in terms of months or even a few years when we plan for the future." She bit her lower lip, and Cole thought she might need more of whatever she was using.

"Xandra thinks in terms of decades leading to centuries," Ebbers continued. "She's a brilliant biochemist. Just coming up with a way to make healthy people live longer would have been enough for anyone else. I mean, she discovered a way to give people about half their lifespan back with no negative side-effects. That's a win."

Tricia looked at her with intense eyes. "The body transformation thing she's doing now? It's part of that?"

Ebbers held her hands up horizontally. "Think of it like climbing a ladder. Her dad ran a chicken farm and was able to put her through school. She got out, worked at a cosmetics firm for a decade and then her father passed away." Her hands moved up an imaginary step. "She sold the farm and dumped her inheritance into creating her own company, Vibrant Passion.

"Her beauty products made her tons of credits. Again, something that would have been enough for anyone else. Her father's death impacted her, though. She started asking the same questions lots of people ask at time like that. Like, 'Why do we have to die?' At the time, lots of people were asking why we seemed to top out around one hundred years old if healthcare had improved so much.

"She set Vibrant Passion to run with managers and went back into the lab. Ten years later she had proof of concept. She had taken that hundred-year lifespan and extended it to one hundred-fifty. Once it was approved for sale to the public, the credits fell on her like raindrops in a thunderstorm. She played it smart, kept it expensive and exclusive."

"Wait," Tricia said, "you're saying the life lengthening process could have been cheap enough for mass consumption by the public?"

Ebbers nodded. "There's really not much to it. It's just a matter of slowing down the degradation of cells in your body as they multiply." She sat up now, ready to explain. "You 'age' because cells in your body die and are replaced by new ones. When you're younger, the cells are better, the little tails they have, called Telomeres, are longer. As you age and the cells reproduce, the Telomeres shorten and the cells degrade with each generation until they can no longer make new cells at all. That's the process she slowed down. She could let everyone live longer if she wanted."

"This would change the world," Tricia said. "How can she just restrict this to the wealthy?"

"Power," Cole said. "She wants power."

"Exactly," Ebbers said. "Credits are only one part of what she needs to carry out her plans. Decades and centuries, remember? She restricts access to the wealthy and those in power so they are available when she needs them. In decades to come, she'll need favors from lawmakers on legislation she wants passed. She's going to want regulatory agencies to fast track her pharmaceuticals. Xandra's laying the groundwork for all of that now."

"What about the body transformation process we saw on the *Candlewax*?" Tricia said. "How does that fit in?"

"That fills two needs. She needs the technology to get to the point where she can not only give clients longer life, but the bodies they want. Her ambitions are expensive. So much so, that even the revenue from Vibrant Passion's cosmetics and life lengthening won't give her the resources she needs. Her plan is to give corporations custom, disposable labor, earn some credits and learn as she goes."

Cole felt his blood run cold. "What do you mean disposable?"

"She rushed things," Ebbers said, drawing closer. "We can transform people in one direction, from base human to a couple different forms we have mapped out. Those were prototypes you found on that ship she hired you to recover." She pointed at Cole. "The one that almost killed you is a Swimmer, meant to work in both aquatic and arid environments. The other with the thick hide and strength is designed to work in harsh mining environments. We can adjust their body chemistry to breathe whatever atmosphere is available. However, that's the limit of what we can do."

"You can't change them back?" Tricia asked.

"No," Ebbers said, "and Xandra doesn't care. She's stuck in the middle of step two of her master plan after working on it for almost ten years and it's driving her crazy. We finally convinced her to pull the plug on the whole thing so we can do it right."

Cole realized Ebbers was most definitely high because she was admitting to serious felonies. Tricia just looked horrified. "What does that mean?" she said. "What do you mean by do it right?"

"We came up with the idea that the transformed workers would be more compliant if we could hold onto their capacity to learn and obey directions, but wipe out their individual personalities. I mean, the plan would be to restore them later. Eventually. It turns out that some people can't adapt to non-human forms. They just freak out and need to be put down."

"My God," Tricia said.

Ebbers looked at her and nodded. "We deployed a batch of Swimmers on Europa in a pilot program for one of the big mining outfits and we had incidents of cannibalism. I warned Xandra it was too soon, but you just can't tell her anything."

"They were eating each other?" Cole asked.

Ebbers closed her eyes and nodded affirmatively. "The Swimmers were going insane. Xandra pulled the plug and scattered them across the ice. They weren't of use to her any longer so she just got rid of them." She inhaled sharply. "She'll probably get around to doing the same thing to all of us at some point. She's a total narcissist. If you aren't of use to her, you may as well not exist.

"When you start working for Xandra at this level, you get the speech. All of us got it. She calls our bodies, 'stupid, frail things' that she wants to improve. See, that's her narcissism. Our bodies aren't good enough."

Cole saw that it was too much for Tricia. It was there on her face and in her posture. The doctor might not realize it because she was sky high, but she was giving them everything they needed to move forward. Cole took a few steps toward the couch and put a restraining hand on Tricia's shoulder.

"That's step two of her plan. What about step three?" Cole said. "What's that?"

"If she can pull off transforming people and change them back, that's everything for her. If she can pull that off, it means our bodies are like clay for her to mold. She can make people look however they want, give them whatever bodies they want, and essentially keep them young forever by just resetting their bodies as they age. If your back gives out or your hips get a little wide, she'll just build you a new body. Best of all, she'll control it. She will be the only one to decide who gets the treatment. Imagine having the power to decide who lives forever and in what body they'll do it.

"Even now, what you don't realize is that while most people will never afford the life lengthening process, they all want to believe they will. People love Xandra for that. She gives them false hope and they eat it up. You can't buy that kind of goodwill."

The revelation struck both of them equally hard, Cole could see. This kind of power was worth killing for. For immortality, people would pay almost any price. Xandra wasn't there yet, though. She still had to solve her immediate problem.

"What's the new plan?" he said. "She's got problems to solve now, so what will she do?"

Ebbers sank again, relaxing. "What she always does. She'll throw credits at the problem until it goes away. She's got all of us geniuses to come up with a solution."

"How many geniuses?" Cole said.

"There's really only about a dozen of us driving the thing. We'll crack the problem. People will be able to change themselves and do it without losing their personalities or eating each other. We'll knock it down."

Tricia stood up and shot Cole a look. "Are we done?"

She was clearly finished whether he was or not. "I think so." He turned back to the woman on the couch. "Doctor Ebbers, we're going to go. If you're smart, you'll stay away from Xandra."

She shook her head and gave him a wry smile. "I don't have anything to worry about because she needs me. You guys, whoever you are, are walking around dead. Lock the door on your way out."

Cole watched Ebbers check a timer on her mobi and carefully reset what looked like a countdown. Then she reached for a clear plastic bag on the coffee table. It had shards of clear crystal Diamond K.

He turned to Tricia. "Let's go."

36.

The *Blue Moon Bandit* slowed from her faster-than-light speed trip back to normal space and Nathan took a look at the nav system to make sure they were in the right place. The sensors pinged and he saw the *Candlewax* floating right where they'd left her.

He flew around to get a good look at things and saw the patch they'd installed on the flight deck was still there.

"Nathan," Duncan said over the intercom, "the ship still looks intact enough to fly." The engineer was getting a feed from the *Bandit's* exterior cameras. "I really need to get aboard to ascertain the state of the engines and mechanical systems."

"Well, I just fly these things," Nathan said, "but in my opinion it's all going to be a nightmare. I'll get us docked and we can go aboard."

He slowed their speed to get up close to the docking hatch. Marla extended a short umbilical and the two ships settled against each other with a slight bump. Nathan looked at Marla. "You have things here?"

"I do," she said.

"Alright, wish us luck."

"I don't need to. Duncan will make it do what you want. I have no doubt."

He smiled as he stood up. "Yeah, me neither."

Nathan made his way back to his cabin to grab his gear. Tricia was already there, zipping up a pair of coveralls with the Milky Way Repo logo. She hadn't said much about the meeting with Ebbers but Cole had filled Nathan in.

"You ready to go?"

"I am," she said, "but I'm worried about you." She walked over and put her arms around him. "She's got you furious and no one makes good decisions when they're angry."

He hugged her back, grateful once again that she was in his life. Being with her made him a better man. It kept him on the path of building things up in order to accomplish things rather than tearing others apart so they could serve as steps.

"You think it's a bad plan?" he asked.

She shook her head. "I think it's bold and loud. Spinning all of this at once will be difficult for her. It may work. Just remember you're still wounded. I've done what I can, but your face is still burnt and you still have injuries from the ball bearings in your arm and leg. Not to mention a concussion. You need to be careful."

"I know this is dangerous, but I feel good for the first time in a long time. After today, I won't worry about the Syndicate or Xandra Ariti. Things will be too loud."

She kissed him. "I hope you're right. Let's go."

They met Cole, Duncan and Richie at the airlock. Duncan and Richie were laden with tool bags containing whatever gear they thought they needed. Cole carried the biggest damn gun Nathan had ever seen.

"You think you'll need that?"

"Well, they almost killed me last time because I couldn't stop them," Cole said. He hefted the rifle. "I don't plan on making the same mistake if things go wrong."

"Good idea," Nathan said. "Well then, let's get started."

They crossed over from the *Bandit* to the *Candlewax*. It was exactly like Nathan remembered, empty, abandoned, and frightening.

The air was thick with decay and the stink of death. At the end of the corridor, where it went left and right, Nathan saw the remains of Izad Mir to his right. He felt the echoes of the wounds he'd received when the mines exploded. Someone else could recover the remains if things went well. He looked at the mess for a moment and then turned left, leading them past the laboratory module. Beyond that, they came to the engineering section.

Cole unslung his rifle in preparation of facing the two creatures Nathan locked inside. The big blast door was still down, though. Duncan stepped closer to look at the door controls and the damage Nathan had caused to lock it in place.

"Looks pretty good, huh?" Nathan prompted.

Duncan just shook his head. "Yeah, you did great."

Nathan knew condescension when he heard it. He'd been a captain too long to know when people were telling him what he wanted to hear. "I don't think you're telling me the truth."

"Well, it's just that now I have to fix all this so we can raise the door to get in." Duncan pointed at the control box on the wall. He removed a plate and pointed at some cables. "The controls for the exterior and interior both run through here, see? All you had to do was disconnect this cable," he reached in and pulled it loose.

"That disables the other side so you can lock it out for safety while you service it."

"Oh, I didn't know that." He felt heat rise in his face, embarrassed at his clumsy attempt to lock the door.

Duncan clapped him on the shoulder. "Don't worry about it. You didn't do any permanent damage."

"It seems to me the critters are the bigger problem," Nathan said. He looked at Tricia. "Was there anything in the lab that could help us? I figure the doctors here had to have some method for keeping them under control."

"That stands to reason," she said. "I can take a look."

"Don't worry about it," Duncan said. "I have an idea."

«»

The five of them, Nathan, Tricia, Duncan, Richie, and Cole stood facing the blast door that kept them separated from the creatures locked in the engineering compartment. Nathan stepped forward and looked through a small window in the door. Through the scratches he could see the thick-hided Mindy and octopus-like Earl, the one Doctor Ebbers had called a Swimmer. That one saw them and leapt at the thick glass. In a crazed fury it beat against the door and the window with its tentacles. The boney claws struck the glass hard enough that Nathan backed away.

He looked at Duncan. "Are you sure about this?"

The big man smiled at him and held up his mobi. He flicked through some menus. "Why would you doubt me? Now that we know what Xandra did, I have no problem running the *Candlewax's* systems. That includes nav, propulsion, and even gravity."

They all crowded around the small window for a better look. Nathan saw the Swimmer hanging from the ceiling inside the compartment. Behind it, Mindy's bulky frame was spread eagle against the smooth metal plates of the ceiling.

"And this won't affect us?" Nathan said.

"Just a second," Duncan said, as he made adjustments on his mobi's screen. "Okay, we're safe as long as we don't step under them. I'm localizing the gravity effect pinning them in place only where they are. Just walk around them."

"And we couldn't do this to them the first time we were here, because why?" Cole asked.

Duncan laughed. "By the time Nathan had control of the ship, you were half dead, remember." He walked over to the door controls and tapped the screen. It rose up slowly and the instant it wasn't separating them any longer, Nathan could hear the creatures howling in frustration. He felt bad for them, but he had no desire to get near them.

Duncan was selling safety, but Cole wasn't buying. He raised his rifle and aimed at the Swimmer, drawing a bead on its center mass. The inky black creature squirmed against the pull of the ceiling as its tentacles thrashed in anger. Nathan was worried Cole's own anger at this thing almost killing him would boil over. He didn't shoot, though. Nathan clapped him lightly on the shoulder and they walked around him into the engineering section.

They approached Mindy and he noticed her anger was more contained. It smoldered in her eyes, but her thick form was held tight. It bothered him to see them contained like this. There was nothing they'd done in their whole lives to deserve what Xandra had done to them. Neither of the creatures displayed anything resembling humanity, though. For now, they were contained. He left it at that.

They advanced through the cavernous space until Duncan and Richie found what they were looking for: a gap in the bulkhead. A loose panel lay off to the side on the deck. Duncan knelt and shined a light into the space.

"Be careful," Nathan warned. "We don't know for sure those two are the only ones loose."

Richie reached carefully into the darkness. Nathan heard something clatter to the deck. Richie took a wrench off his belt and grunted as he worked at something.

"How do you even know what to look for?" Nathan said.

"The error codes I'm getting from the ship," Duncan held up his mobi, showing Nathan the control menus for the *Candlewax*. "Ever since I logged in and took over the system it's been blowing it up with dozens of them. They all come back to one thing, though."

Richie grunted and came out with a cylindrical piece of machinery in his hands. "She was clever, the engineer who blew this up way back when."

"Her name was Hassana." Nathan said. "Is that a pump?"

Richie nodded. "A coolant pump. This is how she did it." He spread his arms wide. "These engines are powered by a fusion reactor, which uses a web of lasers to ignite radioactive fuel pellets. The reactor itself doesn't need cooling, but the magnets that create the magnetic containment field do. The cooling system circulates the heat out to radiators on the hull of the ship to facilitate cooling. She reversed the flow on this pump leading to one of the reactors. The heat built up to blazing temperatures and then she dumped raw water into the system instead of coolant. Water can't absorb heat nearly as efficiently as coolant, so it flashed over to steam. You know what that does?"

Nathan shook his head. "Something terrible?"

"Any given volume of water expands into steam by a factor of one to seventeen hundred. She dumped hundreds of gallons into system."

Nathan was stunned. "She detonated a bomb."

"Exactly," Duncan said. "All those pipes pushing the water out to the radiators erupted." He barked a short laugh. "It must have sounded like the end of the world when that happened. That's probably what cracked the canopy on the flight deck. There's at least one coolant pipe near it leading to a radiator near the bow."

"What about the reactor," Tricia said. "Did it explode?"

Duncan shook his head. "It's trashed for sure, but a ship this size has three and one is still operating. Once the temperature got too high, the lasers stopped and fusion ceased. Kind of ingenious." He pointed at the creatures pinned to the ceiling. "Just keep those beasts off my back and I'll get us underway. We jumped this ship after three years of rattling around in empty space. I don't want any more surprises. When we jump this time, I want all the reactors behaving themselves."

"Then tell us how to help you," Nathan said. "We need to get moving."

———— «‹›» ————

The dormant reactor spun to life an hour later. Nathan smiled and fist bumped Duncan and Richie. "Great job."

"Can we get out of here and away from the deadly beasts, now?" Cole said from behind them. He'd stood guard for the entire hour, keeping a rifle trained on Mindy and the Swimmer.

"I suppose we should," Nathan said. "Let's go."

They exited the compartment and Duncan dropped the door. He made no adjustment to the trapped creatures, though. They remained pinned to the ceiling.

"Okay," the engineer said, "we've got power and my diagnostic shows the engines work. The goose is powering back up as expected and we already fixed the nav system." He looked at Nathan and swallowed. "If you still want to go through with this, the *Candlewax* is ready."

"Oh, I'm most definitely doing this," Nathan said. He glanced back through the door at the transformed humans currently trapped on the ceiling. They hadn't asked for their lives to be disrupted like this. Xandra had just decided they had no value beyond what she could do with them. Then she'd set Atomic Jack loose on him and his crew. It was time to end things.

"Speaking of the flight deck," Duncan said, "I'm going to give it the once over." He walked forward, Cole and Richie tailed him, leaving Nathan alone with Tricia.

She turned to him and put a hand on his chest. "What you're planning is kind of stupid and dangerous. You could just not do it. We could go to Alpha Centauri or even back to Bad Rock."

He hugged her. "If we move, it's going to be because we want to. I'm done hiding from people who want to kill me. I'm not running from the Syndicate anymore," he pointed into the engineering compartment, "and I'm damn sure not running from some lunatic who would turn us into one of those. No, one way or another this ends today."

"In that case, I think I'll stick around."

He smiled. "I wouldn't have it any other way."

They made their way to the flight deck, passing the lab module where Mindy, Earl the Swimmer, Thomas, and so many others had been tortured. They passed the intersection where Doctor Mir had met his end and stepped around whatever remains were spread across the bulkheads and deck. Nathan saw the door to the cabin Doctor Mir had hid in for so many years, waiting for help that had eventually come in the form of Harmony and her crew. There was nothing on this ship of horrors worth preserving.

They entered the flight deck and Cole secured the hatch, his own dried blood still decorated a large section of the floor. It was just the five of them on board now. Duncan was in the engineer's chair, running diagnostics. He'd do it forever if Nathan let him, but it was time to go.

"Wrap it up, Duncan," Nathan said. "Those numbers aren't going to change no matter what you do. You're sure you have control? We aren't about to hijacked by Xandra again?"

"Yeah, I've got us."

Nathan moved to the pilot's seat. He turned to Tricia in the co-pilot's seat. "Strap in and we'll get this show on the road."

37.

The *Candlewax* **dropped** to sub-light speed near Earth, in a low orbit over North America in the early afternoon, local time. Nathan pushed their pre-programmed course into the nav system and the ship oriented itself for re-entry through the atmosphere.

Comms lit up right away and Nathan glanced over at Tricia. "Air traffic control is advising me that we should not have dropped in like that and we should hold our position for an inspection by Protective Services."

"They're going to be disappointed," Tricia said.

"Yeah," Nathan agreed.

The nose of the ship angled up as the re-entry program ran. Super-heated plasma enveloped the ship and flowed over the bow. A warning klaxon sounded as the air grew thicker. The ship began to shudder.

Nathan stared at the patch Duncan and Richie had placed where the missing piece of canopy had been. His eyes were transfixed by the piece of carbon that was glued in place. It would either hold or the heat of re-entry would cook them.

"Stop staring at the patch," Duncan said. "Richie did a good job."

"I know," Nathan said. "It's just really hot outside."

"If you want to worry about something, look at what we're shedding from the hull."

Nathan pulled up a schematic. It looked like the *Candlewax* was melting. Anything attached to the hull that had been damaged by the explosion in engineering three years earlier was blowing off in the hurricane force winds of re-entry. The inner pressure hull seemed to be holding up, though. So far, they had no breaches there.

Nathan breathed a sigh of relief as the ship finally slowed. The plasma envelope dissipated and he took over manual control of the flight. He adjusted course and put power to the thrusters. Now that they were in the thick atmosphere of home, the ship needed thrust to stay aloft.

"Any word from Protective Services?" Tricia asked.

Nathan grunted. "We've been identified as a possible terrorist attack. They stopped all flights out of Go City and I'm sure we have fighters scrambling to us. We'll be over the city in another minute or so, which should keep us safe. They won't shoot at us over a populated area."

"You hope," she said.

"I definitely hope."

Nathan had the ship on enough of a down angle that he saw the New Mexico desert around Go City pass by. Then they were close enough over the city that buildings were under them. He hooked the ship left toward the suburbs. They flew past neighborhoods full of single-family homes, no doubt giving kids playing in backyards something to look at. He hoped nothing else fell off the hull.

Then they were past the neighborhoods and out where the truly wealthy made their homes. Xandra's trapezoid shaped mansion with the four towers was easy to spot from the air. It was so large that it took up enough space to house an entire middle-class neighborhood.

Nathan put power to the forward thrusters to brake their descent. The ship bucked hard, shuddering as their speed dropped. He didn't care. This was the last flight the *Candlewax* would ever make. "Maybe the Swimmer will like her pool. I guess we'll find out."

He swung around over the highway leading to the front of the estate. That's what he wanted. A way for the media to drive right up and see what was happening.

"Brace for impact," he said to Tricia. "This is going to be rough."

"What about us?" Cole said from behind him. "Should we brace too?"

"If you like."

He saw ground traffic veer away from the roadway as the ship dropped. That was good. He was counting on the self-driving vehicles to recognize a threat and detour. The nose of the big ship dipped and he threw the whole thing sideways, crashing the length of the freighter through the front security gate and wall. It spanned the wide concrete driveway and the manicured lawn of the estate.

He reached over to Tricia and squeezed her arm. "Are you alright?"

She nodded. "I'm good. Man, that was teeth rattler."

He unbuckled his harness and stood. "Okay, you ready to do this?"

"Let's get it done."

From their vantage point on the flight deck, they faced the large house. The ship was essentially a new gate to the property. Anyone wanting to get inside would have to go through the ship.

The estate was an absolute mess. The *Candlewax* had crushed the security wall. Pieces of it lay strewn across the manicured green lawn that came with all the credits Xandra could spend on landscaping. The concrete driveway leading up to the main house buckled under the weight of the ship. Nathan felt nothing but joy at having destroyed something Xandra owned and took such pride in.

Two human guards appeared on the driveway from the main house and ran toward them. They were followed by a half dozen humanoid security robots. Media drones orbited the site of the crash, just as he expected. Protective Services would be right behind them.

Nathan tapped commands into his mobi and a hatch in the drive section of the ship popped loose.

Mindy and Earl emerged from the ship. They both howled at the same time and the angry sounds split the air. The two guards looked in their direction just in time to see them charging across the lawn toward them. If their pants were still dry, Nathan would eat his boot.

There was nothing Nathan could do but watch the scene play out. Mindy was slow, trudging across the lawn as quickly as her massive frame allowed. The Swimmer, though, scampered like a puppy who has just discovered new pals. The two guards ran back toward the house as fast as they could, leaving the robots where they stood. The guards were young, but the Swimmer gained ground with every thrashing movement.

"This is all going out live," Tricia said, watching on her mobi. "It's everywhere."

"Good," Nathan said, smiling. "That was the plan."

Earl reached the robots and they engaged each other. All six dogpiled onto the squirming Swimmer and they collapsed in a cluster of violence. The octopus-like Earl rose up, supported by his tentacles and pounded one bot with a sharp white claw. The other security bots assessed the situation and formulated a plan. Four of them secured a tentacle each and they started beating the struggling Swimmer. The human guards made it to the portico and slammed the doors closed behind them.

"Alright, honey, this is where we part ways," Nathan said. "It's time for you to do your part while I do mine."

She reached up, took him by the back of the neck and kissed him. It was long and deep and he lost himself to it. He felt the fear she was trying to hide, like this might be their last kiss. He didn't even entertain the thought. Whatever happened today, this wouldn't be their final embrace. Not even close.

"I love you," he said.

Tricia blinked in the bright sunshine. "Love you, too. Be careful."

———— «» ————

Tricia hustled past the lab and met up with Cole and Duncan near the engineering module. They were standing near a maintenance airlock leading to the opposite side of the ship.

"Okay," she said, "things are getting busy outside. Are you guys ready?"

"We have to hurry," Cole said. "The media is out there, but Protective Services is arriving. They'll push everyone back in another minute."

Tricia nodded. For Nathan's plan to work, they needed the press on their side as soon as possible. Kimiyo had gotten the word out that something would be happening at Xandra's estate. That effort had resulted in the press beating the authorities here, but the gap was closing.

Tricia tapped the controls set into the bulkhead and the doors cycled open. She stepped outside into the bright sunlight and a crush of reporters and camera drones swarmed her. A short woman elbowed her way closest to Tricia, before turning around to face the drone that pointed a camera and microphone at them.

"I'm Alma McKay with System Wide News. Were you aboard this ship when it crashed?" She asked the question with just enough urgency to create some drama, but not so much to make her look unprofessional.

"We didn't crash," Tricia said. "We landed here on purpose." They'd agreed that there wouldn't be a cover story. They were simply going to tell the truth and let people make up their own minds.

The reporter was a pro and never missed a beat at being corrected. "Can you tell us why you landed here? Is this some sort of attack on Xandra Ariti?"

The throng of reporters was larger now that they had someone to focus their attention on. Tricia took a deep breath and addressed the question.

"No, this is not an attack. Not at all," Tricia said. "My colleagues and I work at Milky Way Repossessions and we repossess starships. Xandra Ariti hired us to locate this vessel and return it to Earth.

"What we didn't know was that she was performing illegal experiments on people aboard this ship. If you'll come inside with us, I can tell you everything we know about the solar system's richest woman committing crimes against humanity."

The reporters were stunned silent for all of two seconds, then pushed forward to get inside. Alma McKay was first and followed Tricia as she led them toward the lab. Tricia saw her give Cole a second glance when she saw his rifle, but she stayed with her.

"What can you tell us about what's going on?" Alma said.

"Everything," Tricia said as they entered the lab. "I can tell you everything."

38.

While Tricia dealt with the press inside the *Candlewax*, Nathan waited outside for the authorities. The press had started to ask him questions, but as soon as the door to the ship opened, they abandoned him. He moved out onto the highway and stood in the middle of the road. The self-driving pods and cars had reacted to the crash in accordance with their programming and steered clear of the area.

The authorities were coming, though. He could hear sirens in the distance and drones approached in the air. It was his job to stall them long enough for Tricia and the others to tell the journalists what Xandra had been up to.

He'd been thinking about what Atomic Jack had told him about Xandra's plan to spin the story into one of job creation and altruism. It was true that she had power and influence that his crew didn't. The government might even be compelled to side with Xandra; every rich politician who owed her for their stock returns and youthful bodies would get on her side, slowly silencing and redirecting any version of the story that painted Xandra in a negative light. That could be stymied if they got their version out first. Let her play catch up.

The road was hot enough from the blazing sun that he could feel it through the soles of his boots. The air was almost still, with just a light breeze moving things along in the heat. He looked to his left and saw the *Candlewax* sitting awkwardly across the entrance to Xandra's estate. The hull plating still ticked as it cooled from the heat of re-entry. He breathed deep. It was a beautiful day for payback.

As angry as he felt, a strange sort of calm spread throughout his body. He recognized it from his days flying in the service. It meant he'd done all he could and now, whatever happened, he wouldn't be second guessing himself. There was a certain serenity in that.

He heard a sound on the road behind him so he turned. A long black car stopped a few meters from him and hovered above the concrete road. This one wasn't self-driving. It had a chauffeur. He smiled, knowing who was inside, and prepared himself.

Xandra launched herself from the back of the stretch limo. Her face was so screwed up with anger that he knew his stunt had hit the mark. If nothing else, he'd finally gotten rid of her smirk.

"You!" She screamed as she marched toward him, her white dress and long jacket whirling around her like the outfit was caught in a storm. "What are you doing here?"

He raised his hands and spread them wide, as if to say all of this was to be expected. "We had a deal and you broke it."

"So you crashed a starship into my house? What the hell is wrong with you?"

"What's wrong with me? This is what's wrong with me." He pointed at the burns on his face. "I was tortured by that lunatic you sent. That pissed me off, so I threw a starship at your house. Deal with it."

She stopped by the hood of the car. Her chauffer stood close by, but Nathan could tell he didn't know what to do. It was the middle of the afternoon and the media was all around them. Besides, after Atomic Jack, a corporate goon wasn't going to intimidate him.

"It was just business," she said. "This is why you're small time, Teller. Everything with you is personal. What do you even want from me?"

"I just wanted you to know who brought you down," he said.

She rolled her eyes. "First, I don't care what people say about me. They pretend to hate me now because the services we offer cater to the wealthy. Frumpy women and exhausted men who make their living dragging cargo between asteroids and planets don't earn enough to prolong their miserable existences with our services.

"Second, media activism is a paper tiger. A bunch of slackers shaking their virtual fists doesn't matter to me. Even now, it's not like people are going to get off their couches to do anything. People either don't care at all, or don't care enough to do anything. It's always been that way. It's almost sweet that you thought you could so much as disrupt my plans."

Nathan exploded. "You can't be serious!"

"I have sources that tell me you were out there at Bad Rock when some terrible things happened. I think it could even be called a terrorist attack, right? I mean, a whole building was brought down. And now look at what you've done."

They could hear the sounds of struggle now from the front yard. Nathan figured the action was getting closer but the security wall and ship still formed an effective blockade. The chauffer had his mobi out and from the look on his face, he could see what was happening on the other side of the ship. He showed it to Xandra and she took it from him, her calm demeanor slid away. "You set those things loose on my home? Do you know what they can do?"

He thought about how close Cole had come to dying just over a week ago and how they'd had to hide from her creatures or face a similar fate. Anger welled up within him, threatening to undo his calm, but he kept it together.

"Of course I know what they can do. They almost killed me and my crew. Now it's your turn to deal with them."

She seemed to be taken back by his straightforward answer. "How much is it going to take to make this stop? You obviously have some way to control them, so what's it going to cost me?"

Nathan let a small smile creep over his face and shook his head. "Money won't save you, Xandra. Not this time. All I did was open the door. Mindy and Earl are doing what you designed them to do."

"Who the hell are Mindy and Earl?"

He pointed at the mobi she held. "That's who they are, or were before you stole their identities. You made them into those things. Now you get to deal with them."

"You lunatic. We did those experiments off-planet for a reason. Did you really bring them here and set them loose with no way to control them?"

"Yeah," he said. "Ebbers told us they might eat each other eventually, so you should be safe enough if you just wait it out."

Anger flashed across her face at the mention of Diane Ebbers's name. "You had no right to speak with her!"

"I should mention, when we spoke with Doctor Ebbers, we might have made a little recording, made lots of copies of that recording by the way, and Cole's wife is handing them out like Halloween candy, some for the press, some for Protective Services, we made one just for Saji Vy as well, thought he might get a kick out of that."

Something arced over the security berm before Xandra could respond. They both ducked in response and stared as the remains of a security robot crashed onto the highway behind her limo with the sound of a car crash.

"That's the consequences of your own actions come to find you," he said. "Couldn't happen to a nicer person."

She screamed, filling the air with rage. "They aren't worth this! Don't you understand? I gave them purpose; I took their worthless lives and let them help me in building a new way forward for humanity! They were grateful."

Nathan flinched back from her tirade because that's how she truly felt and nothing he said would change her mind. It wasn't his problem anymore, though. It was up to the authorities now. All he could do was show the world what she'd done.

He looked at the wreckage of the robot on the road. Suddenly aware of how little the security wall meant to a Swimmer like Earl who could jet around on land as easily as a regular octopus could in water, or how Mindy could simply climb it, he started backing away toward the relative safety of the ship.

He pointed to her. "We're not unworthy. Our lives are our own. We're not your property. You don't get to decide our fate. In fact, I think you're about to see just how worthy we are."

"You can't just leave this here," Xandra yelled as her chauffer pulled her toward the car. "This is your mess to clean up!"

As he closed in on the ship, Nathan noticed a drone singling him out as it sped high over the road. It was big one and definitely from Protective Services. Beneath the drone, a dozen black and white vehicles raced along the road toward him.

A metallic voice boomed from a speaker on the drone. "Don't move," it commanded. "You are being detained in connection with this terrorist incident!"

Nathan put his hands up and stood in the middle of the road. There was nowhere to run and it was his job to stall them. The drone pulled up short, rotated, and shot something at him.

He tumbled on the pavement with the impact as a heavy net encapsulated him. After he came to a rest, the drone lifted him off the ground. The net was transparent and he was gratified to see Xandra and her bodyguard similarly trapped. Protective Services was clearly taking no chances. Grabbing everyone and sorting them out later seemed to be their plan.

The drones hauled them to a deserted spot across the highway and deposited them near a crowd of waiting officers. Two of them approached and released them. They slapped restraints on all of them.

Xandra lost her mind as the restraints tightened against her wrists. "You can't arrest me. This is my home. I'm the victim of a violent assault."

An officer wearing sergeant's stripes turned her around to face him. "If that's true, we'll get you free in a few moments, ma'am. Right now, I need someone to tell me what's going on and what those things are on the lawn."

Nathan spoke first. "Ms. Ariti hired me to find and return that ship to her. You'll have to ask her what she was up to with those monsters. They were on board and nearly killed me and my crew."

The group of officers turned toward her. Xandra opened her mouth to say something, but then shut it. The only sounds came from Mindy and Earl fighting security robots on the other side of the highway.

"Well?" the officer said. "What's going on?"

She finally relented. "I want to speak with my attorneys before I make a statement."

"I'll talk," Nathan said. "I have loads to say."

The sergeant nodded to another officer. "Get him in the van with the others and get them back to the precinct. I want to hear his story."

"No!" Xandra said. "Teller, don't say anything until you talk to my lawyers."

The sergeant turned to her. "You're probably in enough trouble. I suggest you stay quiet unless you want a witness tampering charge."

She fumed, but didn't say anything else.

An officer pushed him into a waiting van with steel benches lining either side of the cargo area. Tricia, Duncan, Richie, and Cole were already seated inside. The officer helped him up and he sat down.

Nathan nodded to his crew as the doors closed and threw them a wink. "Hey guys. I think we're just about out of trouble."

39.

A week later, Nathan stood on the set of the System Wide News affiliate in Go City as the evening started. The set wasn't much to look at, just a clear Lucite desk with a couple chairs surrounded by green screens. He had no experience being interviewed by the press so he was nervous. A producer walked up and led him to the desk while a small crew readied things.

Alma McKay appeared from a doorway. Tricia had liked how the journalist fought her way to the front of the reporting crowd to be first on the scene, so when the time came to talk, it was Alma they agreed to speak with. Today, Alma walked directly to the desk and greeted him as she sat down.

"How are you doing today? Ready for the big interview?"

Nathan tried to tamp down his nervousness. "I guess so."

She leaned in close. "Don't worry, you're going to do fine. It's just the 'A' block, which is only twelve minutes. All we're going to do is tell your story."

He nodded. "Sure."

"We're live in five, Alma," the producer called from behind the hovering camera drone. The producer counted them down and Nathan's mouth got dry and his throat threatened to seize up. He grabbed a drink of water from the glass on the desk as the intro music rolled.

She threw a million-watt smile at the camera as they got started. "Hello everyone, I'm Alma McKay and this is *Up Front* on System Wide News. Tonight, we're joined by Nathan Teller, owner of Milky Way Repossessions. He's the man who first exposed Xandra Ariti's inhumane experiments. Welcome to *Up Front*, Mr. Teller."

"Thank you for having me," he said.

"Before we get started, I want to be clear about your legal position with regard to the events of last week. Have you been charged with any crimes?"

Nathan cleared his throat. "I have been formally charged with one felony for landing the freighter *Candlewax* on Xandra Ariti's estate."

"Have you been warned not to discuss the incident with the media?"

"I have," he said. "The authorities have expressed themselves clearly that I should not talk about what happened."

She gave him a carefully practiced look of concern. "Yet, you've joined us on our show tonight?"

"That's correct. I believe Xandra's crimes need to be exposed and my concern is that if it's left to the authorities, some things may be left out. What happened is my story, and I want to tell it my way."

She reached out and gripped his hand. "And you are not alone! Just this evening *Up Front* received a data drop from an inside source we believe to be the recently missing Doctor Diane Ebbers, and I want your reaction to everything she's released."

Nathan was gob smacked. Ebbers had vanished shortly after the incident, and nobody had heard anything from her.

"But first, can you tell us why you chose to crash the ship on Xandra's estate?"

Nathan smiled, now more comfortable with being on camera. "Well, I have to correct your use of the term 'crash'. I successfully landed that freighter right where I meant to."

Alma returned the smile. "Of course. Why don't we back up a little, how did this all start?"

———— «◇» ————

Later that night, Nathan and Tricia were watching his interview. They sat on one end of the Cole and Kimiyo's sectional sofa. The media was running video of the events at Xandra's estate. He had his arms wrapped around her as they watched. Every news station had pieced together clips from myriad sources, everything from security cameras around Go City to their own drone footage and even purloined recordings from Xandra's own security system. It had taken hackers all of a day to break into her system to grab the chaotic scenes from inside the large house. Overlaying the footage was the voice of Diane Ebbers, detailing the massacre on Europa.

Cole and Kimiyo occupied the other end of the sectional while Duncan and Marla were camped out in the corner section. Richie had dragged the coffee table off to the side so he could sprawl himself out on the rug. It was the first night they were back together after a week of talking to investigators from Protective Services.

The hologram display showed Nathan slinging the *Candlewax* into the security wall at Xandra's estate and he winced as he saw the impact. Every time it repeated, he could feel the ship digging into the lawn and threatening to tip over.

"Nice landing," Marla said. "You almost dumped it."

Nathan shrugged. "It's not my ship."

The ship had since been secured by Protective Services and moved to a location where they could pull it apart and investigate what Xandra had been up to.

"What kind of charges is she looking at?" Duncan asked.

Nathan sighed. "The authorities say they're waiting for their investigation to be complete before they make a decision to charge her. There's talk of a grand jury."

Cole grunted. "That's total bullshit. They're going to let her walk."

"We don't know that for sure," Nathan said. "We literally dumped tons of evidence onto Protective Services and the media. There's the ship, the databases, the test subjects, and Mir's notes on all their experimental trials. Not to mention whatever Ebbers did with that data drop."

"Yeah," Richie said, "I heard they have Ebbers hidden away to get her cleaned up so they can interrogate her. It looks like the data drop was automated from a cloud service."

"And in the meantime," Cole added, "Xandra gets to go on all these media shows and proclaim her innocence. No one conducting the investigation can say a word, but she gets to tell her version to anyone who will book her as a guest. By the time her case heads to court, if it heads to court, the idiots who believe her will have their minds made up. They'll think she's being prosecuted for being successful."

"Have you heard anything about Mindy and Earl?" Tricia asked. Nathan knew it still bothered her that there was no way to revert them to their human forms.

"My attorney said they survived the fight at Xandra's estate and are in a containment facility. That's all I know."

"Another lab," she said. "They'll never have a normal life again."

An uncomfortable silence followed as they all contemplated such an existence. For people like Mindy and Earl, what could justice look like?

"Have they made up their mind about charging you yet?" Cole asked Nathan. "Any blowback from appearing on the news outlets?"

"They're still thinking about it, but my attorney thinks they'll stick with the one charge. They aren't happy, but technically all I did was bring Xandra's property back to her as per our contract. But blowing through the flight lanes so I could land a freighter on her estate isn't something the authorities look kindly on. As long as they don't take my pilot's license, I'll consider myself lucky. Right now, I'm out on bail with no travel restrictions, which is nice."

Nathan held up his mobi. "One thing Xandra and Ebbers got right was the way people are reacting on social media."

Tricia put her hand up to block the screen of his mobi. "You really shouldn't look at that."

"It's hard not to when her fans are sending me death threats. They don't believe she's done what she's accused of; some of them think it's all a conspiracy theory to keep people from using her life lengthening process."

"Tricia's right," Richie said. "Don't read that stuff. You know what happened and that's all that should matter."

"I guess," Nathan said. "I just thought that once we put everything out there and gave interviews, people would believe us."

"Thomas is out there doing interviews," Cole said. "People seem to love him; the one-man-with-two-bodies thing. Every time he tells his stories about how he was kidnapped and experimented on, it's another nail in Xandra's coffin."

Kimiyo sighed. "I'm telling you, it won't be enough. Half of the stuff online now is about how Xandra is the innocent victim of a government conspiracy to seize her technology. At the end of this whole thing, she'll just blame it on Doctors Mir and Ebbers. You watch."

"It doesn't help that Mir is dead and Ebbers is an addict," Nathan said.

Richie cleared his throat. "They'll convict her or they won't. What about us? Say we all stay free and clear, what's next for Milk Way Repo?"

Nathan smiled. "We've got our ship and a crew to fly her. I think we go back to work and live our lives the way we want. I used my portion of Atomic Jack's money to pay back my loan for the *Bandit*. There's no one left to run from. Even the Syndicate seems to be ignoring me because of the heat brought down by Atomic Jack working with Xandra. It feels good to worry about no one chasing me."

Tricia patted his leg. "You still have a felony charge, babe."

Nathan waved her off. "I'd rather deal with a prosecutor than the Syndicate any day." He sipped his drink. "I say we get up in the air and go find some ships to repo. I've got a few leads from the banks, so let's get away from all this Xandra stuff. It's up to the government to deal with. Other people's drama doesn't put credits in our accounts, so I think we should concentrate on our business."

Duncan raised a glass. "Now that sounds like a plan."

Marla joined him. "Hell yeah it does. I just want to fly."

Duncan nudged Richie with his foot. The machinist gave a thumbs up.

Nathan looked at Cole. "You in?"

Cole looked at Kimiyo. She shrugged, "As long as you keep coming back."

"I'm in. You got a job lined up or what?"

"I sure do."

If you enjoyed this read...

Please leave a review.

It takes less than five minutes, and it really does make a difference.

Reviews should answer at least three basic questions.
(But won't give the story away.):

- *Did you like the book?* ("Loved the book! Can't wait for the Next!")

- *What was your favorite part?* (Characters, plot, location, scenes.)

- *Would you recommend the book?*

Your review will help other readers discover this book. Consider leaving your review on Amazon, Barnes and Noble, Apple iBooks, KOBO, Goodreads, BookBub, Facebook, Instagram and/or your own website.

Brian Hades, publisher

To leave a review on Amazon

~ Even if the book was not purchased on Amazon ~

1. *Go to amazon.com. Sign into your Amazon account. If you do not have an Amazon account, you need to create one and activate it by making a purchase. Amazon will check to see that your account is active before allowing you to leave a review. Amazon has some restrictions, such as not leaving a bias review. For more information on Amazon's policies please read Amazon's Community Guidelines for book reviews:*

    https://www.amazon.com/gp/help/customer/display.
    html?nodeId=GLHXEX85MENUE4XF

2. *Search for and find The Unworthy by Michael Prelee, then click on the book's details page.*

3. *Scroll down to find the Write a Customer R Write a customer review eview button. Click it.*

4. *Select your star rating. A rating of 5 is best, 1 is worst.*

5. *If you have a photo or video to share, add it to the upload box.*

6. *Add a headline.*

7. *Write your review.*

8. *Press the SUBMIT button*

To leave a review on Barnes and Noble

~ Even if the book was not purchased on BN.com ~

1. Go to barnesandnoble.com and sign up for an account.

2. Search for and find The Unworthy by Michael Prelee, then click on the book's details page.

3. Scroll down to the review section and click on the Write a Review button.

4. Select your star rating. A rating of 5 is best, 1 is worst.

5. Add a review title.

6. Write your review.

7. Add a photo if you wish.

8. Select if you would recommend this book to a friend.

9. Select appropriate TAGs.

10. Indicate if your review contains spoilers.

11. Select the type of reader that best describes you (optional).

12. Enter your location (optional).

13. Enter your email address.

14. Checkmark that you agree to the terms and conditions.

15. Press the POST REVIEW button.

About the Author

Michael Prelee is an award-winning crime and science-fiction author who grew up in rural Northeast Ohio and graduated from Youngstown State University. His first published work is the Milky Way Repo sci-fi crime series published by EDGE Science Fiction and Fantasy.

He won the 2021 Midwest Book Award in the mystery/thriller category for "Lost Little Sister."

Need something new to read?

If you liked The Unworthy, you should also consider these other EDGE titles…

Super-Earth Mother
The AI that Engineered a Brave New World

by Guy Immega

Get ready to explore a new world with Super-Earth Mother

Super-Earth Mother is a thrilling Hard Science Fiction novel that reveals questions about humanities' future; exploring genetic coding, developing artificial intelligence, and building space vehicles that travel beyond the stars.

What will it be like to settle into some 'home-like' planet's environment? How will we survive the journey there? What will happen after we land?

Super-Earth Mother answers these questions and more.

It is the story of an Artificial Intelligence machine named Mother-9 who uses synthetic biology to grow generations of human beings best suited to survive on the earth-like planet Velencia, where the first Human colony of genetically engineered babies will learn to survive and thrive.

Super-Earth Mother is a thrilling quest and the ultimate in sci-fi adventures.

Pishtaco
Lord of the Lost Inca Gold

by Mark Patton

An All-Powerful Evil Shaman Wakes to Protect Lost Inca Gold

Penelope Augusta Gertrude Farquhar, a woman struggling with schizophrenia, finds herself lost in the Amazon rainforest after a fateful airplane crash. But she's not alone: her voices, now personified as historical figures such as René Descartes, Ada Lovelace, and Ernest Shackleton, accompany her on a quest to find the fabled city of Paititi and destroy the evil shaman Pishtaco, who has amassed the lost Inca gold of Atahualpa.

Pishtaco is a thrilling historical fantasy that takes you on a journey through the mystical and mysterious world of the Inca people. Along the way, you'll encounter the pantheon of Inca gods and goddesses, as well as the tribal people of the Amazon rainforest, and learn about their cultures and beliefs. This offbeat adventure is filled with humor, twists and turns, and a unique blend of history and mythology.

Mark Patton's well-researched and engaging writing transports you to another world, while delving into themes of mental health and the nature of reality. Pishtaco is a must-read for fans of adventure, history, and mythology.

The Rosetta Mind
(Book Two of the Rosetta Series)

by Claire McCague

Estlin Hume was living off-grid on 12 acres outside of Twin Butte, Alberta when he got snagged into being translator for first contact.

Home again, he wakes to find himself surrounded by aliens, affectionate squirrels, government representatives, and military personnel. That's nothing new. But he hadn't planned on hosting one thousand three hundred and sixty-one cuttlefish in a massive saltwater tank suspended above his house!

Stuck at the center of the alien contact crisis, Estlin is challenged by ill-advised directives from government officials, trenchant military interference, and random acts of violence from unknown nefarious agents—all of whom are determined to find out for themselves what the aliens really want. No matter the cost! No matter the outcome!

About Claire McCague

Claire McCague is a Canadian writer, scientist, musician, and science fiction fan. She works on sustainable energy systems, plays with words, and owns an excessive number of musical instruments. She's performed with dance bands for decades. As a theatre director and playwright, she's had productions on stages and in fields from the Fraser Common Farm in BC to the Manhattan Theatre Source.

**For more EDGE titles and information
about upcoming speculative fiction
please visit us at:**

www.edgewebsite.com